Last in the Nest

S Wraith Cianán

Foreword

This isn't the first piece of fiction I've ever written, but it is the first I've written with the intention of being published.

To my family, this is with some bemusement, as I haven't written any crime fiction is well over ten years. In the interceding time, most of my literature creations (many unfinished) have focused on action and sci-fi, inspired by a turn in interests from Western fiction to Japanese manga.

Detective fiction came back to me during my move from the UK to New Zealand, during which time I spent a solid month period consuming the words of the both the Golden-Era Honkaku and Shin-Honkaku schools of literature, inspired to give them a try after reading manga based on their works.

Having steamrolled through Pushkin Vertigo's entire collection of Seishi Yokomizo and Yukito Ayatsuji's works, maybe it was natural for an author to turn to thoughts of creating their own mystery novel. Both of these authors were known for their Closed Circle style of murder mysteries – a style familiar to Western audiences by the much-applauded works of Dame Agatha Christie and John Dickson Carr – but I struggled with the idea of creating a unique mystery in the sea of similar gimmick stories.

The idea behind *Last in the Nest* finally became something I thought I could publish only when I blended the classic Closed Circle formula with another style of novel, this one more unique to Japan: that of the Deadly Game Visual Novel.

Visual Novels are a form of video game popular in Japan, remarkable for their unique style of presentation: a first-person text-based story told using textboxes and 2-D character graphics. For video games, they actually present very little in the way of gameplay, intended to serve more as novels delivered through a screen with accompanying graphics. In Japan, this form of literature is very natural: a nice medium between the visual style of manga and more dialogue-heavy written novels.

As visual novels are a medium linked only by presentation, they can cover almost any genre of literature; from romance to sci-fi to horror. But one of the more popular genres for such games is mystery solving. Whilst visual novels as a whole are still mostly relegated to Asia, the few that have trickled across the ocean reflect this shared love of mysteries: series like *Ace Attorney* and *Professor Layton* will be familiar to the Gameboy and DS generation of gamers.

A sub-genre of these mystery solving visual novels that has only recently made the leap to the west, however, is the Deadly Game mystery.

The best way to define such a genre – popularised by franchises such as *Zero Escape, Your Turn To Die* and *Danganronpa* – would be to combine *Any Then There Were None* with the *Saw* franchise, with a dash of *The Hunger Games* to mix the blend. In its crudest form, a group of people unknown to each other are locked into a setting and forced to play a game to escape, with an inevitable part of the game involving you repeatedly having to sacrifice other participants in order to advance. The games blend both the puzzle solving aspect of removing members of your party that may present a danger to your advancement – and more often than not your life – as well as working out who has locked you into this game and why; along with the ever-present psychological horror of watching your group members whittle down over the course of the game. Instead of a typical Close Circle murder mystery scenario where anyone could be *the* killer, a Deadly Game presents the far trickery scenario of anyone could be *a* killer, where simply tracking down one bad egg or unlocking one mystery does little more than pave the way for the next until you're able to take down the mastermind behind your imprisonment.

Whilst this sub-genre has proven to be very successful in a visual novel format, I have yet to find very much in the way of successful pure written novels within in it, besides straight novelisations of the previously mentioned visual novels. One of the trickiest aspects of converting the format into page literature would seem to be length: the first *Danganronpa* game – a franchise that greatly contributed to *Last in the Nest*, so many *Danganronpa* fans may be treated to a few references as they read through – alone chipped in at around 1,103,350 Japanese characters. Using an average of three characters per word, this would put in a word count of roughly 367,783, making it longer than your average *A Song of Ice and Fire* novel. Please bear in mind this is purely dialogue, with the occasional inner monologue thrown in for flavour, as the text-box graphic style removes the need for conjunctions, delivery or visual descriptions. In a world of mystery fiction where anything over 100,000 words is considered unduly excessive, slimming this heavy format down to something more palatable is no easy task.

Have I accomplished it?

Yes, though the length of this foreword should indicate that this was not easy.

Does it live up to the standards of those famed visual novels?

In my opinion, not quite, with plenty of the depth and character drama those games have being agonisingly shelved to reduce runtime. I also find it contributes to a harder mystery overall, as the usual downtime to process and solve each mystery as they come ended up on the cutting room floor as well.

But, if it can introduce people to this sub-genre I've grown to love, and maybe inspire a more dab hand at mystery writing to have a go, I find it's well worth publishing.

As an aside, to lean into its visual novel routes, I've included a series of drawings of each of the characters at the start of the book, including the full-body and head sprites

familiar audiences will recognise. I've also included a few maps and drawings through the story to help with orientation.
I sincerely hope you enjoy *Last in the Nest*.

Drawings

Cuckoo

Shrike

Raven

Rail

Duck

Wren

Map

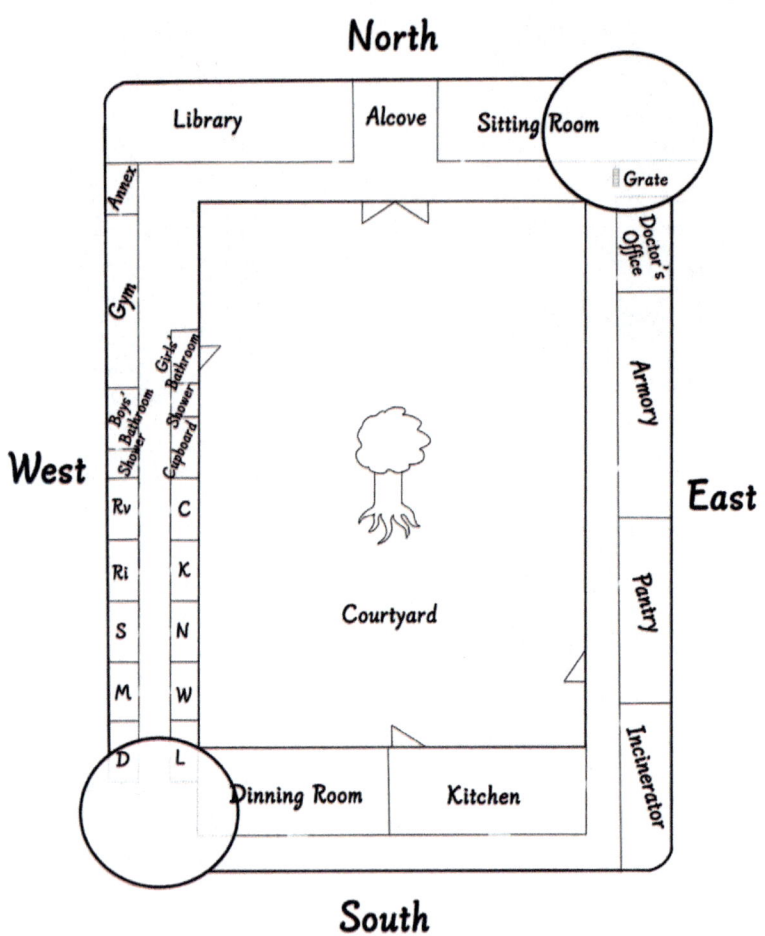

North

Library   Alcove   Sitting Room

Grate

Annex

Doctor's Office

Gym

Armory

Girls' Bathroom

Boys' Bathroom

Shower

Cupboard

West   East

Rv   C

Ri   K   Courtyard   Pantry

S   N

M   W

D   L

Dinning Room   Kitchen   Incinerator

South

Loon

Kingfisher

Mockingbird

Nightjar

Map

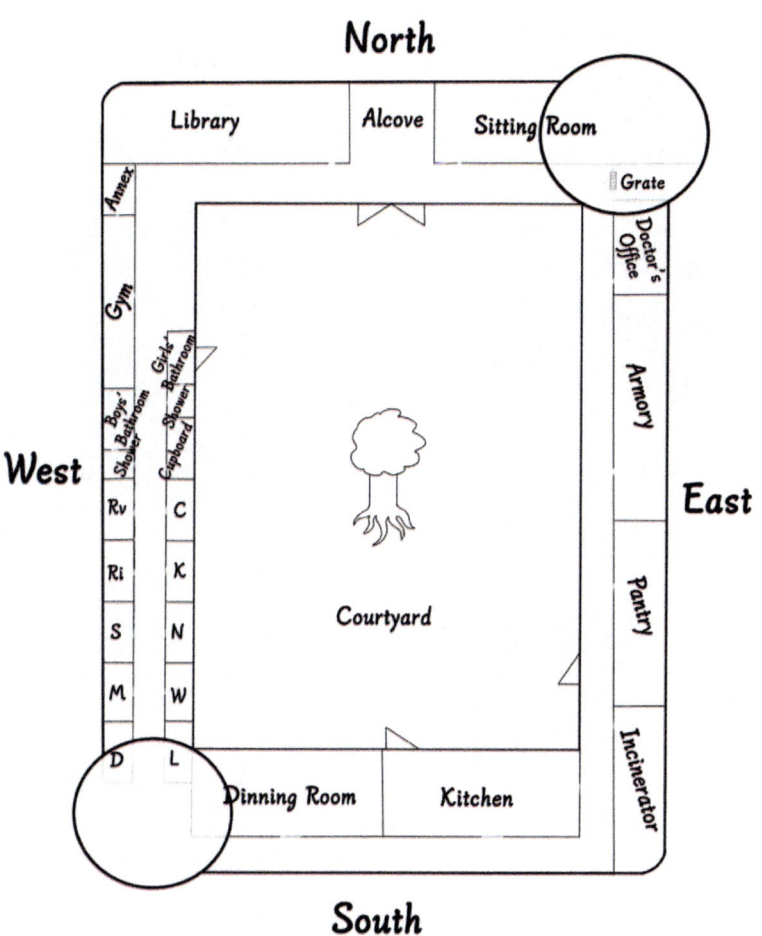

North

Library | Alcove | Sitting Room

Grate

Annex

Gym

Doctor's Office

Boys' Bathroom | Shower | Cupboard | Girls' Bathroom

Armory

West

Rv | C

Ri | K

S | N

M | W

Courtyard

East

Pantry

D | L

Dinning Room | Kitchen

Incinerator

South

Wren

Contents

Tertials

1

He stared into the darkness, and a cheery voice sang back to His ears.

"Hey! Hey there! Are you awake? Heeyyy!"

Why was everything so black? There should be colour, right?

Were His eyes still shut?

He blinked open His eyes, stale air filling His lungs, and took in the face staring down at Him.

It was not a face He knew. Certainly not His own face, He decided.

"Oh good, you're alive!" the boy above Him cheered "I was getting worried! I know people always say 'Check his pulse' in movies, but they never actually show you how to do that, do they?"

It was a bizarre statement to wake up to. He wondered how long He'd been knocked out to worry someone like that.

Though why *was* he worried? The boy was a stranger to Him, wasn't he? So why the concern?

He didn't know him...right?

What *did* He know?

"Hey, can you remember your name?" the boy leaning over Him asked "Or where you are?"

Oh, that was easy, He was—

He was—

Who was He?

He was Him, that was obvious, but there should be a name to attach to Him. Him was only relevant to Himself – there had to be a nomenclature that others would call Him by.

But there was nothing.

Nothing at all.

Nothing that even *felt* like a name.

He felt like He'd thrown open a pantry in His mind expecting to find a wide range of delicious goods, only to find it bare and empty. He tried to look around, beyond the pantry, but in every direction was just more taunting empty blackness.

Who...Who the hell was He?

"I...don't know" He found Himself saying.

Was that His voice? It didn't sound like it – the notes rubbing something inside of Him the wrong way – but it hung in the air when He moved His mouth, so it must be.

The two dark eyes hovering over Him widened. "You don't remember *your* name either?"

Either?

"No" He stated "Do you?"

The boy shook his head, black hair swishing about. "No. Do you remember how we got here?"

Here? Where even *was* here?

He really didn't know anything, did He?

Well, that was a lie. He knew one thing.

He felt wrong, gross, like someone had shoved Him into someone else's body. Every breath of still air that He took felt like it was stolen from another's lungs. Everything in Him rolled in horror, wanting to jump up out of this body and flee to somewhere safe, where everything made sense.

Oh, was He even a *he*?

Shaking hands reached up to His chest.

Yes, He was a he. That at least was comforting.

He was lying down on something hard. The ground, He decided. That was how the boy was able to look down at Him. And beyond that boy's head, He could see the bare branches of a tree.

He sat up, His head spinning and making His whole body feel uncomfortable, the leaves He'd been lying in sticking to His arms for extra discomfort.

"Whoa, hey, be careful!" the boy tried to warn Him, kneeling to steady Him "You were completely out before! Take it easy!"

He decided He didn't like hands touching Him yet. It was too close, too imitate when He wasn't even comfortable with His own touch yet.

He shrugged those hands off as quickly as possible before He took in His surroundings.

He was in a castle, or a prison, He decided. Four intimidatingly high stone walls surrounded Him, with two towers on opposite corners. Anyone who felt like climbing two stories to get to the top of the wall had to contend with rolls of wicked-looking barbed wire. There were no windows He could see from here, just unyielding stone staring back at the courtyard they were in; bare besides grass, fallen leaves and a naked tree.

Even the sky was uninviting here. It was still blue, but it didn't feel like it held an expansive wonder. Just... more emptiness.

It was definitely a prison. Had He done something to end up in a prison?

There was no voice inside to tell Him yes or no; no instinct to go on.

Maybe this boy knew.

"Were we...locked up for something?" He guessed.

2

"I was wondering that too" the boy admitted, apparently unbothered by being shrugged off "But I don't think so. I don't remember everything, but I'm certain I'm not a *bad* person."

That was more certainty than He had. His stomach rolled at the thought.

"Er, that's a nice tattoo?" the boy tried to lighten things up, a nervous smile on his face "Do you remember getting that? That could be a clue."

He looked down at the arm the boy was pointing at, and sure enough, He saw letters. Big blocky letters up His right forearm reading **CUCKOO**.

That felt more wrong than anything else so far. He felt like he was going to throw up just looking at it. He tried scrubbing at it with His finger, even wetting it to try and force the ink out, but there was no reaction.

It wasn't raised and painful like a new tattoo, but it didn't feel like it belonged there either. Like He was going to blink and His arm would go back to being pristine again.

What was wrong with Him?

Why did this feel less like a tattoo and more like a cattle brand? Like a clamp around his neck?

"Do you...want to go inside?" the boy, still trying to be accommodating, offered "It's probably cold out here in bare sleeves."

That comment made Him look down at His outfit. A combination of a green sleeveless vest, a pair of khaki trousers and boots that felt as unfamiliar to Him as the prison. The boy was right: He should be cold out in autumn or winter in such minimal clothing, but He didn't feel goosebumps on His arms, no chill against his skin. Just a gnawing dread.

He wanted to run. If He couldn't run out of this prison, He could at least run out of this courtyard.

"Y-Yeah" He decided.

"Great!" the boy stood up, holding his left hand out for Him to grab "Let's go! Maybe we can find someone who knows what's going on."

He appreciated that the boy didn't grab Him to pull Him up, just left the offer of it. At least he was a quick learner.

It was a good thing the boy offered to help Him up though, because His legs shook like they'd never bore weight before. It took Him a few steps before they stopped vibrating around the knees and began moving like legs really ought to.

At the nearest end of the courtyard was a pair of double doors, a plaque over the top reading 'North Wing'. Pushing through the doors had them enter a grand stone hallway. It appeared the building didn't actually have two stories – just very high ceilings. There were two doors ahead separated by a table in an alcove: one to lead into a library, the other a room with sofas and benches. At the edge of his vision was a stone arch over a staircase that probably led up to the tower, but there was a strong-looking metal grate bolted in front of it.

Strange. Very strange.

3

"Oh hey, I guess this is one of those...er, sitting rooms?"

The boy – actually, no, looking at him stood up, he was really too old to be a boy – the *man* had moved on into one of the rooms, the one filled with sofas and padded benches. The room was homely, dotted with lamps, a red carpet and green walls adorned with paintings of different types of birds in majestic poses, and a roaring fireplace crackling away inside its hearth. But where there should be windows within its architecture, there was just an arch set into the wall filled with harsh grey concrete.

He didn't know what kind of prison this was supposed to be, but somehow the kindly decorations were more unnerving than the bars and razor wire.

They went to move on to the next room, but along the way, He paused at a picture hanging in the alcove opposite the door. Another bird related one: nine chicks in a nest, wailing at an unforgiving sky.

Someone had a theme going on.

"Oh, good! There *are* more people here!"

More people?

He hurried to the library door where the man was standing. Inside was another homely room with carpet and wallpaper, but this time the walls were ornamented with bookcases, with only one bird painting and a clock above a desk at the far end. Between them and that desk was another man, hurriedly putting a book back onto the shelf he was stood beside.

Now there were two people in His life He had to memorise, He realised He'd never really taken in what His companion up until this point had looked like. Curly black hair tangling around his ears, a long black coat with an even longer red scarf he hadn't bothered to take off when they went indoors – He was sure that he was supposed to evoke Edgar Allan Poe, or how some similar gothic novelist may've styled themselves. It was a marked difference from the man in the library: shaggy unkempt ginger hair and a battered green coat over a purple hoodie, with the right sleeve of both cut off abruptly near the elbow to reveal bandages down to his wrist. Whilst His first companion had been nothing but chipper and spry the whole time, this man looked like he hadn't slept in two weeks; the hand holding up the book was even perched on the shelf, as if lifting it to read was too much effort for him to exert.

The new guy squinted at them, his head bobbing around a bit as his vision tried to focus on them. He wouldn't have been surprised if someone told Him he was stoned out of his mind.

"So I'm not alone" the ginger remarked, but there was no breathless wonder in his tone. He was just stating a fact, one that was almost too taxing for him to process.

"Nope, we're here too!" His companion declared cheerily "Any chance you remember how you got here?"

"No" the ginger shook his head, shoving his hands into his pockets "So what do I call *you*?"

4

"Oh, we're…" the black-haired man trailed off and laughed awkwardly "Well, actually, neither of us remember our names!"

The ginger's shoulders sagged. "You too, huh?"

He frowned. This was weird. Three different people losing their memories and waking up in the same strange prison? What were the odds?

"Do you have any idea where we are?" He asked.

"Not at all" the ginger shook his head "And none of these books are any help."

"Hmmm" the black-haired man rocked back and forth on his feet "Well, all we can do is keep looking. You coming?"

The ginger trudged towards them, his posture saying he really didn't want to, but didn't exactly have any better options. "Don't tell me what to do."

He came anyway.

They left the library and crossed the hallway again, slinking past that unnerving barred entryway to reach a corridor with a plaque reading 'East Wing' above it.

He stared down the arrow-straight stone-grey corridor with a shudder. There were still no windows, so if it wasn't for the lights high above them, the whole place would be a dark tomb. It was an unwelcome, claustrophobic change from the empty brightness outside.

The black-haired man didn't seem bothered at all, almost skipping along beside Him, as if this was one great big adventure. Even more unnervingly, the ginger behind them was muttering to himself, too quiet for Him to pick up on any specific words.

He was staring to wish He'd woken up alone. At least then he'd only have to sort through his own thoughts, instead of having to worry about what these people wanted from him.

"Our new friend does make a good point though" the black-haired man abruptly spoke up, looking directly at Him "What *should* I call you?"

He still had no idea. Nothing particularly jumped to mind as a name – no nagging thought or sudden wave of nostalgia. He was Him, and nothing else really seemed important.

Not that He was entirely sure how to communicate that.

"I'm…me" He tried to put His thoughts into words.

He obviously failed, because the black-haired man just laughed.

"I can't call you *Me*!" he laughed "Nothing takes your fancy?"

No, not really. Did that say something about Him?

"I don't care what you call me" the ginger announced "Just don't make it lame."

He frowned. Didn't that mean he *did* care what they called him?

He didn't have time to ponder that idiosyncrasy though, because it was then they heard a massive bang from the nearest door.

"Oh, come on!"

"I think it might need a key."

Another bang.

The black-haired man looked concerned and raced through the door, whilst the other two waited at the threshold.

The plaque on the door read 'Doctor's Office', and that seemed to sum up the room succinctly. There were medical charts on the walls, and a cushioned bed and oxygen canisters against the wall. However, the most interesting thing about the room was a cabinet set into the wall that two unfamiliar people – a handsome man in a leather jacket and a blonde woman in a puffy blue coat – were trying to get in to.

The man was trying to force open the cabinet door, pulling on the handle. Grumbling, he slammed his hand into the door.

"Screw it, I'm kicking it open!" the man decided on, taking a few steps back to get a run-up.

"Wait!" the black-haired man reached out to stop him "I can–"

But before he could finish, the handsome man took a flying kick at the cabinet door. Half expecting the guy to bounce off, He was surprised when instead the door splinted under his booted foot, now droopily hanging by its hinges.

He made a mental note never to piss this guy off, taking a precautionary step back.

"That was cool" the woman commented, speaking up for the first time, her half-lidded eyes widened up at her companion, something that was almost a smile drifting across her face.

The handsome man lit up at the compliment, reaching over and ruffling her hair, leaving yellow strands flapping around her face.

"Well, I knew I kept you around for something" he smiled "You know, you should smile more, you look nice when you do!"

The blonde hid her face behind the strands of hair, but He saw her saw her pale cheeks colouring red.

With the compliments out of the way, they finally they began to focus on the cabinet. A row of transparent glass bottles stared back at them, intimidating labels like "acetaminophen", "sodium hydroxide", "strychnine" and "chlorhexidine" boldly underlined. Something on the top shelf had shattered under the kick that had taken out of the door, and was now leaking onto the row of bottles below, liquid dripping onto their fragile paper labels.

"Huh" the handsome man reached into the now destroyed cupboard, pulling out a glass bottle "Is this medicine?"

"Or poison" the girl suggested.

"I mean, medicine makes sense" the black-haired man remarked, getting over his shock "Since this is a doctor's office."

Both of the strangers jumped in surprise, obviously not having heard the trio approach them.

6

"Oh, hey!" the handsome man startled, looking down at the glass bottle in his hand, little crystals rattling around inside "Shoot, er…This was on me, not her. We couldn't find anyone, and we thought there might be clue as to where we are in this thing, but the door wouldn't open and–"

"Wait, you don't know where you are?" the black-haired man cut him off.

The pair blinked at him, exchanging a look before they both shook their heads.

"No, we just woke up here" the handsome man, obviously the talker of the pair, admitted "We thought it might be a prison, but there's no bars and we have no idea why we're here. We don't remember doing anything wrong."

"So, do you two know each other? Do you remember your names?" the black-haired man questioned, asking all the questions He was wondering.

The handsome man's eyes widened in surprise, whilst the woman fixed the black-haired man with a heavy stare.

"No" the handsome man admitted "Not until ten minutes ago. I mean," he gestured at his blonde friend "In my head, I've been called her Mouse, and the other one Grumpy."

The girl looked down, a flash of disappointment across her face.

"The other one?" the black-haired man questioned.

"Hey, you assholes! Keep up, will ya!"

Perfectly timed, a voice rang from down the hallway.

Reacting to the voice, He leant back out of the doctor's office, seeing a brunette woman wearing what looked like some sort of stylised military cap, leather gloves and a miniskirt striding down the corridor. Her steps faltered as she took Him in, clearly surprised, but she swiftly regained herself and shoved Him out of the way to take His place in the doorway.

"Geez, every time I leave you, you keep multiplying!" she scowled "You need to come and look at this! There's a whole ass library up here!"

"Is there a *way out* through the library?" the blonde asked, her voice flat and downtrodden.

"Er, no, or I would've *said* that!" the brunette snapped "But there's all these broken-ass books in there! You've gotta take a look!"

He frowned. The ginger man had been looking at those same books, but he hadn't said anything about them being 'broken', 'ass' or even 'important'.

Speaking of, where had that guy gone? Wasn't he in the corridor with Him?

"Whoa, nice find! Look at this place!"

Another female voice rang out of the next room along the hallway, which had its door open.

He stepped along to see who this new person was, only to become dazzled by the sight of the room.

It was as if someone had raided an army base. Everyone type of weapon a person could possibly need to fight a battle – from knives, to spears, to grenades, to riot shields – had been crammed into the room. It was an awe-inspiring display of humankind's thirst for savagery.

What kind of prison was this? A doctor's office full of mysterious potions and an armoury, all sitting across from a cozy sitting room and a library. Whoever had built this place must be out of their minds, or at least failed to understand the point of a prison.

At the back of the armoury was the ginger man, frantically messing around with his coat, and a woman wearing some sort of jumpsuit and a cap backwards on her head, walking up to where he was staring into what was definitely a gun cupboard.

"W-Why's this all out in the open?" the ginger questioned, his flustered face burying behind his hair "I mean, this cupboard locks, but the key was just sitting in it. It...seems dangerous, just leaving all these guns out for people to take."

He slammed the door shut and rattled the key in the lock, as if proving a point.

"I don't know; I'll admit, I wouldn't even know how to use one" the woman admitted, turning around and spotting Him in the doorway "Oh, hi there! Is this one of your friends?"

The ginger turned and regarded Him with dead eyes. "No. I met him five minutes ago."

"Oh, well, hi anyway!" the woman greeted him with a chipper friendliness outrivalling even the black-haired man's "Have you explored everywhere yet?"

"No" He admitted, estimating they'd probably only seen a tiny fraction of this place, if the view from the courtyard was any measure of scale.

"I'm slowly making my way round, but it's very lonely by yourself" she admitted, moving past Him to get to the next door along the corridor, this one labelled 'Pantry' "Personally, I find even the most boring of tasks goes by very quickly if you just have a little—oof!"

She was abruptly winded as she opened the door and a child fell onto her. She managed to catch them both before they could crack their heads on the linoleum that did little to cover the firmness of the concrete floor below.

"Hi there!" she greeted the new person with her usual smile "Were you hiding?"

As the person in her arms looked up at her, He could see it wasn't actually a child. Probably something closer to a very small teenager, still with the round cheeks of childhood but the faintest hint of a stubble coming in along his jaw. He peeked up from behind a pair of glasses that looked more like goggles, blue eyes blown wide, like he was about to drop dead from a stress-induced heart attack.

"Yes" he admitted quietly "I heard voices."

"It's ok, it's just us!" the woman assured him "Do you remember your name?"

"Yeah" the boy admitted, stepping back out of her arms with his head bowed "It's Duck."

He tried not to frown. Duck? Now that was a name only parents could love.

"Duck?" the ginger questioned, his voice disbelieving "Why *Duck*?"

"Oh" the boy looked away, gripping his arm "It's on my arm. See."

8

The boy rolled up the sleeve of the jumper and white button up he was wearing, and then the black turtleneck below that, revealing the word **DUCK** tattooed across his right forearm in familiar block lettering.

He subconsciously gripped His own arm, fingers digging into the muscle. More brands. Did all of them have them? Everyone else was wearing sleeves – He hadn't been able to tell.

"Oh, from your tattoo?" the woman guessed, now looking at Him "Oh, you have one too. Cuckoo."

Just hearing the word unsettled Him. It felt wrong, like sandpaper being rubbed up His whole body. He felt pinpricks up his arm and across his face, like water was dripping on them, but rubbing them confirmed that they were still bone dry.

"Do I have one?" the woman questioned, rolling up her own sleeve "Ah, I do! Loon!" Her face fell a little, but she quickly straightened it into her usual perkiness again. "Well, it could be worse. My name is Loon, yours is Duck, and yours is Cuckoo."

He felt His stomach roll. He didn't want that name. *Anything* was better than that.

He hated that word. He hated hearing it. Though he didn't understand why, just hearing the word never failed to unsettle him.

Even the ginger-haired man seemed unimpressed, fixing Him with a confused stare.

"It's not my name" shot out His mouth on instinct.

"Wait, you have names?" the black-haired man suddenly approached them from behind, lured in by a potential development.

"Oh, hi there! We all appear to have identical tattoos" the woman showed him hers, all but shoving it into his face "Duck here has suggested we use them as names, since I at least don't have anything else."

"Oh, that's a good idea" the black-haired man remarked "So I should have one too, right?"

The rolled up the left sleeve of his coat and shirt, but it was the wrong side. He flipped to his right arm and the usual lettering began to emerge.

"Raven" he read, pulling his arm right up to his face "Huh. Do you think there's any significance to that?"

"At least yours is a *name*" He groused.

Not just a brand, He didn't say.

"Yours says Cuckoo, doesn't it?" the black-haired man recalled "I like that. It's poetic. So's mine, actually. We make a good pair."

And maybe it was that camaraderie, that insistence that taking up that awful name meant that He was no longer alone, that there was someone bound to Him in life, that wore Him down.

Fine, He didn't have to like it, but He was Cuckoo.

Cuckoo was Him.

And the others were Raven, Loon and Duck.

"So that leaves…" Raven looked over at the ginger man expectantly.

The man in question wasn't stupid. He was dragging his knuckles up his right arm: the one with the sleeve cut off, so the only thing between his name and the air was a line of bandages. He looked a thousand miles away as he stroked his hand up the cloth wrappings.

Cuckoo felt something squirm in his stomach.

"He doesn't have to" he found himself saying "We'll just make one up. He doesn't have to remove—"

"It's fine" the ginger man cut him off "I don't care."

He did seem to care, holding his breath as he unwrapped the bindings. The whole corridor seemed to hold it breath with him.

Cuckoo expected to see lines of scars, but instead the arm beneath was silky smooth, the only marring being the word **RAIL**.

"Rail" Loon read out for him "Am I reading that correctly?"

Rail said nothing, just staring down at his own arm, his eyebrows furrowed together in visual confusion, as if he expecting to see something else there instead.

Loon just pressed on like nothing had happened.

"Cuckoo, Raven, Rail and Duck" Loon patted the last boy on her list on the shoulder with a gentle smile "Well, with that sorted out, let's keep exploring, shall we? We're not going to find any answers standing here."

She took Duck by the hand and led him away from the room he'd fallen out of, which glancing into revealed was indeed a large panty, stocked with food, bottled water, crates of utensils and even a pile of folded duvets. She moved to the next door before Cuckoo could get a good look, this one on the right of the corridor, and opened it to bright sunshine.

They were back in the courtyard again. Cuckoo could see the door they'd first gone through to their right. There were another two doors in the other two walls: one to the left and the other across from them. Rail crossed the courtyard, mud splattering up his red tattered trainers, to open the opposite door; but it wouldn't budge, standing firm as he pushed and pulled on it, even kicking it in frustration.

"Rail, we probably shouldn't break it!" Loon called to him "We don't want to get into any trouble!"

Cuckoo stared at her from the corner of his eye. She was worried about getting into trouble? *Now*? *Here*?

Rail just grunted as he stepped back from the door, clearly dissatisfied at not getting through.

"Ah, well, about that" Raven winced "Someone already broke something."

As if queued, the other door at the north of the courtyard opened once again, and out stepped the handsome man they'd ran into before, with his two female companions.

10

"So, you have more" the man remarked, pointing over his shoulder as he walked out "We found this one poking around the library."

Emerging into the light after him came the biggest woman Cuckoo had ever seen, a claim he was confident he could make even missing all memories of his life before about ten minutes ago. She stood a full head taller than the man she followed, her jacket cut off at the shoulders, seemingly just to show off that her biceps were big enough to crush Cuckoo's head. He subconsciously took a step back as she raised one massive hand.

And then, to throw him completely, she buried that hand in her messy brown hair – the word **WREN** shifting upside down on her flexing arm – shot him a grin and greeted them in a surprisingly pleasant voice:

"Hi! Nice to meet you!"

Whilst Cuckoo was busy trying not to lose his eyeballs, Duck immediately shuffled to hide behind Loon. Loon threw a little smile over her shoulder, before skipping up to the new arrival and holding her hand out. "Hi there!" she greeted her, friendly as always "I'm Loon! Nice to meet you, Wren!"

The massive woman paused mid-handshake. "Huh? Wren?"

The blonde woman in the blue puffy coat tripped, causing the handsome man to reach out and steady her. The woman in the miniskirt grumble as she sidestepped around the pair into the light

"Loon?!" the second woman questioned, her voice dismissive "The heck kinda name is that?!"

"She's naming us all after the tattoos someone put on us" Rail filled them in, sounding equally impressed about it.

The handsome man seemed to notice the dishevelled shape of a human being at the edge of the courtyard for the first time. "So that would make you...?"

Rail rolled his eyes, pulling his hand from the arm he'd been covering with his hand to show the lettering. "Rail."

The man struggled to pull up the sleeve of his leather jacket, but couldn't roll up the thick material. He gave up and pulled it out of the sleeve, rolling up the sleeve of the shirt beneath.

"Oh crap" he wrinkled his nose "Really?"

"That bad?" Rail questioned, voice flat.

"Worse than Cuckoo?" Cuckoo found himself questioning, determined that he had the short end of the stick here.

The blonde woman sucked in a breath, her hand frozen on her oversized sleeve as she stared at him, but she didn't get to say anything before her male companion was talking again.

"Mockingbird" the man stated, the word dripping with distaste.

Cuckoo grimaced for him. Yeah, that was pretty bad.

11

Mockingbird looked down at his little blonde companion. "Please tell me yours is worse."

The girl just stared at the floor, fiddling with her sleeve. "Kingfisher."

"Why's yours better?!" Mockingbird complained "Can we switch?"

"The hell's a nightjar?" the brunette wearing a miniskirt frowned from her spot next to them, staring down at one of her twig-thin arms.

"A bird" Kingfisher told her, looking everywhere besides at her covered arm.

"They're all birds" Raven realised, pointing at people as he went "Cuckoo, Rail, Loon, Duck, Wren, Mockingbird, Kingfisher, Nightjar. Oh, and Raven. All birds."

Cuckoo felt his breath catch in his throat. Something uncomfortable settled over him; something that made him want to cover up for fear he would never find warmth again. A deep unsettling pit in his belly that had started when he woke up and had only grown when the name of a bird was hung around his neck.

Branded, and then the names of beasts forced upon them. There couldn't be any *good* reason for that.

"We don't actually have to call ourselves those, right?" Nightjar frowned "Because those suck."

"And I suppose you have a better idea" Mockingbird shot at her sarcastically.

Nightjar's whole face turned red, then purple. "Idiots 1-through-8. That's good enough for me."

"So, er" Wren cut in before anyone could argue back "Not to be awkward but, does anyone remember how we got here?"

A silence rang through the courtyard, everyone nervously waiting for someone to speak up first. Someone who had all the answers – who could put their racing minds at ease. But when someone finally did speak, it was only to ask more questions.

"None of you remember *anything*?" Kingfisher questioned, her face twisting into something painful.

"I mean...sort of" Mockingbird admitted, waving his hand in an uncertain motion "It's... kinda spotty up there."

"Well, maybe we can look at this another way" Raven suggested "Does anyone remember what they were doing *before* we arrived here?"

"I was at work" Kingfisher answered instantly.

"Same!" Loon chimed in.

"Well, that's a good start" Raven clapped his hands together "So, do you work together?"

Kingfisher tilted her head to the side. "I work in finance. I'm guessing you don't."

Loon's face fell as she shook her head. "No, I'm human resources."

"I'm in project management" Mockingbird added, raising his hand "And yeah, I also remember being at work before this, if that's of any help."

"I work in security" Wren offered, scratching her cheek.

12

"Yeah, no kidding" Nightjar scoffed.

"No, like...document security?" Wren corrected her, but it sounded more like she was questioning herself.

"You guard documents?" Mockingbird questioned "Like in a library?"

Wren, still thinking, waved her arm to indicate he was close but not quite right. She seemed bothered, bouncing on her toes as her face scrunched up in thought.

An idea sprouted in Cuckoo's head. "As in, *software* security?"

Wren paused for a moment, thinking about that, then lit up. "Yeah, that's it!"

"*You're* an IT nerd?" Nightjar raised a disbelieving eyebrow.

"Something wrong with that?" Wren folded her massive arms, staring down the woman next to her with a look that was almost mean.

Not wanting to get crushed, Nightjar swiftly moved the conversation along. "I'm a bid specialist. Not that anyone cares."

She turned her head to Duck, indicating he should speak next.

"I..." Duck was playing with his fingers as he spoke "I work in personnel management."

"Oh, like me!" Loon lit up again "I knew we'd get along!"

Duck turned his head away, his cheeks dusting with red.

"Now you see *that*" Nightjar jabbed a thumb in his direction "*That's* what an IT nerd should look like."

"We don't *all* look like we suit our jobs" Rail objected, his voice terse.

"What, like you?" Nightjar shot him a venomous stare "So you're not actually a homeless bum?"

Rail looked away with a grimace, beginning to wrap the bandages back around his arm. "I'm a doctor. The in-house doctor for Raptor Tech."

Now *that* got a reaction, with seven people almost speaking at once.

"Raptor Tech!"

"Really?"

"Holy frick!"

"That's where I work!"

"No kidding, you too?"

"Wait, everyone?"

"Guys, guys, GUYS!" Loon raised her voice to be heard above the crowd "Am I hearing this right? We *all* work for Raptor Tech?"

The pit in Cuckoo's stomach only deepened. He thought he was going to be sick.

Of course he'd *heard* of Raptor Tech – who hadn't? Most computers in the world had software patented by Raptor Tech running on them. But did he really work for them? Nothing sprang to mind. Nothing familiar or reassuring.

"Yeah right" Nightjar, as ever, disagreed "I don't remember *any* of you."

Kingfisher opened her mouth to say something, but her words were once again smothered by someone else's.

"Raptor Tech has thousands of employees, including virtual ones, and we all work in different business areas" Raven pointed out "It's perfectly possible we all work for the same company but don't know each other."

"He has a point" Mockingbird conceded; his mouth then up ticked into a smirk as he looked pointedly at Nightjar "Besides, I wouldn't want to remember *you* anyway."

Nightjar's mouth hung open for several seconds as she digested that remark. As it sunk in, her mouth clacked open and shut, her face morphing over and over again into increasingly terrifying images. Then, unable to find the words, she reached down and grabbed a handful of leaves and threw them right into Mockingbird's face, sending him spluttering backwards.

"Well, that's just pathetic" Rail groused, only for him to also get pegged in the side of the head "Wha! What the hell?!"

Cuckoo turned his head to Loon, who he was sure had been the one to throw the second strike. She had scooped up another handful of leaves and was fluttering them down over Duck's head.

"Why me?!" the smaller man sputtered "I didn't do anything!"

"Because I think we all need to take a breather" Loon announced, smearing the leaves all over his head as he tried valiantly to protect his hair "We're all stressed out, and we need to have a little *fun*!"

With that, her next shot hit Raven, who jumped back with a laugh.

That started a battle, with Raven struggling to launch projectiles in her direction whilst Loon fired like machine gun at anyone within reach.

Kingfisher shook her head. "We really ought to be taking this more seriously. Someone— EEP!"

The screech was the result of Mockingbird gathering an armful of leaves and dumping all of them on her head at once, glistening pixels of red and orange clinging to blonde waves.

From then on it was war: a war of screams and laughter. There wasn't any rhyme or reason as to who was hit – Nightjar was taken off her feet dodging a fastball from Raven whilst Rail face-planted the ground after slipping on the remains of a meteoric toss from Wren, mud now caking his trousers. Cuckoo certainly wasn't immune, dodging and weaving left and right to avoid hits, many of them from Duck, who seemed to be gunning for him personally.

Eventually, he ended up in front of a large pile of leaves at the base of the tree, giving him the ammunition he needed to launch a leaf ball back at Duck. It was a good shot, but the smallest of their group seemed to dodge through the air like a pixie, the hit meant for him clocking Wren right on the side.

Wren, who was currently holding aloft a pile of leaves big enough to make a snowman with.

Cuckoo's heart dropped to his knees.

14

"Wren, I didn't mean it" he found giggles unconsciously escaping through his words as he begged for his life under Wren's calculating grin "It was for Duck. Wren, *don't*!"

But words couldn't save him, as Wren launched all of her ammunition at Cuckoo at once in a highly choreographed strike.

He hit the pile of leaves behind him like a falling redwood.

As the air rushed out of his lungs, so did a peel of laughter. It wasn't like all the worries cooped up inside his chest had escaped like butterflies from a cage, but their frantic rustling had soothed until they were less painful, hovering expectantly at the back of his mind rather than howling front and centre.

Loon was right: the mental catharsis was doing them good.

A new sound brushed against his eardrums, a paintbrush of melody across a dim canvas. Cuckoo turned his head towards where this new laugh came from. Near his head was another head, albeit facing the other direction. A beautiful side profile stretched out before him, locks of dark hair in a fan around them.

All the words were robbed from Cuckoo's mouth by this new stranger.

Said stranger who turned their head towards him, green eyes glittering with surprise.

"Oh, hello" was all they said.

Cuckoo searched for something to say, but the sound of laughter turning into argument stole his attention.

"Hey, c'mon!"

"Dude, that's not funny."

"Rail, give them back!"

Cuckoo sat up to see what was going on better. He saw that Rail had grabbed Duck's glasses and was holding them out of reach above his head, and cruel smirk decorating his face.

Nightjar also spotted what was happening. Immediately, she jumped across the courtyard and socked Rail right in the face, causing him to stumble and drop the glasses. "Not funny asshole!" she scowled, handing the glasses back to a grateful Duck "Don't mess with kids like that!"

Duck didn't do anything to refute being called a kid. Cuckoo wondered how old he was. He looked like a teenager, but he couldn't be if he already worked in management. Cuckoo guessed he must be just blessed with youthful looks.

He hoped that Duck didn't turn out to be older than him after all that. That would be embarrassing.

"Hey, you alright?" Loon checked in with her little favourite, smoothing leaves off of his jumper.

Duck's face coloured and he ducked away again. "Y-Yeah."

Loon turned toward Rail, who was still lying on the ground with the demeanour of a corpse, but her eyes first caught on to Cuckoo and the stranger in the leaf pile.

15

"Oh, we have another!" her formerly concerned face broke into another smile "Hi there!"

"When did *they* get here?" Mockingbird questioned.

The stranger stood up from the leaf pile with a chuckle, brushing leaves from their coat. "I apologise, the atmosphere out here was so raucous, I just had to join in. I hope you don't mind."

"Oh, not at all!" Loon stepped forward to shake their hand now "I'm Loon."

"Ah, from your tattoo" the stranger guessed "I guess that would make me Shrike."

Another bird name? That would be Cuckoo's guess, on account of the ornithologically-gifted Raven not speaking up.

Another person reduced to nothing but a beast. A pretty feathered beast, maybe, but that didn't change his feelings on it.

As everyone introduced themselves to Shrike, they nodded along with a smile that may as well have been a blank face. Until they landed on Cuckoo.

"Cuckoo?" they repeated, something questioning in that voice "Huh."

No further clarification. No sign of what was running in their mind. No indication as to why Cuckoo's name, out of everyone's, was so interesting.

"It's curious" was the next thing they said "That they would choose birds."

Cuckoo had been wondering the same thing. Why birds?

For the vulnerability?

"Birds are far more than beasts" Shrike continued, barely pausing for breath "If anything, one could call them the descendants of dinosaurs. The most terrifying creatures to walk the earth, crammed into tiny feathery bodies."

No one could find anything to say to that. To Cuckoo, it felt like the very courtyard itself was holding its breath. He swore he could hear thunder rolling in the clear sky, as if ready to strike them down.

Finally, it was Duck who spoke up,

"So, er" he still had his head down, fiddling with his fingers "Do you remember where you were before this?"

Shrike raised a single long finger to their chin. "Hmmm...I remember being at work, and then something happened."

"Something happened?" Loon questioned, her neck straightening with interest.

Cuckoo's own spine seemed to iron out. This was the first time someone had mentioned anything beyond simply being at work.

"Yes" Shrike's voice grew softer, and for the first time, Cuckoo thought they were truly being serious "I was at work...and then I died."

Across the courtyard, Kingfisher audibly gasped. Anyone who hadn't stiffened at Shrike's previous words were ramrod straight now.

"What the hell?" Rail questioned, sitting up, his voice a sneer "We're *dead*?!"

"No, no" Shrike abruptly shook their head "That's wrong. *I* didn't die. Someone else died. Someone..." They trailed off, face straining with effort, voice so small it was nearly a whisper. "Shouldn't there be nine of us?"

Duck's head whipped towards them, a look of squirrel-ish fear in his face. Loon saw this and put a reassuring hand on his shoulder, regarding Shrike with a cautious look. Mockingbird looked like he was counting heads on his fingers. Kingfisher opened her mouth to say something, but was drowned out once again, this time by the woman next to her.

"There's ten of us, idiot" Nightjar frowned "Can't you count?"

Mockingbird immediately dropped his arms, like he was trying to hide the evidence he couldn't.

Shrike didn't react to the bait though, simply looking between everyone else with a hard stare, eyes flickering like lines of code were rewriting themselves behind them, trying to calculate an impossible equation.

Once again, it was Duck who got things back on track.

"So, do you also work for Raptor Tech?" he questioned, his voice tremoring as he tried to straighten it out into a more confident tone.

"Ah, yes" Shrike almost seemed relieved to change the subject, the relaxed smile crawling back on their face "I do. I'm a psychologist."

Cuckoo frowned. Why would a psychologist be working for a tech company? They'd left something out of that description, *that* he was sure of.

"So, that's all of us" Wren recognised "We all work for Raptor Tech."

"Do we all?" Shrike asked, but it wasn't a real question. It was clear they knew someone there didn't belong.

Cuckoo decided not to draw it out. Better to out himself then let Shrike do it.

"I don't" he admitted "At least, I don't know if I do. The first thing I remember is waking up here."

Raven's eyebrows raised with shock. "You don't remember *anything*?"

"The first thing I remember is you waking me up" Cuckoo shook his head "Before that, everything's just...black."

Thunder cracked above their heads. The heavens opened, and they were all instantly drenched.

Cuckoo swore and looked up at the sky. What had once been an icy blue had somehow darkened into a murderous grey without any of them noticing.

"Inside, quickly!" Loon called, herding them into the North Wing as if they weren't all automatically running in that direction anyway.

They couldn't all fit on the coir matting provided at every door, leaving a squelch of wet and muddy footprints across the linoleum floor. The people with coats and jackets took them off to wring them out, but Cuckoo was forced to stand there awkwardly. He wasn't sure what was underneath this jacket, and he didn't feel like showing his chest off to everyone if there wasn't a shirt. With no spare clothes just lying around, everyone was going to be left a little wet.

Despite it all, a few chuckles and laughs went around at everyone's new bedraggled forms. Raven fretted over the fact his hair had gone flat, Kingfisher wrang her voluminous hair out on Nightjar's boots, Rail took off his red trainers to empty them of water whilst Loon used her cap to flick water at a shrieking Duck.

But all of the humour of the situation drained out of them at Wren's next words.

"Hey, was that here before? Because I don't remember it.'"

She was pointing at the table at the other side of the room, positioned in a little alcove between the sitting room and the library. It had an ornate flower presentation on it, and propped up against one of the vases was a letter.

It was pristine – no sign of having been crumpled in a pocket or carried out in the rain, as if it had just materialised there on command. Whoever had left it there, it had to be before they all met outside.

Without saying anything, Loon stepped forward, ripped open the envelope and unfolded the letter inside.

She spoke as she read, not giving herself time to read ahead. If she had, she may not have had the breath to finish.

"There are ten of you in the nest. For your previous transgressions, as long your situation remains that way, you shall remain here forever. If you wish to leave, you must reduce your number until only the decimator remains. Only one can leave the nest and fly free through the sky.

-Sincerely, The Warden"

A horrified silence swept over the whole group. Everyone was holding their breaths, waiting for Loon to continue, to read out the part of the note that would make sense. But she didn't continue, the paper hanging slackly in her hand with nothing else left to read.

Mockingbird moved first, striding over and snatching the note from her hand. His eyes bored into it furiously, looking for more information, but nothing more emerged.

"That's what it says" he affirmed "Signed by 'The Warden'."

"Like, the warden of a prison?" Loon pondered, head tilting.

"Is that who put us in here?" Wren questioned, scratching her head.

"A warden is someone who oversees prisoners" Kingfisher explained, voice carefully emotionless but hands burrowing into her pockets, only the movement of the skin of her jacket giving away that they were shaking "So that would seem most likely."

So, one person had done this? A single person, managing to abduct ten people and somehow stopping them from remembering how they got here?

In his case, from remembering anything at all.

Was that even possible? It sounded like something out of sci-fi; not something that could happen in the real world.

"Ok, which one of you brats put that there?!" Nightjar turned on the rest of them, balling her fists "That isn't funny you know!"

But there was no response. No one volunteered. All of them just shifted uncomfortably, staring at the note like it was a venomous snake.

No one wanted to address the part about their 'previous transgressions'. That implied there was a reason they were all here – that they weren't just blameless victims.

"What does it even *mean*, though?" Wren questioned.

"That we're trapped in here, idiot!" Nightjar shot at her.

"I think she means the last part" Duck clarified "About reducing our number and the decimator going free."

"Free?" Kingfisher turned to him with a stare that was outright accusatory "There's a way of us to leave?"

"But only if we reduce our number to one" Duck agreed, seemingly unbothered by viciousness of the stare he'd received "And the one who does that can leave."

"How are we supposed to do that?!" Nightjar protested "How are we supposed to make sure there are less of us if no one can leave?!"

A way jumped into Cuckoo's mind. He immediately smothered that thought.

No, that couldn't be it.

What kind of sick freak would come up with something like that?

"Decimator means something, right?" Mockingbird pondered "Like, ten percent, or whatever."

"It comes from decimate" Kingfisher explained "Originally, it was a military term, used to describe disbanding ten percent of one's army. But colloquially it came to mean to destroy on mass. So, I supposed a decimator is someone who destroys things."

Pinpricks ran down Cuckoo's arms. He was right, wasn't he?

"They want us to kill each other."

Everyone's heads turned to Rail, huddling in the corner like a cat in a blanket.

"They want us to kill each other, until only one of us is left" he stated, voice cold as ice "And then they'll set the murderer free."

He knew it.

Everyone else must've been in denial though, because they all stared at Rail in complete shock, as if it was entirely unnatural that he should say such a thing. Rail didn't look at any of them, his gaze fixed on the floor, his hunched posture unchanged from the moment Cuckoo had found him.

Kingfisher was paralysed – Cuckoo wasn't even sure that she was breathing – with her eyes blown wide like glassy saucers. Loon was looking between all of them, fighting to keep the emotions on her face under control. Raven had backed up into the wall, his mouth frozen in a little o. No one else was much better, all of them uncomfortable and verging on denial.

There were only two among them who were unbothered. Duck, who watched Rail with a carefully blank expression. And Shrike, who just stood there with their hands in their pockets, the hint of an easy smile on their face.

Cuckoo envied that level of control over oneself. He had found himself pulling the strap wrapped around his arm until it was almost a vice, the nip of pain from the course fabric digging into his skin the only welcome distraction he could think of to keep him from examining the awful truth of their escape clause in any real detail.

It was Nightjar who moved first, backing away from the entire group with cautious steps.

"What are you doing?" Wren frowned in confusion as she backed up past her.

"You just stay away from me" she warned them off, eyes darting from person to person "You stay back!"

"No one's going to kill you, you moron!" Mockingbird scolded her.

"You can't fool me with your lies!" Nightjar spat back "You stay away from me! I-I know karate!"

"Like hell you do!" Mockingbird rolled his eyes "Stop being ridiculous! No one's going to kill you!"

"A rather bold thing to say. You're so certain you won't be killed?"

Everyone turned to Shrike.

"What did you say?" Mockingbird frowned.

"A person desperate to escape would have little to lose by killing someone they don't even know" Shrike commented "Are you not desperate to leave? Do you not have a reason to escape from here?"

The blood seemed to drain from Mockingbird's face, and then from everyone in the room.

Even Cuckoo wanted to leave, if only because he detested being stuck here at some other person's will. For someone with memories of the outside world, of what they were missing...

Would they really kill each other to escape?

A dark place deep inside himself laughed dismissively at a volume that made Cuckoo shudder: that even good people, provided they were scared and desperate, could do terrible things when cornered.

They...wouldn't do it here, right? He wasn't about to watch the only people he knew suddenly lunged at each other to tear their throats out, right?

He subconsciously took a step back, his back hitting the firm stone wall. It felt like a knife at his back.

"I have an idea!"

Surprisingly it was Wren who spoke up.

"We should each promise each other that we won't kill anyone!" she declared with a proud smile "That way, no one will die!"

Everyone struggled to know what to say to that. They waited for her to declare it an unfunny joke, but the punchline never came.

"Are you serious?!" Nightjar finally found the words "How the hell would *that* work?!"

"We may not have a choice in the matter" Shrike declared, bringing more unwelcome news "If we refuse to play their game, the warden may decide to just kill us all themselves."

It was an even more uncomfortable assumption, one that promised zero escape for them if it was true.

"What the hell, then how are we supposed to get out?!" Mockingbird groaned, putting his head in his hands.

"Other than by doing as the note says?" Duck questioned, getting a series of angry glares in response that sent him reeling "Well...never mind. I guess no one would just agree to do that. Do any of you have better ideas?"

"Anything's a better idea than *that*" Kingfisher muttered angrily, unable to look at him "You can't expect us to just sit here and wait for our turn to die."

"Even if we do kill each other off, do we even have a guarantee the last of us will actually be allowed to leave?" Loon spoke up "It seems a bit much to trust the person who locked us in here to hold their word."

"Not to mention we'd be like, arrested right away" Wren added.

"No one's going to arrest anyone for being forced to kill by a psycho!" Nightjar insisted "That's totally self-defence!"

"Regardless" Loon spoke up again "I think our only hope is to stick together and find the warden. If we do, between the ten of us, I'm sure we can force them to let us go."

Cuckoo shifted. It was a good plan, if it was possible. He doubted it was going to be that easy though.

"Right, so where do we find this warden?" Mockingbird questioned, alive again now there was a mission "They've gotta be in here somewhere, right? Or they wouldn't be able to deal with us if we said no. Are they watching us from cameras or something?"

Cuckoo instinctively looked into the corners of the corridor for little spies. But there wasn't anything out of the ordinary. Just smooth grey bricks without so much as a peephole.

Were they being watched? But if they were, how was the warden doing that?

"There haven't been any cameras so far" Kingfisher shook her head.

"So, if they *are* watching, it must be from a much closer position" Raven spoke up, looking thoughtful.

"You obviously have an idea" Shrike remarked with a big smile "Care to share?"

Raven, who'd previously said nothing since the note had been read, paused for a long moment before he spoke again, and when he did, Cuckoo wished he hadn't.

"It would make a lot more sense if the warden was among us. Watching over his prisoners from within, so to speak."

Something sickening fell amongst the group as they spoke. Duck and Nightjar appeared to turn green. Kingfisher, who'd been stood between them, began to back away towards a corner. Rail muttered something to himself and tried to force his head back down his neck.

It was Mockingbird who got angry, puffing up to a greater height.

"What the hell, man!" he roared, stepping forward and grabbing Raven by the collar of his coat "Why would you say something like that?!"

Cuckoo almost moved to step in, but stopped himself. Mockingbird had the right to be angry by such a statement, and he didn't exactly have any better conclusion to the facts they knew.

"I don't get it" Wren spoke up, looking confused "Is he saying that one of *us* is the warden?"

"That's exactly what he's saying" Duck agreed, slowly shifting towards Loon for safety "He thinks that one of us trapped us all in here to kill each other."

"Or for someone to kill *us*!" Mockingbird stressed, his grip on the startled Raven only getting tighter.

Cuckoo's eyes darted between everyone in the group, watching for anyone making a threatening move.

Just the idea that such a sick person – someone who could trap nine people and puppet them on a string like they were nothing – could be standing in this room with them...

"Could this have something to do with Raptor Tech?" Duck questioned, his voice even quieter now "Some sort of attack on the company?"

"You think a coworker hated our company so much they'd lock ten random employees in a prison to kill each other?" Shrike questioned, hmming contemplatively.

Duck looked away. "Or some sort of outside spy. A hacker or..."

He trailed off, voice softening as he struggled to think.

"We're really all stuck here because we just happened to get jobs with the same company?!" Nightjar shouted, words wavering with distress.

"What else could it be?" Kingfisher spoke up from where she had pressed herself into the wall, tears in her eyes.

Again, silence reigned, no one having any idea what to say to that.

Cuckoo kept his mouth firmly shut. He had no idea if he worked for Raptor Tech. But bringing that reminder up would no doubt bring everyone's worries right down on him. It was Loon who finally spoke up.

"We won't know if the warden is among us if we don't look" she announced "We should search this whole place top to bottom. We may even find a way out if we do."

Again, Cuckoo liked the words, but he had a feeling they would come to naught. Too much effort had been put into this for it to be resolved by the warden leaving an obvious means of escape.

"So, we split up and search?" Duck suggested "Cover more ground?"

"That could give the warden a chance to attack us" Loon shook her head "We should stay in one big group."

That would also give someone *among* them less of an opportunity to kill anyone else within the group, but she didn't say that. Cuckoo noted she was very good at picking what words to say and what to leave out.

She stepped forward and grabbed Duck's hand again, sending a flush of red to his face.

"Come on" she said "We should start now. Nothing better to do. Should we try the East Wing again first?"

"Why are *you* making the decisions?" Nightjar objected.

"Are *you* going to make better ones?" Mockingbird shot at her.

Wren thankfully managed to speak up before Nightjar could. "I think it sounds like fun! Like a scavenger hunt!"

A scavenger hunt for a psychopath where the stakes were death.

Cuckoo turned his head away. He didn't particularly want to go exploring with any of these people. He didn't want to have to deal with the strain of working over what exactly each of them wanted from him. Not to mention, moving in such a large group in such a small space would only make it more likely that they would miss things, or turn on each other.

And, well, if Raven was right and one of them was the warden…

"Alright, let's go!" Loon declared, pulling Duck by the hand towards the East Wing.

With everyone moving off with a purpose, Cuckoo's eyes naturally gravitated to the other person who hadn't moved, still rooted to the spot he'd been frozen in since the message was read, back pressed firmly into the wall to prevent anyone from getting behind him.

Rail was hunched over, picking at the bandages on his arm with chipped nails. The purple bags under his eyes seemed to have impossibly gotten darker and he was back to muttering to himself.

Should Cuckoo say something? He seemed like he was having some sort of mental break, and that probably wouldn't be a good thing if he was trapped in here with him.

What the hell was he supposed to say though? Was there a manual for talking to someone who seemed to be losing their mind?

Please don't go crazy, because I'm stuck in here with you and I don't want to have to start fearing for my own life?

That probably didn't sound good.

Rail was now rocking back and forth, his murmurings becoming more incomprehensible.

Yeah, he should probably keep his mouth shut, in case he made it worse.

"Hey, you guys coming or what?" Mockingbird appeared back in the corridor again, the unlucky nominee sent to come and find them.

Cuckoo sighed and looked away, not wanting to be suckered into this. "Do I *need* to?"

Mockingbird rubbed his neck awkwardly. "Well, I mean, I'm not going to *make* you. But Loon really wants everyone to stay together. And Wren definitely had no issues with physically dragging you."

Cuckoo shifted on the spot. He could understand Loon's idea: force everyone to stay together so she could keep an eye on all of them, make sure no one was getting ideas. But Cuckoo wasn't about to kill anyone.

However, being dragged around by that behemoth of a woman wasn't worth his pride. "Fine" he agreed.

Mockingbird's eyes had now landed on Rail, frowning with concern. "What's up with him?"

Cuckoo just shrugged. "He's been like that the whole time."

Mockingbird didn't seem impressed with that response, walking over to Rail with far more courage that Cuckoo could've managed.

"Hey, dude" Mockingbird addressed him "You doing ok?"

Cuckoo raised an eyebrow. What kind of question was that? Even *he* could tell Rail was anything but *ok*.

Rail said nothing, clacking his jaw shut as he looked away from them both.

24

Mockingbird paused for a moment, before his face settled into a comforting smile, like one might find on an older relative.

"Hey, I know it's scary" he assured him, talking down to him like Rail was a nervous child "I'm quaking in my boots right now. But we're all going to get out of here, ok?"

That was either the right thing to say or the very *wrong* thing to say, because Rail's blank eyes suddenly lit up with a scalding fire. `

"I *know* that!" he spat, almost shaking with the force of his words "Of course I'm getting out of here! I don't care what I have to do! If I have to tunnel out of here, so be it! I won't die here!"

Cuckoo subconsciously took a step back.

Mockingbird also looked taken aback, mind almost audibly whirring as it plotted a new course with this new information.

"Well, that's great!" he settled on, voice cheery "We can all do it together. Ten minds have got to be better than one, right? What do you say?"

The fire in Rail died again as he wrapped his arms around himself, head ducked. "I'm fine. I don't need other people."

"Oh, come on!" Mockingbird still sounded reassuring as he planted a hand on Rail's shoulder, causing the man beneath it to shudder "We've all gotta trust each other, you know? We've all got people we want to see again out there."

Cuckoo grimaced. He didn't. He couldn't remember if he had a massive circle of friends and family searching frantically for him, or no one to notice if he was missing at all.

Some pathetic part of him gave him the feeling that the latter option was more likely.

Rail didn't appear pleased with those words at all, his whole body squaring up as if ready to fight.

Mockingbird though didn't seem to notice and ploughed on obviously. "I've got a bunch of siblings out there that I need to see again. What about you? Got any brothers, sisters—"

He didn't get a chance to finish as Rail abruptly backhanded the hand sitting on his shoulder.

The fire in his eyes was back, but it wasn't just scalding this time. Now it was a wildfire, an unstoppable destructive force of nature that was going to subsume anything around it.

"My sister's *dead*, asshole!" Rail roared right in Mockingbird's face "Thanks for reminding me of that!"

Leaving Mockingbird stunned to the spot, Rail pushed past him, a blur of green charging away into the West Wing, putting as much distance between himself and the disappeared group as possible.

Mockingbird was frozen for a moment, right arm still in the position it had been when Rail knocked it off. It took a moment of adjustment for him to get the use of it back again and scratch his head through perfectly styled locks.

"That went well" he declared, now turning to Cuckoo "Are you going to blow up at me too? You also have a dead sister?"

Possibly.

"I'm come quietly" was what he settled on.

"Oh good" the smile was back on Mockingbird's face "What about your friend?"

"What friend?" Cuckoo frowned, confused.

"You friend with the scarf" Mockingbird gestured into the alcove.

Cuckoo hadn't even noticed that Raven hadn't been in the group that had left. Instead, he was on his hands and knees behind the table, examining the dust on the floor there in what looked like forensic detail.

"Hey, er, which one are you again?" Mockingbird stumbled.

Cuckoo rolled his eyes. He was getting the annoying feeling that this man was either the picture of conceitedness or as dumb as a rock. He wasn't sure which one he'd prefer.

"Raven" he called out "We need to go."

Raven didn't respond to Cuckoo either, now moving the index finger of his left hand along the ground, particles of dirt trailing after it.

Cuckoo sighed with aggravation and walked over to him, standing over him and making a shadow over his head.

"Raven" he tried again.

Raven finally pried his eyes from the floor, looking up at him. "Hmm?"

He'd been so consumed by what was so interesting about the floor that he obviously hadn't heard a thing.

"Loon wants us to stay together" Cuckoo told him, making clear that he wanted no part in this "If we don't go now, they'll drag us after them."

Raven blinked once, taking that in, before peeling his face off the floor. "Ok! Where are we going?"

"They're just leaving the doctor's office, so the armoury" Mockingbird told him, causing Raven to jump in surprise as he processed someone else was in the room.

They followed after Mockingbird, who despite Cuckoo's silent internal pleadings not to, was happy to chat the whole way there.

"So, I don't suppose *you've* got a dead sister on the outside waiting for you?" Mockingbird questioned.

Who words it like that?

"No" was Cuckoo's simple response.

He didn't remember, obviously, but there was no need to tell him that.

"Ah" Mockingbird nodded knowingly, as if Cuckoo had somehow provided him useful information "I've got sisters. Alive ones, obviously."

"Uh-huh" Cuckoo nodded along, trying not to engage.

He had the overt suspicion that this guy was of the mouth-before-brain variety. Who knew what he was going to say next? It definitely wasn't going to be of any help.

26

Mockingbird didn't need engagement to serve as encouragement though. "Five actually. And three brothers. I'm the second eldest of nine."

Cuckoo's eyebrow jutted up. Eight siblings? Geez.

"Which is why I've got to get back to them, you know" Mockingbird continued on "Not that I'd kill anyone. But I can't die here, you understand?"

Cuckoo just nodded without saying anything. Anything could possibly be taken as confirmation that he wanted this stilted, awkward conversation to continue. That he certainly did not.

Mockingbird huffed out a laugh. "You know, dude, you shouldn't ever play poker. Not with that face. If you wanted me to shut up, you could've just said so."

Cuckoo frowned. What was *that* supposed to mean?

He never found out, because that was when they arrived at the armoury, meaning the conversation could finally end.

The rest of the group had crammed into the packed room, poking around the chamber of murder and mayhem. Shrike was running their finger through a cabinet full of knives. Nightjar was twirling a javelin when Wren took it out of her hands and fastened it back into its clasp on the wall. Kingfisher was examining her face in a shield with a frown. Loon was locking up the gun cabinet with a pensive expression, her body turned as if to guard it from the eyes of everyone else. Amongst all of this, Duck was frozen in the middle of the room, arms huddled around himself like he was worried that one of the many sharp implements in the room was going to stab into him if he so much as shivered, eyes watching everyone without stopping on anything.

"I'm going to keep this key" Loon announced, holding up the gun cabinet key "I just...don't think we should have any temptations."

The whole room seemed to tense so badly Cuckoo swore he saw the walls buckling inward.

It was Nightjar who broke it, picking up a grenade and tossing it in her hand with a scoff "This whole room is one massive temptation."

Wren just took the grenade from her and put it back in its box, unable to say anything to refute that.

"This is a little different" Loon told her "Most of these weapons require effort to use, or risk collateral damage. A gun though, well, you just flex a finger."

Well, that put the room in a peachy mood, everyone now avoiding eye contact at all costs.

"I'm going to keep a hold of it" Loon insisted, putting the key in her jumpsuit's pocket "Just in case. At least this way, we can deprive the warden of any easy weapons."

Unless the warden already had a key. But that wasn't something any of them could reasonably guess at.

"Why do you get to keep it?" Nightjar questioned, because of course she did.

"Oh, would *you* like it, Nightjar?" Shrike questioned "If anything happens then, we know to blame you."

Nightjar stared at them, slack-jawed for a moment, before looking away with a tisk. "Keep it, whatever, I don't care."

"We won't get in trouble for taking it?" Mockingbird questioned, his voice weary.

"We've already been locked up here" Kingfisher pointed out, any life that had once been in her voice fully deceased now "What's the worst they could do now?"

Mockingbird paused, looking at her with concern, then nodded. "That's fair."

Cuckoo's stomach clenched. Maybe there was something about seeing a young girl so broken down, but it left him feeling sick in a way nothing beyond his own situation had before.

Did he have a younger sister? Or a younger friend she reminded him of?

...

Nothing, all that was still blank.

He groaned and put a hand to his head. He wanted to take a step back and try and sort through all of this. He was never going to get anywhere having his brain bombarded with all this new outside information. He wanted to pick his brain, see if anything fell into a familiar crack or crevice.

But as he tried to slink out of the armoury unnoticed, Wren hurried after him, standing right next to him like a bodyguard. Just as quickly Loon, fixed him with a stern look, like a mother watching their child reaching for the cookie jar.

Clearly they weren't going to let him out of their sight. If he tried to run, Wren would just drag him back to the group to deal with more upset people. Great.

It didn't take long for the rest of them to give up on the armoury, expressions sullen as they shut the door behind them and moved on to the pantry.

Cuckoo frowned as the noticed a key sitting in the lock of the armoury door. No one else seemed to have noticed it, or commented on it at least. He wondered about taking it, but that would probably just make him suspicious. Should he warn them, maybe?

"Hey, Blank Face, your friend's wandered off again" Mockingbird observed, waving his hand to make it clear he was talking to Cuckoo.

Cuckoo startled, realising Raven was indeed missing again. Glancing over his shoulder, he could see him way behind them, poking around at the grate sealing off the tower entrance.

Had he ever been following them at all?

"I'll get him!" Wren declared, rushing off down the corner towards him.

Cuckoo had a sudden mental image of Raven obliviously ignoring her, and hence being returned to them as a little blob crushed in Wren's massive hands.

The idea of the first person he remembered seeing not coming back...it unsettled him.

Cuckoo ran after them as well.

"Raven!" he called ahead "Stop wandering off!"

Thankfully Raven heard him and turned with a smile just before Wren could reach him. "Oh, hi!" he greeted them "You should take a look at this grate! It's fascinating!"

Wren had just grabbed him by the coat when the promise of something interesting stopped her.

"Did you find something?" she questioned, looking ready to pull him away if he didn't fulfil his promise.

"You know what this reminds me of" Raven declared cheerful, unbothered by the giant currently gripping the back of his collar in a vice "It's like a video game. You know, ones that require you to complete the story of this chapter before it'll let you ascend to the next level."

Wren just stared at him funny. "No?"

Cuckoo finally caught up to them. "How...How is that important?"

"This grate" Raven explained "It's been bolted to the wall with hinges."

Cuckoo blinked at him. Isn't that how doors usually work? Had he somehow gotten doors wrong his whole life?

"No, that *is* usually how doors work" Raven chuckled "Though I'm guessing you didn't mean to say that out loud."

He...hadn't. Cuckoo felt a dagger of embarrassment run through him.

First Mockingbird reads him like a book, now him talking out loud. Was he someone incapable of hiding what he was feeling? That was an unnerving thought.

"But it's hinged on both sides" Raven pointed out "So you can't open it. They may as well have used plain old bolts."

Cuckoo looked at what he was talking about. Sure enough, there were three lines of hinges attached to each side of the grate.

To prove his point, Wren grabbed a hold of the grate and tugged it this way and that. The grate groaned but didn't move.

"Why put in a grate we can't move?" she questioned.

There was only one reason Cuckoo could think of.

"To make sure we can't get up there" he suggested "Or, maybe, to keep someone up there from coming down here."

He didn't need to say who he thought that would be.

Wren stared at the grate in alarm. "You think the warden's up there?"

Raven's question was more interesting. "You think the warden is some eleventh person?"

Cuckoo suppressed a frown. He desperately *wanted* to believe that there was some eleventh person pulling the strings. He already had to be wary of everyone in here. He didn't want to also have to wonder which one of them was the depraved mind who'd done this to them.

Raven was so blasé and perky about this. Was he not concerned at all?

"Maybe?" was all he could say "At least, I hope so."

His voice sounded weak to his own ears. But that just made Raven break into a knowing smile

"Surely you noticed it, right?" he smiled "The grate is hinged from *this* side – meaning whoever did it wouldn't be able to go upstairs once it was complete. The gaps are too narrow to push a drill through from the other side. If it was sealed by the warden, and I can't imagine it would be anyone else, then they're down here with us, not up there."

Cuckoo...*hadn't* noticed that. Raven gave him too much credit.

"But if the warden is down here" Wren pondered "Why lock themselves out of their own tower?"

"That I don't know" Raven admitted, eying the grate "But they must be a reason. If I'm right so far, the one who built this place is a mechanical genius."

Not that that was comforting. It would be far easier to subvert a complete idiot rather than a genius.

Wren thought that over, then clapped her hands together. "We should tell everyone this! We need to stick together, you see. Come on!"

With that she gripped both of them by their collars and began dragging them down the corridor.

Cuckoo squawked and tried to twist out of her grip, stumbling over his feet as Wren's strides were much large than his. But it was like her fingers had little biceps of their own, gripping to him like a barnacle.

Raven found this all funny, laughing as Wren dragged them around the corner and into the first room she found: a kitchen.

It was well stocked, with two ovens and stoves and enough counters to give them all space if they were all going to cook together. It even had a central bar with stools for people to snack at, which Kingfisher, Duck and Nightjar were already sat at, content to leave the actual investigating to Loon and Mockingbird. In the far corner was a partially opened door Shrike was stood by, through which Cuckoo could hear the sound of the rain from the courtyard.

"This is a nice space!" Loon remarked, throwing open an empty cupboard (it appeared all of the cupboards were empty) "There were utensils in the pantry, right?"

"And food" Duck agreed "Enough to last us at least a few weeks."

"We could certainly cook a decent meal for everyone here" Loon announced "I'm not so bad, if I have a few helpers."

"Yes, food!" Nightjar perked up with delight from where she'd been lying with her head on the counter.

"I think she's asking if anyone here considers themselves gifted in the culinary arts" Shrike supplied from their tucked away position.

Nightjar immediately deflated and looked away. "Just say 'Can any of you idiots cook?'. It's less grating."

"Er, I'll just say, no" Mockingbird supplied, raising a hand "I don't think I've ever cooked before."

"Me too!" Wren spoke up, announcing their arrival "I suck at cooking."

"Ah, you're back! Thank you Wren, you're brilliant!" Loon remarked with her usual cheer "Where's Rail?"

Has she *just* noticed he wasn't with them?

"Having a breakdown" Mockingbird supplied with a grumble "I'm a little surprised he's the only one."

"You sayin' something, asshole?!" Nightjar immediately spat, whipping her head around to face him.

"I'm not even looking at you, you dumb broad!" was Mockingbird's immediately response.

"Well maybe a good meal would cheer him up!" Loon spoke up over their argument "Anyone willing to chip in and help?"

Cuckoo tried to shrink back, his collar still stuck rigid in Wren's grasp. He didn't know if he could cook, and he didn't want to find out now. He wasn't even hungry, as if anyone could have an appetite with an anvil hanging over their head.

Raven seemed to be in agreement, his smile turning wry at the idea of eating.

"We should probably finish surveying the place first" Kingfisher spoke up, her voice quiet "We don't want to leave any stone unturned."

"She's got a point" Mockingbird agreed "Last thing we want is the warden jumping out of a vent to kill us as we settle in for dinner."

"Oh, like in that video game you like" Kingfisher nodded.

Mockingbird frowned at her. "What?"

Kingfisher stared back at him, her gaze weirdly heavy. "Don't you remember?"

Mockingbird just blinked down at her. "Remember what?"

Duck picked his head up too at that question. "You remembered something?"

The pause that followed felt unnervingly heavy, as Kingfisher shot Mockingbird an inscrutable stare, ice blue eyes burying right into his soul. Cuckoo felt himself shudder, even if he wasn't the one the stare was directed at.

But the Kingfisher smoothed herself back into indifference and clarified. "I said before, that there were no air vents. And you said that was a good thing, or someone could jump through them, like in a video game you like."

"Oh, did I say that?" Mockingbird pondered, scratching his head "Huh."

"When did he say that?" Shrike questioned.

Kingfisher refused to answer, just staring at Mockingbird like he was dangling a juicy treat over her head.

"You still forgetting stuff, Old Man?" Leave it to Nightjar to break the tension.

"That was one time!" Mockingbird insisted.

"You forgot the room you just came out of" Nightjar reminded him with a smirk.

"One time, and I was still fuzzy from waking up!" Mockingbird insisted "I'm good with orientation usually, I swear!"

"So, we should go and see everything else?" Wren suggested, rocking back and forth on her feet "And then dinner?"

Nightjar groaned disappointedly at the food not slated to come immediately. How was she still hungry in such a situation?

"It probably won't take long" Raven supplied, a slight bite to his words "*You've* already seen half of it."

Cuckoo cracked the slightest of smiles. After all, all he and Raven had seen was a greyish blur whilst trying not to choke.

Maybe Wren could read his thoughts, because she finally remembered to stop throttling them with their own clothing, dropping them back into their own shoes.

"We still haven't found any sign of the warden yet" Shrike commented in a knowing tone "What are the odds they'll make their grand appearance and reveal themselves in the second half?"

Unfortunately, Cuckoo was getting the feeling it was pretty unlikely.

3

Everyone shuffled out of the kitchen in an orderly fashion and meandered on to the next room. Loon stuck her head into the next door, declaring it to be a dining room for them to eat in, which did nothing but get Nightjar complaining that she was hungry again. Perhaps to spare them the whining that would ensue, Loon left that room almost immediately and turned the corner into what Cuckoo's sense of direction – and the plaque above the arched entranceway – told him was the West Wing.

For the first time, there were rooms on both side of the corridor: ten of them, almost identical, with their doors facing each other. Cuckoo would charitably call them cells: monk's cells, specifically. Each one bore a person's name (*brand*) on the front, with a bed, a side table and a rug on the floor. The rugs were even colour-coordinated, one for each person: of the cells Cuckoo glanced in to, he saw that Loon's was red, Mockingbird's was purple, and Raven's was grey.

When they found the warden, Cuckoo wanted to have a word with them about their interior decorating tastes.

Loon didn't seem to agree, squealing over how cute the rugs were. She seemed to be a sucker for cute things.

Everyone was poking their heads through the lines of doors, taking special interest in the rooms marked with their own names on the front. Everyone except Duck, that was, who just leant against the corridor wall, protecting his blind spot, quietly observing everyone.

Was he already wary of everyone? We he expecting someone to attack him at any minute?

Maybe he had a point. Logically, as the smallest of them, he'd make for the most likely target. Thankfully Cuckoo, as the second largest person here, should hopefully be safe.

"We have a bathroom!" Mockingbird's voice called from down the corridor.

Raven turned to the door opposite where Mockingbird had gone through and frowned. "And the girls have a cupboard."

Cuckoo caught sight of a stack of books and pillows inside the cupboard before Raven shut the door again.

"Ours is here" Kingfisher told him, positioned two doors down from Raven "They're slightly offset."

Intrigued, Cuckoo followed Mockingbird through the door labelled with a male icon.

It was a communal bathroom, with several stalls and sinks against the wall, and a blue clothes hamper pushed into the back corner. He ignored them all in favour of the mirror above the sinks, freezing at what he saw.

Ah, that must be him, mustn't it?

For some reason, he hadn't expected to see himself blond. Or for his hair to be in a loose bun, although he left it there for ease. That being said, whilst he still felt like a stranger in this body, he didn't feel any revulsion at his own face.

Those muscles though...they didn't feel right. Poking at them, he felt his finger pring back into the air from the firmness of them.

Yeah, that didn't feel right at all. But why was he so unnerved by the presence of muscles on him?

Why did everything about this body – because his stomach revolted when he tried to call it his own – feel so wrong to him?

Was everyone feeling this way? Or was it just him?

He turned away from the mirror, unable to look at it anymore.

He moved on through the sliding door opposite the sinks to find himself in a shower room. It was empty beyond the appliance itself, a line of five blue towels on hooks and a yellow plastic chair. With nothing but shining white to look at, he stepped out into the corridor where the others were gathered.

"Ok, that means there's a bathroom and shower room each for the boys and girls" Loon announced.

Kingfisher shot Shrike a suspicious look. "So...where does that leave you?"

Shrike merely raised a perfectly plucked eyebrow. "It leaves me in the corridor, talking to you."

Kingfisher's look somehow turned more spiteful. "I meant which bathroom are you using?"

It was like she was fishing for an expected answer, unwilling to budge until she heard what she wanted.

Shrike just stared down at her like a giraffe might look at an earwig, Kingfisher holding their stare with a clenched jaw.

"I think she's asking if you're a boy or a girl" Raven spoke up on Kingfisher's behalf.

Cuckoo couldn't help but hold his breath – the question had been eating at his mind too. It didn't necessarily bother him in any meaningful way, but the curiosity had been nagging at him.

Unlike the rest of the group, it wasn't as if Shrike had any particular features that could easily identify them as male or female. The long hair and pretty face were twinned with broad shoulders and a thin waist. Even their voice didn't bring about any certainty. Cuckoo was pretty sure if he guessed, he was probably going to get it wrong and risk offending them.

Shrike paused for what felt like an eternity, the serene look never leaving their face. Finally, they chuckled and lifted a finger to their lips.

"Hmm...I'll use whichever one isn't occupied" they declared.

A vein seemed to beat in Kingfisher's temple, but before she could say anything, Nightjar got there first.

34

"Not cool, man!" she spat "Which are you?! We ain't having guys perving on us in the shower!"

"I agree" Wren spoke up, folding her arms "It isn't appropriate."

"I wouldn't mind if a girl walked in on *me* in the shower" Mockingbird just had to admit with a shrug.

"See!" Nightjar pointed at him with a furious arm "Point freakin' proven!"

"Guys, enough, enough!" Loon waved their complaints down "I'm sure there's more than two bathrooms in this whole building. We can give Shrike exclusive use of the one we find next. Until then, they can use whichever one they feel most comfortable in."

Shrike almost seemed to preen under the suggestion.

Kingfisher just wrapped her arms around herself, head ducked, mumbling under her breath. "He doesn't seem concerned about what makes *us* comfortable."

Cuckoo rolled his eyes and stepped away from the group, not being prepared to deal with any political commentary being thrown about on the enigma of Shrike's gender.

He stopped in front of the room labelled the same as his brand. He should probably take a look, if only to find out what terrible insult to décor was on the floor of his room. When he pulled the door labelled 'Cuckoo' open though, he had to swallow a scream. His room wasn't like any of the others'.

Blood. Big splotches of red blood all over the room. On the floor, on the bed, on the green furry rug. Heck, it had even made its way up the stone walls and onto the ceiling, an impressive feat considering its excessive height. A *drip drip drip* as drops plummeted to the floor, drilling into his skull. He swore could feel blood spraying onto his face and up his arms, blood sticking to his hands in a gooey mess despite them being visibly dry, a phantom sensation sending shudders through his whole body.

Someone had clearly been violently murdered in here. Or at least, it had been staged to look like it.

The door was suddenly taken out of his hands and slammed shut.

He looked over to Raven, whose pale face told him that he'd also seen what was in the room.

"Ok" Raven spoke up, his voice breathy "I was with you when you woke up, so I know you haven't killed anyone. But they don't know that, and someone's obviously setting you up. So don't say anything, ok?"

Cuckoo's mind was too busy whirring to process his words. Why was his room like that and no one else's? Why him, the one who was missing all of his memories, not just of how they got here?

Why was *he* different?

He hadn't actually killed anyone, had he?

No, there was no way he had. But someone had definitely been killed by *someone*.

Oh god, this was all real, wasn't it? Someone had already been killed, and whoever killed them intended to kill the rest of them, if they didn't do it themselves.

35

Oh god.

Oh god.

He felt sick. His whole body was shaking from his head to his toes.

"Hey" Raven put a hand on his shoulder "Just breath, It's alright, I'm with you. We're not going to say anything for now, ok?"

Raven's hand should've been comforting, but it felt unnatural, and he wanted to throw that oppressive feeling off him. He managed to tough it out though – Raven was trying to help, after all. Best to not upset him.

"Come on" Raven tugged him to follow after the group, Cuckoo doing his best not to bristle under his touch "Looks like there's a gym up ahead. Act normal."

Past the girls' bathroom, the corridor widened as the rooms on the right abruptly stopped. There was only one door on the left, the plaque reading Gym.

The first thing Cuckoo's eyes landed on was a series of dumbbells on the floor sitting next to a pile of shotputs, each weight stylised with a huge spike at either end of the bar; something he couldn't help but consider a health hazard. The second was a weight bench with a massive dumbbell lifted onto it, its spikes left resting at roughly head-height – Cuckoo doubted any of them could've lifted it, except maybe Wren. Finally, it stopped on the rest of the group at the far end of the room – none of them having noticed they were missing – trying to move another cabinet.

The cabinet didn't look heavy, but Mockingbird and Loon weren't able to move it at all. Even when Wren stepped in, she could only get it an inch off of the ground.

Kingfisher turned and looked at them as they entered, her gaze disturbingly blank.

"They think there's a door behind it" she told them "But they can't move the cabinet."

"There's gotta be a dead body in it!" Mockingbird declared, sweat trickling down his brow from the stress he was putting his body under trying to shift the obstacle.

Cuckoo shuddered. He'd be fine without hearing those words, thanks.

Was there really a dead body somewhere in here? That blood had looked fresh.

Raven took in the spectacle for a moment before he announced: "We'll need to roll it. Hold on."

Retreating, he came back from the other end of the room with a pair of metal poles. With Wren lifting up each end of the cabinet one by one, they were able to get it onto the rollers and manipulated out of the way onto its new make-shift wheels.

"That is amazing, Raven!" Loon squealed, which probably would've sounded more like a compliment if she wasn't giving them out like sweets on Halloween.

"Whoa, how'd you learn to do that?" Nightjar questioned, looking genuinely amazed and intrigued.

Raven flushed the same colour as his scarf. "Physics."

"I see" Shrike remarked, eyes burrowing into Raven "What did you say your job was again?"

36

Before Raven could answer, he was cut off by Mockingbird groaning into the now open cabinet.

"More weights" he announced "Damn it, don't they know there's more to a gym than weights?"

He went on for a bit, but the rest of them tuned him out as they faced the tiny door on the other side of where the cabinet had been standing.

"Told you there was a door" Wren declared smartly.

"So, who's going through it?" Nightjar questioned, looking at the only two people who could reasonably fit through it.

Duck buried his face in his collar, whilst Kingfisher tilted her head.

"Is there even any point?" she questioned "There's hardly going to be anything useful in there."

"There could be way out" Nightjar insisted "Have you thought about that?"

"No one's going to put a way out through a door Wren found in half a minute and Raven had opened in less than that" was Kingfisher's annoyed retort "Not to mention one we can't all fit through."

"We still should check inside" Loon declared "Just in case there's any answers for us to find."

Or the warden's hiding in there, she didn't say.

"I'll do it" Duck timidly offered "I don't mind."

The offer took Cuckoo by surprise. Up until this point, Duck hadn't seemed interested in exploring the prison at all; just standing back and watching them as Loon dragged them all from room to room. Why the sudden interest?

Loon whirled around to face him, gripping Duck's hand in both of hers, her delighted, smiling face that had somehow gotten impossibly brighter moving just inches away from his own.

Oh, *that* was why.

"You will!" she cheered "Thank you Duck! You're so brave!"

It was a bit overblown for Cuckoo's taste, clearly meant to boost Duck's fragile ego. It worked though, his ears tinging with red and a more confident set falling to his shoulders. He looked dazed, like a man who'd never drank clean water before had just sipped from an oasis.

"We'll be right here for you" Loon reached up and patted his head, nothing but pure affection in her eyes "Just let us know if you get into any trouble, ok? You're not going to be alone."

It wasn't much of a promise, since Loon was hardly going to fit through there herself, but none the less, Duck looked at her with wonder, like he'd never been shown affection in his entire damn life. The heavy eye contact was uncomfortable enough to have Cuckoo averting his eyes, feeling like he was intruding.

Nightjar huffed, aggravated. "Are you just going to stand there staring at each other? Because I don't have to be here for this."

Loon just shot an unimpressed narrow-eyed stare at her, whilst Duck flinched and all but threw himself through the tiny door, scrabbling noises echoing in the walls as he shuffled in the limited space.

"Go Duck!" Wren cheered "You can do it!"

"Good job kid!" Mockingbird called with a smile "We're relying on you."

"So don't die" Nightjar blunted added.

Everyone sent her a dry look.

"Really?" Raven asked, wincing.

"What?" Nightjar scoffed "If he dies, *I'm* not getting his body out of there."

Of course she was thinking about herself.

It was an awkward pause as the eight of them remained stuck outside, just listening to the scraping and shuffling of Duck moving around inside the dark room. He must be moving by hand, since none of them had seen any torches as they moved around.

Hopefully the lights wouldn't go out, or – without windows – they'd definitely be screwed.

Finally, Duck stuck his head out.

"I think it's an annex" he declared "There's just junk in here. I've checked all the walls, but this is the only door in and out."

Collectively, everyone's spirits sunk.

"That's it then" Kingfisher folded her arms around her body as if giving herself a hug "The next room is the library, so we're back where we started."

"We've checked every room then?" Mockingbird realised "But we didn't find any way out."

"So, we're really trapped here?" Wren asked.

"That's obvious" Nightjar rolled her eyes.

"That food won't last forever though" Loon realised "How do they expect us to restock?"

"There has to be a way out" Raven announced "If only because there has to be a way *in*."

Everyone stared at him, causing him to duck his head with an embarrassed smile.

"Finally, someone asking the right questions" Shrike chuckled.

"How the hell is *that* the right question?!" Nightjar protested.

"*We're* all in here, aren't we?" Shrike pointed out "And this place is furnished. In order to do that, there must be an entrance through which both we and the furniture were brought."

"Couldn't they have bricked it up afterwards?" Kingfisher suggested.

"I doubt we would have remained unconscious that long" Shrike shook their head "And we would have seen signs of the wall being recently patched up. But everything in here is infuriating well-polished."

They were right. Everything in the prison sparkled with freshness. Cuckoo doubted the ovens had ever been turned on or the beds slept in.

It was like the whole place had been built specifically to house them.

But why do that? And who would have the funds to do such a thing?

"Er, maybe we were, like, craned in?" Wren spoke up, not sounding certain about her words "Like, someone got a big crane and winched us over the wall."

The stares the group sent her were positively exasperated.

"So, then they wouldn't have to make a...hole...?" Wren tried to suggest, her voice slowing as the ridiculousness of the suggestion caught up with her "I'll shut up."

"Please do" Nightjar rolled her eyes.

"There must be a method of leaving this place" Shrike continued, ignoring the interlude "We just haven't found it yet. It must be incredibly well hidden."

Raven looked like he wanted to say something, but before his mouth could fully open, it was blasted shut by another one of Loon's inspiring speeches.

"There must be!" she declared "And we'll find it! The ten of us working together, I'm sure we can do it!"

Cuckoo held back a sigh. Big words when one of them was already missing and everyone was too busy grating on one another to really get along.

She hadn't forgotten the bit where they were being encouraged to kill each other, had she? No, she was too smart for that.

"Well, good luck with that" Nightjar declared, straightening her hat "I've searched every inch of this place and found nothing, so I'm getting food."

"Wait!" Loon called out "We should stay together!"

She kept saying that. It was like she was worried if she didn't keep an eye on everyone, they'd go and take the warden up on his offer.

But Nightjar didn't so much as slow her pace as she strode out of the gym, boots making a piercing clacking noise on the linoleum floor.

Cuckoo was a little amazed. How was her stomach settled enough to eat? His certainly wasn't.

"I, well, er" Wren shuffled from foot to foot awkwardly "I'm...also hungry. Can I go too?"

Loon sighed, taking her cap off to brush a hand through her short hair and resettling it on her head, still backwards. "Ok. Just stay safe."

"We'll be fine!" Wren declared, rushing off after Nightjar.

Cuckoo believed her. No one was going to be stupid enough to take on a muscled giant.

"I haven't seen the rooms in the North Wing yet" Shrike declared "Anyone fancy coming with me?"

"I will" Raven offered "There's something I need to check."

39

The two of them filed out, Raven shooting Cuckoo a look as they passed. He wasn't sure if it was supposed to be reassuring, or maybe a subtle warning to keep his mouth shut about the state of his room.

There was no chance of that – Cuckoo didn't think he could trust anyone here with such damning information.

Mockingbird followed them out with a little huff, Kingfisher right on his heels.

That left just himself, Loon and Duck in the gym.

"I'm going to keep looking in here" Duck told them, still on the floor, half out of the annex "Maybe there's something that could help us."

"Ah, thank you" Loon smiled at him "You're so thoughtful."

Duck looked away, his face red. "Ah, that's going a bit far. Everyone should do their best to help each other in this situation."

"Not everyone knows to step up and do the right thing in a crisis" Loon assured him, crouching down to get more on his eye level "Don't downplay yourself, ok? You're worthy of all the praise you're getting!"

Cuckoo shuffled awkwardly. They'd completely forgotten he was in the room, obviously. Thankfully the discomforting praise and overdone staring was all they did. Duck shuffled back into the annex and began pushing out some of the items he found there.

A set of ceramic dishes, a wooden crutch, a stack of empty crates, a mop and bucket, and even a pair of wheeled pallet movers. Nothing that was going to help them. No wonder they had been relegated to a junk cupboard.

With the list of unhelpful items only growing, Cuckoo became acutely aware of the fact that he was standing around doing nothing. Loon wasn't even looking at him, and he was beginning to realise that whilst she had encouraging words for everyone else, she'd never said anything to him ever since he'd outed himself as the odd-one-out in the courtyard.

Well, she didn't have to say he was so *unwanted*.

He shuffled backward out of the room, determined to leave if he wasn't needed or wanted. His eyes drifted over the gymnastics stack horse, the rowing machine and the chalk board against the wall. Loon didn't so much as look up at him, the human instinct for eyes to follow natural movement somehow evading her.

His footstep took him through the North Wing, wondering if he should check out that other corner room beyond the pantry that he'd missed seeing on Wren's magical mystery tour, even if the others had seemingly not found anything useful in there.

No one had mentioned finding a body, and yet someone had clearly been killed in his room. So, what had happened to them? It was one thing to lose an entrance, but a body too?

He paused at the grate Raven had been so fascinated by before, tugging on it experimentally to prove that it didn't move. Beyond it, stairs circled up the tower in a spiral.

This was the only place they hadn't been able to access. But if it was hinged from this side, the warden mustn't be able to get up there either.

If everything about this place was custom built, why leave this here?

Was it some sort of trap, or a distraction?

Click!

His head automatically turned down the corridor to find the sound that had just assaulted his hearing.

Rail was coming out of the doctor's office, a hand in his coat pocket. He turned and locked the door, tucking the key away in his one of his trouser pockets.

Cuckoo frowned. What was he doing?

Rail looked up and caught eyes with him. But before Cuckoo could say anything, Rail's whole body recoiled in terror, and he fled down the corridor like his coat was on fire.

Cuckoo considered going after him, but he wasn't sure what he would say when he got there. He didn't think he was someone who was good at comforting others, let alone someone as skittish as Rail.

Another sound caught his attention, this time a cry of dismay from the sitting room.

Peering in, he saw what he'd apparently been missing whilst standing useless in the annex.

Someone had found a dart board and had hung it up on the wall of the sitting room. Mockingbird and Raven were the competitors, with Mockingbird mourning a terrible shot. Kingfisher was perched on a padded bench with her usual passive expression, whilst Shrike was picking around one of the bricked-over windows at the end of the room.

The game was more interesting than watching Duck plunder the cave of wonders, so Cuckoo paused in the doorway to watch them. Mockingbird had apparently never played before, his grip on the dart flimsy and the little projectile missing more than it hit. Raven on the other hand seemed to be doing ok – even with him squinting at the board – his darts hit more than they missed, and getting more and more accurate as the rounds went by.

It only took a few more rotations for a winner to be easily decided.

"How are you so good at this?" Mockingbird groaned.

"I'm really not" Raven assured him, pulling his dart out of the 20 on the board "You're just...really bad."

Mockingbird just looked even more upset. "Is that supposed to make me feel *better*?!"

Kingfisher herself now glared at Raven, not happy that his words were upsetting her friend.

"Ah, well, would you like another round?" Raven asked "You're getting used to it now, so I'm sure you'll do better this time."

"What so you can kick my ass again?" Mockingbird scoffed "Nah, I need an opponent on my level."

His eyes skimmed over Kingfisher, then Cuckoo, frowning as he didn't find was he was looking for. Then they locked onto Shrike at the far end of the room.

"What about you Shrike?" Mockingbird asked, a cunning smile on his face "You going to join in or just stand there looking pretty?"

Shrike turned towards him, raising a finger to the side of their head in thought.

"Alright" they finally agreed "I will. But" A razor-sharp smile broke out onto their face. "Only if Raven will play against me *properly* this time."

Raven looked taken aback. "What do you mean?"

"I mean that I have no intention of playing against an opponent who throws matches" Shrike insisted.

Mockingbird looked between them in confusion. "What? Threw the match? How?"

Cuckoo was trying to work that out himself. It certainly didn't *look* like Raven had thrown the match — even for the short time Cuckoo had watched, his play style had remained consistent the whole way through. Hell, if anything, it only got *better* over time.

"Let me guess, you have a desperate need to be liked?" Shrike just continued on, their smile becoming more and more duplicitous "You won't win anyone's favour by lying to them."

Mockingbird was just becoming more and more visibly confused, but Raven seemed to be trying to hide behind the upturned collar of his coat, which implied Shrike wasn't wrong.

"So, either you use your dominant hand this time, or I get to use my left" Shrike finished with a flourish "How's that?"

The silence of the room, stunned by Shrike's little monologue, was broken as Raven chuckled uneasily.

"Well," he swapped the remaining dart in his right hand to his left effortlessly "I didn't expect anyone to notice."

Shrike shrugged. "Most people only see what they expect to."

"For the record, I'm pretty ambidextrous" Raven admitted "But, yeah, I default to my left."

Cuckoo had to manually set his jaw back to normal. He'd been with Raven since he woke up and it hadn't even occurred to him that he'd been using his left hand the whole time. Was Shrike just that observant?

That felt both awe-inspiring and terrifyingly unsettling at the same time.

"Ah, you somehow didn't notice either Cuckoo" Shrike was chuckling "You're a lefty yourself — I thought you of all people would pick up on such an obvious tell. Were you off being distracted again?"

Cuckoo felt his cheeks flush. Such a blatant criticism wanted to send him into hiding, maybe behind the door or under the sofa. The fact it was Shrike who said it somehow made him feel even worse, like looking stupid in front of them was some great mortification.

"Wait, so, you were messing with me?" Mockingbird questioned. If he'd been a dog, Cuckoo was sure his ears would've flattened back against his head.

Kingfisher was also glaring at Raven; somehow her silent stare was scarier than if she'd cursed him out.

"Like I said, I'm pretty ambidextrous, so it didn't make a difference" Raven assured him gently "You're just a bit impatient is all. If you'd stopped and thought about your line before you shot, you would've won easily."

"Well, there's an easy way to determine that" Shrike determined "If Raven plays against me and his performance doesn't adjust, we'll know he was being genuine."

They said that so easily, and yet, there was absolutely nothing genuine in that grin on their face.

Raven's expression seemed equally false as he smiled back. "Alright. Assuming you're not a secret darts genius."

"Oh, I assure you" Shrike laughed "*That* is not one of my talents."

Cuckoo shuffled uneasily towards the door. The sitting room had suddenly become very claustrophobic, like two dragons were about to do battle in the tiny space. He both desperately wanted to watch their bout, and yet didn't want to know the outcome.

Peering out the door, he saw Loon and Duck pass him. They must have finished investigating the annex. Loon was carrying an armful of boxes and Duck was carrying what looked like a cookbook.

That item reminded him of something Nightjar had mentioned, about all of the books in the library being broken. He hadn't had a chance to question her about that, with all the excitement that had come before. Rail had also been in there, but he hadn't mentioned anything odd about them.

The library was just next door. It wouldn't take him long just to take a peek.

"Do you want to join us, Cuckoo?" he heard Raven ask "We could pair up. You and me, Shrike and—"

"So you can deflect attention off yourself?" Shrike immediately pounced on his words, not letting him finish.

"So no one feels left out" Raven snidely corrected them.

Mockingbird was clearly feeling left out, trapped by the bench Kingfisher was sitting on with no way past the still sniping pair, nearly backing up into the fireplace in his haste to escape.

"Look" he spoke "If you two are just going to flirt with each other the whole time, or whatever this is, we're leaving."

That was a mistake, as twin sets of eyes bored into him, suddenly finding a common enemy.

"Oh no, *stay* Mockingbird" Raven insisted.

"Yes, we need a judge" Shrike chimed in "One who's seen Raven's play for himself. To ensure this is fair, after all."

"Oh, I couldn't agree more" Raven agreed, but with a shark-like grin.

"You walked right into that one" Kingfisher quietly added, looking away with half-lidded eyes like this was all so boring to her.

Mockingbird was cornered, Kingfisher was apathetic, and Cuckoo knew he needed to excuse himself before he could get pulled into whatever bizarre measuring contest this was.

"I'm just going to the library" he spoke up, already sidling out of the door "I'll be back. Start without me."

And with that, Cuckoo fled what he determined was probably going to be the most frightening game of 501 ever played, never being so grateful for his two good legs before.

He didn't linger in the corridor too long. His eyes kept drifting to the corners, looking for any of those hidden cameras. He couldn't see any, but that didn't explain why he felt like he was being watched.

Mercifully, the library was void of people. The room was lined with bookcases, with several small metal bird faces above them that he hadn't noticed before. He diverted his eyes one he determined there weren't any cameras in them, finding the staring discomforting.

In the middle were two more free-standing bookcase, shelves stuffed to the brim with paper. But he couldn't help but note that, while the bindings of the books were ostensibly different colours, they were the same five or so colours repeated across the room. They were all also block colours, and exactly the same thickness. Approaching the closest bookcase to the door, he could see that none of the books had titles, and none of their spines were creased, as if they've never been opened before.

What in the world?

He pulled down a bright green book at random. The cover was pristine, no indication of what it was about, so he flipped to the first page.

It must be a poetry book, because all the first page contained was a poem.

Ten little birds sat in a nest.
One boasted he could fly, before he was ready.
He fell to the ground, his course true and steady.
And then there were nine little birds in the nest.

Nine little birds sat in a nest.
One sheltered his siblings through storms and the tide.
But one sibling grew prideful, and cast him aside.
And then there were eight little birds in the nest.

Eight little birds sat in a nest.
One grew big and strong, their presence firm, sturdy.
He was pushed away, screaming for mercy.
And then there were seven little birds in the nest.

Seven little birds sat in a nest.
'I shall never die', screamed one to the heavens.
The sky threw down lightning, and burnt all his feathers.
And then there six little birds in the nest.

Six little birds sat in a nest.
One stared at the horizon, lost and all hopeless.
The wind pulled him under, leaving him breathless.
And then there were five little birds in the nest.

Five little birds sat in a nest.
One slept nice quiet, under his brother's wing.
Without warmth he passed silent, 'The poor little thing!'
And then there were four little birds in the nest.

Four little birds sat in a nest.
But one could not bring himself to feel safety's charms.
He threw himself forward, into nature's crushing arms.
And then there were three little birds in the nest.

Three little birds sat in a nest.
One cried for his brother, a useless endeavour.
The wind ripped right through him, he was silent forever.
And then there were two little birds in the nest.

Two little birds sat in a nest.
One sat apart from others, his voice ever silent.
He was hence swept away, head held high, defiant.
And then there was one little bird in the nest.

One little bird sat in a nest.
All lonely he shivered, as days ticked on by.
Solo he leapt, flying free in the sky.
And then there were no little birds in the nest.

It was, quite frankly, the most appalling poem Cuckoo had ever read. Its barely followed its own structure, and the rhymes grated in his ears with how forced they were. It was like some golem who had only ever heard *about* poems had tried to write one.

He turned to the next page, hoping for something less grating. But instead, the left page was blank, and on the right was just the same poem.

He frowned, flicking through the book. But every flick was the same, all the way to the end of the book: blank on one side, terrible poem on the other.

He put the book back on the shelf, deeming it a dud, a prank someone had left. He pulled down the next book, this one in a red binding, only to see the same poem staring back at him.

Had someone messed with every book on the shelf? In the case?

Or was it the whole library?

Cuckoo crossed the room to one of the large free-standing bookcases in the middle, putting it between himself and the door. He pulled down one of the books, only to be greeted by the same poem on the first page.

Why would someone give them a library, and then fill it with books containing only one single poem? To drive them mad?

To drive them mad enough to kill each other?

Who would do something so insane?

The words of the poem began to spin on the page, creaks and groans as a shadow fell over the pages. He looked up, the case swaying once before it toppled, giant maw sweeping down towards him. There was no time to move or run. Before he could even scream, there was an agonising pain through his body, blood gargling in his lungs, the sound of a chuckle in his ears as he drowned in—

Cuckoo gasped, and he felt like he stepped back into his body again.

What? What the hell was that?!

He looked up at the bookcase, staring at its upper shelves as he waited for it to move. Even though the...vision was over, he found he couldn't breathe as he waited.

But nothing. The bookcase stayed as rigid as a stone guardian, as it should.

Cuckoo wet his lips and tried to turn his attention back to the book in his hands, but his whole body was still shaking.

It wasn't like he'd experienced a daydream – it was as if he actually lived it, and was then thrown back to where he was now. He could feel the crushing pain in every inch of his body like he'd actually been trapped under a falling bookcase.

He heard a creak, and a shadow begin to fall over the page—

Cuckoo's feet began to move before he could think, jumping back and away from the toppling bookcase.

He didn't quite make it though.

Cuckoo was tangibly aware of the sound of fear and pain: what it should sound like when a human was being hurt, even if he didn't remember hearing it himself. Maybe it was just something intrinsic within the psyche of every human being. But the crunch followed by wail of pure unbridled agony was a sound he didn't think he could've imagined in a lifetime, sending chills up his spine just hearing it.

It was so unsettling that it took a few moments for him to realise that *he* was the one screaming.

4

The screams in his ears were deafening, but no matter how hard he tried, Cuckoo couldn't make himself stop.

He tried to focus on his ringing ears – maybe they would distract him from his leg – but it didn't work. No matter how hard he tried, his brain refused to engage with anything but the agony below his knee.

His head was a mess. He wanted to run. He wanted to cry. He wanted to grab a machete and cut the damn thing off to stop the pain, as illogical as that was.

There was no room for logic here though. There wasn't room in his head to contain it among the pain pain pain—

"CUCKOO!"

A voice finally managed to cut through the fog in his head.

Twisting his head, he could see down his body, and the bookcase resting far too close to the ground to have a whole lower leg holding it up. He could see the door, where Duck and Raven were trying to push through the narrow entrance at the same time.

"Cuckoo!" Raven cried out again, finally forcing his way in "What happened?!"

"Holy frick!" he heard Nightjar swear – or at least it sounded like it ought to be a swear – pushing Duck aside to peer in the door herself "How the heck did you do that?!"

Cuckoo wanted to scream out that he hadn't done anything, that he didn't understand what was happening, but his throat was now raw, and he felt like he was choking on tears with every breath.

"Help me get this up!" Raven cried out, sounding like he was going to cry himself as he gripped the end of the bookcase "Hurry!"

Nightjar, surprisingly, didn't argue about it. She immediately ran to help him, pulling up at the same time he did.

The bookcase just barely budged, something in Cuckoo's leg cracking at their ministrations.

Cuckoo wished he'd just died. That he hadn't had that…vision and just let himself be crushed. At least it would've been quicker.

"I'm sorry I'm sorry I'm sorry Cuckoo!" he heard Raven chant as gentle hands patted his head "Stop standing there and help us!"

He was addressing the three in the doorway: Shrike, watching with a pensive but concerned look on their face; Duck, stood next to them as a statue to unmitigated horror; and Mockingbird, pacing up and down the corridor in a panicked shock.

They didn't move, causing Raven to let out a shriek of rage and lunge at the bookcase, trying to lift it himself and making no progress. Nightjar moved to copy him, only to stop when Shrike finally spoke up.

"Raven, think about this" they said in a firm voice "Even the four of us together aren't going to be able to lift that with all of the books on it."

"I know!" Raven insisted "But I—"

"So, think of moment dynamics" Shrike continued "How do we increase turning motion without increasing force?"

"With distance!" Raven yelled out "I know that I—" He cut himself off, his eyes darting about as he thought furiously. "Leverage. I need a pivot."

"Exactly" Shrike assured him calmly but firmly "Decide what you need, and we will get it."

There was another moment as Raven thought like it was his life that depended on it. But finally, he settled on an answer, dark eyes blazing with determination.

"Shelves" he decided on "I need two shelves. And books."

There was an immediate scramble, Raven rushing to one of the other bookcases and throwing books to the side to grab the shelf they were on, tearing it up from its supports with a violence Cuckoo hadn't expected of him. Nightjar did the same on another shelf, whilst Duck grabbed the now scattered books and began piling them either side of Cuckoo's body four high.

If he'd been in his right mind, Cuckoo would've seen the plan coming into fruition. The books were to become pivots, with the shelves having their ends shoved under the bookcase to serve as levers. Now a person could stand on the raised end of the shelf and use their entire body weight to lift the weight of the bookcase, not just the strength of their arms.

But he couldn't focus on that, because he was too busy focusing on how much he wanted to die. What was the point of even getting him out if it was going to keep hurting this much?

"Come on" Shrike grabbed Mockingbird by his jacket and dragged him into the room "You're heavier than me. We need that."

With the still stunned Mockingbird in place and Shrike standing behind Cuckoo to pull him out, both Raven and Mockingbird jumped onto the shelves, the pivots creaking into life.

The bookcase just barely lifted a few inches, and Cuckoo saw white sparks flying behind his eyes. Shrike grabbed his shoulders and tried to pull, but his leg caught on something. Cuckoo swore his heart screeched to a stop – that it had just given up beating from the pain.

"It's not enough!" he heard Shrike shout.

Nightjar scrabbled at the bookcase to help, but her leather gloves struggled to grip the wood. Duck was frozen to the spot, just staring at Cuckoo in horror with his arms hanging limp at his sides.

The shelves seemed to groan, like they were considering giving way under the weight.

"What do we do?!" Nightjar demanded.

"I'm thinking!" Raven insisted, but it sounded more like he was panicking.

The day was saved by Wren, leaping through the door out of nowhere. She took in the scene in an instance and, without thinking, grabbed the edge of the case, managing to lift it another inch with only one arm. That gave Shrike the extra room to pull, and finally Cuckoo came free.

Just in time. A second later, both shelves broke in half, sending both Raven and Mockingbird stumbling to the floor. Nightjar and Duck jumped aside just before the bookcase could cut off their toes.

Cuckoo remained staring at the ceiling, refusing to look at his leg. If everyone's gasps of horror were any indication, nothing good would come of it.

As he predicted, getting him out from under the bookcase didn't make the pain any better. In fact, impossibly, it seemed to get worse. He threw an arm over his eyes, both to block out the now painful light and to stop any more tears from escaping.

The embarrassment was almost as bad as the pain. He wanted everyone to stop looking at him like a roadside attraction. Raven's hand was petting his hair again and he felt like he was being torn apart – simultaneously he wanted Raven to get his hands off him, and also bury into the warmth of kindly attention in the hope it might drown out the pain.

"So, was this a freakin' accident or what?" Nightjar asked, her usual irritation creeping into her words.

"Of course it was!" Raven insisted, at the exact moment the petting on Cuckoo's head stopped dead "It has to be. Right?"

"You tell me, smartarse!" Nightjar snapped back.

"Someone put out a death threat to all of us, one of us nearly gets killed and you think this is an *accident*?!" Mockingbird's voice reached an incredible pitch and volume as he spoke up for the first time.

"No one here is going to kill each other!" Wren stated decisively.

Shrike sighed. "This is getting us nowhere."

"I don't...I...I" Duck stuttered somewhere further away "I d-don't know what to do! You...Y-You...L-Loon! Loon!"

"What is it? What happened?" Loon's voice also entered the room, followed by a gasp "Cuckoo! What happened?!"

"The b-bookcase fell on him" Duck reported, his voice wobbling in panic.

"Was pushed on him more like" Mockingbird grumbled.

Loon paused for a while, but when she spoke again, she was decisive.

"We need a doctor" she declared "Rail's a doctor, right? Has anyone seen him?"

"I can make a guess" Shrike reported "I will go and retrieve him."

Footsteps left the room. Even so, Cuckoo still felt crowded.

"Can someone get a chair?" Loon suggested "Maybe two?"

"If we lift him, he's just gonna scream" Nightjar objected, even as more feet padded out of the room.

Cuckoo wrinkled his nose. Had he screamed when he was moved? He hoped not. He didn't remember that.

"We should probably wait for the doctor anyway" Wren agreed.

"Cuckoo" Raven's voice called out to him "Can you look at me?"

Cuckoo didn't want to, but Raven sounded too concerned for him to hide away.

He dreaded the idea of seeing a look of pity, but Raven's eyes were pure worry when he pulled his arm away to look into them.

"Just hold on a bit, ok" Raven tried to assure him "We're getting a doctor. You're going to be just fine."

The voice was soothing, but Cuckoo knew the words were pretty lies, just designed to give him a tiny smidge of hope to hold on to. The pain wasn't going to miraculously vanish because Raven wished it to.

To his horror, his mouth moved in a pitiful whimper before he could stop it. "I just want it to stop."

Still Raven's eyes didn't turn to pity, which he was immensely grateful for. Just a watery sadness deeper than most oceans.

"I know" he said quietly "I'm sorry."

"I have a chair" Kingfisher announced as she walked in the door "What happened in—"

She dropped the chair she was holding with a scream as she saw him.

Encouraging.

"Yeah, I know" Mockingbird sympathised with her morosely as he used his own chair to herd her out of the doorway "Somone pushed a bookcase on him."

"Whad'ya think you're doing spreading crap like that!" Nightjar snapped at him.

"No one pushed anything on anyone!" Wren joined in, just as angry "This is an accident!"

"We don't *know* what happened" Loon silenced them all, a bite in her words she usually careful to leave out "For now, can we all worry about Cuckoo, instead of our own skins?"

This did a good job of shutting up the room.

Cuckoo felt another blinding spark behind his eyes, rubbing them to try and making it all stop.

"Here we go, one doctor" Shrike announced as if cued, pushing Rail into the room.

Rail took in Cuckoo on the ground with slack-jawed horror. Then he began to full-body shake, like a seizure was starting.

"Ah, no time for that" Shrike insisted, steering him by the shoulder further into the room "You can panic later. Patient now."

"I...what?" Rail seemed out of breath, as he looked around the room from person to person "What am I...what?"

"You need to help him!" Raven insisted.

"Help?" Rail looked down at Cuckoo's leg before looking away, his face somehow paling even further "How? Why me?"

"You're a *doctor*" Nightjar reminded him, her voice communicating her displeasure with his attitude quite succinctly.

"You can t-treat him" Duck added "R-Right?"

"Treat him?" Rail stared down at Cuckoo like he was an exotic zoo animal "I don't treat people! I diagnose them! I don't even...I..."

He couldn't even finish the sentence, running his nails down his bandaged arm. He looked to be on the verge of hyperventilating.

"A doctor's a doctor!" Nightjar complained "You helpin' or what?!"

"Don't pressure him" Kingfisher insisted, back in control of herself "Not all doctors do first aid. Besides, that leg more like something you'd need surgery for anyway."

"We can get him surgery once we make it to safety" Loon decided, gently putting a hand on Rail's shoulder "Rail, is there anything at all you can do for now? Something you've read about, maybe? Even if you've never done it before, it's worth a try."

Cuckoo wanted to argue – he didn't exactly feel up to being Rail's first guinea pig patient. But instinctively trying to pull his leg away wrenched another scream from his throat, and he didn't ever bother *trying* anymore.

Rail jumped at the scream, before slapping himself on the cheeks hard with both hands. He paused for a moment, took a breath, and then looked down at Cuckoo with laser focus.

"What happened?" he asked.

"Bookcase was pushed on him" Mockingbird immediately answered.

"*Fell* on him" Wren corrected harshly, as if that was important.

Rail didn't seem to breathe for a moment, his eyes bugging out of his head as he took in the bookcase lying just a few feet away. He pinched his hand harshly, which seemed to bring him back to himself.

"Did he free himself?" he questioned.

"*We* did" Nightjar told him.

That just made Rail look *more* concerned. "H-How long was he under there?"

"Five minutes, maximum" Raven declared "We got here as soon as we heard him yell."

"Oh, that should be fine then" Rail relaxed a little, kneeling by Cuckoo's side next to his leg "Ok...um...examine the leg. Yes, I'm going to examine the leg."

Cuckoo was not at all assured by the fact he sounded like he was reading from a medical textbook.

"Ok" Rail's hand hovered near the leg "I'm gonna have to roll your pants up. Just, let me know if it hurts, ok?"

For a delicate moment, everything was fine as the trouser leg was pulled up. But then something caught, the leg was raised just a fraction, and Cuckoo's throat let Rail know in no uncertain terms how much it hurt.

"Ok ok!" Rail winced as he immediately backed off, many people in the room clutching their ears "I'm not going to touch that for now. Um...now..."

"Earmuffs" Nightjar snorted "We need freakin' earmuffs."

That triggered a vengeful snap into Cuckoo.

"Screw you!" he spat up at her, not feeling the slightest bit remorseful.

"I can't do anything with him in this much pain" Rail decided on, shuffling uncertainly in place "Painkillers...Were there painkillers in the medical office?"

He didn't check while he was in there? What kind of doctor was he?

"There was a cabinet full of pills and liquids" Kingfisher remembered "I'll be back."

"You'll need the key" Rail declared, passing it to her "Remember to lock up and bring it back."

"You took that?" Mockingbird questioned, but Rail didn't even look at him let alone answer.

She hurried out the room, pushing past Duck harshly enough to send him careering into a bookcase. Thankfully, this one didn't fall over.

"Alright, painkillers are coming" Loon encouraged the doctor "What next?"

"Next? Um..." Rail leant over to examine what of the leg he could "It doesn't look like anything's been punctured, and it seemed like his boot saved his foot. So...I could splint it?"

"And what do you need for that?" Loon continued to ask encouragingly.

Rail paused for far too long before answering. "Two pieces of wood, and bandages. And...a towel, I guess, would do."

"I-I can get b-bandages!" Duck announced, fleeing the room.

"Towels are in the shower room!" Mockingbird called after him.

"Will these do for wood?" Wren questioned, holding up two pieces of the broken shelves.

"They need to be longer – as long as his leg" Rail shook his head.

"Great, this had to happen to one of the tallest guys here" Nightjar rolled her eyes "We couldn't–oof!"

That last sound was made as Mockingbird thrust a still intact shelf into her arms.

"Hold this" he said retroactively, taking a step back.

"Hey, don't just push things at me you piece of–HOLY!"

Mockingbird's foot raised up and crashed down onto the shelf in her hands, cutting her off succinctly. Whatever kung fu magic he was using worked, as the shelf split in half neatly along the grain of the wood, leaving two almost identical long pieces.

"Will this work?" he questioned, taking the pieces out of Nightjar's still stunned hands and passing them to Rail.

Rail's mouth opened and closed a few times, a hint of fear in the corners of his eyes, before his shaking hands were able to grasp them. "Er...yes. Yes, these will do nicely. But I can't begin to splint it until we get some–"

"Painkillers!" Kingfisher announced, arriving with an armful of little transparent glass bottles "I think anyway. I don't know any of these names."

Rail frowned. "You didn't bring back the key."

Cuckoo wanted to curse him out. Why the hell was that important?! Just give him the damn painkillers!

Kingfisher seemed equally confused. "Do you need it?"

Rail shuddered. "It just shouldn't be left unattended."

Mockingbird groaned and left the room. "Fine, I'll get your damn key! If that'll make you happy!"

"Rail" Loon directed the doctor back on track "Cuckoo's in pain. Which one should we give him?"

Thank you, Loon!

"Read them out?" Rail suggested.

Kingfisher let all of the bottles rest on the floor, picking up the first one and reading the label.

"Chlorhexidine" she read out first.

Rail stared at her funnily. "That an antiseptic, not a painkiller."

Kingfisher tossed that bottle aside and read the next one. "Acetaminophen."

"That's...ok" Rail hesitated "We could really use something a bit stronger."

Kingfisher set that one aside, moving onto a bottle with white crystals in it. "Sodium hydroxide. Wait, that's not medicine."

Rail frowned. "That belongs in a *chemistry* lab. Drinking that would just burn him inside out."

Cuckoo groaned. He already felt like he was burning from the inside out. How much worse could that be?

Kingfisher picked up a bottle full of clear liquid. "Strychnine."

"That's straight up poison!" Rail all but shrieked, his hair standing on end "Where did you get these from?!"

"The doctor's office" Kingfisher told him, picking up the next bottle "Hydrogen Peroxide."

"Another antiseptic" Rail explained "Were these all stored together?"

"Same shelf" Kingfisher confirmed, onto the next bottle, squinting at the liquid-damaged label "This is sodium hydroxide again, I think. The label's damaged, but the contents look the same. And this one..." She moved onto the next bottle. "3-methylmorphine."

"That's good!" Rail cried out "Um...how big are the tablets?" He glanced at them. "Right, two of those."

"He'll need water" Raven pointed out.

"I'll get it!" Wren announced, nearly tripping over Shrike by the bookcase and colliding with the returning Duck on the way out.

"So, someone was keeping poisons in the same cabinets as medicines?" Shrike inferred from the previous conversation.

"We are being told to k-kill each other after all" Duck reminded them, passing Rail the bandages "O-Of course they'd make it e-easy."

If the room could possibly get more down, it was now.

"We need a towel too" Rail reminded him.

Duck blinked at him. "Oh. S-Sorry. I d-didn't hear."

"I'll get one" Kingfisher offered, standing up "There are some in the shower room."

It didn't take long for Wren to come back with a cup of water, a minute after Mockingbird gave Rail back his precious key, not that it cheered him up any. Cuckoo was all too happy to swallow down the tablets, regardless of their bitter taste. Heck, he would've done it without the water. Anything to dull the pain.

The effect was immediate. A second after swallowing them, Cuckoo felt like a gentle blanket had been laid over him. The pain in his leg didn't go away, but it settled into nothing more than a dull ache. His whole body felt like he'd jumped into a hot tub on a freezing day.

"Yeah, he's definitely feeling better" Shrike chuckled, obviously recognising something on Cuckoo's face.

Raven sighed with relief, relaxing for the first time since he'd entered the room.

"Yo, that's some good stuff!" Nightjar remarked, a wicked grin breaking out onto her face "Can I have some?"

"Absolutely not!" Loon cut in "Well Rail, do you need our help to splint it?"

But Rail was frozen, halfway through cutting the bandages with scissors sourced from the desk at the end of the room. He looked very unsettled, not even noticing Kingfisher returning with a red towel and holding it out to him, the scissor clattering away worriedly in his shaking hand.

"That's...not right" was all he said.

"We shouldn't be splinting it?" Raven guessed with a concerned frown.

"No, those pills shouldn't be acting that fast" Rail explained, running his left hand through his hair, almost cutting his scalp open as he forgot about the scissors in that hand in his anxious panic "We should've had to wait at least a few more minutes."

Cuckoo for one was more than happy with that fact they hadn't had to wait. He felt great, where before he'd felt like he was on the verge of death. What was so wrong with that?

"Well, they are" Mockingbird just shrugged "You wanna get this over with before he nods off?"

Nods off? Actually, yeah, he was feeling tired. His eyes kept drooping shut.

Maybe it would be better if he just slept for a bit now. He could worry about everything in the morning.

"Ok, Mockingbird, you get that side, Nightjar, that side" Rail declared, shakily removing the belt from his trousers "Wren, when I tell you, I'm going to need you to pull tight. As tight as you can – no matter how much he screams."

Screams? Wait, what? No, he was feeling great. Why would he be screaming?

Rail folded his belt up into a wad and passed it to Raven. "Put that in his mouth. We don't want him to bite his own tongue off."

Whoa, what?!

Cuckoo opened his mouth to object, but before he could get a sound out, Raven obediently shoved the belt in, the scent of leather clogging up his nose and mouth.

Rail ignored his cry of alarm, picking up the red towel and wrapping it around his leg. The bandage he'd wrapped around his hand wound across the towel, before he passed the end of it to Wren.

"I am very sorry about this" Rail apologised, sensing little vibrations of discomfort running through Cuckoo's body "It will be over quickly."

And somehow, those green eyes held firm and steady as he spoke. They were almost reassuring, and for a moment, Cuckoo could believe Rail was a doctor.

"Ok, now!"

Cuckoo never did get to find out how a leg was splinted. As soon as Rail gave the order, an agony somehow worse than the bookcase landing onto him ricochetted from his leg throughout his entire body. Blinding sparks flew through his eyes before his vision went black.

o

"...nothing you could've done, ok. It was gonna suck no matter what you did."

"I know, I know. I just...don't like screwing up like that."

"I mean, at least of all people, it happened to *him*. It would've been worse if it was one of us."

"You shouldn't say–"

"Hey, he's coming to! Cuckoo! Can you hear us?"

Cuckoo managed to force his eyes open with a groan. Everything felt too bright, and the discomfort he felt within his own body was even worse than usual. His vision took several seconds to clear up into defined shapes, where he could see Raven, Loon and Rail peering down at him.

"Cuckoo? How are you feeling?" Loon questioned "Are you with us?"

He felt like shit, to be honest.

"I wish I wasn't" he answered, his throat parched and dry and still tasting like leather – something Raven picked up on as he all but shoved the rest of the glass of water Wren had brought between his lips.

"You passed out back there" Loon explained "But Rail did a great job with your leg! You should be able to walk on it!"

"With help" Rail quickly added "Definitely don't put any weight on it. You're going to need surgery when we get out of here, and the last thing an actual doctor needs you doing is making the damage even worse."

Cuckoo glanced down at his right leg for the first time. He could see the splint – the two shelf pieces bound to his leg in a vice by the bandages and the towel. The painkillers must still be in effect, because it felt more like a dull throb down there rather than the agony he'd been unwillingly getting used to.

He noted that he'd been moved from the floor to the two chairs Mockingbird and Kingfisher had brought, his leg elevated up on the second one.

Beyond it, everyone else was still packed into the room. Mockingbird was pressed into a corner, not even looking at Kingfisher standing at his side. Nightjar was pacing the room, full of frantic energy. Wren was ringing her hands, looking for something to do. Duck was a statue again, half hiding behind Loon. And Shrike was poking away at the fallen bookcase.

All of them, besides Shrike, had only one thing in common: staring at Cuckoo, his pain and humiliation the most entertaining thing in this prison for them to gawk at.

A tiny part of him was grateful they were concerned enough to stick around. A much larger part of him wished they'd all just go away and leave him to be miserable.

At least Rail also looked miserable, gripping onto the nearest bookcase like it was all that was holding him up, not that he'd ever looked anything verging on *happy* before. He wasn't even looking at Cuckoo, his gaze fixated on the junction between the bookcases and the wall.

"Thanks" he told him, not saying what he was actually thinking.

That he didn't want Rail treating him again unless he was already dead.

Rail somehow managed to look even more uncomfortable, stepping back away from Cuckoo and putting his hands in his pockets.

"Don't ask me to do that again" he demanded quietly.

"Oh, believe me, no one here is in a hurry to get under your magic hands, Mr Bedside Manner" Nightjar scoffed, folding her own arms.

"We should do our best not to get injured" Raven pointed out "We can't expect Rail to patch us up for every mistake we make."

"Yeah, particularly if he's the next one dead."

The whole room stared at Mockingbird when he said that, Rail in particular turning ashen at his words.

"You got something to say, asshole?!" Nightjar scowled at him.

"I'm just going to say it as it is" Mockingbird stated firmly "No way Cuckoo could pull that bookcase down by himself. There wasn't an earthquake, and if anyone of you can look me in the eye and say it fell by total coincidence right after we've been given an ultimatum to kill each other, then I get to call you crazy. Someone pushed it on him."

Tremors wracked through Cuckoo's entire body at the thought. The exact circumstances of the bookcase falling hadn't been important before now, but it was a hard point to refute.

If it wasn't for the vision, he wouldn't just be in pain, but dead.

"B-But who could do that?" Duck questioned "It was s-so heavy."

He might have phrased it as a question, but he was looking up at Wren as he said it.

"Hey! I wouldn't kill anyone!" Wren insisted "Killing's just wrong!"

"Even to get out of here?" Mockingbird questioned.

"Especially so!" Wren snapped back "I'm not mean enough to think I deserve to get out of here more than anyone else!"

"What, you don't have anyone waiting for you on the outside?" Mockingbird asked doubtfully.

"Of course I do!" Wren still refused to get angry, just looking hurt "I have friends! Eight very good ones! But I couldn't—"

"I think we can stop the accusations against our giant companion for now" Shrike smoothly cut in like a butter knife "Both before she squishes Mockingbird like a gnat, but also because she's not the only one capable of moving this bookcase."

They knelt down at the far end of the object that had captured their attention so thoroughly.

"It's a little hard to see, but if you look here, someone has cut notches into the base of the bookcase" they reported "Would everyone please confirm what I say is correct?"

A couple of the other free bodies checked the bookcase, all of them agreeing with the assessment. For Cuckoo that was a relief – at least he had more words than just Shrike's to confirm something he wouldn't be able to examine himself.

"I see," Raven realised, eyes wide "With the base cut out, the bookcase was incredibly unsteady. All it would've taken was a small push from the other side to tip it over."

"Exactly" Shrike smiled "Even the 90-pound Duck could have done it."

Duck frowned, but it wasn't exactly something anyone could refute.

Cuckoo felt like something had crawled into his skin with him. Someone here really had tried to kill him.

Logically he shouldn't take it personally. He was just alone, and none of them knew each other. But it felt personal. His life was all he really owned at the moment, and someone had tried to take it.

Even though they hadn't succeeded, they'd left him in a hyper-vulnerable position that made his skin crawl.

"So, you're saying someone went and sawed out the bottom of the bookcase, knowing that Cuckoo was going to stand under it?" Loon questioned.

"He only left the sitting room a minute before it fell" Raven interjected "And he didn't tell anyone he was going to the library."

"Is that true?" Loon asked, looking down at Cuckoo.

"*I* didn't know I was going until I left the sitting room" Cuckoo confirmed "It must've just been random chance."

"I think we're assuming that this is too well planned" Shrike stopped that line of thought "Cutting the base would've taken time and made noise. We only found that letter when we were all together – it was still in its envelope. Most of us have been together since then, so it's highly unlikely the bookcase was sawed by one of us."

Cuckoo agreed with most of that point. They were all together for most of that time, and the only one who'd been alone for any significant time was Rail.

He winced at that thought. He could picture Rail, never the picture of stability, running around with a hacksaw. And they *had* found him alone in the library. But it was a dangerous road to go down, suspecting someone based only on an alibi. And they hadn't found any tools that could saw a bookcase when they'd been touring the prisoner.

Assuming things would surely just make the situation worse.

"So...it was already sawed before we got here?" Kingfisher guessed "Why?"

"The same reason we've been provided with an armoury and poisons among medicines" Shrike smartly responded "This mysterious warden has made it clear that they want us to kill each other. There's probably all sorts of clever tricks and traps for us to use for murder around this place if we can find them."

That...was a thought Cuckoo didn't want in his brain. It was one thing to set a killing game ultimatum – it was another to put weapons in their hands as they did so.

Someone really did want them all to die.

But why? Why would anyone do this?

For some sort of sick amusement?

And Cuckoo had almost been their first victim.

"So, if *anyone* could have pushed it, then does that mean we don't know who did it?" Wren tried to guess.

"Well, they would've needed to *know* about the unstable bookcase, so that could be of help" Shrike suggested helpfully "Certainly the warden would've known about it. And anyone particularly observant could've potentially spotted it."

"So, *you're* a suspect then" Nightjar pointed out "Mr Know-It-All."

"Potentially I would be – but I've never actually been *in* the library" Shrike pointed out.

"Unless you're the warden" Mockingbird chimed in, his voice sharp "Then you would've."

"I am not" Shrike sighed, like Mockingbird was too stupid to comprehend "I would not have volunteered that information willingly if I was."

"So, anyone who's been in the library before" Kingfisher inferred before Mockingbird could object "Who would that be?"

No one was quick to volunteer themselves as suspects.

Cuckoo could think of a few names. Rail, Raven, Nightjar. But it didn't feel right to start slinging mud at people – they'd need a lot more proof than that, or everyone could start blaming each other and the whole group would fall apart even further that they already were.

"And of course there's one more suspect" Shrike added "Cuckoo himself."

Cuckoo felt the world drop out from under him.

"You think I did *this* to myself?" Cuckoo questioned, barely able to believe the words were leaving his mouth.

"Oh, maybe not on purpose" Shrike waved their hands in a calmly manner "But with a bookcase so unstable, simply putting a little weight on the side you were standing on would potentially be enough to tip it. Say, if you leaned on it."

"That must be it!" Loon finally spoke up, her formerly worried face now looking hopeful "Just a tragic accident!"

Cuckoo tried to think that over. *Had* he leant on the bookcase before it fell?

He didn't remember doing so, but that vision had thrown him. Maybe he'd grabbed it to steady himself from the images of seeing his own death play out in front of him.

An accident. Not someone trying to kill him.

That thought settled better with him.

"Was anyone in the library with you when it fell?" Mockingbird asked him, clearly not convinced.

Cuckoo tried to think about it. He hadn't seen anyone before his vision, but he'd been so out of it after that that anyone could've walked in. And the bookcase had been obscuring the door from view.

He didn't get to say any of that though, because his eyes finally caught onto Rail.

Rail had thrown himself back against the wall, twitching away. He was clutching his arm, scratching at the bandages so harshly Cuckoo was worried he'd tear them. There was a low chuckle in his throat, the sort of building madness you hear in a horror movie to let you know who the serial killer is.

"We're all going to die" he was saying in a breathy laugh "We're all going to die in here."

Everyone's hackles immediately went up, some taking a cautious step away from him. Only Loon steeled her nerves enough to approach him.

"Rail, it's ok" she tried to assure him "We're all in here together. We're going to stick through it, and we're all going to find a way out. No one's going to die. Ok?"

She went to put a hand on his shoulder, and Cuckoo had to restrain himself from shouting a warning to her. He had a deep-seated fear that Rail might bite her if her hand got too close to him.

But he didn't bite, instead shying away from her, eyes rolling like a trapped stallion as he laughed mockingly.

"We're all going to die here" he kept saying, chuckling like it was his own private joke "We're all going to die. They're going to…my life…they can't–" He began violently shaking his head, enough for Cuckoo to feel sick looking at him. "They can't take that away too! They can't! They can't take that from me! They can't take anything else!"

Tears streamed down and plopped to the carpet like the start of a typhoon. He was clearly going into a panic attack.

"No one's going to take your life, Rail" Loon was still trying to reason with him, approaching him slowly like a cornered hound "We're all going to look out for each other. Just listen to what I'm saying and we can–"

That was apparently the wrong thing to say.

"NO ONE'S CONTROLLING ME!" he suddenly shrieked, pulling back and forcing himself back into the corner of the room, almost seeming to glitch against the background in his frenzy "No one gets to control me anymore! They don't get to take anything anymore! My sister…My sister! Cuckoo! They can't force me to do anything! I…I have to get out of here! They can't…They can't–!"

But he didn't elaborate what the heck that rambling speech was about. Instead, he took in a gasp of air and launched out of the corner, crashing into the bookcases hard enough to dislodge books, and pushing past the crowd to escape the room.

"Hey!" Nightjar called after him, but he was long gone "We just gonna let that bag of crazy run around here?"

"Don't be rude" Raven frowned at her disapprovingly "He was just scared. We all are."

Cuckoo didn't say anything, but he could see both points. That was certainly unhinged, but there was such an undercurrent of grief to the whole performance that Cuckoo felt more sad than scared, though that might just be because Rail was gone and no longer a present danger.

Why had Rail called out to *him* though? It wasn't as if he'd made any effort to talk to him before. They didn't know each other. And what was it he wanted him to do? It was so unexpected, a tiny moment of lucidity in the middle of the ramble, that it had caught Cuckoo too off-guard to say anything at the time.

"We shouldn't leave him by himself" Loon agreed with Nightjar, once again fighting to retain control of the group "I don't think he'll hurt anyone. But he might hurt himself." Immediately Wren shot to attention. "Don't worry! I'll get him!"

"Don't hurt him!" Loon called after her as she also left "Just make sure he's safe!"

With Rail now gone, and no quick answer as to what had happened to Cuckoo, the room rapidly became restless.

"Well, I'm going" Mockingbird announced "We're not going to find anything in here."

"I'll go with you" Kingfisher declared without pausing for breath.

61

"No" Mockingbird held out a hand to stop her from following him "I...I need some time alone. To think things over. Just...leave me alone."

As Kingfisher's face fell, Mockingbird kept ignoring her, setting out alone.

"Well," Loon finally spoke up, her tone as perky as ever "I think what we need is a good meal! It's coming up on 17:00. I think with the cookbook we found and some stocks from the pantry, we can make a good meal for everyone."

"I'm not sure Cuckoo is safe to eat" Raven remarked "He's pretty...spacey."

Spacey? Was he? Cuckoo tried shifting on his seat, only for the whole room to sway.

Oh, yeah, that wasn't fun. He should probably stay here.

"It'll probably take a while to make enough food for everyone" Loon thought it over "Maybe something simple, like soup? And something for the side?"

"I saw some bread buns in the pantry" Kingfisher supplied, still looking miserable at being ditched by her favourite person "And some olives, I think."

"Great!" Loon cheered "You have a great memory, Kingfisher! Do you think you could help me out?"

Kingfisher froze, but recovered quick enough to not arouse suspicion. "Yes, I think so."

"Awesome! You're on ingredients!" Loon squealed with delight before turning to Duck, grabbing both of his hands in hers "You'll help me with the food prep, right Duck?"

Duck's face flushed a deep red that might as well stay there permanently by now, barely able to meet her eye. Cuckoo got the impression he really wasn't used to pretty girls giving him attention.

"Y-Yeah" he stuttered out.

"Great!" she cheered again, still holding his hand as she pulled him out of the room, Kingfisher following on her heels.

Nightjar rolled her eyes, seemingly at the world, before storming out as well.

With only Raven and him in the room now, it felt almost bare. The atmosphere had been almost suffocating before, but now it felt suffocatingly quiet and absent.

"Well, that was a turn for the exciting" Raven remarked "I guess I should go and find you a cane or something of the like. I haven't seen any wheelchairs around—"

"Wait!"

As Raven moved to leave, Cuckoo desperately grabbed his sleeve. Where Cuckoo had wanted to be alone before, now he dreaded being stuck here with only his thoughts and no way to fend off an attack.

"Don't..." his cheeks burned with embarrassment, but that was better than being left by himself while he was this vulnerable "Don't leave me alone."

Raven's face softened. "Alright, I'll be back."

"No!" the word jumped out of him.

God, how pathetic was he? One near-death experience and he was jumping at everything.

They'd already proven no one was out to kill him. How much more reassurance did his stupid brain want?

"Cuckoo, I'll be coming back" Raven assured him "But I'm not sitting on the floor. I'm going to get some water, and a chair, and I'll be right back." His smile turned bashful. "I'll admit, I don't like being alone either."

Cuckoo flushed again. It wasn't necessarily that he didn't *like* the concept of being alone – he'd just never *been* alone before. He'd woken up with Raven and been around other people ever since. The only time he'd been alone, *this* had happened to him. It might've scarred his programming a little.

"Right" was all he could think to say.

Raven swept out of the room, and immediately Cuckoo's worst thoughts pounced on him.

What the hell had just happened?

Had he really caused that bookcase to fall himself?

It had to be that – what were the odds he'd wandered into the library and someone passing by had just happened to see him and decided to kill him?

Yes, it had to be an accident, nothing else made sense.

But that didn't explain the vision.

He'd been calling it a vision in his head, because he had no other word for it. But it wasn't as if he'd been out of his body looking at something. More like he'd lived through the moment of his death and then had been snapped back in time a few seconds, as stupid as that sounded.

Sure, he may not remember anything from before a few hours ago, but somewhere inside himself, he was confident that he shouldn't be experiencing something so blatantly supernatural.

First locked inside a prison, his memories taken away, then branded, then having visions about being killed.

What the hell was this?

What the hell was *he*?

Was he even human?

No, he was definitely human. Perfectly, normally human.

But such things weren't supposed to happen to normal humans.

Were the others having visions too? Was he supposed to ask them, or were they afraid that he would look at them like they were crazy, like he worried they would look at him?

"Told you!" Raven's triumphant arrival with a new chair blissfully shut up his thoughts "Sorry, stopped at the bathroom. You don't need it, do you?"

Cuckoo didn't feel like moving at all, for now. The *idea* of moving made him want to puke.

"Can we just stay here?" he asked.

Raven chuckled and placed the chair down beside him, just as the clock on the table next to them changed to 17:00. "No problem with me."

Raven sat down, folding one leg over the other primly. "You're very lucky you know."

Cuckoo blinked at him. "Huh?"

"The bookcase could've killed you" Raven pointed out "It might feel awful now, but if you hadn't seen it coming and gotten out of the way, I'd be crying over your body right now."

It was a little flattering to hear someone say that, especially after they'd only known you for so little a time.

That was the only reason Cuckoo could think that he would open his mouth and say:

"Oh, I did see it coming."

Raven blinked. "What?"

He should've played it off, but maybe because of the trauma, or the painkillers, it all just came spilling out unbidden.

"I had a...vision, I guess" he explained "I saw the bookcase fall, felt it crush me, felt myself dying. And then I was back upright again, like it had never happened. So, when I heard the bookcase moving again, I moved without thinking. Not quickly enough apparently."

Raven just stared at him, his mouth forming a perfect O. Cuckoo flushed and squirmed, sending a jolt of pain up his leg.

This was it. Raven was going to think he was crazy. Heck, he *sounded* crazy, even to himself. If he hadn't been the one to experience it, he would've laughed at the thought.

Raven finally broke the tension with a chortle. "Cuckoo, are you magic?"

That...was not what he expected to hear.

"I...don't think so" was the best Cuckoo could offer. Who was he to say no, when he didn't even know who he was.

"Hmm" Raven just smiled comfortably, not seeming bothered at all "You really are fascinating, Cuckoo. I'm glad it was you I woke up next to."

"Really?" Cuckoo questioned.

"Really" Raven declared without a pause "You're quiet, so I guess you must do a lot of thinking. But you're also very honest, with your words and your face, even when things don't make sense to you. Maybe it's because you don't have any memories. But I think, out of everyone, you're the one I can trust."

Someday, Raven was going to say something to him that didn't make him want to hide under his own hood. For now though, he didn't want him to stop. Not when it made him feel this light inside.

Was this what having a friend was like?

5

It was a long, uncomfortable hour that followed, Cuckoo's eyes trained on the clock on the table, if only so he didn't have to think about the throbs in his leg behind the splint. Raven would occasionally get up to pick at one of the books, as if hoping for some kind of miracle that one of them would be different, maybe even hold all of the answers to this place (not that any of them did). For the rest of the time, he looked lost in thought, occasionally asking Cuckoo about things around the prison and questioning if he'd noticed anything odd about the pantry, the bathrooms, the alcove. Each time, Cuckoo would just shake his head.

No, he hadn't seen anything in this prison that was any odder than anywhere else they'd already seen. To be honest, with his memory what it was, he wasn't even sure he was qualified to remark on any odd structures when, arguably, this was the only structure he remembered knowing.

Raven found that logic very funny, but he had a habit at giggling at *everything* that came out of Cuckoo's mouth, so it wasn't exactly a high bar to please him.

There was clearly *something* on Raven's mind though, thoughts dashing in binary flashes behind his eyes. But Raven seemed to be reluctant to divulge what was bothering him until he'd worked it through his own head first.

He didn't ask any further about his vision, something Cuckoo was grateful for. He didn't want to talk about something he didn't understand himself.

For his latest ponderance, Raven had gone and gotten another book, sitting next to Cuckoo to read it. But he didn't read it like normal person: he practically had the page up to his eyeballs, like he was secretly trying to lick it.

"Do you think there's some sort of detail in the paper?" Cuckoo guessed.

Raven jolted and almost dropped the book. "Sorry?"

"The paper" Cuckoo reiterated "If you get any closer to it, you'll be eating it."

Raven laughed. "Ah, no. It's more stupid than that I'm afraid. My eyesight is shockingly bad. To tell the truth, it's a miracle I did so well in that darts game – I could barely see where the board was."

Ah, he had been squinting, hadn't he? Cuckoo suddenly felt a shoot of pity for Mockingbird – he probably wouldn't take finding out he lost to an almost blind man using his weaker hand very well.

"Do you need glasses?" Cuckoo questioned.

"Most likely" Raven agreed "But I didn't wake up with any, and there aren't any in here. So, I guess I'm just going to have to deal with everything being fuzzy."

Cuckoo felt bad, but there wasn't much he could do about it. If there were no glasses, Raven would just have to cope. But he wouldn't have to cope alone.

"You stay with me" he decided "I'll be your eyes, if you make sure I don't get left behind."

The statement surprised him as much as Raven, but he found he didn't want to take it back.

Raven looked a little flustered as he buried his face in the book again. "Ah, I'd appreciate that. We'll look out for each other in here, us disabled ones."

He peeked out from the top of the book again, eyes strangely shy.

"Are you going to look out for me when we get out of here too?" he questioned.

Cuckoo frowned. "Well, outside of here we can probably get you glasses."

"Ah" Raven deflated behind the book again "Of course."

Cuckoo felt like that had been the wrong thing to say.

"Don't you have family out there?" he asked, Mockingbird's voice in his head "You won't need me if you have them."

"Well, yes" Raven sounded contemplative "But...well..." It took him a while to figure out what to say. "I think I'd like you to stay anyway."

Cuckoo felt like a rock had been dropped on his head, body swaying dizzily. He hadn't thought for one second what he would do when he left this place, having nothing to draw from. But knowing someone wanted him around – that he wouldn't be entirely cut off in a world he didn't know.

Why did that sound so nice? It should be grating to have to deal with other people, shouldn't it? It shouldn't be worth the extra anxiety of having to look out for more people than just yourself, right?

But sitting in this room, the two of them looking out for each other...it felt...nice. Content.

Maybe Raven meant what he said as a whole: that he wanted *everyone* in the prison to get out of here and stay together. But he's only said it to Cuckoo, and that made it feel special.

Special enough to sprout flames in his heart.

"Thank you" he breathed.

Raven stayed ducked behind the book, shoulders curling. "You don't have to thank me for anything."

He didn't say anything more than that, his focus back on the book as he nearly cut off his own nose trying to turn the page.

The books were still bothering them *both* then. Why make every book in the prison seemingly identical? It almost felt like an escape room – that there was some hidden clue disguised amongst the hidden objects.

But if the books were a clue, did that mean there were *other* books in the prison that may provide other clues? Duck had been carrying a cookbook before, which must have contained recipes for him to have been carrying it, but where had he got it? The annex? Or maybe...

"Hey, Raven" Cuckoo spoke up "There were books in that cupboard by the bathrooms, right?"

Raven sat up, blinking up from one of the books he'd been examining in forensic detail. "Er...yes. Why?"

Cuckoo shuffled on his seat. "It's just, maybe there's something in them that could tell us where we are?"

Raven just kept blinking at him. "You don't think all the books have the same poem in them?"

The words spinning on the page, creaks and groans as the shadow fells over the pages, giant maw sweeping down to–

Cuckoo pushed the memory from his head.

"They do in the library" he agreed "But maybe the books hidden away have clues of how to get out of here."

"Oh, like hiding clues in a treasure hunt!" Raven gasped, standing up "Ok, you just wait here, I'll go get them!"

"No" Cuckoo reached out and grabbed his sleeve before he could leave, wincing as his leg responded to the change in weight "I want to go."

Raven peered down at him strangely. "You don't have to."

Cuckoo felt himself shrinking into the seat. "I know, but...I can't stand being useless."

He hated it. It made him feel like dirt.

But also, he worried that if he stayed in this room any longer, completely helpless and vulnerable, the fear would get the better of him and he'd go crazy, just like the books.

He was still doing all he could to avoid looking at that fallen bookcase.

Raven paused for what felt like an eternity, before his face spread into a smile that felt dangerously close to pity.

"Alright, let's go" he said definitively.

Cuckoo expected him to go rush off and find a crutch or something, but instead he bent to take Cuckoo's arm, dragging him up with it. Cuckoo yelped as a bullet of pain ran through his whole body, but it dulled into an ache by the time he was stood up on one leg, Raven taking his weight through the arm over his shoulder.

Cuckoo grimaced, not liking the vulnerability of the position. But it would have to do for now – he couldn't expect to just hop there.

He looked down at his feet. His right boot had been removed at some point, probably when he was unconscious, leaving his foot bare and twitching.

"Can you...help me put that back on first?" he asked, nodding at his stray boot.

"Oh, sure!" Raven declared, cheery as ever.

He set him back down on the chair, causing Cuckoo to hiss with pain again.

"Sorry" Raven apologised and he knelt by Cuckoo's foot with the boot "Ah, we might have problem. This won't fit on there."

Cuckoo could see the issue. The splint extended past the point where the boot's high top would sit. There was no way to fit it.

He sighed. "Guess I'm barefoot then."

He could only hope the linoleum floor wasn't too cold.

Raven paused for a moment, then lit up. "No, we can't have that! Here!"

He turned his legs to sit on the floor and took off one of his loafers.

"You can have mine!" he declared.

Cuckoo recoiled instinctively. "Er, no thank you."

"Relax, it won't hurt" Raven assured him "It just slips on, see."

Sure enough, the shoe sat happily on his foot, the only pain being from the minor jostling of slipping it on there. Luckily, they appeared to be the same foot size, even if Raven's shoe did look cartoonishly formal next to his other boot.

"What are *you* going to wear though?" Cuckoo asked, not wanting Raven to be in any discomfort.

"I'm putting on your boot!" Raven announced as he did exactly that, tying up the monotonous laces "Ta dah!"

If Raven's shoe looked silly on *his* leg, then his looked even stupider on Raven's, slacks slipping out where they were only half tucked in. Not that that stopped Raven from jumping to his feet and showing it off like it was a proud new fashion statement.

"Right then" he extended an arm again "Let's try this again, shall we?"

Cuckoo groaned in anticipation of what was coming.

o

Moving wasn't easy; little prickles of pain ran through his lower body every time he had to move his weight-bearing leg, the broken one swinging in the air between them like a rampaging pendulum. But it had to be better than just sitting there, watching everyone rush around him and hoping no one would take advantage of his vulnerability.

"You ok?" Raven checked, his face feeling too close as he turned it towards Cuckoo.

"Yeah" Cuckoo huffed out in a breath between hops.

It was getting a little better, each step tiring him more but letting the pain fade a little further, getting more and more manageable with every step.

Raven chuckled and looked away again. "You don't have to force yourself to be so strong, you know. There's always chaff like me to do the work for you." He looked down, eyes looking sad. "I promise I won't mess up. I can do *this*, at least."

Cuckoo tried to make sense of *that* statement, but it was too much of a rollercoaster ride for him to follow. Chaff? Screwing up? What we he talking about?

Before he could begin respond to that, a series of bangs boomed from down the hallway.

"Hey!" a voice echoed after them "What are you playing at, dude?! Come on!"

The pair looked at each other, a silent exchange, and then hobbled towards the noise.

Said noise was coming from Mockingbird, hopping from foot to foot as he rapped his left fist on the boys' bathroom door, his right fight buried in his jacket.

"What's the problem?" Cuckoo asked.

"What does it freakin' look like?!" Mockingbird snapped at him "The door's been locked for ages and I need to pee!"

Cuckoo frowned. "How long?"

"I don't know, too damn long!" Mockingbird swore, smacking the door again "Come on! It's not funny! I'm bursting here!"

"But" Raven looked concern "The door doesn't lock."

Mockingbird turned his attention from the door to shoot Raven a poisonous look "What?!"

Raven shuddered and almost took a step back, nearly causing Cuckoo to fall, but then seemed to swallow his nerve. "The door to the bathroom doesn't have a lock. The individual stalls do, but not the main door."

Mockingbird shot Raven and then the door a now incredulous look. He then hunched over, seemingly in pain, clutching his hand to his stomach. With his free arm, he pushed down on the handle and shoved the wood with his shoulder, but the door didn't budge. It certainly seemed to be locked.

"They must be holding it shut" he seethed "Come on! Don't be an ass! This isn't funny!"

Cuckoo tried to think it over, examining the door the best he could leaning on Raven. There was no keyhole, but there did seem to be a tiny gap between the bottom of the door and floor. If someone on their hands and knees were to–

He winced as a bolt of pain shot from his leg up his body. Damn it!

"Raven, can you look under the door?" he asked "See if anything's blocking it?"

Raven obliged, shifting Cuckoo to lean on the wall. He knelt down and shoved his face up to the gap, a beam of white tracing across his face.

"There's something shoved up against the door, something green maybe" he declared "I could be the hamper, I guess. Was that green?"

Mockingbird went careful still, his face emptying of colour. He even seemed to be holding his breath as his eyes blew wide and a trickle of sweat ran down his face. Cuckoo was about to ask him what the matter was, when he shook himself out of it.

"Who–Who the hell would do that?!" Mockingbird protested.

Cuckoo tried to think that over. He couldn't think of why someone would need the whole room to themselves.

Raven sat up, a pondering look on his face. "What if it's Shrike?"

Cuckoo look down at him with a frown. "Why would they do that?"

Mockingbird took that as gospel though, banging on the door with his fist again. "Shrike, is that you in there, you asshole?!"

"I mean, Loon told them to use whichever bathroom they were most comfortable with" Raven recalled "Maybe they put the hamper up against the door so no one could walk in on them?"

It was a solid theory. It certainly made the most amount of sense.

Mockingbird groaned and leaned his head on the wood, his left hand gripping his right through the leather of his jacket. Then he puffed up his chest and crossed the corridor to the girls' bathroom.

"Don't you *dare* rat me out!" he shouted back at them as he pulled the door shut behind him "I'm desperate, ok!"

The girls' bathroom door slammed shut with a finality, leaving Cuckoo and Raven alone once again.

Raven stood up again and rested his hand against the door. "We can't leave it blocked though, can we? There's ten of us – we can't be expected to use one bathroom for as long as we're stuck here."

Cuckoo tried not to feel uneasy. "If it's just Shrike, then why aren't they saying anything?"

Raven nodded thoughtfully. He tapped his fist on the door primly.

"Shrike!" he called in "It's ok if it's you. Can you just call out to us, let us know you're ok?"

Nothing but silence and a faint white light drifted from under the door.

Cuckoo felt the hair on his arms raising. He didn't want to think anything bad had happened but, well, it was almost as if he could see that bookcase collapsing on top of him again.

Granted, there weren't any bookcases to fall on top of Shrike in the bathroom, but...

"What if they're injured?" he found himself saying.

Raven stared at him with concern. "W-What?!"

"If they're injured and they can't answer" Cuckoo repeated himself.

Raven's eyes widened, his pupils taking over his whole eyes. Without saying anything, he turned and charged into the shower room next door.

"Shrike!" Cuckoo heard him call, and sound of banging again "Huh? What going on?!"

"I was wondering that too" a second voice came from the other direction, the way they'd just come.

Cuckoo turned against the wall, wincing a little at the pain. He saw Wren and Kingfisher coming up the corridor.

"We think Shrike's in the boys' bathroom, but they've blocked the door and aren't answering" Cuckoo filled them in.

Kingfisher just seemed content that they weren't in the girls' bathroom, but Wren frowned with concern.

"How long have they been in there?" she asked.

Cuckoo bit his lip – Mockingbird hadn't exactly said.

"A while, I think" he decided upon.

Wren didn't seem to like that answer, walking up the door herself. "Shrike, if you feel more comfortable answering to a girl, it's me. Can you talk to us?"

"My goodness, so many people calling my name. I almost feel wanted."

Cuckoo was startled as Shrike's melodious voice wandered down the hallway, emerging from around the corner, and not the bathroom.

Anxiety spiked through Cuckoo's whole body. Shrike was the only one with a good reason to barricade the door. If it wasn't them in there...

Wren looked equally anxious. "Can the door be locked from the outside?"

"It doesn't lock at all" Cuckoo told her what Raven had said "It's barricaded."

Finally, Kingfisher seemed to grasp the seriousness of the situation, looking as worried as Cuckoo and Wren were.

"So...someone's hiding in there?" she guessed.

Cuckoo picked up on what she was implying. "You mean the warden?"

Kingfisher hugged herself, looking away. "Who else?"

"My, my" Shrike didn't seem bothered at all, a lazy smile on their face "What a conundrum. Are we sure there's no other way in?"

As if prompted, Raven leaned out of the shower room, face panicked. "I can't get this one open either!"

"There's another door?" Wren guessed.

"There's a sliding door from the shower room" Raven confirmed "But it's not opening!"

"Is it locked?" Wren asked.

"It only locks from *this* side!" Raven insisted.

Cuckoo swore he could feel his own blood pumping through his veins. Maybe it was the adrenaline, but when his hopped his way along the wall to the shower room, he didn't feel so much as a twinge of pain.

It could just be a coincidence. Maybe someone just wanted to cool off and sealed the bathroom so they wouldn't be bother. Maybe they'd slipped on the white tile and banged their head. That had to be more plausible than some insane nutbag picking them off one by one when they were alone.

It had to be something like that. It just had to be.

The adjoining shower room was empty, the white tiles spotless, the four blue towels hung up along the wall not showing any signs of being used, the yellow plastic chair underneath them still dry. Of course, with all the excitement of the day, it wasn't as if anyone had been hurrying to use the shower. On the right wall was a sliding door with a window, a white sheen from the bathroom lights dancing beyond the frosted glass. A large manual lock was obviously used to the secure it from this side, but it didn't look like it could be manipulated from the bathroom side. Raven was trying to pull the door open, even planting his foot on the doorframe, but it didn't budge.

"Can you..." Raven trailed off as he tried to get his breath back from the panic and excursion "Can you look through the window? I can't reach."

The window was pretty high up, Cuckoo's eyes were only just able to clear the window ledge. Not that it did him any good – all he could see was the white light reflecting beyond the artificial frosting.

Of course a shower room wouldn't just have a window you could look through, but it was still maddening that they couldn't see through.

"Step aside" Wren called, gently moving Cuckoo out of the way and sending Raven scrambling.

Cuckoo saw muscles for days flex as she pulled on the door. He thought he heard a creak from the other side and the door tremble, but ultimately it didn't move.

Wren mumbled something, then lifted her elbow and smashed in the window, miraculously not cutting herself open.

Raven winced. "That did open from this side, you know. You could've just slid it."

But Wren didn't seem to hear him, too busy attempting to fit her head through the now open window.

"What the hell's going on down there?!" he heard Nightjar yell, boots clacking in the distance, Kingfisher scrambling to intercept her before she could bring more chaos into the situation.

Wren finally pulled back from the window with a frown.

She looked over at Cuckoo. "Can you look through there? My head's too big."

He tried again, standing on the toes of his good foot. This time he could see the pristine white of the far wall. He could see the counter, upon which sat a pair of sodden brown trousers resting to the right side of the sinks. Tucked neatly below the basin was a familiar pair of red shoes, though Cuckoo couldn't remember who he'd seen wearing them.

Wait, was that a bloody scalpel on the left side of the sink? Yes, definitely – a drop of plasma frozen in place at the end of the blade.

And there was something red just within the corner of his vision, but the window frame stopped him from being able to see what it was.

"I think someone's injured" Cuckoo reported, dread rising within him.

"Can you see who's in there?" Wren asked.

"No, it's too high" Cuckoo informed her "I'd need to– Whoa!"

He gasped as Wren grabbed him around the waist and lifted him up about a foot, shoving his head through the window frame.

The movement caused his head to sag, and he found himself looking down the door towards the handle. It was blurry at the edge of his vision, but he thought he saw something leading towards the stalls.

"Wait! Wait!" he called down "Someone's tied a roll of bandage to the door and around the leg of the stalls. That's probably why it's not opening."

"Can you grab it from there?" Wren suggested.

Cuckoo tried to judge the distance, but it looked further than his arm could reach. "Maybe someone with a knife could cut it, or a pair of scissors?"

"There's scissors in the library" Kingfisher recalled.

"I'll get 'em!" he heard Nightjar shout outside the room, footsteps trailing away.

Cuckoo tried to get his arm through the window in anticipation, but it was impossible to get both his head and arm through the tiny gap.

"Can you get Duck too?!" he called after her "We'll need someone smaller than me!"

"He should still be in the kitchen with Loon, right?" Raven suggested.

He heard Kingfisher take in a deep breath. "I'll find him."

More footsteps echoed in his ears as she hurried off.

He heard Shrike's chuckling from the shower room now. "Well, that's a *flattering* position."

Cuckoo felt his cheeks flooding with red. It wasn't as if he'd *asked* to be grabbed and have his head shoved through a window!

"Shut up!" Raven came to his defence "It's not like *you're* helping!"

As they waited, Cuckoo tried to spot anyone in the room. He couldn't quite see the nearest corner where the door was, and the stall doors were all closed, but there wasn't anyone on the floor that he could see. But now he could get a better look at the red stain...

His heart clenched. That was definitely blood splatter. And not just a little, enough to spray across the whole corner and wall leading up to the sink, snaking in waterfalls down to the floor.

"S-Someone's bleeding!" he found himself yelling.

He didn't want to say dead, despite the fact he knew it had to be true. He didn't want to put that out there.

Suddenly the strong grasp around his waist was gone, and he shrieked as he was sent plummeting to the floor, right onto his bad leg. He dropped immediately, a shout of agony bouncing off every wall.

"What was that for?!" Raven demanded, dropping to Cuckoo's side "Rail said not to put weight on his bad leg, remember!"

He was about to shout back that he hadn't done anything, but stopped when he realised Raven had been yelling at Wren. Now she'd dropped him, she was tugging on the door with all her strength, eyes white with panic.

"HEY!" her voice was almost shaking the door by itself "If you're injured, SAY something!"

Nothing.

"We're coming!" Wren called out to them "Just hold on! We're going to save you!"

Cuckoo flinched at the word. Deep down, he knew whoever was in the bathroom was beyond saving.

"Are they still in there?!" Mockingbird was back from his trip to the girls' bathroom, peering into the shower room "What the hell?! How badly did they need to go?"

"There's blood across the floor and up the wall" Cuckoo reported, gritting his teeth against the pain.

"Someone's been injured in there!" Raven finished for him.

Mockingbird didn't look like a man that was easy to unnerve, but something about that fact he took the news so well bothered Cuckoo. His eyebrows didn't so much as cant, mouth pressed shut in a line.

"Do we need to get Rail?" he suggested calmly.

"Oh, I don't think that's necessary" Shrike chimed in, voice like the melody to an old children's fairytale, the ones where the wolf would eat both the grandmother *and* the girl "The game is already afoot."

Suddenly Mockingbird looked confused as he finally noticed Shrike in the corner. "Wait, if you're in here, who's in *there*?"

The thought suddenly struck Cuckoo. In all the excitement of the trapped door, he hadn't thought about *who* was in bathroom. If it wasn't Shrike, then...

There wasn't time to ponder it. At that moment, Kingfisher arrived with the pair who had been cooking, and a few seconds behind her, Nightjar appeared with the scissors. It didn't take long to fill them in, and then for Wren to boost Duck up through the window with the scissors. In the time it took Raven to help Cuckoo up from the floor, the door was sliding open.

It was immediately clear what had been holding the main door to the bathroom closed. It wasn't hard to spot, a swipe of blood directing their eyes right to it like an arrow.

It wasn't the blue hamper, still tucked against the wall in the far back corner.

Instead, wedged in the corner behind the doorstop was Rail. Sitting up against the door, a line of cuts up his right arm, slicing through his brand until it was illegible. A trickle of blood spilled down his head, his neck, his coat, onto the revolver lying limp in his lifeless right palm.

Secondaries

6

Far away, something was ringing in Cuckoo's ears. It was a high pitched and shrieking, but he couldn't move to block his ears from it. A death toll singing through the silence as a soul left for another plane.

His eyes were fixed to the body. Rail's head leant forward, eyes half-lidded and mouth twisted in aguish. His left hand, the hand that had shook as he'd tightened the brace around Cuckoo's leg just hours before, was now an immaculate white palm amongst the speckles of red and grey that showered the rest of the surroundings. Little rivers of crimson ran down his unbandaged right arm, where little nicks from what looked like a knife littered the pale skin in a perfectly space lines from wrist to elbow. Red hair was turning to brown, with a maddening drip, drip, drip from the gaping exit wound on the right side of his skull being the only thing to pierce the ringing.

That wasn't...what was he looking at?

He swore he could feel that blood dripping on his arm, his face; sliding across his skin as snakes of red, warm and scratchy like tears.

What the...

In the next moment, the sound snapped back, and the dripping was lost under a cacophony of footsteps and a woman's screaming.

"Don't look, Kingy!" he heard Mockingbird bark as he herded Kingfisher and Duck out of the room they'd just entered, blocking the door to anyone else coming in "Oh god!"

"What the hell!" he heard Nightjar curse behind him, having just managed to duck around Mockingbird before he blocked the door "Fudgin', bloody hell!"

"What?! What's happened?!" Loon called from outside.

Cuckoo tried to pry his eyes off of the corpse, distracting himself from the blood and scattered brain matter with any thought he could grab on to.

Maybe it was presumptuous to call it a corpse. Maybe Rail was still alive. This could all just be one mean prank on behalf of the doctor.

As if anyone could find this funny.

They should check for a pulse. They always did that in movies, Raven had pointed out before. Though like Raven, Cuckoo had no idea what he'd be looking for. Was it supposed to be obvious? A beating in the wrist that anyone could find?

He eyes fell to Rail's now unbandaged arm, the line of fresh cuts laddering up the pale flesh, the letters of his brand all but obliterated in a hail of methodical destruction. He averted his gaze quickly.

He was about to ask Raven to check for him – maybe he would have better luck with Rail than he'd had with him – but he stopped as he took in the man holding him up. He wasn't panicking, not even pale really; there was still colour in his cheeks. But he was rigid stiff, eyes focused on the body with an intensity that Cuckoo couldn't bring himself to break.

Thankfully, Wren had followed the same train of thought as him, and was kneeling down to check Rail's undamaged wrist, mindful to keep out of the blood speckles in a complex game of hopscotch. Her massive hands were trembling so badly it was a wonder she could feel anything through them, but before long she was pulling back and regarding him with a look of both grief and fear.

"He's...dead" she reported, voice ladened with forced control just to get the words out. Cuckoo clenched his fist, feeling his nails digging into his skin. It wasn't the words he wanted to hear. He didn't want to accept them. He turned his face away from the corpse, trying to understand the feeling welling up inside him.

It was revulsion, or shock. It felt more like...familiarity.

Why did he feel like he'd seen this before?

Why would he have seen a dead body before? And why was that the only thing to feel even vaguely familiar in all this time?

His eyes caught onto the counter containing the two skins on the wall, next to the worst of the blood splatter. He took in the strange sight of the drenched brown trousers to the right of the sink and bloody scalpel in a smear of blood to the left.

Something was wrong here.

"Dead?! Of course he's freakin' dead!" Nightjar swore – through her biting words, Cuckoo could hear the panic vibrating her throat "His brain's up the freakin' wall!"

"Someone's dead?!" Loon squeaked from outside, trying to force her way past the sobbing Kingfisher and protective Mockingbird "Who?!"

Duck managed to duck under the arm the stiff-as-a-board Mockingbird had on the doorframe, peering back into the room with searching eyes, as if to check if there really was still a body where he last saw it.

"The d-d-doctor" he clarified for his friend, voice stuttering "H-He's dead."

"Bugger's gone and topped himself!" Nightjar clarified with her usual subtly.

The words jolted Cuckoo a little bit, his eyes focusing down on the swipe of blood on the floor. He hadn't let that run through his head before, but they had to be right. The room was completely locked, and Rail had the gun. It had to be a suicide.

Right?

The tragic taking of a precious life by someone who'd found this claustrophobic situation too much to handle. That had to be the explanation.

Right?

Rail had been crazy. He had to have taken his own life. That was the only answer that made sense.

Right?

"He's done what?!" Loon finally managed to push her way into the bathroom, the hair

76

spilling out from her cap now frizzy and her clothes a mess, like she'd been pulling on them. She didn't get any better once she was in the bathroom, her whole body first freezing, and then putting her hands to her mouth in shock, her nails digging into her nose so hard it began to redden.

"Ah, we should'a seen this coming!" Nightjar mumbled, pinching her nose.

"S-Should we?" Duck questioned "He s-sounded like he w-wanted to live."

And that was what was bothering Cuckoo. Maybe it all was just bravado, but for Rail to have turned so quickly from posturing he was going to tunnel out of there if he had to, all the way to taking his own life? What could've happened to turn things so quickly for him?

He'd mentioned a dead sister before. Did that suddenly just get to him? But why now?

"I told you to watch him!" Loon cried out, staring at Wren with hurt eyes.

"I did, h-he got away from me!" Wren insisted, voice filled with distress, still kneeling by the body "I looked everywhere for him! How was I supposed to know that he was in the one room I couldn't get into?!"

"How could he even have gotten a gun?" Mockingbird questioned, his voice shaky as he looked at Loon "You still have the key to the gun cabinet, right?"

"Of course I do!" Loon insisted, pulling the key out of her pocket "See, it's still here!" She looked down at the revolver in Rail's hand before hastily averting her eyes from the gore. "I don't even remember seeing a gun like that in there. Not one with a...spinny thing in the middle."

She must mean a revolver, like the one in Rail's hand. But if Loon was right, and it hadn't come from the gun cabinet, where could it have come from? Was Loon just mistaken...or lying?

"Huh" Mockingbird looked uncertain as he looked away, his shoulders quivering under the shoulder pads of his jacket.

"He probably swiped the key and then put it right back!" Nightjar insisted "That's what I'd do!"

"You getting any ideas Nightjar?" Mockingbird questioned, pouncing on her statement immediately.

"Of course not, I'm not stupid!" Nightjar spat back "I'm not gonna kill anyone after telling you how I'd do it, and I'm sure as hell not killing myself!"

"Can you stop yelling?!" Wren demanded, tears in her eyes "Please!"

The bathroom fell blissfully silent at her cry, everyone avoiding eye contact with each other and the body.

"Are we *certain* he killed himself?" Mockingbird finally asked, his voice surprisingly quiet and pondering "I mean, absolutely positive?"

At the same moment, two voices rang out.

"Of course he did!"

"No."

Cuckoo and Loon stared at each other in surprise, the tension in the room suddenly thickening impossibly more.

Beneath his arm, Cuckoo felt Raven's shoulders tense ramrod straight.

For a moment, everyone was silent, heads ping-ponging between the two who had spoken. The tense fog was only removed when it was cut to ribbons by a familiar chuckling.

"Well, this is awkward" Shrike's voice chimed in, Cuckoo straining to obverse them in the mirror behind him where they were leaning on the wall "But it sounds like you agree with me, correct Cuckoo?"

Suddenly all eyes were on him now. Crap...he didn't even know why he'd said that. It had just slipped out.

Trying to hide his anxiety, he stared down at the swipe of blood on the floor.

"This body" he had to reduce it to that; he couldn't think of who that body used to belong to "It's been moved."

"Hah?!" he heard Nightjar pacing in the back of the room "What d'ya mean it's been moved?! There was no one else in here!"

"But there had to be" Cuckoo found himself saying "This body...it didn't die in that position."

Out of the corner of his eye, he swore he saw Shrike's easy smile turn into a predatory grin.

"What the fudge?!" Nightjar cursed behind him "He blew is brains out, alright! Why does it matter *where*?!"

Did she always curse like that? Like she was being kid-friendly?

Duck shuddered and reached to grab onto Loon's jumpsuit. Mockingbird drew in a breath, holding his head high as if trying not to throw up, and retreated back to the shower room. Even Wren stepped back from the body, nervously looking between it and Cuckoo.

"If he had died there, the blood would up the wall next to the body, right?" Cuckoo guessed, really not knowing enough about this subject to be talking, but it didn't look like anyone else was going to say anything "But it's not: it's across the room."

There was another round of ping-ponging, this time between the body and the blood spatter across the floor and up the wall.

"Oh" Duck suddenly spoke up, voice surprisingly calm considering the situation "T-This swipe mark," He gestured with his foot in the direction of the sweep in the blood extending from the body's feet. "It m-must be from s-someone dragging the body."

Oh, yeah. Cuckoo forgot about that. That made it a lot more obvious, didn't it?

Shrike was chuckling again. "Good observation, Cuckoo and Duck. A point to you both. Now, where do you think he was shot from?"

"Hey!" Wren barked "Don't turn this into a game show, you psycho! A man is *dead*!"

"And so will we be" Shrike smartly retorted, effectively shutting her up "Rather quickly, if we don't determine if there's a killer in our midst. Any thoughts, Cuckoo?"

They expected him to guess where Rail was shot? He had no idea! Somewhere on the left of the room, obviously, but they wanted an exact spot?! He just knew the body had been moved, hadn't he already done his part?!

Duck was silent, just staring at him pointedly. He obviously wasn't volunteering to help this time.

After a moment of pause, where Cuckoo swore he could feel his thoughts leaking out of his ears, Shrike stepped up to him, holding something out.

"I made this, back there" Shrike offered, shoving the item in his face "Do you concur this accurately represents the bathroom in its current state?"

The item was a piece of paper Shrike had drawn on (did they have that on them the whole time? What for?), with shapes roughly corresponding to the layout of the room. The body against the door, the blood up the wall at 90 degrees to the sink, the bandage that had been holding the shower room door in place. It all seemed reasonable.

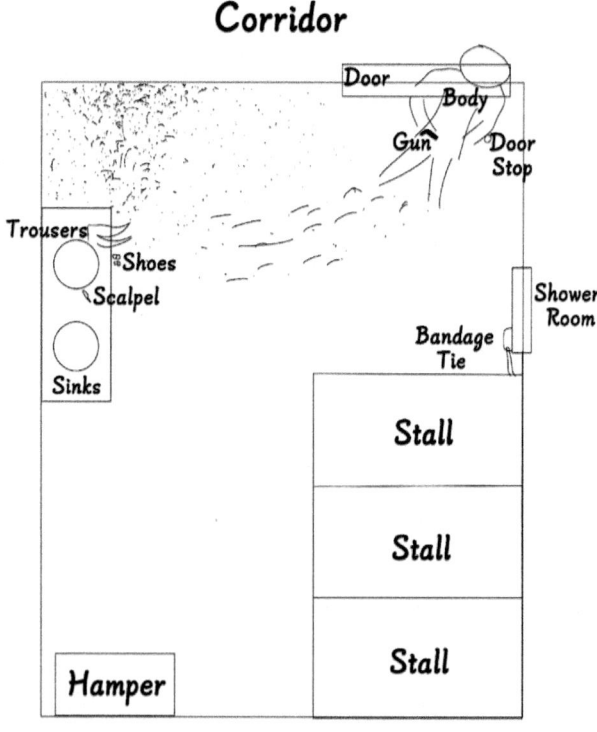

Corridor

"Yeah" he nodded "I guess."

"I think so" Raven nodded, also seeing the piece of paper "Somewhere on the left of the room?"

Shrike hmmed to themselves as they twirled a mechanical pencil between their fingers, eyes narrowed with distain and frustration, like the pair of them were the stupidest people they'd ever had the misfortune of meeting.

Cuckoo tried to hold back his frustration. It felt like Shrike had set him an impossible code to crack, a twisting shapeshifting matrix of unlinked numbers, and then had the nerve to gloat when no one could read it.

"Maybe the clue is not the body itself, but what the body doesn't have" they suggested pointedly.

That clue didn't make any sense either. What was the body *missing*? The right side of its head, obviously. But what did—

Duck suddenly gasped, pointing. "Pants!"

Cuckoo conceded, that was a good spot. The obvious gunshot exit wound to the body had been so all-consuming in his mind he hadn't processed the fact that Rail was sitting in his coat and underwear, his legs completely bare, nothing but a fresh bandage running around his left leg. The unwound bandages weaving down from his elbow were also damp, a clue to where he'd been.

His eyes slid over to the trousers sitting next to the sink, trying to avoid the dripping scalpel sitting opposite them.

"And that's a point to Duck" Shrike announced "You're slacking, Cuckoo."

Why him? It wasn't like anyone else had said anything either.

"So...he was by the sink with his trousers" Cuckoo guessed "And then was shot there."

That didn't explain the scalpel or the wounds on his arm though. Had he been attacked with the scalpel first, fought off the attacker and then been shot? But why start with a scalpel if you had a gun?

And how did he not see his attacker coming? They would've had to pass behind him to reach his left side where he was shot from. He would've seen them in the mirror, regardless of which door they'd come from. So how could they have possibly surprised him, when Rail didn't seem to trust anybody?

Nothing made sense.

"The hell was he walking around without pants for?!" Nightjar demanded.

"They're wet" Wren commented, pointing at the little pool of muddy water under the draping pant legs "He...went swimming, maybe?"

Duck, who'd just been about to say something when she spoke, looked up the large woman with a stare of complete disbelief.

"Where?!" Nightjar demanded again "Does this *look* like a resort?!"

"There's not exactly anywhere to go swimming around here, big guy" Mockingbird pointed out from just inside the shower room door.

"You shut up, you prick, I already said that!" not done with causing drama, Nightjar now turned on her favourite enemy.

"You said it like a moron, you weren't helping anyone" was Mockingbird's immediate and rather pathetic response, speaking with his fists clenched in his pockets.

"Please don't fight" Loon quickly stood between them "This isn't helping! And it's disrespectful to Rail!"

"*He* was the one walking around with no pants!" Nightjar argued "You think he deserves respect?! Pervert!"

"Do you have any idea how stupid you sound right now?" Mockingbird shot back, teeth gritted. "Will you take this seriously! Someone's dead!"

Cuckoo could feel a headache coming on, like he was listening to a group of screaming school children. He'd have to interject now, as Nightjar searched for a suitable comeback.

"He wasn't walking around with no trousers" he corrected "He came in here and took them off. That's why his shoes are in here, right by the sink."

There were no interjections to that statement, just Mockingbird looking a little smug, so Cuckoo deemed it safe to go on.

"He was washing his trousers" he continued "They got all muddy during the leaf fight, and it looks like he injured himself leaving the library. That's why he came to the bathroom, and brought the bandages with him. The scalpel was probably to cut them. He took them off by the sink, bandaged his leg and tried to scrub the stains out."

This theory seemed to finally, thankfully, shut everyone up, as they mulled over that possibility.

"That would make sense" Wren concurred "It's not like we found any spare clothes in here, or any laundry stuff. If he wanted to be clean, he'd have to wash them himself."

There was now a prideful smirk on Shrike's face. "Very nice, Cuckoo. We should see if your hypothesis has merit."

With that, they crossed the room over to the bloody wall at a right angle to the sink, trampling through all the blood and grey matter like it was nothing but a puddle. Cuckoo felt like throwing up.

They strode up to the wall and put their face almost level with it, cheek hairs grazing the blood. Then, grin widening, they put the mechanical pencil back in their coat pocket and withdrew a folding knife instead.

"What the hell?!" Mockingbird jumped back through the doorway to the shower room as if protecting himself, his left hand coming out of his pocket, ready to fight "How long have they had that?!"

"You're carrying a weapon?!" Loon exclaimed, sounding horrified.

Nightjar scoffed behind them both. "You think they're the only one?"

Loon turned to her, alarmed. "You too?!"

81

Prompted, Nightjar withdrew a paring knife from her own jacket pocket. "Of course I do! Someone's threatening to kill of us! I want to be ready for the bugger when he shows his face!"

That did nothing to ease Loon's horrified look. Neither did Shrike, who then started picking at the blood and plaster on the wall with their own knife.

"Hey!" Wren jumped forward, doing her best to avoid the blood, grabbing them by the shoulder "You shouldn't mess with that! We need to leave everything for the police!"

The was a ring of silence through the bathroom.

"Y-You think the police are coming?" Duck questioned.

A strangled sound made its way out of Nightjar's throat. "Is this idiot for real?! You think the *police* are going to show up?!"

"Of course they are!" Wren insisted, turning to them both as Shrike shrugged her hand off "Ten people are missing! They're going to come looking for us! And when they get here, we need to make sure the crime scene hasn't been touched so they can investigate!"

Hadn't they already touched it already? By snapping the bandage and checking his pulse, let along walking in all the blood.

"What police?!" Mockingbird jumped in with an argument "I mean, don't get me wrong, me and that broad over there aren't much for agreeing with each other. But do you honestly think the police are going to just barge in and save us?"

Nightjar began shrieking again, at the exact same moment Wren began to argue how wrong they were – that they just needed to stick together and have a little faith – and Loon tried to soothe them all with patient calls for quiet and understanding. Duck shrank back like a bomb had gone off all around him, which mirrored how Cuckoo was feeling at that moment.

Whatever Shrike had been digging at in the wall finally came free. A flash of gold arced across the room, landing squarely at Duck's feet. The little tinging sound it made as it landed silenced the room.

A mushroomed bullet whirled once in a circle, before stopping with a cheery jolt.

Cuckoo felt bile in his mouth.

"Well," Shrike wiped the blood from their knife on the edge of the sink cabinet and folded it away with a flourish "I guess the body really was moved then. A point to Cuckoo, for being the only one to notice."

The chord of tension in the room tightened again, as the possible implications of that rang out in everyone's minds.

"That's...it's not possible" Loon insisted "Someone would have to be in the room for that to happen."

"Well, I guess that must be it then" Shrike shrugged, apparently unbothered by that logic.

"Well, how the hell did they get *out* of the room, then?!" Nightjar demanded "Both doors were blocked!"

"Yeah!" Wren chimed in "We had to break in!"

"Could they have tied the shower room door from the outside?" Mockingbird suggested, looking down at the remains of the bandage on the floor.

"I could barely get my head through" Cuckoo pointed out "Let alone an arm and a head."

"It's very d-difficult" Duck agreed.

"So does that mean *he* did it?" Mockingbird questioned, waving his arm at Duck "I mean, he was the only one who could get his head and arm through there."

Loon gasped with horror at him. "You can't throw around accusations like that!"

"I c-couldn't!" Duck insisted, waving his arm frantically "I couldn't kill Rail! The w-window is too high!"

"There's a chair in here" Mockingbird reminded him "You could've reached it using that."

"So, we're looking for someone small then?" Nightjar continued the line of thought, scowling at the rest of the group with barbed eyes "It must Duck or Kingfisher then! Or Shrike! You're pretty puny—"

"I c-couldn't reach!" Duck's pleas got louder with desperation "Even with the s-scissors, I can only j-just reach! The distance from the w-window is t-too far!"

At that suggestion, Mockingbird began to shut the shower room door. "Kingy, I need the—"

He was cut off as the door shut, his voice a just mumble through the broken window.

A few seconds later, his left arm reached through the window, flailing around to try and reach the doorhandle. It was the wrong arm to be reaching with, considering where the handle was, but ever so, it was still a scissor's distance away from the handle where the bandage had been tied.

"Forget it" Loon shook her head "There's no way someone could reach from there, even if they could tie a knot with one hand."

Mockingbird mustn't have heard her, as it took a moment more to for him to finish flailing around and make his way back through the door.

"Nope, can't be done" he shook his head.

Duck sagged against Loon, obviously relieved he was no longer suspected of doing something so awful.

Wren frowned. "Could they have used a tool then? Like how we used the books and shelves to lift the bookcase. Or the poles to move the cabinet. Something to—"

"Let's forget the shower room door for now" Shrike cut her off "Should we consider how, instead, they may've escaped through the main door."

"Oh, of course!" Nightjar scoffed sarcastically "They just phased through the dead body! How could I not have seen that coming!"

83

Shrike shot her a truly spiteful look. "Are you truly going to contribute nothing but snark and insults? You're going to select *that* as your role?"

Nightjar just stood there, slack-jawed with shock. Mockingbird let out a little whistle of admiration.

"It can't be done" Loon insisted "It wasn't possible to get through the shower room door with the bandage tie in place, and Rail's body stopped anyone from leaving that way. No one got out, it was only Rail in the room. It's a suicide."

She said it so definitively that Cuckoo found himself staring at his own feet in doubt. Could he have been wrong? Maybe blood and bullets just did strange things, and it wasn't like television at all. Had he caused a fuss for nothing?

"Perhaps" he heard Shrike say "Or maybe the body was moved *after* they left the room."

"Oh, come on!" Nightjar spat, her fire back "How were they supposed to move a dead body when they weren't even in the same room?!"

Shrike hmmed contemplatively, which Cuckoo had come to recognise as their irradiated noise, as if they were a teacher talking to toddlers. "Maybe Wren is right, and they used a tool in the room to help them."

"What TOOLS?!" Nightjar now roared "THIS IS A FREAKIN' BATHROOM, NOT A STORAGE CUPBOARD!!!"

"Dude, if you know, just tell us" Mockingbird also complained "This guessing game crap is getting really old."

Cuckoo reached up to cover his ears from the onslaught, but as he did, he found himself looking at Rail's legs. They weren't bloody underneath. Had he really be dragged through all that blood to get there? Had someone wiped the blood from his legs? But why would they do that?

His eyes flickered up the counter. Could he have been wearing his trousers after all?

No, his legs would be wet then, considering the trousers still were. But they were bone dry.

What was he missing?

As his eyes moved from the sink to the body, they drifted over his own leg. The splint around it, made so quickly by Rail, a last gesture of kindness, woven with unsteady hands from shelves and bandages and a red towel. He'd never get to truly thank Rail for that.

The towel...

Wait.

His eyes flew past Mockingbird, who'd moved just out of the way of the door enough to see through. He could look right through to where that line of four blue towels was hanging.

Was he right?

"Can I talk to Kingfisher for a moment?" he asked Mockingbird.

Mockingbird narrowed his eyes at him, but didn't argue. He disappeared off to the side for a moment, before coming back with the girl in question.

She looked like shit. She wasn't crying anymore, but her face was warped with signs of overwhelming grief and shock. Her jacket appeared to be tightened impossibly further around her, until he swore he could see her elbows through it, whilst strings of blonde hair stuck to her wet cheeks.

Almost on instinct, Cuckoo's hand went to rest reassuringly on her shoulder. But before he could touch her, the young girl reared back, almost hitting the wall, eyes white with fear.

Cuckoo tried not to feel stung. It was a horrible situation – he couldn't blame her for doubting everyone.

"Hey!" Mockingbird immediately barked at him.

"Sorry, Kingfisher" Cuckoo addressed her, making sure to keep his hand within sight "When you got the towel for Rail to fix my leg, it was from the girls' shower room, right?"

She simply nodded, eyes still white like blooming orchids.

"How many towels were there when you took it?" he asked.

There was a pause as she thought over the answer. He wasn't sure how this would solve the mystery, but it had to lead somewhere. If there was anyone he could trust to remember such a detail, it would be Kingfisher after all.

"Five" she answered quietly "There were five towels."

"And there's only four behind you, right?" he wanted to check, in case he'd somehow missed one in panic.

Kingfisher blinked, and then looked over her shoulder to count. "Yeah."

"There should be five" Cuckoo stated definitely "Five blue towels, five red towels. Or possibly more, since there are more boys than girls. No one took a towel from this shower room, right?"

Silence. No one owned up to such an action.

"So, the towel is the missing tool, right?" Cuckoo guessed, encouraged by Shrike's brightening expression "I don't know *how* it was used exactly, but that's what you're getting at—"

Raven abruptly gasped beneath his shoulder, causing Cuckoo to startle. He'd been almost silent since they'd entered the room – so silent he'd wondered if he'd fallen asleep.

"The napkin trick!" he gasped.

Cuckoo wished he could say that those words prompted a big revelation about how the body was moved, but in reality, he just found himself staring at the side of Raven's head dumbly. Not that anyone else was saying anything else either.

"Oh, er, hold on!" he slid Cuckoo's arm off of his shoulder, holding his weight up with just the arm around his waist "I can show you! Can someone get me one of those towels? Oh, and er..." He looked up at Wren with a bashful smile. "I need you to move the body."

Wren seemed genuinely struck dumb for a moment, before her face turned thunderous. "No!"

"Please!" Raven insisted "It's important! We won't know how the trick was done otherwise."

"I'm not moving the body!" Wren insisted "That's tampering with evidence!"

"No one's gonna yell at you about it, moron!" Nightjar couldn't resist jumping in "If we don't find out who did that, maybe your sorry ass will be next!"

Wren looked between her and body, obviously torn.

"We can't move him, that would just be wrong" Loon agreed, her voice quiet "We—"

"See!" Wren cut her off "It's just wrong!"

"What's wrong will be dying in here because you're being a f—!"

"W-We can use the g-girls' bathroom!" Duck's voice suddenly exploded into the air "They're identical, r-right? So, the t-trick should work just as well as in here!"

Kingfisher and Nightjar looked sulky about it, and Loon clearly wasn't happy about it, but now the suggestion was out there, it was a difficult one to shoot down. And therefore, it was with a great deal of grumbling and eyes avoiding each other that they filed out of the crime scene and into the girls' bathroom across the hall.

For ease, they entered through the girls' shower room, one by one watching their step to avoid the muddy footprints all over the bathroom floor. One of the girls must've gone out into the courtyard after the rain had begun.

As everyone filtered inside, Raven laid down one of the four remaining towels on the floor in front of the main door, the edge stopping just beyond the edge of the doorframe.

"Cuckoo, do you mind being my dead body?" Raven asked, but Cuckoo got the feeling it wasn't a question.

And so, with everyone watching, Cuckoo was sat down on the edge of the towel, whilst Raven squeezed through the partially closed door to the corridor and shut it behind him.

There was an awkward pause, with everyone staring at Cuckoo, and the man in question trying desperately to avoid looking back at them or anything else in the room. Just being in here felt like some kind of violation.

He tried to stare ahead best he could, so he couldn't be accused to looking at something he shouldn't; his eyes fixing past the audience onto the big wooden door at the far end of the room. The boys' bathroom didn't have a third door. A storage cupboard, maybe? For women's items?

Before he could get stuck on that mental image, the whole world shunted as the towel was pulled below him. He was yanked backwards into the bathroom door, hitting his head with a thunk against the wood, whilst the towel was whipped out from both under him and under the door to join Raven in the corridor.

"Ow!" he found himself yelling, seeing stars blossom behind his eyes.

For a moment, there was silence. Then the door cracked open behind him, shifting Cuckoo's prone form the extra inch required for Raven to speak through.

"Sorry!" he called apologetically "I guess that's why it's only supposed to be done with dead bodies!"

Some shuffling later, and Cuckoo was pulled away from the door onto the hastily sourced shower chair to let Raven back in. With Rail being pulled behind the door stop for extra leverage, him sitting up against the door would be sufficient to stop anyone from getting in without a lock.

Good, his head hurt. After the library, he was really getting sick of being Raven's physics guinea pig.

"I did warn you" Raven pointed out.

"What warning?" Cuckoo scoffed, rubbing his aching head.

"You didn't hear me count down?" Raven frowned, then smiled "Wow, these rooms are really soundproof, aren't they? No wonder no one heard the gun shot."

Cuckoo put his head in his hands. That complicated things. He had been wondering if it would be possible to narrow down a time of death to when no one was in the West Wing, since no one heard the gun shot. But if the bathrooms were functionally soundproof, then someone could've been in the next room and they wouldn't have heard it.

That meant Rail could've died any time between him leaving the library to the moment Mockingbird had been unable to force open the bathroom door: from 16:45 to 18:00, roughly.

A 75-minute time period where people were moving in and out of multiple areas. There was little chance anyone had a solid alibi for that whole time.

Someone had killed Rail, and they had no way of finding out who it was.

"This was murder" he muttered to himself "Rail was murdered. One of us was murdered. And we don't know who did it."

A silent fog of grief and disbelief wrapped around the room, as everyone took that fact in, and what it meant. The bookcase falling was ambiguous, it could've been an accident; but there was no mistaking this. Someone was actively trying to kill them all. A trojan horse amongst the code, looking to eradicate everything around it.

They still hadn't found hide nor hair of a mysterious warden. So did that mean...

Could Raven have been right?

Was the warden among them, and preparing to kill them all?

Mockingbird broke the silence, sagging against one of the stalls with a look of relief.

"Well, at least now we're agreed on that" he remarked "That means someone's started the game, right?"

"It w-would be appear so" Duck nodded, watching the entire room from behind Loon.

"Killing people is not a game" Loon told them with a tight look on her face "And we don't–"

"How did you even know how to do that?" Wren cut her off, turning to Raven with a worried look.

"Yeah, you worked out how the bookcase came down in the library too, and how to get to the hidden door in the gym" Nightjar reminded everyone, staring at Raven with hard eyes "You some sort of murder mystery freak or something?"

Raven began messing with his hair furiously. "Well, er, I mean, I can't say I haven't read a few of them. And, well, I'm really good at puzzles, I guess. But I couldn't have done it without Shrike–"

"I recon he did it!" Nightjar spoke up, pointed at him with suspicion.

Cuckoo dug his nails into the skin around his eyes. As illogical as it was, he didn't want to think someone in the group could've done this. He wanted to put it all on some mysterious foreign force beyond their control. It was safer that way – he wouldn't have to eye everyone he was now relying on with suspicion.

But they hadn't found any evidence of someone else in the prison. It was just the ten of them, and one of them was dead. So, if there really was a warden, they had to be here, right now, in this room.

Someone who had a spare key to the gun cabinet, or had managed to get the key from Loon without her noticing. Someone who was not only willing to kill, but to make a game out of it.

What kind of sick freak were they dealing with?

"What, no!" Raven paled "I just know these things, you know! I couldn't have done it!"

"So, where's your alibi?" Mockingbird now jumped in "Do you have one?"

"Everyone stop it!" Loon tried to corral them "Alibis? We don't need *those*."

"I think we do" Kingfisher disagreed, eyes darting and wary.

"Of course we need them!" Nightjar scoffed "How else is puzzle freak over there going to prove he didn't get his jollies killing one of us?!"

Cuckoo looked up to find Shrike – no doubt they would have opinions about this. But they weren't in the room, and he struggled to remember if they'd come with them from the boys' bathroom. Maybe they knew how quickly the mood would turn and wanted to vanish before they were turned on. After all, every accusation they were levelling at Raven right now could just as easily be thrown at them.

"I didn't do it!" Raven insisted, sounding on the verge of tears "I have an alibi!" He turned to Cuckoo with tears in his eyes. "Tell them, Cuckoo!"

But Cuckoo couldn't help him. 75 minutes was too long for someone to have a solid alibi. It only would've taken a few minutes of distraction for someone to have killed Rail and set up the crime scene, especially with all of the implements besides the gun being sourced from the shower room and Rail's own belongings. It was just too long a time period to account for fully – a time when anyone could've disappeared for a few minutes to get some air or go to the bathroom.

Wait a minute...

"When we the last time anyone used the boys' bathroom?" he asked.

There was a round of silence amongst the boys, the girls staring at them expectantly.

Mockingbird waved one hand defensively, the other still in his pocket. "Don't look at me! You saw how *my* attempt went!"

"*You* went to the bathroom, didn't you?" Kingfisher spoke up, looking pointedly at Duck.

Duck squeaked. "M-Me?!"

"Yes, you" Kingfisher narrowed her eyes at him "That's where you said you were going, anyway. When you foisted getting ingredients for dinner onto me."

Duck blinked at her for a moment, and then his expression filled with wonder. "Oh, I did! R-Right as we s-started cooking! But there was n-no dead body then!"

"I probably went at about the same time as you then, not long after Loon announced she was making dinner" Raven supplied, eyes lowered guiltily "But yeah, I didn't see him either. I would've said something if I had. He must've arrived after I left."

This wasn't helping. But then again, it wasn't as if anyone was going to admit to seeing Rail in the bathroom – that would get them pounced on immediately. He didn't want to say it, but if anything, it would make just as much sense for a girl to have done it, relying on the fact the murder happened in a boys' bathroom to alleviate suspicion.

"So, if both Duck and Raven went to the bathroom at about 17:00, and neither saw Rail in there, he must have been killed some time in the hour that followed" Cuckoo inferred "Where was everyone in that time?"

"I was with you!" Raven was quick to jump in "Well, except when I was at the bathroom. But other than that, I was with you the whole time!"

That was *almost* an alibi. With it being unclear who used the bathroom last though, it wasn't a perfect one. The last person to have used the bathroom could've easily seen Rail walk in and killed him.

"I-I was helping Loon with the c-cooking!" Duck also supplied "N-Neither of us could have done it!"

"I was running to get ingredients for part of it" Kingfisher admitted quietly "But I was back and forth the whole time – there wasn't enough time for me to have committed a murder." She looked over at Nightjar. "She helped for a bit. But then she disappeared somewhere when the job was half done."

"You little rat!" Nightjar spat at her.

"So where were you, then?" Mockingbird jumped in, all too eager to stoke the flames "What's *your* alibi?"

"None of your fudgin' business!" she spat in return.

"Oh, stop looking for trouble, she was with me!" Wren sighed, pinching the bridge of her nose "She was helping me look for Rail. But we didn't find him. We couldn't exactly check the bathroom."

"Were you together the whole time?" Cuckoo questioned.

"Until the last few minutes, yes" Wren agreed "Then we ran into Kingfisher, and she said she wanted to go to the bathroom but didn't want to be alone. So, I said I'd take her. We ran into you right after that."

"Oh, so that really is a phenomena? Women really do go to the bathroom in packs?" Shrike had miraculously appeared in the shower room doorway, arm behind their back, eyes twinkling with mischief.

Wren just shot them a poisonous look. "Leave her alone! People are getting hurt, she was scared!"

Kingfisher was also staring at the new arrival, daggers in her eyes. "What about you?"

"Yeah!" Mockingbird jumped in "Come on smartarse, what's *your* alibi then?"

"They don't need an *alibi*!" Loon insisted, her voice cracking "Rail—"

But Shrike cut her off before she could finish.

"Oh, I was wandering around, all by my lonesome" they cheerfully admitted "Just singing my happy tune."

"That's not an alibi, dude!" Mockingbird protested "That's just *sad*!"

"Speaks the only man with no alibi whatsoever" Shrike pointed out, tone not changing.

Mockingbird turned flustered. "Well, yeah, I was in my room."

"Right next to the bathroom" Shrike reminded everyone.

"Yeah, I know it's a rubbish alibi!" Mockingbird's face now turned red "But I didn't do it!"

"Can you prove you didn't?" Shrike questioned.

"Of course I bloody can't!" Mockingbird shot back "None of us can!"

"If n-none of us have alibis, we can't d-disprove anyone" Duck remarked, looking around the room worriedly.

Cuckoo tried to think. Was there really no way to prove who did this? Would they have to just live with the suspicion, knowing there was a killer amongst them?

"The towel."

Kingfisher's voice was soft, but it caught the attention of the whole room.

"The towel was removed from the bathroom, so the killer must've taken it with them" she recalled "If we can find it—"

"Then we can find out who killed him!" Mockingbird lit up, grinning down at her "Nice work Kingy!"

Kingfisher looked away, hiding her face behind her hair.

"So, we should start a search sweep!" Wren suggested "Everywhere people have been in the last hour! I—"

"I'm afraid that won't be necessary."

Shrike took their arm out from behind their back and threw what they had been hiding onto a heap on the bathroom floor.

Cuckoo nearly threw up again.

It a towel, one had clearly been blue at one point. But now it was turning brown where it had been swept through puddles of blood.

There wasn't any need for discussion. This had been what the killer had used to escape the bathroom.

"I found it in the cupboard across from the boys' bathroom" Shrike explained "I thought the killer might've been in a hurry to hide the evidence, and picked the closest hiding spot."

"So it was you then!" Nightjar jumped on their words.

"Why would I bring it here if I was the one to hide it?" Shrike pointed out, eyes flattening into an annoyed glance "I actually checked there since everyone had initially gathered outside the bathroom – all of us were in the vicinity of the cupboard, and could've stashed it there during the commotion over the locked bathroom door."

Cuckoo stared down at the towel, pondering it. It was possible – a slight of hand disposing of the evidence. But there was one person who definitely could've done it before they all got there, without having to worry about other people seeing.

Raven realised it too, turning to Mockingbird. "You were outside the bathroom when we arrived, right across from the cupboard."

Mockingbird turned on him with a worried stare. "You saying something?"

"He would've been covered in blood from handling the towel if it happened right before you got there" Kingfisher quickly pointed out.

"Exactly!" Mockingbird nodded quickly "I wasn't covered in blood!"

"So that solves it" Loon spoke up, quick to exonerate him "We should–"

"I...don't know about that" Raven admitted slowly "You were hiding one of your hands. And then you went into the girls' bathroom–"

"Oh come on!" Mockingbird cut him off, sweat on his brow "I was the one who *found* him! Why would I be trying to get into a bathroom I knew was locked?!"

"Everyone–"

"You could've *known* it was locked" Shrike pointed out, ever the agent of chaos "What better way to throw off suspicion than putting on a pretence in front of two witnesses?"

"Everyone, we can't–"

"That's not funny, man!" Mockingbird complained, having now turned red down his neck, hands flapping in his jacket pockets "I really needed to go! If I'd actually committed a murder in a bathroom, I would've gone when I was *in there*!"

"HEY, he didn't commit a murder!" Loon shouted her voice above the rest, finally managing to complete a sentence "*THERE WAS NO MURDER!*"

The strange statement effectively shut them all up.

"Eh, what're you talking about?" Nightjar frowned "Didn't we just prove–"

"We've proven that someone moved Rail's body" Loon cut in, her words biting "A sick joke someone's playing desecrating a corpse like that! But it's not murder!"

"You can't know that" Kingfisher looked at her funny.

"*I* have the key to the gun cupboard!" Loon insisted, holding up the key to demonstrate the fact "No one could've taken a gun, except for the person who found it before I took it! Which I why I've never seen a round gun like that! I was the first one into the room when we went in as a group, and the only one who got there before me when we woke up was Rail!"

A horrified silence hung in the air.

"So...Rail had to be the one to take the gun" Kingfisher inferred "So...he really did kill himself? And someone just moved the body?"

"B-But why?" Duck stuttered, looking horrified.

Cuckoo frowned. That solution didn't sound wrong, but it rubbed him the wrong way. He wasn't sure why. Maybe the coincidence of someone killing themselves when they knew that murders would be coming was too big for him to accept. Why would someone do that, knowing that everyone would assume there was a murderer on the lose?

And if Rail had killed himself, why would someone got through the effort to stage a suicide as a murder disguised as a suicide? What would be the purpose of that?

Yes, Rail had found the armoury, and could have taken a gun, but why would he have taken a gun before they even knew they were in danger? And there was no guarantee he was the first one there: what if someone had found it first and just not admitted to it?

But Loon seemed so sure. Did she know something he didn't?

He wasn't seeing things that weren't there, was he?

He decided to test her theory.

"But what kind of person would do that?" he asked.

Loon's face screwed up, and for a moment, Cuckoo thought she was going to hit him. "A screwed up one!" she settled on, her voice a hiss "And that's all there is to it!"

"It would be...rather convenient, wouldn't it?" Mockingbird's shaking voice cut between them "That someone would go to such lengths to muddle a suicide. You don't–"

"Shut up!" Loon snapped, causing the entire room to snap back a step – all except for Cuckoo, leaving him in position to be grabbed by the arm and hoisted up from his seat "Dinner will be ready in fifteen minutes! We're eating in the dining room!"

Saying nothing more, she dragged him out of the room.

7

"Hey! Hey, wait!"

Loon was less supporting him so much as holding his weight as she dashed through the corridors back to the kitchen. His working leg began to ache from the rapid hopping he was forced to complete, whilst his broken leg screeched with agony from being shaken back and forth.

"Can we stop?!" he found himself gasping from the strain "Please!"

But she didn't reply, didn't even look at him. She just kept dragging him onward — leaving him silently wishing for Raven to come back — until they made it to the kitchen, where she all but threw him down on one of the bar stools.

"What the hell were you thinking?!" she spat right in his face.

He shrank back from the face staring down at him. Her eyes were wild and angry, hair standing on end under her hat. This wasn't the carefully constructed Loon he thought he'd gotten to know.

"That...you're very scary?" he found himself admitting.

Her eyes softened for a moment, taken by surprise by the honest admission. But they hardened again just as quickly.

"Do you understand what will happen if they know that Rail was *murdered*?!" she hissed, her voice low, as if she was expecting someone to walk in.

The words caught him by surprise, causing him to sit bolt upright.

"Wait, you *knew*?!" the words burst out of him.

"Of course I knew!" Loon hissed back "I knew the moment I saw him! All the blood was to the right of him, meaning he was shot from the left! Obviously someone else shot him, and then put the gun in his right hand by mistake!"

That took a load off Cuckoo's mind. For just a moment, he wondered if he'd been going crazy, seeing things that weren't there. That was how strong Loon's certainty had been. Now know he knew he was right the whole time, he felt like a thousand-pound weight had been lifted off his chest.

"But...why wouldn't you want the others to know?" he questioned "There's a killer amongst us—"

"If they know that, then *more* people are going to die!" Loon all but shrieked at him, her hands flying outwards, her right hand hitting into the pot still boiling on the stove "Ouch! Son of a cow! Ah!"

Cuckoo flinched back again at the change in volume, even before she burnt herself. Something was obviously distressing her — something more than Rail being dead.

"Do you think the warden will kill us, for us figuring out that we know they killed Rail?" he tried to guess.

Loon had stepped over to the sink, running her stinging hand under the water to sooth it. She shook her head, not even dignifying him with enough effort to turn around and look at him

"I don't care about any warden" she admitted quietly "If they're here, then there's nothing we can do about that. I'm worried..." Her shoulders came up, and her voice seemed to drop impossibly quieter. "I'm worried about the others."

Cuckoo tried to nod along. He thought he understood what she meant – if the warden had made their move, then none of them were safe. Any of them left on their own could be next.

"We can keep them safe" he reassured her "We can sleep in shifts, make sure no one's left alone, not leave any food or drink unattended–"

"I'm not worried about some shadowy figure killing us" Loon stopped him, finally turning back to him with a grave face "I'm worried one of *them* is going to kill us."

She nodded her head towards the West Wing, making it very overt who she was talking about.

Cuckoo's heart froze in his chest.

That was something he couldn't prepare for. He couldn't watch eight people at all times. It wasn't possible.

If others in the group, people who weren't the warden, were willing to kill, then more people were certainly going to die.

He could still feel Rail's shaking hands pulling the bandages tight on his leg before he passed out. Just as vividly, he could see Rail's anguished blood-less face barely more than an hour later.

His whole body was shaking.

"The warden gave them all a motive: kill everyone else, and you get to leave" Loon stated firmly "And no one wants to stay here."

"B-But" Cuckoo's tongue tripped over his words "No one would *kill* people just to get out of here!"

It wasn't conceivable. No one would do that, right? Not to people they *knew*, even a little bit. It was different from before, when they were all strangers locked together in that North Wing. Since then, they'd worked together. They'd explored together. They'd *bonded*, right?

Or was Cuckoo just the fool, latching on to the only people he'd ever gotten the chance to know? Onto the people who'd helped him without judgement when he was screaming.

Cuckoo didn't want anything to happen to any of them. He couldn't imagine a world where someone could.

Loon's face gave nothing away. Slowly, she raised her arms, and wrapped them around herself gently.

"I might not look like it," she said carefully "But I have eight kids waiting for me at home."

"E-Eight?!" Cuckoo tried not to let the surprise show on his face.

Eight kids! That couldn't be right! She surely couldn't be any older than *him*, let alone old enough to have had that many kids!

"All adopted, obviously" Loon corrected him, a little blush on her face at the insinuation "With all this haze in my head, I don't even remember their names, or their faces. But I know they're out there, and that they need me."

For some reason, this made more sense to him. The way she'd taken charge so easily, her firm but gentle hand, her carefully-pulled words, her affection towards the young-looking Duck. Yeah, Loon would make a great mother.

"Do you understand?" she asked him, her face carefully blank "Why I need to get out of here?"

Cuckoo felt his steady heartrate suddenly skyrocket at her words, the room turning deadly silent. It occurred to him that they were alone, just the two of them, in a room full of sharp objects.

"You...You wouldn't *kill* anyone though?" he stuttered "Right?"

His eyes flickered towards the door, but he knew it was useless. He could hardly run like this.

"Of course not!" Loon insisted, some fire coming back into her eyes, but not enough to burn him "I would never be able to look my kids in the eyes if I did!" She settled down again, tone dropping to a murmur once more. "But if I remember them, even when my own name was taken from me, then why can't the others have people they need to get back to? Friends, loved ones, family...People they *would* kill for."

And that...that was something Cuckoo couldn't refute. Mockingbird had mentioned having siblings. Wren said she had friends on the outside. Even Raven had implied he had something to return to. They all had reasons to not want to stay here, beyond concern for their own lives.

Well, except for himself, of course.

No matter how hard he thought about it, he couldn't picture anyone waiting for him. Everyone before he woke up in that courtyard was a black curtain he couldn't pull aside. Was he so disliked that he truly had no one worth remembering?

"Hey" he looked up and saw Loon staring down at him with kindly eyes "There's someone out there who loves you, I guarantee it. Everyone has someone: no one's ever truly alone, even if they think they are."

He tried to feel her words, but they didn't reach his heart. For whatever reason, he couldn't bring himself to believe her.

"H-Hey!"

They both startled as Duck poked his head through the door.

"Are...we r-ready to start c-cooking again?" he questioned, looking between the pair of them with a confused expression.

"Ah" Loon looked to the side, like she was thinking quickly "Er, we need more pepper, Duck. Can you go get some more?"

Duck frowned. "D-Didn't we already–"

"Pleease, Duck?" she pleaded sweetly, drawing out the word with a smile.

For a moment, Duck's cheeks coloured, responding to a simple gesture like he'd never been smiled at before. Then he ducked his head back around the door, clearly embarrassed.

"S-Sure!" he called back to them "B-Be right back!"

It was only when the sound of his footsteps faded that the smile slipped from Loon's face, and she turned to look at Cuckoo again.

"I don't think anyone here would ever kill anyone, under normal circumstances that is" she told him "Even with an incentive, I don't think most of them would. But if they believed someone had already started killing – if someone has already removed the pin from the grenade, it becomes a lot easier to throw."

Cuckoo's mouth felt dry, as he finally understood why she'd brought him here. If Rail had been murdered, then that meant anyone of them could be next. So, under such circumstances, why not hurry and kill everyone else so you can leave before the warden – or anyone else – could kill *you*?

It was a terrifying thought. One he didn't know how to handle. One that made his shoulders tremble at just the thought.

Maybe it was because he had nothing else, but he didn't want to lose anyone else, including to each other.

"And I just told them that there's a killer in here with us" he groaned, feeling sick from his head to his toes.

The way Loon looked down at him...it was scary. Somewhere between pity and resentment.

"Yes" she said "I doubt they bought *my* excuses."

She leant her face towards his, causing him to lean so far back he nearly fell backwards off the stool.

"So, if anyone dies tonight, that's on you."

o

With Loon's words paralysing him – and no one showing up to help him out either – Cuckoo stayed exactly where he was on the stool in the kitchen, sitting back and watching Loon and Duck finish their work. Seeing them rushing around to make a meal for ten – well, now nine – he almost wanted to ask if he could help. But just as he

96

thought about opening his mouth to speak, Loon would catch his eye with that disappointed stare, and he'd shut it again.

It resulted in a very awkward fifteen minutes, Cuckoo stuck on his stool with nothing to do but drum his fingers against his leg, the motion soothing to him, like they were dancing on a keyboard. That was, until Loon sent Duck out to gather everyone for dinner.

With her little helper otherwise occupied, Loon began to gather up that plates and bowls, stacking them next the soup pot to carry through to the dining room. However, it became quickly apparent that there were too many items for her to carry herself.

"Can I help?" he offered.

Loon raised an eyebrow at him. "How?"

That...was a good point. As if prompted, his leg began to ache.

Also prompted by her question was Raven, who appeared in the doorway.

"Hey, you're here!" he smiled at Cuckoo, and he wasn't going to lie, it felt nice to have someone smiling at him after Loon's displeasure and Duck's indifference for anyone who wasn't Loon.

"Can you help with this?" Loon gestured to the dishes, just as Raven slipped an arm under Cuckoo's shoulders.

"I'll send someone through" Raven assured her as he helped Cuckoo out of the room "Can't have anyone missing dinner!"

It might be selfish, but Cuckoo couldn't help but feel a warmth in his chest that, after his screw up before, Raven came to find him, and came to *him* before the edibles.

"Hey" he turned his head to look at Raven as they walked to the next room "Er...nicely done. Back there. With the towel trick."

Raven's smile seemed to get impossibly brighter, his free arm scratching at his brow.

"Ah, thanks!" he smiled "Glad I could be of some use!"

Cuckoo frowned. His didn't like that insinuation. Raven had been nothing but useful.

He didn't get a chance to ask about though, because at that moment, they stepped into the dining room.

Cuckoo hadn't seen the dining room yet. It reminded him, with a shudder, of the library – a red carpet with green and gold wallpaper. Some cabinets ran around the edge of the room, but a glance over at them determined that they were all empty. The majority of the space was taken up by a large table, with seven seats around it. Three more arrived just after them, carried by Wren: the three chairs from the library.

"Hey!" Raven called out to the room "Can someone help Loon get the dinner through here?"

"I'm freakin' busy here!" Nightjar shot back where she was setting out place mats, Mockingbird following her with cutlery for the table.

Wren stood up from where she'd been about to sit at one of the chairs she'd brought in. "I'll go."

Just as she left the room, Duck reappeared, dragging Kingfisher behind him.

"F-Found her!" he announced cheerfully.

"I was just getting a ladle" Kingfisher insisted tiredly, snatching her hand out of Duck's with a moody stare as she held up a ladle in her other hand "You didn't need to *drag* me back. I was coming."

Raven put Cuckoo down in the nearest seat, next to the head of the table, just as Wren and Loon came through from the kitchen with the soup and the bowls and plates.

"Someone needs to get the bread and olives" Wren told them all.

Her eyes particularly landed on Shrike, sitting at the far end of the table. They blissfully ignored the unsubtle command, smiling away as they picked at their teeth with a toothpick.

With an aggravated huff, Nightjar slammed down the last placemat in front of Cuckoo.

"Fine!" she groused "I'll go and make myself *more* useful!"

She stormed out towards the kitchen, Mockingbird following her with a fed-up sigh.

Cuckoo couldn't help but feel even more useless, as he sat back and watched as everyone took their places at the table. Raven sat next to him with a smile, whilst Kingfisher stood up from her seat abruptly when Duck sat next to her, moving to the far end of the row. One by one they took their turns with the ladle to scoop out their own serving; naturally something Nightjar complained about once she and Mockingbird came back.

"The hell, you're just helping yourselves without waiting for me?!" she screeched, slamming down the bread board, causing the stack of napkins stashed on top of it to jump.

"That's a jerk move" Mockingbird also complained, wincing as he set down the olive tray.

"Isn't the best part of the soup in the middle, anyway?" Kingfisher pointed out dryly "Just sit down."

Mercifully, Nightjar didn't have any further commentary, and after a scramble for the bread, napkins and the last two servings, everyone took their place.

That being said, once the food was doled out, it wasn't as if anyone was hurrying to eat. Wren took a bite out of a piece of bread, but instead of continuing with the meal, she just sat there and chewed it until it was pretty much paste. Raven's bread didn't fare any better, with him slowly dissecting it into smaller and smaller strips. Kingfisher stared blankly down at her soup as if she didn't understand its purpose, whilst Nightjar leant on her elbow, twirling her spoon between her fingers with no sign that she intended to use it. Mockingbird was slumped in his seat and hadn't even taken his hands out of his pockets. Cuckoo locked eyes with Duck, sat across from him; despite the fact he was the one to help make the food, he was merely playing with his napkin. The only one with an appetite was Shrike, who was using their toothpick to reach for the olive tray, making off with one morsel after another in rapid sequence.

Everyone was doing their best to ignore the empty seat between Shrike and Wren, as if not verbalising it would help them forget that there used to be ten of them, and now there were nine.

Finally, with no one else showing any signs of moving, Loon slammed her hands down on the table, jumping to her feet.

"Ok, I'm just going to say it!" she announced "Rail is dead! There's no way around that!"

An uncomfortable chill ran down the table at her words, eyes flickering to the empty seat.

"He's gone" Loon continued, voice softening a little "He took his own life. He made his own decision."

Someone at the table scoffed. Cuckoo couldn't turn his head fast enough to see who it was.

"And we can't let that hang over us" Loon ignored the interruption, her eyes lowering to the table in thought "It's tragic, and we can morn him, but we can't let grief trap us here forever. As tragic as losing one of us might be, we can't let it define us."

Duck's napkin dropped to the floor. He coughed out an apology and reached down to get it.

"It's true we don't know each other" Loon stood up a little straighter, now looking them all in the eye "And we have no reason to trust each other. But we're also nine people in the same situation. None of us are here by choice, and we all have people we need to get home to. People we would do anything to see again."

A few people at the table squirmed, Cuckoo included. He didn't need to be reminded he wasn't one of those people.

"Whoever put us in here wants us to fight each other – that much is clear" she admitted "So we're going to show them we're not the mindless beasts they're trying to make us into. We're people, and we're going to get out of here like people. We're going to work together and find a way to escape. Maybe we won't succeed tomorrow, maybe not the day after, but at some point, we will get out of here. And we're going to do it by all of us pulling together!"

It was a rousing speech, and it did leave Cuckoo feeling a little better than when he first sat down. A few others at the table were sitting up a bit straighter too, Raven's eyes all but gleaming. But others, especially those at the far end of the table, weren't having any reaction.

Loon seemed to pick up on this, taking a moment to think it over.

"Duck" she put a hand on the man in question's shoulder, causing him to jump "You've stood by me and been a pillar of strength for me. It's thanks to you we're all having this meal together."

It wasn't exactly glorious praise, but it had Duck lighting up none the less.

99

"Kingfisher" Loon now addressed the blonde girl, who seemed to lack the energy to even be surprised "You already have this whole place memorised. Any time we need something, you know exactly where to find it. Nothing escapes your mind!"

The girl in question seemed to shrink further in her seat, but there was now a tiny smile on her face.

"Raven" she now turned to the man sat beside Cuckoo "You've figured out every trick and trap so far. Your analytical skills are incredible!"

Raven's whole face seemed to light up at compliment, mouth wide and eyes bright. Cuckoo tried not to worry over how such a simple compliment had such a dazzling effect on him.

"Wren" she moved along the table "Your strength amazes me."

"Of course" Wren mumbled around the now granulated bread in her mouth.

"But you also care so much" Loon followed her statement up with "Thank you for looking after us, and I hope you'll continue to do so in the future."

That seemed to appease Wren a little bit, her grimace from before raising into a full grin.

"Nightjar" Loon seemed to take a moment to think about this one "Well, I think I'd be panicking a lot more if I didn't have you to panic for me."

"What kind of freakin' compliment is that?!" the woman in question roared down the table.

"At least it's a compliment, you moron" Mockingbird grumbled, sliding down further in his seat, until Cuckoo became concerned that he was going to slide right off under the table.

"I jest, I jest" Loon quickly cut in before an argument could spring up "Nightjar, through all the words, you've been helping us since the beginning. I haven't forgotten that."

For once, Nightjar had nothing to say. A pensive look crossed her face, before fading into a triumphant smirk.

Loon then moved onto the man next to Nightjar. "Mockingbird, you've been so encouraging to us all, like a big brother. Thank you for keeping our spirits up when we needed it."

Mockingbird couldn't even bring himself to look at her, his gaze fixed firmly on the wall behind Wren's shoulder. It looked like all of that previous energy he'd been radiating had been sapped right out of his bones.

"Cuckoo" she turned to the man seated to her left, making him hold his breath in anticipation "You're so honest. You don't say much, but you think things over with such a level head. And you've been so strong, throughout everything. Don't ever think you're a burden on anyone here, because you're not."

That...wasn't what he was expecting to hear. He wasn't sure he *wanted* to hear it either. Tears pricked at his eyes, causing his picture of the room to go blurry.

"And Shrike..."

This time Loon trailed off, her mouth opening and closing as she searched for words. An awkward blanket fell over the table as everyone looked between their fearless leader, who was struggling to find something to say, and Shrike, who's usual serene smile hadn't so much as faltered.

Cuckoo could understand the problem. He also found it difficult to compliment something about Shrike that didn't involve their physical appearance, and that would no doubt ring hollow after the sincere, personal compliments everyone else had received.

"You're better than you let yourself think you are" she finally settled on.

Those strange words signalled in the first time Cuckoo got to see a crack in that perfectly polished exterior. For a moment, Shrike seemed to freeze in time, their smile reducing to a pressed line. But then the moment lifted, the smile – so obviously fake, how had Cuckoo not recognised that before? – came back into their face, and nimble fingers moved to snatch another olive.

"I'm *exactly* what I think I am" was their bizarre response, just before popping the olive into their mouth.

If the comment made any more sense to Loon, she didn't show it, just smiling happily at all of them as she reached forward to grab the ladle from where it was resting in the soup pot.

"I'm so proud of all of you" she told them "And I can't wait to prove that warden wrong and escape here with all of you. Because I have faith that, with our combined skills, we can do it! And when we make it back to our loved ones on the other side, I'm going to introduce my kids to my eight new best friends! Because I for one wouldn't want to be stuck in here with anyone else!"

A few smiles were cracked around the table as Loon filled the ladle and raised it up, like she was toasting with a glass.

"So, we're going to do this for Rail!" she cheered "We're going to get out of here without anyone else dying! I guarantee it! So just stay beside me and, I promise, nothing else will happen! We're going home!"

And with that, she raised the ladle to her lips and downed the entire spoonful of soup.

The table went into uproar. A few people laughed. Other groaned. At least one person yelled out:

"Don't drink from that, we have to use that and now it's got your lips all over it!"

Duck was smiling, his face more positive than Cuckoo had even seen it, scrambling to fill his spoon and raise it to his lips to mimic the woman he clearly adored, even after such a short span of time.

Even Cuckoo couldn't help but hide a grin behind his palm, the spirit of the room infectious. He picked up his spoon and dipped it into his soup, ready to join in—

Static screeched behind his eyes, the whole world glitching and stretching like a puzzle coming undone.

101

But as quickly as that spirit had been raised, it was crushed.

A feeling of nausea, a burning in his throat and stomach so powerful he wished he could dig his spoon through his skin and stab at his insides to release that twisting, churning horror. Tears streaming down his face and as the pain overwhelmed him, crashing to the ground with a—

He was jolted back into his seat, staring at his full spoon in horror.

That wasn't...was it? From before...

He threw his spoon down into his soup.

"DON'T EAT THE SOUP!" he screamed.

All noise was killed in an instant as everyone turned to stare at him. He felt goosebumps down his back at their confused, suspicious stares. But a tiny sound to his right focused their attention on someone else.

Someone they couldn't afford for it to be.

They could do nothing but watch as Loon — her face contorted and horrified — first gagged, then gargled, and then bent forward and spewed red all over the table.

8

In the moments after Loon collapsed, there was silence.

In the moment after that, there was screaming.

Duck dropped the spoon that had been at his lips, scrambling forward hysterically and grabbing onto Loon like a baby to its blanket. The others capable of moving scrambled back from the table like it was on fire. Cuckoo wanted to as well, the soup and bile Loon had spewed up before her collapse flooding dangerously close to where he was sitting. He swore he could feel phantom spatters of that blood across his body, like she'd hurled all over him and not the table, but a glance at his arms showed they were immaculate. He'd felt the same way upon seeing the blood in his room, and at the sight of Rail's body, right? Why did this keep happening in response to the sight of blood?

Was it another type of vision? But this didn't appear to be a flash forward...

"It's poisoned!" Wren was barking right in his ear, putting her arms out as if to stop others from getting close to the table.

"HOW?!" Nightjar screamed, her voice reaching octaves that were even more piercing than usual.

"More importantly, *what*?" even Shrike wasn't unaffected, their usually controlled voice wavering with panic.

"The soup?! The ladle?!" Raven cried out, his eyes darting to Kingfisher, who was frozen to the spot.

"I-It has to be the soup, right?" Mockingbird stuttered, face slack-jawed with horror as Loon's body twitched on the table "That's what *he* said anyway."

With that he looked at Cuckoo with a glare that should've killed him on the spot.

It was at that moment, with Mockingbird so pointedly calling attention to him, that Cuckoo realised just how perilous a position he was in. He could feel the weight of six accusatory, suspicious stares on him.

He was abruptly yanked up and to the side, his jacket balled into one of Wren's massive fists.

"WHAT DID YOU DO?!" she screamed right in his face, her own visage twisted with rage and grief "WHAT DID YOU PUT IN THERE?!"

Cuckoo felt his heart rate spike, the world slowing down as his mind searched for a way out of this. How was he supposed to tell them that he saw it coming? That this was the second time his vision had glitched and he felt himself die?

He was already being suspected of murder; he didn't need to tell them all he was going *crazy*.

"He just tried to kill us!" Nightjar shrieked, pointing at him, her face turning as white as sheet and then blood red "Someone stab him!"

Wait, what?! No no no no no... He had to think quickly!

"Wait, he might've just seen it coming again!" Raven tried to jump in, his voice frantic "Like he did in the library!"

"What did you say?" Shrike's voice was so quiet, Cuckoo nearly missed it.

Especially since Wren went back to screaming in his face at that exact moment. "WHERE'S THE ANTIDOTE?!"

"I-I don't know!" the words slipped out, even as his brain screamed at him that this was exactly the wrong thing to say. He was used to Wren being gentle and a bit silly – he didn't know how to handle this outright quivering rage.

"DON'T LIE!" Wren began shaking him, and Cuckoo swore he felt his neck snap "IF YOU DIDN'T DO IT, HOW DID YOU KNOW NOT TO EAT THE SOUP?!"

He vaguely heard people shouting for her to stop, leaving him hanging by his jacket with his head lolling towards the table. He cringed as he realised the blood and soup Loon had thrown up was slowly crawling towards him, intensifying that splattering feeling all over his body. He tried to shuffle further into his seat – even with everything that had happened that day, he wasn't broken enough to want chunks of vegetables and white crystals all over him.

White crystals...

"The crystals!" he quickly shouted out, hoping this would be enough to spare him "I saw white crystals in my soup!"

He waved his arm frantically towards the table.

Wren peered over at the table, face still bleeding suspicion. But after a few unbearably tense moments, she dropped him back into his chair.

"He's telling the truth" Shrike informed them with a blank face, using their spoon to scoop up some soup from their bowl and examine it closely "There's salt crystals in here."

"S-Salt?!" Nightjar squeaked, hands up by her face "Salt did *that*?!"

She nodded at Loon, who appeared to be seizing on the table as Duck wailed with horror over her. Cuckoo tried to avert his eyes – that glitch had had the unfortunate effect of letting him know the exact hell Loon was currently going through. He could still feel the burning in chest and stomach, ebbing too slowly.

"Certain salts are highly corrosive, and can cause burns" Kingfisher recalled, her eyes wide "Like phenol, and sodium hydroxide, or–"

"So, are we dead?!" Mockingbird cut her off, sweat running down his brow as he stared at Loon in pure horror "Like, are we going to go like *that*?!"

"Did you drink the soup?" Shrike questioned him.

"N-No!" Mockingbird shook his head.

"I did."

Cuckoo turned his head with horror towards the small voice that had spoken. Raven was clutching his own wrist, staring down at the table with a vacant expression.

His hands felt sweaty. Was Raven about to hurl and then drop into agony, like Loon just had?

"Me too" Kingfisher also admitted quietly, staring at Loon with wide-eyed horror.

"Frick!" Nightjar suddenly cursed, turning and hitting the wall "No, no, this isn't happening! This can't happen to me!"

"J-Just calm down!" Wren tried to calm her down, her voice reverting to being soft and shaky "If you've swallowed any, we'll just—"

Nightjar though just screamed loud enough to drown her out, smashing her fists into the wall a few more times before collapsing with a sob.

"I can't die here!" she sobbed, clutching her knees "I have people waiting for me! People who actually give a crap about me! I can't die here! I just can't! I can't!"

Cuckoo felt his mouth go dry. It was a very sincere statement, one he hadn't expected from Nightjar of all people. Words filled with so much grief it made him uncomfortable just listening to them.

"You're fine" Shrike assured them "If you'd drank anything that corrosive, your mouths would be burning right now. Salts are heavy — it probably sank to the bottom of the bowl. She was just got unlucky that she downed an entirely serving in one go."

Nightjar looked up from her curled up position, her eyes hardening. "You better not be lying, you little freak. If you're lying, I'll use my last strength to smash your freakin' head in!"

"No, he's right" Kingfisher backed him up "If we'd drank poison, we wouldn't be standing right now to complain about it."

"G-GUYS!" Duck now turned to them with a scream, and Cuckoo didn't possess the words to describe how horrified his face looked "W-WE NEED A DOCTOR!!!"

At that moment, Loon's head began crashing onto the table, her hat flying off onto the floor.

"The doctor's dead, moron!" Nightjar shouted from her seat position.

Cuckoo's stomach plummeted with horror. He'd been so absorbed with the fact that someone had *murdered* Rail, he hadn't thought about what they'd deprived them of. Without a doctor, none of them had medical training. None of them had any idea how to help Loon, or if they even could.

Wren swore and picked Loon up, putting her over her shoulder.

"There'll be something in the doctor's office!" she barked "We need to go, now!"

"I locked the doctor's office after we took the medicines back" Kingfisher recalled "And I gave the key back to Rail. He wouldn't stop fussing until I did."

"Does he *still* have the key?" Mockingbird questioned.

"It'll be on his body if the killer didn't take it" Raven suggested "I can go get it."

Cuckoo fell ill himself at the idea of having to grope a dead body, let alone the dead body of a friend who'd been murdered. But Raven showed no signs of such disgust as he hurried out of the room towards the boys' bathroom.

With Raven on his way, Wren carried Loon out of the room, the hysterical Duck on her tail, flailing around in a panic like he wanted to do something but didn't know what would help. It didn't take long for the other four to follow them.

"Hey-HEY!" Cuckoo yelled out, but none of them came back for him "Wait, I need help!" He grabbed the edge of the table and forced himself onto his one working foot. He managed to hop along for a few steps by clutching the table, but as he tried to cross to the wall, he didn't quite make it. His bad foot came down to steady himself, and he collapsed forwards with a thud.

If it wasn't for the fact that the dining room was carpeted, he would've shattered his face.

His cheeks burnt. He felt humiliated. Walking was the simplest of human actions after breathing, and he couldn't even do that.

His harsh feelings towards himself became even worse when he heard a familiar chuckling above him.

"You're not having a good day, are you?" Shrike remarked.

He tried to turn his face away from that amused smirk, only to end up staring at a mixture of soup and blood trickling down from the table onto the carpet.

"Others are having worse" he admitted quietly.

For once, Shrike didn't seem to have a quip for that. "Hm...I suppose that's one way to view it. Granted, to others, their mere existence could be nightmare enough."

Cuckoo wondered who they were talking about. Kingfisher, with her vacant stares? Raven, with his self-depreciating comments? Duck, with his closed-off demeanour? Or themself, maybe?

"Well, I'm not cruel enough to leave you lying on the floor ass-up" Shrike announced, their voice returning to its usual melodic state "Come on, let's go watch the fireworks." As they helped him up though, he spotted Loon's hat on the floor.

"Wait, wait" he grabbed the hat before he stood up as straight as he could "Ok."

It was initially a silent walk to the doctor's office, Shrike apparently having nothing interesting to say. Cuckoo would put it down to shock, like him, except Shrike didn't strike him as a person who was ever shocked.

They waded through death so easily – Cuckoo both admired them for that and felt unsettling chills run down his spine whenever he thought about it.

He looked past their unbothered face at Loon's hat, currently clutched in the hand on Shrike's shoulder. It, rather miraculous, seemed to have avoided getting any blood or bile on it.

"So, if anyone dies tonight, that's on you."

Well, wasn't that prophetic.

"This is my fault" he muttered to himself.

"Oh, is that an admission?" Shrike asked, voice playful.

"N-No!" Cuckoo quickly shook his head "I didn't put anything in the soup, but..."

He stopped himself, wondering if it was safe to admit this to Shrike of all people.

Shrike turned their head towards him, and he was surprised at what he saw. The usual smirk and dancing eyes were there, but for some reason, up close, they looked very wrong. There was a strain at the corner of their mouth, and the edge of their eyes almost seemed to droop a little.

Maybe he was just an awful person, but looking at someone who was usually so in control, and seeing how fractured they were underneath that all, it sent a flush of warmth and confidence through him. That he wasn't alone in how poorly he was handling this.

"Loon was concerned after we found Rail" he told them "She was worried that, after I told everyone that there was a murderer amongst us, people would begin killing each other to escape. And now she's dying, so she was right."

Shrike hmmed, looking ahead again. "You think this is because of *you*?"

"What else could it be?" Cuckoo questioned.

Shrike paused a little, before nodding their head softly. "Yes, I think you might be right."

Well, wasn't that a bitter pill to swallow. It was one thing to think it yourself, it was another for someone to second it.

"Although..." Shrike added on "Maybe not in the way you just implied."

Huh?

"Are you...going to elaborate?" he questioned.

"Perhaps" was the strange answer "But only if you answer one question for me."

Cuckoo felt apprehensive. Subconsciously, he knew whatever Shrike wanted to ask, it must be pretty heavy, if they had to corner him with emotional blackmail first. It certainly couldn't be good.

"Raven said you 'saw it coming, like you did in the library'" Shrike recalled, eyes turning to burrow into him "What exactly did you see in the library?"

That...was exactly what he *didn't* want them to ask.

He had absolutely no idea how to respond to that. He'd barely made it through telling Raven without his cheeks bursting into humiliated flames, and that was with a man who both already withheld crucial information from the group for Cuckoo's sake, and who he'd already began to feel himself trusting. How was he supposed to tell Shrike – someone who scared him on more than one level and made him feel small on all the others.

"HEY! Cuckoo! We have a problem!"

Thankfully, he didn't have to answer, as Raven came swooping in to save him one more; this time, racing around the corner behind them to catch up.

"Rail didn't have the key?" Shrike guessed, turning the pair of them to face the newcomer.

Raven paused for a moment, hunched with his hands on his knees. He seemed really exhausted, considering he'd only ran to the bathroom and back.

"Worse!" he panted "The body—His body's gone!"

Cuckoo's brain shorted out.

"What?" judging by Shrike's expression, so had theirs.

"It isn't in the bathroom!" Raven insisted "The blood's gone! So's the gun and the pants and the shoes! Even the bullet hole! It's like nothing ever happened!"

That seemed weird. Maybe someone could've moved Rail's body to another room for privacy, and so the men could pee in relative peace. Even the cleaning of the blood could've been an act of kindness. But who would go through the effort to cover up a bullet hole? Who'd even had the *time* to?

Shrike was very still for a long moment. Then they turned back in the direction they'd originally been going, dragging Cuckoo with them.

"We need to see the doctor's office" they announced "If I'm right..."

Whatever they thought they were right about, they didn't say.

Yet, somehow, that didn't give Cuckoo any amount of unease compared to Raven, who had buried his head in his hands and was mumbling to himself the whole way.

He couldn't be certain, but he could've sworn he was muttering:

"Why them? It should've been me. It should've been me..."

o

The key to the doctor's office may not have been in Rail's pocket, but it *was* in the door it belonged to. Ot was standing proudly out of the keyhole of the opened door, daring to gleam in the light of the bustling activity inside.

It was almost enough to distract from Loon shivering and moaning on the bed at the far end, Duck frantically clutching her hand and patting her forehead with a wet cloth whilst Wren led a search for any medicines they could find, as if they'd know which ones to use and how to use them.

"It was already in the door when we got here" Kingfisher told them, her eyes wet but voice flat, before they could even ask.

Cuckoo frowned. Things were getting curiouser. Not only had someone cleaned up the crime scene, but they had also brought the crucial key back to where to belonged. Why though?

"Whoever killed Rail — they must've brought it back here after they cleaned up the body" Raven recognised.

Kingfisher stopped, frozen. "Rail's body is missing?"

"Vanished, apparently" Shrike told her "Along with everything in the bathroom we left behind."

"I don't understand" Raven muttered "We were all together in the dining room after we left the bathroom. How could someone have done that? There was no time. Maybe to bring the key here, if they were careful. But to make a whole body disappear again..."

Cuckoo straightened as he realised what Raven meant.

"Again?" Shrike questioned, but Cuckoo's mind was whirring too loudly to take in their confusion.

It was just like the body that had made the bloodstains in Cuckoo's room. That had also disappeared. And they still hadn't found it after all this time, amongst Wren and Nightjar tearing the whole building apart looking for Rail...

Where were these bodies going? And why hide them in the first place?

"Why did they take the body?" Cuckoo pondered to himself quietly "To dispose of it somehow? But where?"

Where was there even to take bodies? The whole prison was sealed. There was nowhere to go.

Kingfisher turned pale, pushing past them into the corridor.

"Well, that seems important" Shrike remarked "Feel like following her?"

Unfortunately for Cuckoo's already aching leg, she'd gone all the way to the far end of the corridor, right back to where they'd started. Namely, the room opposite the kitchen – the only room he hadn't been into.

The room wasn't decorated with cheerful tiles or wallpaper like the others. Instead, it retained its hard stone walls, leaving it dark and gloomy. At the far end was a large green machine with a hatch door. Kingfisher first placed her hand on the machine, then checked through the hatch door.

"Nothing, it's empty" she admitted with what sounded like a relieved sigh "And it hasn't been on."

"An incinerator" Shrike remarked with wonder, passing Cuckoo off to Raven so they could take a look themselves "You're right, completely empty, like it's brand new."

Cuckoo noticed a common theme. For all the prison seemed old, everything in its shone like it had never been used. Not so much as a scuffed skirting board or a chipped drawer – even the library books had no creases in their spines or folds in their pages. Like it was all impervious to age or wear.

This place...it couldn't have been built just for them, right?

"You can see the chimney stack for it from the window in my bedroom" Kingfisher explained "I thought it was worth checking, just in case."

"Good thinking" Shrike commented, shutting the hatch door and pressing the push lock down into place, hearing it lock with a satisfying click when sufficient weight was applied down onto it "But no, Mr Warden must have more interesting places to stash a body."

"We should probably look for it though" Raven suggested "I could probably get a few guys together, search from top to bottom."

Cuckoo doubted they would succeed. They still hadn't found the first missing body, let alone a second. But he could understand people's need to be busy – to force themselves to think about anything else.

"Well, we certainly can't leave it outstanding" Shrike agreed "But who will care for Loon?"

It wasn't a question; they were looking right at Cuckoo when they said it.

"Me, I guess" Cuckoo groused, as if he had any qualifications for looking after a dying person.

Which is how he found himself sitting with Duck at Loon's side, changing out her sick bucket and trying to force her to drink. He had no idea if he was helping or killing her, and couldn't bear to look at her face, especially after black burns began to form around her mouth. He tried to look for any kind of antidote that could help, but when they didn't know what she'd swallowed, they could hardly think of anything to combat it.

He even located the pain killers Rail had suggested to give to him, but he had no idea how to make Loon swallow them with her mouth continually filling with saliva and bile. Why couldn't Rail be here right now...

After the first hour, Duck's fight seemed to go right out of him. He would just silently dab her face, any light that had been in his eyes crushed in the blackness, until an unnerving calm took over his once nervous body.

Cuckoo tried to keep his eyes trained on the floor. He didn't want to look at Loon, in case she opened her eyes and looked back. He didn't think he could take it, if she looked at him with those same eyes that just hours earlier had reminded him that this was *all his fault*.

In the end, nothing they did mattered. At 21:30, roughly three hours after she'd drank the soup that she herself had made, Loon finally stopped breathing.

9

It didn't feel like a tragedy, but a mercy.

It was a callous thing to think, but when the blood stopped streaming from Loon's mouth, her limbs settled and her chest rose no more, Cuckoo wanted to cry with relief rather than grief.

Duck was frozen to his seat for what felt like an eternity. Then his face began to morph, cracking and tearing apart in a visceral yet silence snarl of rage. But almost before Cuckoo could worry about it, the mask came back down again, and he was a just a boy once more. A child who began to cry, but his tears were silent, refusing to let go of her hand even in death.

Cuckoo kept glancing over at Loon, at blackened lips parted for a breath that would never come. They'd never hear that firm but kindly voice again.

As stupid as it was, Cuckoo didn't want any of the other voices racing around his heart to fall silent.

There was a full half an hour where he and Duck sat in silence, no idea what to say to one another. What was there to say?

In four hours, they'd lost two of their number. The doctor and the leader – the two who were going to get them out of there.

They'd lost them both.

Even the others, who'd been on a scavenger hunt for Rail's body, didn't seem surprised as they filed back in, eyes more resigned than panicked as they had been after Rail's death. Grief given the form of numb acceptance rather than disbelief and horror.

"No body?" Cuckoo guessed by their despondent expressions.

"Not with us" Raven nodded, gesturing to himself and Shrike.

"Or us" Kingfisher agreed, looking at Mockingbird.

"It's like it vanished completed" Nightjar remarked, herself and Wren the last two to arrive "What the hell?! Bodies don't just vaporise into thin air!"

On the contrary, in this place, that seemed to be exactly what happened to them.

"Do you think…" Raven pondered quietly "There maybe is a way out then? There would have to be, to remove a body."

"We've all been through this place multiple times" Mockingbird shook his head "There is no way out. It's like whatever entrance they used to get rid of Rail just…vanished." He pinched the bridge of his nose with a trembling hand. "I don't get it."

"It's almost like…" Kingfisher spoke up, her voice breathy "It's almost like someone just…pressed delete. On all the things they don't want us to find."

No one really knew what to make of that statement.

The silence it gained was broken cruelly, with the build-up of a laugh.

Cuckoo knew that laugh, but as it built it took on harsh climbing notes, like someone smashing their hands wildly into piano keys when you expected a concerto.

Shrike threw their head back, green eyes almost rolling out of their sockets as what sounded like the last day's worth of stress burst out of them in a roar of madness.

Cuckoo almost forgot to breathe. Shrike had been intimidating up until this point, sure, but only in how flat they'd been. It was like watching a complete absence of humanity – not because there was no emotion, but because it was the same emotion – the same saccharine smile – through every moment. Like a statue had come to life but only knew how to do one sultry expression.

But this laugh…it was almost beyond human. It was cry of a killer who'd finally tasted their first blood, or an animal whose lifelong mate or cub had just been murdered in front of them. It was beyond anything that could be defined as sadness or insanity – just terrifying.

And then it abruptly cut off in a breath, head tilting so one rolling eye could look at Cuckoo.

"It's not real, is it?" they whispered, only audible by how effectively Shrike had managed to steal the sound from the whole room "It's all fake. *We*…"

It was like they ran out of breath before they could finish, choking on the last word, a hanged man's final gasp.

"The hell are you talking about?!" Cuckoo expected it to be Nightjar, but the shout of pure anger came from Mockingbird "Two people are *dead*! You think that's *fake*?!"

But Shrike said nothing to that, just canting their head forward again so their hair fell in front of their eyes, hiding their expression.

"So, nothing we do matters" they whispered "Does it?"

Maybe it was narcissism talking, but Cuckoo wondered if they were still talking to him.

"The hell it does!" Mockingbird roared again, reaching forward as if to grab Shrike by the collar "What are you playing at?!"

But Shrike just ducked around him, eyes still hidden as they fled the room.

"HEY!" Mockingbird shouted after them, but he got no response.

"Er…" Wren was nervously playing with her fingers as she looked at the others "Should I, you know…?"

She nodded out the door, clearly asking if she should follow them.

"Ah, don't bother!" Mockingbird spat "If they're just going to be a prick!"

Kingfisher shook her head, her expression forlorn. "I think it all just caught up with him. It's probably best to let him cool off."

For reason, that just didn't seem right. Whatever that breakdown was, that helplessness, it was more terrifying than anything Cuckoo had ever seen.

It felt unnervingly like watching an animal's death throes.

"Forget them" Nightjar shook her head, looking like all the fight had been drained from her "Now what?"

Silently, everyone stared at Loon's body.

Whenever they weren't certain, it was Loon who always had a game plan. Loon who had controlled almost their every action like a vice grip. Now they were stranded in a foggy wilderness with no guiding hand.

"D-Do we..." the whole room held its breath as Duck spoke up for the first time since they'd left the dining room "Do we know who d-did this?"

Four heads slowly turned towards Cuckoo, causing a shudder to run through him.

"It can't be him!" Raven was the only one to come to his defence.

"He was in the kitchen, whilst the rest of us were all together the whole time" Mockingbird noted bitterly "And he knew the soup was poisoned."

"He already said how he knew that!" Raven insisted, his voice now desperate.

Cuckoo's cheeks reddened a little. It was difficult to feel bad when someone like Raven, a man who'd only known you a few hours, was defending you so ardently.

"Well, if it's not him, it's Duck!" Nightjar pointed out "And do you really think *he's* capable of poisoning his girlfriend?"

Cuckoo looked over at Duck, who was clutching his sleeves in a death grip. He didn't appear to be breathing as the blood began to drain from his face. He looked like he could be sick at any moment.

Cuckoo could sympathise. Nothing hit harder than a group of people accusing you of murder.

Quietly, he picked up Loon's hat from where he'd left it on top of an oxygen canister and passed it to him. He hadn't had a moment to give it to him before now; it hadn't felt right.

"Here" he murmured "I think you could use it."

Duck immediately snatched the hat from him, fingers twisting into the brim so hard he swore he heard the cardboard inside creak.

"S-Something's wrong" Duck muttered, seemingly to himself "I shouldn't...I...What's wrong with me? I—"

"It technically could be *anyone*!" Raven cut him off, directing their attention to the other group in the room, who were apparently continuing to bicker over their heads.

"I didn't go near the damn soup!" Nightjar insisted.

"None of us did" Kingfisher agreed.

"Both of you collected ingredients" Raven pointed out, a shake of panic in his words "You could have contaminated them then! Which means there are other suspects!"

"Good point" Mockingbird now chimed in, turning to Nightjar "How do we know the ingredients were safe?"

Wren didn't say anything, no pleas for calm or strange statements. She just folded her massive arms and looked done at the floor, hair falling over her face like a curtain. She looked like a child who was expecting to be told off for messing up.

Cuckoo found himself staring down at his own legs. Raven's argument was good, bar one detail.

"What if" he said, balling his fists "The soup was poisoned *after* Rail died."

Silence reigned for a minute.

"That's an interesting statement" Mockingbird remarked, wetting his lips "Did you *see* someone put something in the soup?"

"No" Cuckoo shook his head "Honestly, it was Loon who predicted it actually."

He told them all what Loon had predicted only a few hours ago, about how now someone had been murdered, it would alleviate the consciences of everyone who wanted to leave, assuring them it would be perfectly satisfactory to commit murder now their lives were on the line.

The silence that followed his words felt heavy, oppressive, like a massive weight was pressing down on all of their necks.

"But, if that's right, it could *only* be Cuckoo or Duck" Kingfisher recognised breathily "They had the soup in sight at all times."

"Or Wren" Mockingbird added "She carried the soup."

Wren was still too busy staring at the floor to hear them, so Nightjar had to defend her herself.

"How was she supposed to poison in soup she was carrying with both hands?!" she insisted, turning to Kingfisher "It's more likely it was on the ladle *you* brought!"

"No way" Kingfisher shook her head in response to the accusation "Duck saw me get the ladle from the pantry when he came to get me; I didn't have time to do anything to it."

"So that's *two* alibis that rest on Duck" Mockingbird remarked "Wouldn't it be simpler if *he* was the one who actually did it?"

Another creak came from Loon's hat. Cuckoo began to fear for its safety. Despite the obvious reaction though, Duck said nothing in his own defence, just staring down at the hat.

"Or...any of us could've done it" Cuckoo admitted "We *all* handled the soup, when it was being served."

Everyone took a sharp breath in at his words.

"Is...that actually possible?" Kingfisher questioned "That no one noticed someone pouring poison into the pot?"

"Like anyone here is crazy enough to do *that* in the open!" Nightjar scoffed.

"If someone was so crazy as to kill eight people to escape" Raven spoke up, his voice quiet "I don't think they'd think anything of acting so openly."

"You think they wanted to kill *all* of us?" Kingfisher questioned, her eyes almost popping out of her head.

"There was no way they could've known that Loon was going to make a toast" Raven pointed out "They would've assumed that we would all eat together. In that case, without Cuckoo stopping us, it would've been too late for any of us to stop by the time someone showed symptoms. We would all be dead, one after another."

A tense air seemed to drift through the room, like a ghost had just walked through all of them.

Finally, Wren's face twisted, and something settled on her shoulders, like she'd just made a firm decision. Without a word, the usually talkative giant stormed out of the room like she was on a holy mission.

Mockingbird followed her out. "Where are you going?"

"Like hell I'm letting this happen again!" Wren's unsettlingly determined voice snapped back, loud enough to boom in Cuckoo's ears, even from down the corridor "No one else is dying, not on my watch!"

Her words sent Nightjar and Kingfisher running after them both, leaving just the three boys in the doctor's office.

"Thank you" Duck murmured once, not really indicating who he was talking to.

Cuckoo hoped it wasn't him. There was an undercurrent of bitterness to the words, like he should've spat them instead of stating.

He fixed Loon's cap firmly to his head, flattening his hair and pulling the brim down over his eyes in the opposite way as to how Loon wore it, before pushing off his chair and heading out to follow the others.

"Sorry" Raven said once he'd left "I shouldn't have left you back there."

"Oh, don't worry about it" Cuckoo shook his head "We were all stressed."

The gap that followed was awkward. How were you supposed to thank someone who'd repeatedly defended you again a murder charge, even when they barely knew you? In comparison, all Cuckoo had done was make fun of Raven's eyesight and shot down his alibi for Rail's murder.

Why was he so loyal? What the hell had Cuckoo done to inspire *that*? They'd only known each other a few hours; surely he couldn't have done anything so notable in that time. He genuinely didn't understand, and it bothered him more than he cared to admit.

"You don't have to thank me" Raven spoke up with a chuckle, like he could read his thoughts "I genuinely don't think you've done anything wrong here. Besides, you're my friend."

Friend. It was the first time someone had called him that, or at least, that he could remember. The word felt strange, like he wasn't used to hearing it in his ears. It caused blood to rise into his face.

Somewhere in the prison, a massive crashing sound sounded, followed by multiple people shouting.

Cuckoo sighed and shuffled to the edge of his seat. Whatever was going on, he owed it to Loon to make sure no one else got hurt.

"Can you help me here?" he asked Raven.

"Oh!" Raven suddenly lit up "Hold on! We found something for you in the gym!"

He ducked out of the room for a moment, before returning with a crutch – one with a padded top designed for people to lean on. It even looked to be around the right size for Cuckoo.

"Now you won't have to depend on me anymore!" Raven declared cheerfully.

Cuckoo was fairly certain he'd never used a crutch before, if only for how unfamiliar it felt trying to use his armpit to balance on it. Raven hovered nearby the whole time, but it still took an inordinate amount of time and far too much strain for them to negotiate the length of the hallway, by which point his armpit was already starting to chafe.

Damn leg. If anyone tried to kill him in this state, he would have little choice but to lie down and beg for it to be quick. If he didn't see it coming first.

He got a good measure of what the crashing was for on the way there, when Mockingbird and Kingfisher ran past him, arms filled with ornaments from the sitting room and some of the more liftable dumbbells from the gym. Nightjar then passed with what looked like a letter opener and a toolkit. Duck emerged from the pantry with numerous cooking implements, still in their wrappers, depositing them in the armoury before running back again. Just as they reached the massive double doors, Wren pushed past them with what looked like every sharp or heavy implement she could expect to find in the kitchen.

The floor of the armoury was a mess, covered in what looked like every potentially deadly implement the group could find.

It was a few more runs before Wren was satisfied, by which point the needless curtains from the sitting room and the towels from the bathroom had also been classified as 'potentially lethal'. With the prison cleared, she then moved on to patting everyone down. She pulled a scalpel out of Mockingbird's right boot, and then went after Nightjar's knife.

"Like hell!" she swore "I need that!"

"If everyone gives up their weapons, then everyone is safe" Wren declared, grabbing her by the scuff of her collar as if prepared to shake the knives out of her clothing "No exceptions."

"I need this to keep *me* safe!" Nightjar insisted "We can't all have rippling biceps you know!"

"*No exceptions!*" Wren stressed again, this time actually shaking her.

"Shrike got to keep *their* knife!" Nightjar tried pleading.

"Only because we haven't found them yet" Wren declared "When we find them, I'll confiscate that too. Now cough it up!"

Finally, reluctantly, Nightjar gave up her knife. And after a bit more pressing and shaking, gave up her second knife. They were thrown onto the pile of murder amassed just beyond the armoury's doors.

"Done!" Wren declared with satisfaction as she slammed the doors shut "Now no one else can die!"

Cuckoo felt that was a gross oversimplification. If someone wanted to kill, they would find a way to do so.

Raven seemed to agree, his fingers fiddling with his scarf. "Loon, was poisoned, remember? Did we account for that?"

"We don't even know what she was poisoned *with*" Mockingbird pointed out "It could be anything."

"Ten bucks It came from Dr Death's Box of Poisons in the doctor's office" Nightjar sulkily grunted.

"The medicines you brought to the library" Raven turned to Kingfisher "You said you took them back, right? And locked the door?"

"Yes, with Mockingbird and Nightjar" Kingfisher confirmed "I locked the door behind me and gave the key back to Rail."

"She did" Mockingbird confirmed "I saw her." He narrowed his eyes at the group "And don't go accusing any of us of taking anything. Not like any of us were left alone long enough to grab anything."

This must've happened when Cuckoo was unconscious from the splinting. But with everyone else agreeing on that interpretation of events, Cuckoo had no reason to doubt them.

"Someone probably grabbed the poison and hid it before we could gather all the bottles!" Nightjar spat "You just *had* to grab everything and throw it around the library for everyone to reach, didn't you!"

Kingfisher didn't respond, didn't even look at Nightjar, seeming entirely unfazed by the accusation.

"Leave her alone" Mockingbird jumped to her defence "At least she remembered to bring the key back – you almost left it in the door."

"And yet the key made its way from Rail's pocket *back* to the door" Raven pondered, stopping Nightjar from retaliating "Did Rail go back himself? Or did he already have the scalpel on him in the library?"

Cuckoo frowned. Rail was the one who kept locking the door and hiding the key – why would he do all that just to go back there himself and leave the key behind?

"Did anyone get that key?" Wren questioned.

"I-I have it" Duck admitted, still hiding behind the pantry doorframe.

"Keep it, and go lock it" Wren told him "We have to make sure no one goes helping themselves to the drugs in there."

Cuckoo was suddenly glad he'd kept those painkillers in his pocket.

Duck immediately scampered off towards the doctor's office, pushing through the throng of people to make it through.

"Can't we just lock the drug cupboard, rather than the whole office?" Nightjar questioned "What if we need bandages and stuff?"

"Ah, that would be impossible" Raven admitted, rubbing his head with a bemused smile.

"This idiot broke it" Kingfisher pointed over her shoulder at Mockingbird "Because he was too impatient to wait for a key."

It was a much-needed moment of levity in the tense atmosphere, getting a few chuckles.

Surprisingly, the response from Mockingbird wasn't explosive. He just turned his head away, buried his hands further into his pockets and muttered:

"Like any of you had better ideas."

"I'll keep the armoury key" Wren announced as she locked the massive door in question "Any objections?"

"None here" Raven held up his hands in surrender "I doubt you would need a weapon to kill anyway. And you'd certainly be the hardest person for anyone here to kill."

Sure enough, no one objected, not even Nightjar.

"What about the gun cupboard key?" Mockingbird questioned "Can't that open the armoury?"

"Loon still has it, and we're locking her in the doctor's office" Cuckoo pointed out, remembering seeing the key when she first took it (and trying not to think about the fact the two people who'd first been at this doorway with him were now both dead) "Besides, it's too small to fit that lock. It's more like a locker key than a door key."

Wren pulled the key out of the armoury lock and paused, her massive shoulders hunching as she muttered a "Huh."

"That's not a good huh" Raven recognised.

"This key is actually two keys" Wren explained "Watch."

Slowly, she pulled the two sides of the large key, one in each direction, until it slid apart into two halves. It was very clear that neither half could open the door without its partner, too much detail on each side to go without. The armoury key had never left its lock, so it was the first time anyone had seen the trick.

"Should we split them, then?" Kingfisher suggested "Nothing against you Wren, but..."

"It would be safer" Raven agreed, finishing for her "Then if someone did manage to take Wren by surprise, we wouldn't be in immediate danger."

"So, who gets the second key?" Nightjar questioned.

Wren thought about it for a moment, before she held the second key out to Cuckoo.

Cuckoo felt a wave of relief run though him. He didn't really know Wren all that well, and if she'd given it to someone who'd already accused him of murder, he wasn't sure what he was going to do.

However, the key was barely in his hand when Nightjar's shrieking voice almost deafened him.

"ARE YOU SERIOUS!" she screeched "YOU'RE GIVING IT TO **HIM**?!"

Cuckoo quickly buried the key in his trouser pocket before Nightjar could make to snatch it.

"He's injured, so he's the least likely to go out and try and kill someone" Wren explained her logic "No point in giving him a knife or an axe if he can't chase someone with it, or a grenade launcher if he can't aim it with one arm."

Nightjar let out a laugh, but it was dangerously close to a shriek of fear.

"You can't be so *stupid*!" she laughed "He's going to kill all of us!"

Cuckoo almost tumbled back from the force of her words. Did she seriously believe that?

"Don't say that!" Raven immediately jumped in, face red with anger "He's never hurt anyone before!"

"Can you seriously say that with a straight face?!" Nightjar shot back, now addressing the group "Everyone knows how freakin' suspicious this guy is, right?! How just *looking* at him puts you on edge! He's obviously the freakin' warden!"

Cuckoo was forced to watch in horror as everyone looked away, none of them saying anything. Even Raven let his mouth clack shut, a bead of sweat running down the side of his face.

How had he managed to upset them all? Some of them he'd barely talked to, let alone said anything that could've convinced them he was a psychopath who would lock ten people inside a prison – himself included – and bait them to kill each other.

"I–" his throat felt like a desert as he forced the words out "How could you think that? That I'm the warden? I...I don't..."

He couldn't finish the sentence. He hunched over on his crutch, trying not to be sick.

"It isn't anything personal" Kingfisher spoke up, her voice as emotionless as ever as her eyes drifted to the side, fixed on a point up the corridor in the direction of the North Wing "You seem nice. But you're the only one who doesn't remember anything, you're the first to notice every murder, and the person who died is always someone who singled you out. If someone among us is the warden, you're the most likely suspect."

Hearing it spelled out so frankly, and no one else speaking out to refute her words, made tears prick at Cuckoo's eyes. He didn't think he was someone so weak as to be affected by mere words, but two people were dead – two people who'd done nothing to deserve it – violently murdered in fact, and no one could find a single word to defend him against having done it.

Since when had he cared so much what these people thought of him? They were all just people he'd met today, right? He shouldn't give a damn what they thought of him! He hadn't before!

But then, why was he hurting so much inside?

"S-So what if he's the w-warden?"

It wasn't the words he was expecting to hear, and especially not the person he would ever expect to say them.

Cuckoo hadn't heard Duck return, but he was waiting in the corridor with them. His head was ducked, Loon's hat doing an unnerving job of covering his eyes, so Cuckoo couldn't tell how he was feeling. His words gave away nothing – not raised in volume, no particular empathises or implication of mood. Just a statement of fact.

"The w-warden's stuck in here too, r-right?" Duck questioned, his whole body vibrating with some kind of adrenaline "We don't k-know anything about him. W-Why he's doing this, or if he even w-wants to."

Everyone was stunned a bit speechless by his words.

Raven pondered that. "I suppose that could be true. They're in here too, and if the same rules apply to them, they have to be the last one alive to leave. So, if they don't do their job, they might not be able escape either. Under those circumstances, they *may* be an unwilling participant themself."

Cuckoo tried to follow. Were they saying that they thought the warden was just another puppet, marionetted by someone even higher above them?

"E-Exactly" Duck nodded along, pulling Loon's hat down further over his eyes "Why would he w-want that?" He let out a shuddering breath. "W-Who would ever want the job of forcing such n-nice people to k-kill each other?"

A harsh silence swept through the group as that question hung in the air above their heads, needle-point ready to crash down upon them.

"Duck?" Kingfisher questioned, choosing her words carefully "Are you–?"

"I am n-not the warden" Duck answered quickly and decisively "But I d-do not hate them for Loon dying, or whoever did it. Everyone's just trying to get out of this n-nest. I do not hate them at all."

His voice was almost steady and more confident sounding that it had been all day, the stutter that had been plaguing his words almost gone. It was almost like listening to Loon instead.

"I c-can be angry later" he decided, even as his lips pulled back into something nasty "But for now, all my energy is focused on s-surviving. B-Because that's what Loon wanted me to do. I am not going to kill anyone. B-But I w-will not die here. Because I c-can't let her be forgotten. S-She was...unforgettable."

He finally seemed to run out of steam, sagging with an exhausted breath out.

"Well, *I* hate the freakin' warden!" Nightjar announced, venom spitting from her eyes as she glared at Cuckoo "And I need him dead to get out of here! So, I recon we deal with him here and now, before he can kill *anyone else*!"

Raven sucked in a breath of horror, staring at Nightjar like a huge realisation had crashed down upon him. Before Cuckoo could question him about it, his own eyes became fixed on Nightjar as well.

As she roared, she pulled another tiny pocketknife from somewhere on her body, her leather gloves crunching as she launched it at Cuckoo. It flew past his ear and embedded itself in one of the little gaps between the bricks in the wall, a pinging sound ringing out as the blade waggled in the grout from the force of it.

Cuckoo swore if he'd actually managed to eat anything tonight, then his trousers would've turned brown.

Immediately four simultaneous voices rang out:

Mockingbird: "*Deal* with him?! What the heck?! What do you mean?!"

Kingfisher: "You're being rash. We don't even know if the warden is the one killing us, or if killing them will let us out."

Raven: "He's not going to hurt anyone! Don't you hurt him!"

Wren: "Nightjar, if you have any more of those hidden, I'll lock *you* in there with them!"

Nightjar glared at all of them, her body vibrating with rage. She was practically spiting fumes as she stormed past them towards the kitchen.

"Don't worry!" she snapped back over her shoulder "If I had any more on me, I'd have *gutted* him!"

Cuckoo tried to swallow but his mouth was too dry. He was pretty sure Nightjar hadn't been seriously trying to kill him in front of everyone, or he probably would've had another vision. But that didn't mean she wouldn't try later.

What kind of a person was he that people kept trying to kill him?

"We can't afford to fall apart like this" Wren groused, running a hand down her face "I think everyone needs to get some sleep. We can work out a plan for escaping this place in the morning."

"You...expect us to sleep?" Kingfisher questioned "With a killer on the loose?"

"We're only going to make mistakes if we stay awake" Raven pointed out, scratching at his eyes "We *do* need to sleep at some point."

"So, we could sleep together?" Wren suggested "Then no one could attack any of us." She fixed them all with a determined stare. "I'll protect you all, with my life if I have to. I won't let anyone else down again!"

Cuckoo wondered what she meant. Rail had done everything possible to get away from her, and she couldn't have reasonably saved Loon without noticing something was wrong with the soup. Who did she think she'd let down?

"Or the killer waits for us to fall asleep and then collapses the roof of us" Mockingbird refuted "No way. With all the traps in here, I'm not taking my chances. I'm sleeping in my room. I'll just barricade the door."

Kingfisher wrapped her arms around herself as she asked: "Can...Can I come with you?"

Mockingbird shifted awkward on the spot, taking several moments to think of how to reply. "Sorry, it's probably best if we're not together. If I get attacked, at least I know you'll be ok."

Kingfisher's eyes widened, looking incredibly hurt – disproportionately hurt for the reasonable excuse. It was a pair of very teary eyes that looked away from him.

Cuckoo wondered how long it would take her to get the hint that whatever interest he'd had in her before was long gone with everyone's nerves so frayed.

"To be honest, I don't think it would do any good" Raven told her gently "It's not possible to barricade the bedroom doors."

Mockingbird blinked at him. "Why not?"

"They open outwards, so it's impossible to barricade yourself in" Raven explained "All you'd be able to do is barricade someone *else* in from outside."

"So…" Cuckoo was hesitant to say anything after the previous body blow, but they needed to come up with something "We sleep in our own rooms and scream loud if someone comes in?"

Kingfisher shot him a dry look. "You'd like that, wouldn't you?"

Well, clearly *that* was the wrong thing to say.

"I haven't tested it" Raven commented "But if the bedrooms are soundproofed like the bathrooms, it wouldn't do us any good to scream. It might be better if someone stayed up to keep watch."

"I can do that!" Wren offered immediately.

"Weren't you the one saying we needed sleep?" Mockingbird pointed out "Besides, what if *you're* the killer?"

"I'll stay up and watch with her" Raven offered, rolling his shoulder "I'm not really tired. We can sleep in the morning, while you look for a way out."

Cuckoo frowned. Hadn't Raven been rubbing his eyes before? Surely, he was tired. Why would he volunteer to say up if he could barely keep his eyes open?

"I can do it, if you're tired" he offered.

Raven smiled gently at him. "I appreciate that, but…" He looked like he was considering his words carefully. "It should probably be someone they all trust."

No one spoke up to refute that.

Well, that was a kick in the teeth.

"I mean, *I* trust you!" Raven hastily amended "Let me do this for you, and you can watch out for me in the morning. Ok?"

And how was Cuckoo supposed to turn down an offer as kind as that?

"Ok" he agreed "So, you and Wren stay up. We can switch at…four maybe?"

That was about eight hours. Surely, they could last that long.

But then again, they're lost two people in half that time.

"This all sounds g-good to me" Duck yawned "I-I'm going to bed. A-Anyone coming with me?"

"I'll come with you that far" Raven offered "I can patrol the West Wing, whilst Wren stays on this side. After two hours, we'll switch."

Hence, Cuckoo found himself trailing after Raven, Duck, Mockingbird and Kingfisher as they took their opportunity to head to back to the bedrooms.

They passed the kitchen, where he could see Nightjar sitting at the bar, leaning on a beer bottle. There were several other brown glass bottles around her, in varying stages of drank.

Loon must have been planning a party after dinner, but Nightjar was happily – or miserably – downing the party drinks all by herself.

He wondered if he should say anything. He was concerned for her, and she should be told that were all going to bed. But he doubted anything he could say would be welcomed right now.

Predictably, Nightjar spotted him in the doorway through the haze over her eyes, glaring at him through the red.

"The hell d'ya want?!" she spat at him "To laugh at me, ha?!"

"W-What?!" Cuckoo squeaked "N-No, I–!"

"Cuckoo, you ok?" thankfully Raven came back for him "Hey Nightjar, wow, party of one in here, huh?"

"Shut the hell up!" Nightjar swore at him, her leather gloves squeaking on the glass as she tightened her fist around the bottle "Did I freakin' ask fer yer opinion, Pretty Face?!"

"Oh dear" Raven stood up to her anger commendably well, just sighing "Well, most of us are going to bed. Wren and I will be keeping watch so you can sleep in peace. Might want to clean up in here when you're done."

Nightjar seemed so stunned by his smarting statement that she shut up, giving the boys time to escape unscathed.

It was a few steps along to the dining room, where Cuckoo tried to keep his eyes inside his head.

The room was completely cleaned up – table and floor pristine. The blood and bile that had trickled onto the floor had been immaculately cleared, the carpet back to its fuzzy red. If they'd wanted to go back and investigate the crime scene, nothing would await them but their own anxious faces reflected in varnished mahogany.

How were these crime scenes being cleaned up? Even if someone had time, how had they not been noticed?

"Something interesting?" Raven pondered, pausing his steps to wait for him again.

It hadn't escaped Cuckoo's notice that, despite being capable of walking much faster than he could hobble, Raven insisted on staying by his side after his encounter with Nightjar.

"Don't trust me on my own?" Cuckoo groused, still smarting from his earlier silence "Worried I'm going to murder someone?"

Raven just laughed. "Oh Cuckoo, I don't think *you* want to hurt anyone. In fact, I've never felt safer than when I stand next to you."

It was a weird statement, but Raven was a weird guy. It was a little flattering, to be honest, to be trusted so openly.

Though, it did bring to mind another weird statement Raven had made earlier that day. One that, even with all of the other things that had happened in the hours since, Cuckoo hadn't been able to get out of his mind.

"To be honest, I was far more worried about someone attacking *you* when you couldn't get away" Raven admitted "Statistically, next to you is the safest place to stand – any attacker would go for you first."

Ah, yeah. Exactly what Cuckoo wanted to hear as they reached the bedrooms; Duck, Mockingbird and Kingfisher closing their doors behind them. None of them said anything to him, no good nights or good lucks.

"Hey" Raven looked at him gently "Don't hate them."

The statement caught Cuckoo by surprise.

"Huh?"

"You *really* shouldn't play poker" Raven joked before his eyes turned downcast "They don't *hate* you – not really. They're just grieving, and they want someone to blame. None of them are bad people. When the warden is unmasked, when he's dethroned for good, everything will be ok." He fixed Cuckoo with an inscrutable stare. "We have to trust each other in here. Or we'll never make it out alive."

It was a difficult statement to swallow. Cuckoo wasn't sure he could follow through with it. He knew logically that no one would be acting this way if it wasn't for the warden pulling all their strings, dangling their freedoms over their heads.

But that didn't mean he didn't feel a burning inside him when he pictured Nightjar's rage, Mockingbird's demeaning stare or Kingfisher's indifference.

Maybe that was *his* grieving.

Maybe that just meant Raven was a better person than he was.

"Grief, huh" he muttered.

"It's a terrible thing, isn't it?" Raven pondered beside him "Turning men into beasts."

Cuckoo kept his eyes fixed on the corridor floor, to try and keep his expression neutral. He burnt his gaze into the shiny blue linoleum, tarnished only with a spattering of muddy footprints between the girls' bathroom and the gym up ahead.

He wondered if the rain outside had stopped now.

He wondered if it would ever stop.

Cuckoo's eyes danced over to the door of his own room, for the first time noticing it was located on the same side of the corridor as the girls' rooms. Staring at that firmly closed door, he wondered if the crime scene in there had been cleaned up, just like Loon's had been.

"Oh, I suppose you can't stay in your own room, can you?" Raven recognised "Well, Rail isn't going to be using his, and it's right next to mine, so you can stay there."

Cuckoo tried to repress the shudder that ran through his body at the thought of sleeping in dead man's bed, Rail's lifeless missing body flashing before his eyes, overlaying the memory of blood spatter all over his own room.

They still hadn't resolved that. Whose blood *was* that, and who had put it there, and why *his* room? Raven had said not to tell anyone, but it felt like a heavy rock in his gut every time he thought about it, slowly eating him alive. Not that he could tell anyone - not with all of this suspicion on him.

But Raven didn't seem to be bothered by those thoughts. He didn't hesitate as he opened the door with Rail's name on.

Thankfully, Rail's body wasn't in there. Just a regular empty cell, with a bed, table, black rug and a clock.

Sitting on the bed, Cuckoo had to remind himself that Rail had most likely never stepped foot in here, that this was nothing more than a hotel bed.

"Well, if you need anything, just peek out of the door and shout, yeah" Raven smiled "I'll see you tomorrow."

His hand paused on the doorframe. The same hand he'd been buried in when he said that troubling thing...

"Wait!" Cuckoo called after him, stopping him from leaving.

He had a feeling, if he didn't ask now, he wouldn't get a chance again.

"Hm?"

"What...What did you mean?" he asked hesitantly "When you said 'It should've been you'?"

Raven just blinked at him, trying to work out when he'd said such a thing. But then he deflated into a sheepish smile.

"Whoa, I must've been really out of it if I said *that*, huh?" he remarked, eyes fixed on the floor "I just thought it was ironic, that I was still here when others were dead."

Cuckoo didn't understand. "What's ironic about that?"

Initially, Raven didn't say anything, just scuffing what had once been Cuckoo's boot against the floor. But he eventually worked himself up to it with a sigh of resignation.

"Do you remember when we first woke up, and we all stood in a circle in the courtyard and talked about what jobs we had?" he asked quietly.

Even if it hadn't been earlier that day, Cuckoo would've remembered. The horror of realising everyone there had something in common that he didn't. The outsider-ness that had yet to go away.

But with it being Raven to ask the question, it brought to mind something that Cuckoo had been too distracted to put together before.

"You said you worked for Raptor Tech" he recalled "But you never said what you *did* for them."

Raven's smile seemed to turn impossibly more miserable. "That's because I don't remember."

Cuckoo's breath caught in his throat. "You don't?"

"I know it's there" Raven shook his head "Every time I think about the me before I woke up today, I see it. It's like it's dangling in front of me, but when I reach for it, someone pulls it higher and higher away from me. Whenever I drop my guard, it comes back, but no matter how quick I am, it's always faster."

Cuckoo's throat felt dry. It was bad enough having absolutely nothing to draw on, but knowing everything you needed was right there and yet held maddeningly out of reach had to be agonising.

"Maybe this isn't a good thing, but I think my job was ingrained into my very being" Raven admitted "Like I was born to do it. And now it's been taken from me, it's like I've lost my purpose. Like someone cut every sinew in my body and I don't know how to move without it. That's why I think it's ironic."

"I still don't understand why you think that" Cuckoo admitted.

Raven's eyes were still plastered to the floor, seemingly unable to look at him. Cuckoo noticed with growing horror that they were turning watery.

"Loon and Rail had a purpose" he stated sadly "Loon was an amazing people person – a great team leader that brought the best out in all of us. And Rail was a doctor who could've helped so many people. And yet they're both dead, and the one with no purpose is still alive."

Cuckoo wanted to say something, but before he could find the right words, Raven was back to monologuing; though his voice was softer this time, maybe ashamed or worried about being overheard.

"When we first found that letter, from the warden" he continued "I thought, oh, I understand why I'm here now. I'm here to die so the others can escape. It all just made sense to me. Useless things exist to be disposed of, after all. But now others are dead and I…"

Cuckoo was so struck dumb with horror that he forgot how to speak in the face of these terrible words. It left him emotionally unprepared to deal with the smile Raven shot his way – a horrible smile that made Shrike's look truly authentic in comparison.

"So, if we somehow stay alive in here, and you need to kill someone to get out" Raven continued on, his voice waving only a little bit "You can kill me, ok? I don't mind, if it helps you get out of here. That can be my purpose."

"NO!"

The word surged out of him in a burst, the same burst that had him leap from the bed to try and grab Raven before he could leave. He didn't make it, crashing to the floor once again, but any humiliation was immediately squashed by abject panic.

"Hey, careful, you'll hurt yourself" Raven scolded him, kneeling to help him back to the bed.

But Cuckoo took the chance he was given to seize him by his scarf, gripping the fabric with fingers that dug into the material like anchors.

"Don't you *ever* say something like that!" he shouted right in his face, the surge of adrenaline so great he couldn't bring himself to stop even at the obvious sight of Raven's discomfort "No purpose, what kind of hack line is that?! That's bullshit!"

Raven cringed away from him, but Cuckoo just held on tighter.

"You know where I'd be without you?!" Cuckoo continued shouting, tears pricking at the corner of his eyes "I'd still be on the floor of that library, buried under a bookcase! We'd all still be in the bathroom, not knowing there was a *murderer* among us!"

"Shrike already knew that one" Raven looked aside as he talked "They were just messing with us."

"But you figured out *how* they did it!" Cuckoo stressed "Because you're smart! If any of us are likely to figure a way out of here, it's you, you know that?"

A tiny smile formed on Raven's face, but it still felt hollow.

"And for one," Cuckoo admitted, cheeks reddening "I'd be going out of mind if you weren't here to stand by me and cheer me up and defend me all time. Maybe *that's* your purpose here – to keep us all moving forward, no matter what gets thrown at us!"

He heard Raven's breath catching, before a blank expression settled on his face. It was somehow more reassuring than the smiles – it felt more real.

"Perhaps" was all he said on that matter "But this isn't anything to be worrying over when we're tired. You should get some sleep."

Cuckoo wasn't certain he'd managed to put either of their minds at ease – he wasn't good at words, they didn't come naturally to his brain – but Raven clearly wasn't in the mood to talk any further. He just helped Cuckoo up onto the bed, pulling back the covers and yanking the mismatched shoes off his feet. It felt weird sleeping in the same trousers he'd been walking in all day, but there was no way to remove them past the splint without cutting them off, and he wasn't going to be known as the naked wonder if none could be sourced that were capable of clearing the splint.

"Try not to worry, ok" Raven tried to reassure him "You'll need a level head for tomorrow."

"Hey" Cuckoo grabbed his sleeve, stopping him before he could turn to go "Promise me you'll be alive by tomorrow."

Raven's jaw dropped open, taken aback. His eyes skittered around the room, trying not to look at him again.

"I can't say that" he admitted quietly.

"You're going to" Cuckoo told him fiercely "You're going to promise me you'll be alive by tomorrow. And then, tomorrow morning, I'm going to come find you, and we're going to escape together. So, promise me."

It didn't make any sense, for him to be this attached to people he'd only met this morning. Beyond the horror of seeing two dead bodies, the only concern he should have with them is the existential horror of seeing something that was one alive have life no more.

But that wasn't it.

He mourned Rail and Loon. He was miserable that he wouldn't ever hear them growl or preach at him again. He wanted to see Rail get better, and Loon hug her children again. He wanted to thank them both for getting him here, knowing he couldn't have done it without them. It was a bone-deep terror but also pre-emptive grief that held his body hostage every time he thought about another one of their number dying, especially Raven.

Maybe it was because he had no other people in his memory to think about – something as simple as not wanting to lose the only people he had in his life. But even if it was as superficial a reason as that, it was powerful enough to leave him breathless.

He clenched his fist around Raven's scarf, knuckles whitening as they refused to let up on the red fuzzy material for even a second. If Raven didn't agree, he thought he might die.

Raven's eyes were still looking away, but he finally managed to give Cuckoo what he needed to hear.

"I promise" he murmured "I will be alive by tomorrow. Just...make sure you get some sleep, ok?"

The wave of relief that swept through Cuckoo's body at Raven's words finally allowed him to let go. Released, Raven wasted no time rushing for the door, but paused before he shut it.

"Get some rest, 'Ku" he assured him "Everything will be better in the morning, I promise."

Coverts

10

Cuckoo *wanted* to get some rest, if only because Raven had asked him to, but despite his best efforts, he lay there, staring at the ceiling for what felt like hours, unable to calm his racing mind.

The clock at his side said it was only 00:00, but he disagreed. It had to be 5:00, at least. Yet maddeningly, the little red numbers just blinked back at him, unwilling to change just because he wanted them to get closer to morning.

How was he expected to sleep like this, knowing there was a killer among them, who'd killed two of their friends just metres away? Heck, when Cuckoo was sleeping in one of their rooms?!

Grousing aside, it wasn't just his fears for his own safety that was keeping him awake. More, his mind couldn't stop running over the events of the day. Waking up, exploring, the fight in the leaves, the death threat, the blood, the library, finding Rail, Loon…

He should probably be tired after such a day, but his mind was too busy racing, trying to put together pieces of the puzzle, despite not knowing how many there were or what the completed product should look like.

Rail's body going missing bothered him significantly.

Why would someone move it? Was there something on the body that could identify his killer that they all missed? How had they even managed to move it, in a building full of anxious people watching everyone's every move? And why had they gone through all the trouble to return the doctor's office's key?

He hadn't seen the boys' bathroom since they'd found Rail. Raven said it had all been cleaned up, but had anything been left behind that could be a clue?

The boys' bathroom was only three rooms along – no reason he couldn't check it out. Maybe it would put his mind at ease and let him sleep.

This tiny room he'd been sentenced to may not have a window, but the red light from the clock illuminated his crutch against the wall. He couldn't see his shoes, but he was hardly going to need them. He was only going a few steps.

The hallway light was still on, with no light switch he could see to turn it off. The prison was so silent now: the lights didn't hum, and not even the sound of any wind was able to penetrate the thick walls. It was the uncomfortable kind of silence – the one that made static ring in your ears, that made you wince every time you took a step because even that was too much noise.

A peek down the corridor told him that not everyone was asleep. Raven and Wren's doors were open, as expected. But so was Nightjar's – clearly she hadn't gone to bed yet. The one-man pity party must still be going into the morning.

Cuckoo braced himself against the bathroom door, not entirely prepared to see that speckled blood again. His eyes met the cupboard across the way, where the bloody evidence of the crime that had occurred in here had been hidden. It was cracked open a little. Had Shrike left it like that?

He shook his head, braced himself, and forced himself through the doorway into the bathroom.

Raven was right: everything was gone. The whole room was spotless. No body, no blood. Running his hand along the wall, he could feel that the hole that Shrike's knife had dug out had been sealed, the paintwork perfect but also dry – as if the terrible events of that evening had been simply brushed over.

It wasn't even just the obvious things: the cut bandage roll that had sealed the shower room door shut was gone; the water stain Rail's washed trousers had left on the floor had been moped up; and, most concerningly, the broken windowpane in the door had been fixed.

The last item was what bothered Cuckoo the most: theoretically, one could paint over the blood with fast-acting paint. But who'd been going around changing *windowpanes*? No one had had time to do that.

He looked at the corner where they'd found Rail, now unobstructed. It was bad enough Rail had been murdered – who thought it was acceptable to go and mess with his body? Depriving them even the right to bury him?

It made his head hurt just thinking about it.

Thankfully the headache seemed to be exactly what he needed, as wave of tiredness washed over him. He wasn't going to solve anything tonight, but at least he could keep his word to Raven.

He stepped back out of the bathroom, shutting the door behind him, but something felt wrong. Something that hadn't been there when he'd made his way to the bathroom.

His foot was wet.

He looked down at his left foot in wonder, admiring the little puddle it had trodden in. It could've been from someone mopping up the bathroom to remove the blood, except he was certain the floor of the bathroom had been dry.

And the hallway hadn't been wet when he made his way up there. He was sure of that. Peering along the corridor, he noticed the stretch of floor leading up to the gym was shiny.

Had someone moped it? Why?

The area was very specific even – they'd started at the girl's bathroom and worked their way up to the gym, but hadn't done a very good job, letting water run down the corridor to meet Cuckoo's foot.

And then, that uncomfortable silence was broken by a creaking sound.

Cuckoo frowned. He was sure that came from the gym.

"Hello?" he called out, trying to keep his voice low so as not to wake the others behind him "Is everything ok?"

For a few seconds, there was nothing. And then a whispered voice:

"I'm fine."

It was a male voice, hushed quiet until it was barely audible.

"Raven, is that you?" Cuckoo asked.

Another pause. And then:

"Yes."

Cuckoo would've questioned what he was doing in the gym, how that was supposed to be keeping watch, and why he was mopping floors in the middle of the night? Stress maybe? Was stress-cleaning a thing? But another wave of tiredness hit him, and he just wanted to go to bed.

"Are you ok?" he questioned out of politeness.

"Yes. Go to bed."

Well, he was hardly going to argue with that.

"Ok, see you tomorrow" he whispered back, but got no reply.

He didn't so much as get into bed as collapsed on top of it, crutch clattering as it hit the floor. He didn't feel the pain in his leg anymore – nothing but the welcoming arms of nothingness.

o

Cuckoo's sleep was so deep he slept right through the door opening and was only aroused by the person who had done so when they violently shook him.

"Cuckoo! Cuckoo wake up! Please!"

He cracked one eye open with a groan. Despite his heavy eyes, he could make out Kingfisher standing over him right away.

"What?" he murmured, not appreciating the interruption.

Kingfisher reared back for a moment, looking horrified. "I need you to get up and see if *you* can see what *I'm* seeing. Sorry, I couldn't find anyone else. No one else is in their rooms."

Cuckoo turned his head to the look at the clock. The numbers 03:08 stared back at him. What the hell? Why were people who should be asleep up and about at 3:00?

Where were Raven and Wren? Weren't they supposed to be keeping watch for people doing this?

"What is it?" he repeated, burying his face back into the pillow "Can it wait until morning?"

"No, it can't" Kingfisher insisted "The incinerator's on."

Now *that* got his attention.

Cuckoo's head flew up in alarm. "What?!"

"There's smoke coming out of the incinerator chimney" she told him "You can see it from my room."

It was a bit of a scramble to grab his crutch from where he fell, and for Kingfisher to help him put his shoes on, but thankfully her room was directly across from his, which made up for the time lost. He felt an absolutely awful shoot of agony up his leg the second he moved, the painkillers having worn off by now. He felt ever grateful he'd remembered to grab the bottle of them back in the doctor's office and downed two completely dry as Kingfisher pulled him along.

The girls' rooms were almost identical to the boys', but since they faced the courtyard, they had windows. Not much of one, but still window. They were the narrow slit-type ones you saw in ancient castles – clearly not big enough for a person to fit through, barely enough room for a glass pane even. In fact, they were almost invisible from the outside. But it was possible to see directly across the courtyard to the East Wing from them.

Sure enough, grey smoke rose into a black sky from the top of a chimney stack atop the East Wing.

There hadn't been anything in the incinerator when they checked it earlier. What an earth could someone be burning at this hour? They had barely touched anything in here.

Suddenly, he had a horrible feeling.

"I think I know what happened to Rail's body" he breathed.

Kingfisher flinched, but said nothing, turning towards the door.

"We need to see for ourselves" she said definitively.

It felt like it took an age to follow the corridors around the U-bend of the prison to reach the East Wing. Cuckoo felt slightly less like he was going to trip over on his crutch at any moment, but he was grinding his teeth with how long it was taking to regain his balance after every step. He wished Kingfisher would run ahead, but she remained walking at his side. Maybe the importance of turning off the incinerator before it could destroy vital evidence had been lost on her, or she just didn't want to be left alone in a place where two people had been murdered.

Hence, it was together that they entered the incinerator room.

Cuckoo felt sick. He was suddenly glad that Kingfisher hadn't ran ahead.

The incinerator was definitely on, the roar of its engine flooding their ears the moment the door was opened. A wave of uncomfortable heat swept over them, originating at the hatch door.

Cuckoo swore he'd seen Shrike lock that same door only hours earlier. But it had been violently forced open with a ferocity that a simple push lock shouldn't require – the hinge and handle of the lock lying on the floor in pieces some distance away. The reason for the heat was very apparent: the door was propped open slightly, enough to see the dazzling orange glow behind it.

And the thing that was propping the door open was very clearly a human hand.

Both he and Kingfisher cried out at the same time. She ran to find the off switch, whilst he hopped forward to grab the hand and try and pull the body attached to it out of the fiery depths.

When he pulled though, he heard a sound like bones snapping, and he fell back to the ground.

There was a thud as something heavy landed back inside the incinerator. At the same moment, the engine sputtered and died as Kingfisher found the kill switch.

Cuckoo looked down at what had landed in his lap when he fell. It was a right hand, but *only* a right hand. The palm was aching pink with the visible swelling of healing burns, the fingernails cracked and bloody; but the top was still pale and whole, beside a few scrapes to the knuckles, like it hadn't been pulled out an inferno.

However, from the wrist down was nothing was a blob of black mutilated flesh, with the brittle remains of a bone poking through.

Cuckoo wasn't afraid to admit he shrieked with horror and backed away, the hand falling from his lap to the floor between his legs. He tried to back up even further, his stomach rolling at just the sight of it, but ran into Kingfisher, who had also dropped to her knees with a shriek with horror.

"Is that…" she looked reticent to even state the thought "Is that…Who…?"

To be honest, Cuckoo had no idea. Was it possible to determine gender from a hand? It was pale, but both Loon and Rail were, and any hair colour that could've helped them had been long since burnt away.

He dreaded the thought, but maybe there was something *in* the incinerator that could help identify which body it was. A scrap of clothing, or hair maybe.

Trying to settle his stomach as best he could, he used Kingfisher's head to push himself up to his feet and lifted up the hatch door again. The stress and fear of what he was about it do helped black out the pain he ought to be feeling.

The engine may be off, but the heat still blasted his face, and he could see the orange light within the machine slowly dying down. It left him with pretty poor lighting to determine what he was looking at.

It was definitely a human body pressed up against the wall nearest to him – he could make out another arm and two legs. They were laid faced down, too far down for Cuckoo to even think of reaching in to turn them over for any obvious indication of gender, and he couldn't see another door in. Everything had been burnt completely black, and he swore parts seemed to be melting, though he did his best not to look at those parts. He couldn't see any hair, but the head was tucked away too much for him to get a good view. Likewise, there wasn't any indication of clothing, but maybe that was the first thing to burn?

Nothing. There was nothing he could use to determine who this was. The hand was the only thing that had survived, presumably because it had been left outside the flames.

He pulled away from the hatch, feeling nauseous. This was just a mess. Why would someone do this?

"I don't kn–"

He didn't get any further than that, because at that moment, Kingfisher let out another ear-piercing screech. This one was so loud it didn't just blow out Cuckoo's ear drums, but probably those of anyone asleep in their rooms on the other side of the prison.

She was looking at the upturned side of the hatch door, all the blood drained out of her face.

When Cuckoo turned to look at it too, he had to bite his tongue to keep from screaming as well.

Along the underside of the door were a series of bloody scratch marks, ones that so easily matched the fingers of the hand currently lying on the floor.

Suddenly, the fact the push lock had been so violently broken despite being easy to operate made horrifying sense. It had been broken by being forced open from the inside.

Whoever had been placed into the incinerator hadn't died earlier that evening at all. They'd been thrown in alive.

o

Cuckoo's eyes stared down at the hand in horror, at the chips in its nails and its finger pads worn down through layers of skin.

He thought Loon had died horribly, but surely *this* had to be worse.

Kingfisher was also staring at it, taking in the burnt palm and melting stump, the pristine pale flesh only broken over the knuckles and fingertips. She first paled, then turned green, before her faced flushed a deep red that was almost purple. It may be him misinterpreting, but she almost looked angry.

"He...She...Someone else is dead" she gasped.

Cuckoo froze still, keeping silent. For a moment, he thought Kingfisher was going to reveal something he didn't know.

But the moment past, and she began looking around the room, eyes building fire in their depths as they locked onto the floor nearer to the door.

"They didn't die here" she declared "That's where...the body was dragged in."

She was pointing at a pair of muddy marks, spaced about the width of a shopping trolley, on the floor. They slid into the room in almost perfect parallel, dead-ending at the incinerator. Their tails slinked out of the door, bending around the corner, the door frame appearing to be chipped a few inches off the ground where whatever had made the marks had run into it.

It only took a few steps to follow them into the courtyard, the door frame there also scuffed from another hit.

The drag marks continued across the courtyard in awkward sweeps, piles of mud thrown up around their trenched path, finally ending at the big wooden door in the opposite wall.

Cuckoo recognised it immediately. It was the only door from the courtyard that had a lock. The one that was never unlocked.

Thinking along the same lines, Kingfisher crossed the courtyard, mud immediately turning her white trainers brown. Thankfully it had stopped raining, so she didn't get wet, but when she turned the handle of the door, it remained shut fast.

Kingfisher paused for a while, apparently not foreseeing that inevitable outcome, before turning back across the courtyard to where Cuckoo was waiting on the mud-slathered coir matting.

"Do you know where that goes?" he asked.

"I...have a theory" Kingfisher managed to get out, her eyes flickering about like she was looking at a puzzle invisible to Cuckoo's eyes "Can you find everyone?"

It was an odd request. Maybe she had something to announce. Did she know who was dead? Who had killed them?

"I can't say now" she shook her head, knowing what Cuckoo was thinking "There are things I need to know, and we need to find everyone. I'll go through the south and check the kitchen and dining room. You go north and check the library and the sitting room."

Before he could get a word out of her, she took off in the direction she had indicated.

He used the long walk along the East Wing to settle his thoughts and his stomach. He hadn't eaten anything all day, and he was pretty sure if he tried to eat, it would all just come up again.

Someone else was dead. Another one of their number had been killed, and the killings were only getting worse as they went on.

Was that going to be all of them? We they really all going to die in increasing awful ways, nothing but entertainment for the warden, whoever they were?

Cuckoo's whole body shook violently, as it trying to throw the thought away from him.

No, no one else was dying. They were going to gather everyone together, and no one was going to go anywhere alone. They were all going to stay together until they could find a way out of here.

Well, that was if he could find anyone.

The sitting room and the library were both empty, with no signs anyone having been in there recently. The dartboard was still hung on the wall from the early game. The only strange thing was that one of the padded benches had been removed from the sitting room and was lying in the middle of the corridor neared the barred entrance to the tower. There was no sign of blood, or someone being injured by it, and no one in sight, so Cuckoo used his crutch to shove it up against the wall so it wouldn't serve as a tripping hazard.

That wasn't the only trip hazard though. Just outside the alcove, the table had been shoved to the side, and a painting was lying on the floor.

Cuckoo was momentarily confused, not sure where this painting – nine bird chicks chirping in a nest, of course – had come from. The library and sitting room all had similar paintings, but he didn't think this was one of them.

It was only when he looked up at the alcove, he was able to place it.

This was the painting that had hung on the wall of the alcove. Now it had been removed, he could see what it had been hiding: a series of shiny brass pipes, one of which contained a lever.

Now, it's common knowledge that if one were to dangle as tantalising a prize as a shiny golden lever in front of a curious onlooker, they will be almost overcome with the urge to pull it. Cuckoo barely registered following his instincts to do so.

There was a pop, then a hiss, then a groan. Abruptly, the whole wall of the alcove began to shudder.

Cuckoo jumped back the best he could, nearly tripping over the painting behind him.

The wall at the far end of the alcove slowly began to rise, the dirt on the floor Raven had been so preoccupied with earlier swirling in the new air current.

Beyond the door was almost pitch black, the light from the alcove keeping his eyes from adjusting. But he could taste the salt in the air, and hear the sound of waves hitting rocks.

Some part of Cuckoo had been trapped in a very pitiful, dark place ever since that bookcase had fallen. At that smell, that sound, the weak, pathetic little spark deep within rose from its tomb and gasped out a breath of joy.

This had to be it! The way out! It was here all along!

He had to tell Raven! He had to tell everyone!

He blundered back into the hallway like an elephant learning to use its legs for first time, wiping out the poor person who'd had the misfortune of trying to pass the alcove at the same time.

"Sorry!" Cuckoo apologised instinctively.

Duck stared up at him from beneath Loon's hat, ignoring the pair of water bottles that fell from his hands; one thunked to the floor between his feet whilst the other rattled away down the corridor.

"...A-Are you ok?" the younger man questioned "You look d-drunk."

Cuckoo felt drunk. Drunk on life, on the joy of knowing they were all going to live.

"I found it!" the words burst out of him in a rush, at a volume that made Duck wince "We have to find everyone, come on!"

He didn't hobble back to the bedrooms, but flew on the fluffiest cloud imaginable, leaving poor Duck nothing more than a dinghy tossed in his wake, scrambling to grab his water bottles and run after him.

136

It wouldn't have mattered if there had been an earthquake, or a bomb going off; he wouldn't have felt or heard it. He'd never felt so alive.

"Everyone!" he bellowed down the corridor "I've found the way out! We can go! HEY!"

But this didn't have the effect he was looking for. Instead of everyone rushing out of their rooms in joy, an empty silence echoed back.

Cuckoo's grin faded a little. "Hey, anyone there? *Hey!*"

But there was still no response.

It was then Duck caught up to him.

"N-No one's here" he told him smartly "They all d-disappeared."

All of them? That was just weird. It was 3:00, where did they all go? It wasn't to the incinerator — he and Kingfisher were the first ones to find it, or there wouldn't have been a hand hanging out of it.

He'd taken the north of the prison, and Kingfisher the south, but the south was the shorter route. She should be back by now. And if everyone wasn't with her, where were they?

Raven had been so insistent he went to bed. So why wasn't *he* where he should be?

It was then he noticed something, something that may've already been there when he left his room, but he'd been in too big a hurry to notice.

Someone had moved one of the stack horses from the gym next to his door.

He was thrown for a moment, but then Raven's words from before echoed in his ears. *'They open outwards, so it's impossible to barricade yourself in. All you'd be able to do is barricade someone **else** in from outside.'*

Had someone tried to barricade him inside his room? Had Kingfisher had to move the obstacle to get to him? That would certainly explain why she only came to him after checking everyone else's rooms.

But who would do such a thing?

"Kingfisher!" he called out "Was that there before?!"

Finally, someone did emerge from one of the rooms. But it while was the person he expected, it was not where he'd expected her to appear from.

"You're here."

Both he and Duck jumped, turning to face behind them.

Kingfisher poked her head out of the gym, panting and her brow sweaty.

"We-" she wheezed "We have another problem!"

All that joy that had encompassed Cuckoo's entire being was sucked out of him in an instant.

He wasn't sure what he was expecting when he entered the gym, but somehow, this almost felt peaceful.

The room had been mostly emptied by Wren's insistence on moving all dangerous items to the armoury, leaving the floor bare and exposed. Bare, except for a grey rug sitting in the middle of the floor where there hadn't been before, and the weight bench: the massive spiked dumbbell on top unable to be moved.

And at the far end of the room was Wren; her massive form slumped forward over the weight bench, balancing awkwardly on the tips of her toes. The only sign on any distress was a bulge in the back of her jacket, just above what was clearly a smudged footprint, and a few spots of blood on the floor beneath her.

Walking around to her side only confirmed what Cuckoo had already suspected.

The was no life in Wren's eyes anymore. The spiked end of the dumbbell — the only weight in this prison she couldn't lift — had pierced her whole chest. The gentle giant had died without struggle.

11

It was an icy, impudent rage that filled Cuckoo as he stared at the body of the woman who'd done everything possible to keep them safe. There was no sadness: he was pretty sure he'd ran out of tears to shed for the dead. But the rage refused to die, bubbling up in him like a shaken bottle of fizzy pop about to explode.

There was no reason for this! He'd found the way out! There was no reason to kill anyone anymore!

That rage exploded out of him in a roar as he kicked the rug in front of him – the resulting pain too shallow to penetrate the fog in his head – his whole vison spinning so badly he could barely see Kingfisher and Duck at the other end of the room.

Spots of red filled his vision, and he wondered if he was going blind.

He blinked and blinked, but even as his vision recovered from the haze, the red remained.

Blood. He was looking at a patch of blood on the floor.

His kick had partially rolled the rug over, and he could see blood underneath. Someone had tried to clean up a crime scene, but hadn't managed to hide everything, and so had thrown down the rug and hoped no one would look under it.

Underneath the rug was a pool of blood the size of grapefruit, a few scattered white crystals and shards of glass, a mixture of small transparent and large brown shards. All of those were intriguing, though nothing without context.

But what was next to them was an undeniable clue.

A single muddy right boot print.

Raven.

Cuckoo stared down at the rug in horror. He recognised it immediately. Every bedroom had a rug in varying colours. This grey colour was definitely Raven's.

Raven was wearing *his* boot on his right foot.

Wordlessly, he placed his left booted foot next to the footprint.

...It certainly looked the same size.

"...could be nothing" Kingfisher's voice managed to penetrate the fog around his head "It could even be planted, designed to make us think it was him."

Those words pulled the garrot away from his throat. He wasn't sure how he was supposed to breathe if Raven – kind, supportive Raven – had done this. But if someone was trying to frame him, that would make more sense.

The doctor, the leader, the protector. Their most vital members were being taken away, one by one, making their situation all the more hopeless.

So, did that mean...the body in the incinerator...could that be...

He shook his head violently and stood up tall.

He turned to the body he could actually identify. Biting his tongue, he reached into one of Wren's pockets, then the other.

No armoury key. Great. At least they knew *why* she was the next one targeted.

He patted the second key in his trouser pocket.

Well, that probably meant *he* was next.

"We're figuring this out" he said determinedly "Come on."

He squeezed in between the pair at the door and a pair of muddy pallet movers pushed into the corner to reach a bucket of coloured chalks. Next to it was a mop in a second bucket, both wet and muddy.

Damn it, that was probably Wren's killer he heard last night, mopping up after themselves as they framed Raven blatantly under their noses. They'd even pretended to be him when they called out!

He could've ended all of this last night if he hadn't gotten so damn tired!

Or he could've been the next victim in the incinerator...

It wasn't worth thinking about that. He dragged the bucket of chalks into the hallway. They were for use on the scoreboard in the gym, but they'd work just as effectively on the stone corridor wall.

"Right" he picked up the blue chalk as Kingfisher and Duck followed him out of the room "We're going through each murder, one at a time, and we're finding everyone's alibis. The warden's one of us, and we're going to catch that bastard before we walk out of here right under his noise."

"You think they're a man?" Kingfisher questioned.

"You think he's one of *u-us* three?" Duck asked, eyes staring up at Cuckoo beneath the brim of Loon's hat suspiciously.

"Fine, *they*, and no" Cuckoo shrugged "It could be any of us that are still alive. Until we know who the fourth body is, we have to assume everyone who's body we haven't seen could be the warden."

In blue chalk, he wrote the names: **Cuckoo, Kingfisher, Duck, Shrike, Mockingbird, Nightjar, Raven**

"Fourth b-body?" Duck questioned.

"There's another body in the incinerator" Kingfisher told him, shuddering in leu of an elaboration "We don't know who it is."

Duck didn't ask any further, merely turning down his eyes and nodding sadly.

"First, Rail" Cuckoo picked up the black chalk and wrote **RAIL** beneath the list of names "He died in the boys' bathroom between 17:00 and 18:00. Where was everyone during that time?"

"I was in the k-kitchen" Duck spoke up first "So I c-couldn't have done it."

"But you *did* leave to go to the bathroom" Kingfisher pointed out.

Duck frowned at her. "But he wasn't d-dead then."

"We don't know when he died exactly" Cuckoo reminded him "All we know is that you and Raven used the bathroom at about the same time around 17:00. Neither of you saw each other, and so we don't know what order you used it. Theoretically, the last person to use the bathroom could've killed him. If that was you, you're a suspect."

"That's not f-fair" Duck protested "How am I s-supposed to have an a-alibi then?"

"You don't have one" Kingfisher pointed out "But then, neither does Raven."

Cuckoo conceded that point. He wrote the names **Duck** and **Raven** under Rail's.

"W-Well Loon couldn't have d-done it" Duck pointed out "She was in the k-kitchen the whole time."

"Loon's *dead*" Kingfisher rolled her eyes "She's obviously not the warden. That's why her name isn't up there."

Duck peered up at the list of names and took stock of the fact her name wasn't up there. "Oh."

Cuckoo felt the chalk slip in his fingers. He was starting to wish he had better company for this.

"I was in the library the whole time" he supplied to get the topic back on track "The only time I was alone was when Raven went to the bathroom, and I obviously couldn't have committed a murder when he was in there. So that should be me excluded."

"And y-you're injured" Duck nodded "You p-probably couldn't k-kill anyone like that."

That was a point Cuckoo hadn't thought of. Granted, he thought he could probably shoot someone with only one leg, but dragging a body around on a towel would be an impossibility.

Cuckoo went to scratch his name off of the list, but Kingfisher spoke up.

"You may not have killed Rail" she conceded "But how do we know you're not the warden?"

"Huh?" Cuckoo was confused.

"I'm saying" Kingfisher stressed, her voice tense "How do we know the warden is the one killing us?"

That was a thought he was sure all three of them had been thinking, but Cuckoo didn't want to hear out loud. It brought Loon's worried words to mind: that people would start killing because the warden had started it.

"We can't prove it with any of the others" Cuckoo conceded "But we can with Rail. Rail's murder was the first one, before we knew for certain that someone was trying to kill us. Not to mention the killer would've needed a way into the gun cabinet. And with Loon guarding the key the whole time, it's more likely to be someone with their own key – such as the one who set this whole place up. So, anyone with an alibi for Rail's murder can't be the warden."

The image of the bookcase collapsing, the feeling of his ribs crushing into lungs, jumped to the front of his mind, but he crushed it quickly. That could still be an accident, a coincidence – in the end there was no way to prove it. And adding it to the list of murders just complicated things: it wasn't as if they'd established where everyone was when the bookcase fell, and it was too late to ask them now with half of them being dead and most of them missing. Plus, it didn't take away from his statement about the gun – it needed to be someone who could've gotten in without Loon's key. The odds of someone taking the key from Loon and then slipping it back without her noticing were too monumental for it to be anything else.

Loon had raised the idea of Rail taking the gun himself, but why would he? And why would someone so flighty and suspicious let another person near his gun? It had to be some third party with a second key – it was the only thing that made logical sense.

Kingfisher pursed her lips in irritation, but finally relented. "Fine. You're off the hook."

It was with a little bit of satisfaction that he crossed his name off the list. Take that, Nightjar.

"You can cross me off too" Kingfisher told him "I couldn't have killed Rail."

"Weren't you by yourself for some of it?" Cuckoo reminded her.

Kingfisher opened her mouth to argue, then shut it with a clack. She squeezed her eyes shut, seemingly calming herself down, before she finally spoke.

"I left a few times to go and get food supplies from the pantry" she admitted "But it was only a few minutes at a time. Not enough time to shoot someone and manipulate a crime scene. People would've noticed if I was gone for that long."

That...was a good alibi. Duck and Loon may've been cooking, but they surely would've noticed a several-minute disruption to their ingredient train.

"It's s-still possible" Duck suggested quietly.

Kingfisher shot him a poisonous look. "How?! You saw me!"

Duck flinched, but after fingering the brow of Loon's hat, he pressed on with a deep breath. "You could've, if you used m-multiple journeys to do it. You went to the pantry three times after N-Nightjar left. You could've s-shot him on the first loop, tied the door on the s-second, and then m-moved the body on the third. That would have b-broken your time up enough for us to n-not notice."

Cuckoo felt his eyebrows crawl into his hair. That was a level of deductive reasoning he hadn't expected of Duck. Maybe Loon's death had brought him out of his shell somewhat.

"It is possible" Cuckoo agreed "I'm sorry Kingfisher, you're staying up there."

Frustration mounted in Kingfisher's eyes, but she let it go without a fuss as Cuckoo wrote her name under the others in the column.

"What was Nightjar's alibi?" he asked.

"She was with me at first" Kingfisher explained, instantly able to recall it "But after twenty minutes she ditched me."

"W-Wren said she and Nightjar were looking for R-Rail" Duck finished for her.

Cuckoo twirled the chalk in his hand. "Did Wren find her immediately after she left you?"

Kingfisher scrunched her nose in thought, then shook her head. "She didn't say."

Cuckoo nearly swore. They couldn't question Wren about it now, and Nightjar could just lie. He may've pressed the chalk into the wall a little too hard as he wrote Nightjar's name.

"Shrike was by themselves, and Mockingbird was in his room by himself" he added, their names going on the list "So all we've actually done is eliminate three people, one of which already had an alibi and the other two are dead."

He'd hoped they'd be able to narrow it down more than that. But everyone alive who wasn't himself didn't have a clear alibi for Rail's death, and just because they were in the clear for the murders after that didn't mean they weren't the warden.

He pinched his nose. In the end, all he'd done was proven what he already knew: that the warden could be anyone.

"Right" he moved onto the next chalk, a purple one, and wrote **LOON** as the next column "What about Loon? Who could've poisoned the soup?"

"Duck" Kingfisher supplied immediately "You."

"Y-You too" Duck pointed out "Y-You brought the ladle."

"It obviously wasn't the ladle" Kingfisher rolled her eyes again "It was the soup."

"Did anyone l-look at the ladle b-before you put it in the s-soup?" Duck questioned "It was a-already out of it's p-plastic wrapper when I f-found you."

"I barely looked at it with you dragging me away like that!" Kingfisher insisted.

"I don't think any of us have alibis for that one" Cuckoo admitted "As Raven said, we all reached over the soup to grab things and pour our own servings. Any of us could've slipped something in at that moment."

"W-Wouldn't that be hard?" Duck suggested "With us all w-watching?"

It wasn't the first time that had been mentioned, and Cuckoo couldn't figure out if he was right. Was there enough time? How long would it take to pour poison into a soup? Could it be done surreptitiously?

"Nightjar caused a fuss when she and Mockingbird came back from the kitchen" Kingfisher suggested "Everyone was looking at her then. Could *that* have been when it was poisoned?" She then narrowed her eyes. "Unless one of the two of you did it. You could've tampered with it in the kitchen."

She had a point. When else could the soup have been poisoned? It seemed unlikely, too risky, to have acted in the open like that. But what other option was there? Unless it was Duck, no one else had been left alone with the soup. That had to be it, right? It couldn't have been at any other time, right?

"So, that means it c-couldn't have been Nightjar?" Duck suggested, ignoring her barbed words.

"Or Mockingbird, since he was behind her" Cuckoo agreed, watching Kingfisher deflate with relief at his words "So neither of them. But everyone else is up there."

He wrote down the next list of names: *Cuckoo, Duck, Kingfisher, Shrike, Raven, Wren.*

"W-Why's Wren's name up there?" Duck frowned "She's d-dead."

"Technically she could've killed Loon" Cuckoo pointed out "And then someone killed her."

Duck straightened, a flinch in his shoulders. "T-Two killers?"

"Everyone has a reason to get out of here" Kingfisher reminded him "Just because a person's dead doesn't mean they couldn't have killed before."

It was a conundrum. If someone couldn't be removed from the list because they were dead, it was going to be all but impossible to determine a killer.

He moved on to the orange chalk, writing **INCINERATOR BODY** next.

"How can we work out who killed him if we don't know who he is?" Kingfisher questioned.

"Or s-she, or they" Duck corrected her "It could be N-Nightjar or Shrike." He looked up at Cuckoo expectantly. "C-Couldn't it? You s-said you didn't k-know who it was."

Cuckoo worried his lip as flashes of the molten flesh in the incinerator swept through his brain. No, there was no way to tell whether that lump of carbon had once been a man or woman. It could be Nightjar or Shrike as easily as Raven or Mockingbird. Wren was the only one it couldn't have been – the hand that had fallen out too pale and small – but she was dead anyway.

"Do we have any way of narrowing this down?" he questioned "Kingfisher, when did you see the smoke?"

"A few minutes before I woke you" she admitted "I tried other rooms first, but you were the only one still asleep."

Yeah, there was that. The thing that had been bothering Cuckoo.

"Why was everyone up at 3:00?" he questioned, his eyes landing on Duck "Wren and Raven should've been the only ones awake."

Duck looked away, his hands playing with the lids of the two water bottles jammed into his trouser pockets.

"I...couldn't s-sleep" he admitted "I n-needed to get water. I knew there were some b-bottles in the p-pantry. Wren said not to d-drink out of the taps – the water might be d-dangerous."

That wasn't a dumb idea – better the sealed bottles than the tap that could potentially be tampered with. Although Cuckoo wasn't sure how they'd go about doing that.

"S-So why were *you* up at 3:00?" Duck now turned to Kingfisher.

Kingfisher also looked way. "You're not the only one not sleeping."

Cuckoo now felt bad for sleeping. Had *he* been the only one able to? What kind of monster did that make him?

"Do we know when the others left?" he questioned, trying to distract himself "Did you see them go? Or where they went?"

Both shook their heads.

Cuckoo sighed, pressing the chalk against his head. With no one seeing anyone leaving, no one had an alibi. Great, just great. Weren't Wren and Raven supposed to be keeping watch to make exactly sure this didn't happen?

Well, obviously Wren had caught them in the act and died for it. He could only hope that the same thing hadn't happened to Raven.

Although...

"The pool of blood in the gym" he found himself saying "Could it be from Raven? Or whoever's in the incinerator?"

Kingfisher's head whipped towards him, her hair practically standing on end. "Huh? It's from Wren, isn't it?"

"I don't think so" Cuckoo disagreed "Wren was impale a few metres away, and besides the wound that killed her, she wasn't injured. There was no reason for her to form a pool of blood across the room. Someone else was injured in the gym, a few steps away."

"Huh" Duck considered it "So s-someone walked in on Wren being m-murdered, and the m-murderer also killed them in there, then t-threw them in the incinerator."

"They weren't killed here, just knocked out" Cuckoo winced "They were thrown into that incinerator alive."

Duck appeared to turn green, something Cuckoo couldn't fault him for. He'd barely kept his stomach upon realising the same thing.

"S-So it has to be R-Raven then, in the i-incinerator" Duck suggested "I mean, w-who else was awake?"

Cuckoo clenched a fist to force Raven's smiling face out of his mind. "Or he's the murderer who threw them in there. At the moment, I might hate it, but he's the most likely suspect."

He wasn't sure if Raven being a murderer who would defile a human like that was any better than him being dead.

Kingfisher began pulling on a strand of her hair hard enough to break it. "We don't know that the body in the incinerator has anything to do with the gym. Wren could've injured her attacker before she died, and they walked away. We can't know whoever killed her is our second body, or vice versa."

That was a good point. Wren was certainty big enough to have injured her attacker before she died.

They were making too many assumptions here – too many mysteries were still unsolved for them to guess at the order of events.

Left with no choice, he wrote the names of everyone presumed to be alive under the new heading, putting questions marks beside everyone who wasn't currently with him.

"Y-You're not putting yourself down?" Duck questioned.

Cuckoo looked at him strangely, then looked down at his leg.

"The body was dragged across the prison and then lifted five feet up into the incinerator through the hatch door" Kingfisher explained "No way he could do that."

"Oh" Duck nodded along "S-So, that means we couldn't have done it either. R-Right?"

Cuckoo thought that over. It wasn't a stupid idea – whoever put the body in there had to have some pretty decent upper body strength. Duck was probably only a little taller than the hatch door itself, and Kingfisher only had a few inches on him. They couldn't have lifted a body up to head-height, at the very least not without help, and he couldn't think of any reason why someone *would* help them.

He rubbed both of their names out.

That actually left a pretty small list. Just Nightjar, Mockingbird, Raven and Shrike – and one of them had to be *in* the incinerator. Though they were physically capable of doing it, it must've taken some pretty serious determination to haul a body that far and that high.

Although, there was *one* person capable of heaving around a dead body with no issues. He was just about to write a fifth name when he paused.

Unless...

"The incinerator?" he questioned "Is there any chance it could've been on since midnight?"

Duck frowned at the odd question.

"No" Kingfisher shook her head "I only saw the smoke at 3:00. I remember looking out the window when the clock chirped at midnight, and there was no smoke."

Her clock told her when the day changed? Did they all have different clocks in their rooms then? He didn't remember hearing that.

"Are you certain?" he decided to check "You're sure you remember that correctly?"

Kingfisher narrowed her eyes, glaring at him menacingly. "I don't *forget* anything."

Cuckoo felt a rush of terror go down his spine. As illogical a statement as it was, he believed her.

So did Duck, who he swore stopped breathing for a moment, before shaking himself back to life when she said nothing else.

"And, I mean, you saw a b-body, right?" Duck questioned "I-If it had been t-three hours, it would probably be just a-ash. Right?"

That...was an unsettling thought. And also far too accurate.

"So that means..." Cuckoo muttered as he selected a red chalk from the bucket.

He wrote the name **WREN** and then drew an arrow to before the **INCINERATOR BODY**.

"You think Wren died first?" Kingfisher guessed.

"I think so" Cuckoo admitted "I think I nearly walked in on her murder."

Both Kingfisher and Duck straightened with alarm.

"At midnight, I went to the bathroom to see if I could work out what happened to Rail's body" he admitted "I didn't, but when I came out, I saw the corridor floor had been mopped, and there was someone moving about in the gym."

He was expecting a gasp or some level of astonishment. But Duck just kept staring at him with suspicion, whilst Kingfisher was carefully blank, wrapping her arms around herself again.

"Did you see anyone?" she questioned.

"No" Cuckoo admitted "But I *heard* someone."

If anything, that just made the atmosphere more tense. Cuckoo pushed down the urge to back away from them both.

"W-Wren?" Duck questioned.

"No, it was a man" Cuckoo corrected him.

"Which man?" Kingfisher asked.

Cuckoo winced. He wasn't looking forward to this bit.

"I thought it was Raven, and he didn't correct me" he admitted "But I only thought that because I knew he was supposed to be on watch. If everyone was up and about during the night, it could've been anyone."

And boy was he kicking himself for that. Maybe investigating the gym would've got him killed, but if he'd just checked which rooms were occupied or not, rather than just going by which doors were still open...

"Any *man*" Kingfisher stressed.

Duck looked down. "I-If we can trust what C-Cuckoo is saying."

A fair point. He may not have even witnessed the clean-up of the murder, that was just his assumption. But if that wasn't what the person in the gym was doing, it was once heck of a coincidence.

"It's not like he could've done it" Kingfisher pointed out "If he couldn't drag a body into an incinerator, he definitely couldn't rush up on Wren and take her by surprise. Therefore, he has no reason to lie."

A wave of relief rushed over Cuckoo at Kingfisher jumping to his defence.

"Oh" Duck's head got impossibly lower, hiding himself completely behind Loon's hat "S-Sorry."

Cuckoo wrote down the names of all of the men thought to be alive except for himself.

"I-It can't be me!" Duck chirred up when his name was written.

Cuckoo frowned. "Do you have an alibi?"

Duck opened his mouth to say something, but then put his head back down, no comment made.

"Did the man stutter?" Kingfisher suggested "Like Duck?"

Duck looked up at her, confused. "W-What stutter?"

Kingfisher raised an eyebrow. "The one you talk with."

Duck seemed genuinely confused. "I-I do?"

Kingfisher and Cuckoo exchanged a look. He didn't know? Had it never occurred to him? It made Cuckoo pause for just a moment, chalk tilting slack in his hand. Had Duck always stuttered?

147

"Well, anyway, there was no stutter" Cuckoo put the conversation back on track "Otherwise I would've *known* it was Duck."

Duck raised his head again. "Oh! T-Then it c-couldn't be me!"

"But it's not like you stutter on every word" Cuckoo pointed out "And whoever it was said very little."

"I...err..." Duck scratched his head under the hat "People s-stutter when they are nervous, r-right? I-I w-would be n-nervous if I was caught c-cleaning up a c-crime scene."

A good point.

"You also don't wear boots" Cuckoo realised, looking down at his feet "*If* that boot print really did come from the killer."

Duck seemed to perk up at that suggestion. "Of course! W-Why else would they t-try to hide it?"

It wasn't the best evidence, considering the dubious authenticity of a single muddy boot print in a pristine room. But with two pieces of evidence in his favour – as well as the sheer unlikeliness of *Duck* successfully pushing *Wren* onto a sharp object – Cuckoo scrubbed Duck's name from the list. Now it just read **Raven** and **Mockingbird**. Both of them wore boots on their right foot.

"We can take Mockingbird off" Kingfisher suddenly announced.

Cuckoo tried to understand that logic but came up empty. "How?"

There was a pause, like Kingfisher was weighing her options before she spoke.

"Because he couldn't have poisoned the soup" she finally announced "So it wasn't him in the gym."

Cuckoo tried to see where her sudden confidence had come from. He wasn't seeing a link between the two crimes.

"T-There could be more than one killer" Duck reminded her.

"I know" Kingfisher acknowledged "But whoever poisoned the soup also killed Wren."

The chalk nearly dropped from Cuckoo's hand in shock.

"I-I don't know why you t-think that" Duck stuttered incredulously.

Kingfisher folded her arms, her voice haughty. "Were you only paying attention to the boot print? Look what else was under the rug!"

Now Cuckoo thought he understood. He hadn't touched them, but he'd seen them.

"There were white crystals" he recalled "Like in the soup."

"So, the poisoner had them in their pocket when they killed Wren, and some spilled out" she confirmed with something almost approximating a smirk on her face "Ergo, it could not have been Mockingbird."

Something felt wrong with that statement. If they had already raised the idea that the boot print was to frame Raven for something he may not have done, why couldn't the crystals have also been part of the cover up?

"W-We don't even know if they're the same!" Duck protested "T-They're just white r-rocks!"

"Occam's razor" Kingfisher insisted.

Cuckoo frowned. "What's that?"

Kingfisher rolled her eyes. "The idea that the simplest solution will inevitably be the correct one. There were white crystals at two crime scenes only a few hours apart: the simplest solution is that they are the same crystals."

She ended the sentence with a stern look, clearly determined to make this point stick.

Cuckoo didn't feel as certain. In fact, there was something about Kingfisher's absolute certainty that was unsettling him.

The smudged footprint on Wren's back flew through his mind.

Was that a genuine clue though? It seemed to point to a very obvious suspect, but if they had to assume evidence had been tampered with, could they trust *anything* in the gym to be safe?

"We don't know for certain that the crystals have anything to do with the murder" he pointed out, watching Kingfisher carefully "They could've been planted after the murder, or left there hours ago. They could've been in *Wren* pocket when the killer attacked her for all we know."

He swore Kingfisher's face turned poisonous for a moment, but she relaxed it pretty quickly. "So, you're saying Wren was the poisoner?"

Of course that was what she focused on – the only theory that explicitly linked the crystals to the murder.

Cuckoo just crunched his nose. This whole crime scene was just off. Which evidence was planted and which was genuine? Why was there a single blood stain several feet away from Wren's body when her only injury appeared to be the bloody spear wound? Why had someone mopped the floor of the corridor if Wren had been attacked in the gym? Had they also cleaned up parts of the gym? Why was Wren even *in* the gym at midnight anyway? And where was Raven in all of this? Already dead in the incinerator? Or a killer himself maybe?

There was the last set of clues: those glass shards – one set clear, one set brown. Cuckoo swore they were familiar, somehow.

"I don't think we can eliminate anyone on the evidence alone" Cuckoo decided "Leaving a single boot print and scattering salt around a crime scene would be easy enough for anyone. Sorry, Kingfisher."

Kingfisher's face reddened, but she recovered unnervingly quickly.

"Could it have been Shrike then?" Kingfisher suggested "He's masculine-sounding enough."

"D-Does he wear b-boots?" Duck questioned.

A slight pink tinge jumped to Kingfisher face as she whipped her head away. "Were any of us seriously looking at his *feet*?"

Cuckoo felt his own face redden as he fiddled with the long stick of chalk in his hand. Well, good to know it wasn't only him who'd been stuck staring at their pretty face.

Duck, who probably who probably didn't realise there were people besides Loon in the world, just frowned. "If we d-don't know what f-footwear he wears, then we c-can't exclude him. Right?"

Cuckoo thought it over. The voice didn't have Shrike's usual cadence, but it was only a whisper. Maybe they'd been able to keep it flat for three whispered sentences.

He jabbed the chalk into his temple with frustration. Trying to match the voice to any of the others was just causing it to jumble in his head. If he thought about it any harder, it was going to overlay, and they'd never figure it out.

Shrike's name went on the list, as a precaution if nothing else.

Damn it! The killer had been right there!

Reluctantly, he stepped back and took in his work.

~~Cuckoo~~ **Kingfisher   Duck   Shrike   Mockingbird   Nightjar   Raven**

RAIL	LOON	INCINERATOR BODY	WREN
Raven	Cuckoo		
Duck	Duck	Raven ?	Raven
Kingfisher	Kingfisher	Mockingbird ?	Mockingbird
Nightjar	Shrike	Shrike ?	Shrike
Shrike	Raven	Nightjar ?	
Mockingbird	Wren		

"You know, w-when you look at it like that" Duck remarked "If there is only one k-killer, it would have to be either Raven or S-Shrike."

Cuckoo didn't really want to think that. If all these crimes really were just committed by the warden, it could only be one of the two of them.

If it wasn't for that stupid motive, this would be so easy to narrow down. But when *anyone* could be a killer, and they didn't even know the identity of one of the murdered parties, this was the best they could do.

They couldn't even be sure if *this* was right. They didn't know *how* the soup was poisoned, *when* Wren exactly died, *where* Rail's body had gone, or even *who* the fourth body was!

This whole thing couldn't be solvable. If solving the puzzle of who killed who was supposed to be their way out, they'd all die *long* before they could narrow down a true suspect.

A way out.

Oh, how could he be so *stupid*?!

Had he really been distracted so easily?!

"We don't need this!" he declared, feeling a thousand pounds lighter just thinking about it "None of this matters! We already have a way out!"

Now *that* got the desired reaction.

"We can leave?!" Kingfisher gasped, eyes wide.

"Y-Y-You're k-kidding, right?!" Duck stuttered out, his whole body tensing impossibly further.

"There's a door in the alcove!" Cuckoo dropped the chalk into the bucket "I couldn't see out, but I heard the sea! I could smell it!"

Kingfisher bounced on her heels, her usually impassive face lit up. "Let's go! We can leave!"

She took off down the corridor, Duck chasing after her. One of his water bottles went tumbling out of his pocket again and he had to chase after it.

Cuckoo almost made to follow them, but paused as he reviewed the wall again. There were three people still running around this prison, and at least one of them was a killer, possibly even the warden. If they left, were they stranding them with a killer?

Was he leaving Raven and Shrike here to die? Were they already dead?

He shook his head firmly. He couldn't think like that. He wouldn't be of any help to them with a broken leg. They needed the police, or the army. Help in the useful sense.

If they made it outside, he could get them that help. But they needed to make it out before the warden showed up and stopped them.

He chased after the other two without another thought.

o

Cuckoo didn't actually manage to catch up to the others until he reached the alcove. His whole body ached as he dragged himself along, his head spinning a little with exhaustion.

Whatever he'd done to get these muscles, it hadn't provided him any stamina. Running around this hellhole was wearing him down.

Maybe he had one of those sitting down careers? That could explain why he felt so unfit – like he wasn't cut out for physical endurance.

Well, hopefully he would find out soon.

Kingfisher looked a little tired herself, drinking from one of Duck's water bottles as she leant against the wall.

"Thanks" she thanked him, handing it back to him when she was done "I guess I got a bit excited."

"I-It's understandable" Duck reassured her, twisting the cap back on.

Cuckoo could agree with that. Bone-weary tiredness aside, he swore he could feel lightning sparking out of his fingers with excitement.

Then he frowned. The door was closed.

He hadn't imagined all of that, had he? That wall had definitely opened up, right?

No, he could see the lever was back in the place he'd found it. It had just been closed. Had it been closed manually? Or did it close by itself over time?

He shook himself. That wasn't important. They were leaving, and they weren't coming back.

"You ready?" he questioned, gripping the lever.

"I'm not staying in this prison a moment longer" Kingfisher declared, shuddering.

Cuckoo was a little surprised – he'd expected her to want to look for Mockingbird first. Maybe she was just that desperate.

"Let's go" Duck nodded along, playing with his cap anxiously.

They were both looking up at him with a brightness and determination he hadn't seen since that fight in the leaves – like little kids who were waiting to see Santa for the first time.

He'd never questioned how old they really were before, but in that moment, they looked so young.

Something prideful and protective puffed up within him.

He pulled the lever, hearing gears grinding in the walls. Once again, the farthest wall began to lift upwards, salty wind hitting the three of them in the face.

Kingfisher's face split into a delighted wide-eyed smile, the first one he had ever seen from her. Duck's breath caught nervously, dropping his half-filled water bottle and making no effort to run after it as it rolled into the stone tray beneath the former wall. Their eyes couldn't adjust to the darkness well enough to see outside, not with the bright lights of the prison behind them. They'd be running out into the unknown.

And yet, none of them were afraid as they poured into the darkness, all too happy to leave the light behind.

For a moment, Cuckoo was blinded, stumbling on the uneven surface. It was rock beneath his feet: wet slippery rocks that had him moving cautiously, less his crutch slip beneath him. He could hear the waves ahead of him, as his eyes focused on something pale in the distance.

"Duck, do you see anything that way?" he heard Kingfisher question from his right.

"No" was Duck's response from his left.

The horror of what they were saying caused Cuckoo's vison to snap to life. Ahead of him, the rocks stopped at a thrashing ocean, spray spitting at his feet. A dock stretched out ahead of him, a mechanical seesaw contraption at the far end; but beyond that, there was only open dark ocean, rolling under a layer of white fog that blocked the horizon.

He looked left. Nothing but more ocean and fog curling around the west side of the prison.

He looked right. Nothing but even more ocean and fog twisting around the east side of the prison.

He didn't need them to say it. He didn't even need to travel to the south side of the prison. Seeing that told him the truth, and it felt like ash in his mouth.

"This is an island. We're still trapped."

Alula

12

Duck turned very still at Cuckoo's words, eyes fixed on the horizon as he rang his hands. Kingfisher on the other hand began to visibly panic, her feet beginning to pace.

"We-We can't be!" she insisted "We got out! We made it! We're free!"

"We're not" Cuckoo shook his head "We can't walk from here."

He didn't want to point out the obvious – someone must have gone out before him. Someone who discovered the lever behind the painting. And yet, no one had come back to them, cheering that they'd found a way out, or promising that they would come back with help. Maybe because of inherent human selfishness, but deep down he knew that wasn't the case. Someone had come out here and discovered the tragic truth behind their situation, then said nothing to spare them all the pain.

They couldn't escape.

"A-A boat!" Kingfisher suggested "We could take a boat! There's a dock, so there must be a boat!"

They all glanced towards the dock. There was nothing on it, no sign of barrels or crates of cargo. The wood was perfect, no scrapes or knicks from items being dragged. Not even any seaweed or limpets clinging to it, as if it was built just yesterday. The only thing that stood out was the structure bolted to the far end.

It was T-shaped, with a pivot in the centre of the top rung. Two ropes hung down into the water. Cuckoo could make a guess as to what they were for. You would attach a hook to one rope, and a weight to another. Then you could lift heavy cargo from the water or from boats. A simple pivot lift.

But again, the ropes weren't frayed. The wood gleamed with untouched varnish. It had clearly never been used.

The dock and the lift were brand new. Probably the only thing that had ever been on it was *them*, when they were first brought here. There was no boat.

"There is no boat" Cuckoo found himself saying, the fight leaving him like his ghost had left his body.

He had to watch the spirit crush in Kingfisher's eyes, a sheen of impassive coldness lowering over them like a curtain drawing. He felt like shit watching it.

He hadn't thought to keep an eye on Duck. He only realised that was a mistake when the smaller man charged past him, throwing his hat down onto the dock and diving feet-first into the water.

"Duck!" he yelled, forcing himself after the smaller man to the end of the dock "What are you doing?!"

154

"I can s-swim it!" Duck insisted, looking back at him in the water, buried in churning sea up to his neck "I can m-make it! I k-know I can! I'll g-get help!"

"You have no idea how far it is, or what's out there!" Cuckoo insisted "Get out and we'll come up with a plan!"

"I-I can't! I have to m-make it!" Duck insisted, and those might have been tears running down his face or just sea water "I p-promised Loon I would m-make it! So, I have to t– !"

Abruptly, before he could even finish the word, he was pulled under. He didn't sink under of his own account. It was too sudden, too sharp, too straight down. It was a pull, not a dive.

Above him, the pivot tilted to the right with an audible clack.

"NO!" he heard Kingfisher scream out as she rushed forward.

Cuckoo swore his brain shorted out for a minute, but when he saw a few bubbles break the surface, it broke something in him. He dropped his crutch, prepared to jump in after him.

Darkness all around him. Below, he could see ropes standing taught, piercing the world below. A large rock hung from two ropes to his left, whilst another smaller rock sat attached to a single rope directly below him.

Suddenly, something was ripping through his leg. It worked its way up, slashing at his belly and arms. He tried to whip around to see what was tearing at him, but every time he turned, a dark shape would turn away faster than his eyes could move. He tried to find Duck, he had to help him, but blood was clouding the water around him, agony screaming in his brain as his vision faded–

A snap, and he was back on the dock, a sharp pain coming from the injured leg he was now resting his weight on.

"Dammit!" he swore, putting his arm out to stop Kingfisher, who was taking off her coat in a panic "Don't! There's something in the water!"

Some sort of trap, maybe? Set up by the warden to kill anyone who thought of trying to swim to escape?

Shit! This couldn't be happening! Not now!

Kingfisher just stared at him with horror-filled eyes. "I thought...I thought...I–"

Above them, the pivot clacked to the left, a rope coiling to the surface on the waves. A moment after, Duck's head finally broke the surface.

"HELP!!!" he screamed, his voice piercing, one arm flailing through the air "THERE'S S-SOMETHING DOWN HERE! D-DON'T COME IN! PLEASE! L-L-LOON!!! I'M S-SOR–!"

Finally, his screams were silenced as he was pulled under once again, just as abruptly as before.

The silence on the dock was only broken by the clack of the pivot above them again, a death rattle in the air. A second rope emerged from the waves to join the first, coiling around each other like sea serpents.

155

A few bubbles broke the surface in a clump, a tint of blood red on their shining exteriors; but then the ocean resumed its prior fury, smoothing over Duck like sand over a blemish, the frothing red all that remained, toing and froing in the surf.

He never came up again.

o

"Shit!" Cuckoo swore, pounding his fists against his thighs "SHIT!"

All he could do was scream. There was nothing more he *could* do. He couldn't jump in there, or he'd succumb to the same fate as Duck, if his leg didn't drag him down. There wasn't a convenient rope or paddle he could throw in to pull him out, if that would even do any help.

The tertiary agony of those gashing wounds was still reverberating through his body – an unsubtle reminder of one thing.

He was completely helpless.

Dammit, if Loon had wanted anyone to survive, it was Duck! How many more people was Cuckoo going to let down?!

They were all going to die here...weren't they?

Kingfisher crumpled, her knees hitting the dock like her strings had been cut. But she didn't try to dive in, just peered under the dock in the hope Duck had surfaced there.

Nothing. Just more blood gathering on the surface in clumps.

It felt like forever they were planted on the dock. Neither of them really thought that Duck was going to surface after all that time, not as the little pool of blood rocked back and forth mockingly on the waves, but it felt like a betrayal to turn their backs on him.

If they turned away, they were admitting that there was no hope. No escape. That they were trapped here.

For a terrible moment, Cuckoo remembered that letter – that warning that they were imprisoned here for their 'previous transgressions':

Had they really done something to deserve this? Were they really such terrible people they deserved to be tortured here?

Duck's hat, his constant reminder of Loon's care, sat morosely on the wooden planks. A taunting reminder of their failures.

What could a kid like Duck had done to deserve being mauled like that?

It seemed like hours, but it was probably minutes, before Kingfisher rose to her feet.

"We need to go" she declared "We need to prove that this is indeed an island."

There was a determination in her voice that Cuckoo couldn't understand. He felt like every breath was effort, like there was glass in his lungs that pierced him every time his chest moved. How was she not feeling the crushing weight of knowing that they could never escape? That they were all going to die at the whim of some terrible monster calling itself a warden?

But her shoulders were held high as she bent down and picked up his crutch, holding it out to him.

"Are you going to lie down here and die?" she questioned "Or are you coming with me?"

There was a fight in her eyes, and it was contagious. He could feel it licking through his body, breathing life into his limbs.

There had to be some way off. After all, the last person alive got to leave. So, there must be some method for them to escape. Something in the prison they had missed.

Raven and Shrike were still in there, right alongside Mockingbird and Nightjar, maybe. He couldn't leave them to die. He had to find a way to get them out of here!

Or else, why was he still alive?

He seized the crutch from her and propped it up under his arm again.

"There may be something we've missed" he declared "We haven't searched outside yet. We should trace the whole prison, inside and out. Find what we've been missing."

It felt like he could breathe again.

They left the hat behind, the only memorial they had. There wasn't a body to mourn; just foam and blood churning in the waves.

The pair didn't drift too far from one another as they walked around the outside of the prison. The rocks provided a shelf of only a few metres between shear stone walls and thrashing waves. As they rounded each corner, they hoped to see a convenient dingey or portcullis that gave away a hidden boat launch. The sign of wet footprints exiting the surf from a hidden mooring. Heck, a bridge would be welcome.

But no such miracle emerged. There were no footprints, no structures. Every time they turned, their hope was smothered by jagged rocky edges and pelting spray despite the lack of wind, until they saw the dock come back into view again. It was untouched. Whatever had killed Duck hadn't emerged from the waves.

"There's nothing out here" Cuckoo declared, leaning on his crutch to take the weight off his aching leg "It's just a rock. The prison and the dock are the only things here."

Kingfisher curled her fists with frustration, but then relaxed and sighed. "The clue for how to get out must be inside somewhere. Somewhere we haven't looked yet."

Cuckoo tried to think about it. They'd searched the whole place, hadn't they?

Well, everywhere except for behind that iron grate, but no one could get through something that was bolted to the wall. Unless there was some way to get past it?

Well, it had to be worth a try.

"I think we missed something" he turned to Kingfisher "I don't know how—"

WHAM!

Somewhere ahead of him, a thundering sound sprinted along the beach and assaulted their ears, the rocks under their feet trembling with the force of it.

The pair of them exchanged a look, before sprinting forward as best they could.

There wasn't any sign of distress at the dock. No sign of Duck's body or whatever monster had attacked him. The pivot was still standing there cheerfully, hat still perched in place. It was clear such a catastrophic crashing sound could not have come from there.

Kingfisher gasped next to him, pointing at the prison. "The door!"

Sure enough, the entrance by which they had come was once again sealed. It was an almost perfect design — the sliding section slotting so perfectly into the wall that the seams were almost invisible.

Cuckoo felt his heart begin to race again. "Are we…trapped out here?"

He tried to calm himself, think about this logically. But it was hard when all he could think of was being stuck out here, on hard rocks with tossing spray and the threat that whatever was in the water may not stay in there forever.

Kingfisher was back to pacing, pulling her hair and muttering about how "it couldn't end now" and "she needed to find her first".

He looked around, trying to work out if there was any way to open the door from outside. But the only things even near to the door were a torch held in a golden bracket, and beneath that a large plant pot filled with stones, with some of the blue and white pebbles having fallen out onto the ground. Nothing that even looked like a lever.

Out of frustration, he grabbed one of the larger pebbles and launched it out to sea with scream.

The pebble got more air than he expected, fuelled by his grief and frustration. It sailed right over the waves and into the fog beyond.

And then nothing.

No splash. No thud. No sound that indicated the pebble had landed. It was as if it was still falling, like it had been thrown off the edge of the map.

Cuckoo frowned. He bent forward to grab another large pebble, but when he did, he stood up too quickly and hit his head on the bracket above.

"Ouch!" he yelled, his hand rushing to his head.

Seriously, how much more abuse was his body going to take today?

He heard Kingfisher gasp, and a now familiar grinding noise behind him.

The bracket was golden, the same as the lever. Pushing it up, with his head at least, had activated the same door opening mechanism.

He didn't hesitate. The mystery of the soundless pebble no longer interested him. He just rushed through to the inside of the prison before he could get locked out again, Kingfisher right on his heels.

They stopped just inside the alcove, having to stop themselves from hugging in relief. If they were going to be imprisoned, they'd both rather it be inside, where there was food and beds.

"Did…Did someone try to lock us out?" Kingfisher guessed, almost panting with relief "The warden?"

"I don't know" Cuckoo admitted "It might be automatic. How long were we out there?"
Kingfisher thought about it for a moment. "About half an hour?"

Cuckoo was impressed with her rationality. He thought it had been hours.

"So, we wait half an hour: then if it doesn't close, we know someone shut us out" he settled on.

Kingfisher nodded. "I'll get the clock from my room."

She dashed off, and he found himself envying her speed. The lump in his throat reminded him that even if he escaped from this place, he'd be shackled to this useless leg for a long time.

As he waited for her, he looked back at the still open door. Something wasn't right. Something about the tray that caught the door on its way down.

It had been pretty empty before, just a little bit of dust that had drifted in from the outside. But now there was some kind of stain on it. Like someone had dropped hot glue onto it – that same kind of texture with a dollop of red putty in the middle. Who was running around here with hot glue?

Suddenly the penny dropped. Duck had dropped one of his water bottles into the tray. That was the water bottle. That was what the door falling had done to it. It had crushed it to paste.

He shuddered. If it did that to a partially filled water bottle, what could it do to a human? Another reason not to step outside. Mis-time it and you could end up squished to putty. The warden had made it clear. They didn't want anyone going outside. Anyone who tried had to contend with a trap door and some sort of murderous device in the water.

"That's not a good look" Kingfisher remarked as she arrived back at the alcove "You look like a ghost."

"You don't want to get caught under there" he said as an explanation, gesturing to what had once been the water bottle.

She blanched too, nearly dropping the clock in her hand.

It was on that charming note they waited. Kingfisher had been pretty spot-on with the time, the clock from her room reading **04:12** when she arrived. It was hard to believe only a little over an hour ago, he'd been sleeping peacefully, thinking they were going to escape in the morning. Now three more people were dead, he didn't know where Shrike or Raven were, and his mind felt so empty.

Was that what grief was supposed to feel like? This numbing emptiness?

It felt too much like what he'd felt like when he first woke up with nothing.

God, he was so tired.

They didn't say anything as they waited. There wasn't anything left to say to one another. There was no easy comfort like talking to Raven or Shrike; not even the comradery that had began to swell in the air when the group had been all together. Talking to Kingfisher always felt like a battle against a wall, like she'd shut him out the moment they'd met and had no intention of letting him see weakness if she could help

159

it. Come to think of it, she'd been just as awkward with Duck, and only a little better with everyone else. Even standing next to Mockingbird, she'd been pretty cool with him on the whole, only letting the emotions bleed through when he wasn't looking.

Seriously, had they done something to her? What was this wall of silence that she put up, and what the hell was it hiding?

"Do you always intend to say everything you think?" she questioned, looking away from him "Or are you just an idiot?"

...He'd said that all out loud, hadn't he?

Well, that was awkward.

"No, I...I..." he tried to think, but it was like his brain was trudging through swamp water "I'm sorry. I'm just really tired."

Kingfisher said nothing, just staring off into the middle distance. Further conversation was clearly not wanted.

Half an hour of even more awkward silence passed. Then 45 minutes. Cuckoo struggled to keep his eyes open through all of it, leaning against the table to stay upright and catching his head slipping forward every few minutes.

Kingfisher seemed fine, unshaken for someone who'd been awake all night with no sleep. She just kept staring resolutely away from him.

When 50 minutes passed, Cuckoo called an end to it.

"It mustn't be automatic" he declared, pulling the lever to shut the door "It would've gone off by now. Someone did shut us—"

Before he could finish, the heavy stone door crashed down in front of them, jolting the earth and nearly deafening them.

They both full-body shuddered. Neither were in a hurry to run through there again. Not until they *knew* they could leave.

What had just minutes ago been a symbol of hope was now just a reminder of how much hopeless danger they were in.

Cuckoo turned to look outside of the alcove. In all the time they had been waiting, no one had passed them. The corridors were silent and empty.

That was bothering him more than he cared to admit. There should be five of them still alive, and yet he hadn't seen any of the other three since he fell asleep.

Shrike. Raven. Mockingbird. Nightjar. Where were they? And which of them were dead? His eyes meet with the metal grate at the end of the wing. Something in his brain was still bothering him about it, even through the weighty exhaustion it was under.

Did it look different somehow? Had the angle changed? But how was that possible?

"I have idea" he announced to Kingfisher, walking towards the iron grate "I know Raven said—"

He didn't get to finish.

All he managed to register was something hard hitting into the back of his head, and then black silence.

o

Pain.

Throbbing pain.

Not the same kind of shooting pain that occasionally climbed up his leg and paralysed his whole body, but a deep burning pain that came in waves and ricochetted through his head.

Cuckoo groaned, tucking his head under his arm.

Why pain? Why was he always in pain?

What had he done to deserve all this?

What, had he killed someone before he arrived here?

Cuckoo opened his eyes, only to send another blinding bout of pain through his head.

Groaning and trying not to cry, it took several attempts for him to be able to raise his head, a shower of dirt falling from where it was perched on his bun.

He was where he remembered being before – in the middle of the North Wing, staring at the iron grate. Around him were the shattered remains of one of the smaller flowerpots from the arrangement that had been on the table.

It didn't take much effort to work out he'd been hit with the pot, and that had knocked him out.

He managed to sit up, looking around for both Kingfisher and his crutch. He found the latter just a few feet away, but the girl who'd accompanied him was missing.

"Kingfisher?" he called out, but got no reply.

It took a few attempts to get the crutch under him so he could stand – eventually he found that shuffling over to the nearest wall was the only way to do it, and it left him dizzying and shaking.

It didn't matter how many times he groaned and sobbed though; Kingfisher never showed up.

He reached into his pocket for the bottle of painkillers, but they were gone.

Great, just great. Had Kingfisher taken them? Or whoever had knocked him out?

He looked over at the table where the remains of the flower arrangement stood. Also on there was the clock, now reading **05:31**.

30 minutes? He'd been unconscious for 30 minutes?

Behind the table, the alcove door was still shut. Kingfisher hadn't gone back outside, then. So where was she? Why did she just leave him here?

"Kingfisher!" he called out, louder this time, but still she didn't emerge.

What could have happened in 30 minutes? Had someone knocked him out and taken Kingfisher?

Or had Kingfisher done this to him? But why would she need to?

Unless...

He reached into his other pocket, feeling his heart sink as his fingertips touched fabric and not metal.

His half of the armoury key was gone.

If the person who had attacked him was also the one who had killed Wren, then they had both halves of the key.

This was bad! He had to make it to the armoury! He couldn't let them reach those weapons!

He didn't want to think about the fact it had been half an hour already, and that any amount of chaos could've broken out in that time.

He limped into the East Wing, following a trail of soil spotting along the floor.

"Kingfisher!" he yelled "Where are you?!"

His heart plummeted when he saw the doctor's office was unlocked. Had Duck opened it before they left? Surely he would've mentioned if he'd been robbed of the key.

The room had been clearly ransacked – bottles tossed onto the floor and cupboards thrown wide open with their paper contents scattered about the floor. One of the oxygen bottles had been tipped over on the floor, one of the tossed papers lying up against it, its valve showing it was half empty. Had the team who'd collected all of the dangerous items done that, or someone else?

This felt more like purposeful destruction.

Loon's body was missing – something that Cuckoo was starting to expect by now. The only question was if Duck had managed to get the gun cabinet key from her, or if whoever had taken the body (the warden he guessed, because who else would care?) had it.

What the hell was wrong with this place?

His head throbbed with agony as he stepped back into the doorframe, leaning on the wood to steady himself as the world spun.

He probably had a concussion or something. He really ought to sit down.

...No! He couldn't do that! Kingfisher could be in danger, dammit!

He had a mission, and he was going to see it through to the end, no matter what!

When he was able to step out into the corridor again, next door his eyes fell on was the armoury, where the trail of soil dead-ended in an arc. Cuckoo was horrified to find that the key was in the lock. He threw the double doors opened with a gasp, dreading seeing bare walls and an open cabinet.

He took stock of the pile of instruments lying on the floor, the exact number of weapons on the wall, the closed gun cabinet without a key.

Nothing *appeared* to be missing.

But why go through such efforts to take the key and open the door if you didn't plan on taking anything?

It didn't even look like anything had been disturbed. Nothing had been stood on or shifted. Like they'd only gotten as far as the threshold and then turned around.

Nothing about this made any sense.

He looked back into the corridor. Following the trail of soil from the flowerpot, someone had knocked him out, getting soil all over themselves in the process, and then travelled to the armoury, before turning around and going back to the doctor's office without taking anything. But the trail ended there, not enough granules left to mark where the person went next or what they'd been doing in there.

And there was still no sign of Kingfisher.

"KINGFISHER!" he tried bellowing one last time, wincing as the sound bounced through his aching head.

This time he heard a groan, coming from the pantry door next to him.

He hurried over, kicking aside a partially filled water bottle lying in the doorway.

"Kingfisher?" he called out to her, blinking to adjust his eyes.

The pantry lights were off, and the lack of windows meant that he was initially staring into a void. He fumbled for a light switch, but almost as soon as the lights buzzed into life, he wished they'd stayed off.

A few feet away from him was a body, lying face-down on the floor, as he had been not long ago. But unlike himself, this body had a stream of blood coming from their head, which had pooled underneath them. The blood went back several metres — clearly they'd been attacked further in and had nearly crawled all the way to the door to look for help.

And it wasn't hard at all to determine who that was.

"KINGFISHER!"

He didn't care about his own pain now, collapsing right by Kingfisher's head, just managing to avoid kneeling in her fanned-out blonde hair. Something was clawing at his throat, and it felt like a scream.

How could this happen?! Why was it every time he got close to someone, they died?! Was someone personally attacking him?!

Why was he somehow still alive while everyone else died around him?!

As he despaired though, Kingfisher groaned, her hands scrabbling on the floor.

She was still alive!

"Kingfisher?" This time he was almost breathless as he pulled her into his lap and turned her over, a little shower of dirt hitting the floor like a waterfall.

She was pale. Almost as pale as Rail had been. Her eyes were unfocused, blinking as they tried to focus on the face above her.

He wasn't a fool — there wasn't much left in her.

"This is my fault" he found himself saying, a sob in his words "It's my fault. I'm sorry. I'm sorry."

"Cuckoo" a little smile broke out onto her face "I got her. She can't hurt anyone anymore."

Cuckoo didn't understand. She'd got who? Nightjar? Was Nightjar also dead?

163

"Don't worry" she kept assuring him "I don't regret anything. And if she remembered...she wouldn't be able to *live with herself*."

She barely got the last three words out, her breath stolen from her lips as she coughed up a splodge of far too red blood.

"Don't talk" he whispered, not sure why his voice was coming out so weak "I'll...I'll find someone, I..."

He trailed off, not sure what he was talking about. Who was he going to go to? The doctor was dead. Neither of them had seen anyone else in hours. Any help would have to be provided by him.

He had no idea how to treat a headwound. Was the bleeding the problem, or was there something else he should be watching for?

He couldn't save her...could he...

Cuckoo was unfortunately getting used to seeing dead bodies. But this was the first time he'd found one that was still alive, still hurting. Still fighting to gasp for air, because even through the pain, she still desperately wanted to live.

It was horrible. He didn't want to look at her anymore. He didn't want to feel that phantom blood spray across his body when he hadn't made it here in time to suffer that. But looking away felt too much like leaving her alone when she was vulnerable.

He knew too much about that fear to do that to someone else.

God, what use even was he? What was even the point in him being here?

"Cuckoo" Kingfisher repeated, her face still smiling, but now her eyes were watering "Don't blame yourself for this. My sister...I know you didn't mean to kill her. I was suspicious at first, but you're a good person - I truly believe that. Not like me. Not like me at all."

Cuckoo didn't understand. What was she talking about? Who did she think he'd killed? Loon? Wren? Who was her sister supposed to be?

The sensation of blood on his arms felt more and more like a pair of shackles chaining him to the ground.

"I'm sorry I lied" she apologised, pulling him out of his frightened thoughts, her voice unsteady "But when Mockingbird and Nightjar didn't know me...I didn't know how to say it. I remember most of it, I think. I remember them, all of them, and you – our harbinger of chaos."

Cuckoo's breath caught in his throat. She remembered everyone from before they arrived here?! She'd known all of this from the start?! Did she know why they were here?! Why hadn't she said anything?!

And what the hell was a harbinger?! It certainly didn't *sound* good.

"I thought I knew who the warden was" she admitted "I thought I could stop him. But I was wrong, in the end. So wrong. About all of it."

"W-What do you mean?!" Cuckoo demanded, his voice stuttering "Who's the warden?!"

"Please get out of here" she instead requested in favour of ignoring his question, her voice growing faint "Don't let my last two brothers die."

Cuckoo felt like he was flailing in panic. He could feel Kingfisher slipping, and he couldn't do anything about it; nor did he have a clue what she was talking about.

Brothers? Sisters?

Didn't Rail also mention a dead sister?

"Who are you talking about?!" he all but screamed out "Who's your sister?!"

Kingfisher inhaled a breath, her eyes glazing over.

"Cuckoo."

That was the last thing she said. She breathed out one last time, before going still.

That scream crawled up Cuckoo's throat, but this time, he let it fly free.

13

He wasn't sure how long he stayed on the floor, holding onto Kingfisher. He felt that he lacked any energy, like he could just melt into the floor and become one with the stonework.

After the last 12 hours, who could blame him? Why should he bother to get up? Just so he could find another dead body of a friend?

He wanted to go back to 12 hours ago, when he didn't care about any of these people. When they could've just died and he would've felt nothing more than passing fascination.

He wished they'd never helped him. He wished he'd never gotten to know them. He wished he was the one dead.

Don't let my last two brothers die.

Who did she mean? Raven and Mockingbird maybe? But she hadn't seemed particularly close with Raven. Why would she call him her brother?

And who was this sister she thought he'd killed?

Why did Kingfisher not mention that she had memories of before the prison? That she apparently knew them before they all arrived here? Was it just her, or was everyone hiding memories close to their chest?

Was it truly only Cuckoo who didn't know anything?

No wonder they'd found him suspicious.

There were too many unanswered questions, too many things he didn't understand. And three people still missing.

What kind of person would he be if he just sat here and died?

He couldn't let the warden run about unchecked. If he did, what did the others die for? What was he still alive for if not to stop them?

He didn't know where he found the strength, but he was somehow able to gently put Kingfisher's lifeless head aside and get to his feet.

Taking a deep breath, he looked down at the dead body of the woman who'd been by his side that night. Who'd turned to him when she was afraid and uncertain.

The right side of her head was a mess, blonde strands matted with blood. Some of those strands still had speckles of soil sticking to them.

So much blood had spilled onto the floor – tufts of ripped hair swimming in it – that Cuckoo struggled to believe it had once been contained within a single body. Kingfisher had even crawled through some of it to make it to the door. Tracing it back, it started at a massive splodge of blood against the wall.

A strike to the right side of the head. So, a left-handed person must've done this.

Who was left-handed? Raven was. Cuckoo himself was, but he hadn't done this. Nightjar and Shrike held their knives in their right hands, so not them. Mockingbird might be, with him always hiding his right hand in his pocket, but...no, he'd held his dart in his right hand. Surely that meant he was right-handed.

So, Raven then. It couldn't be anyone else.

His stomach churned, conflicted. On the one hand, that implied Raven was still alive. On the other, Raven couldn't have done this, right? Raven had been so determined to die, so why would he kill anyone?

Cuckoo had made him promise to stay alive until morning. Was this somehow the only way?

Was this *his* fault?

He felt bile rise up his throat, a culmination of everything from the previous 18 hours finally catching up to him and putting its hands around his throat. He tried to make it out of the room, but his crutch caught on something and he tripped, his stomach releasing its contents into the corner. He hadn't eaten anything all day, but somehow there was something for him to dispel.

When his head began to feel dizzy and his arms weak, his stomach finally gave up, letting him push away from the smelly puddle he'd produced. As he scrabbled to get up again, his foot clinked into something.

A glass bottle, its liquid contents half empty. The skull and crossbones on its label stared back at him, eyes dancing over the words 'STRYCHNINE. Warning – May Cause: Pain, Muscle Spasms, Weakness, Delusions, Death'.

Strychnine was a type of poison, right? That's what Rail had said. But what was it doing here?

He cursed under his breath. The doctor's office was unlocked – anyone could've gotten their hands on the poisons in there. But why was it *here* specifically? If Kingfisher had been poisoned, why hit her? Had she refused to drink it?

His eyes followed the bottle over to what appeared to be a set of spare duvets folded against the wall. One of them had been tossed aside, lying on the floor next to an entire sea of brown beer bottles.

Had someone been sleeping in here? Or more than one person, maybe? Surely one person couldn't drink *this much*.

But it was when he laid eyes on the remaining pile of duvets that his heart stopped.

There were imprints in the soft down. But they weren't the imprints of anything human. Even as someone not accustomed to such items, he knew what he was looking at.

They were the imprints of guns. One long-barrelled rifle and two handguns. And maybe the imprint of a knife next to them?

Someone had taken them out of the armoury next door, and then stashed them in here under the first layer of duvet to hide them.

He felt his heart drop to his feet. Now there were three guns and a knife out there unaccounted for. How had that even happened? The gun cupboard was locked, wasn't it?

He quickly shuffled out of the room, sparing only one last look back at Kingfisher's body. He knew he was become desensitised, but he also knew that if he thought about that too long, he would find himself on that floor with Kingfisher.

He rushed to the room next door, where that dreaded key stuck out at him as it had before. This time though, when he peered in, his eyes locked on the gun cabinet.

There was no sign of the key anywhere.

He didn't leave it at just that though, stepping forward around the other implements to reach the door and test it.

Still locked.

It sent a rush of relief through him, but only for a moment. Yes, at least the remaining guns were safely locked away. But that didn't explain the missing three. If the doctor's office key was still on Duck's body at the bottom of the ocean, how had someone gotten in to hide Loon's body and steal the gun cupboard key? The door hadn't been kicked in, it was just standing open normally.

He found himself wandering in a daze, turning the armoury key over in his hand. Puzzles raced tauntingly through his thoughts, fleeing from his grasp before he could turn them over for their solution, forever stuck as just links of code, as 1s and 0s in his mind.

Was the gun Rail was shot with one of the guns that had been hidden?

Who had hidden them?

When had they hidden them, if Loon had the key in her possession from the moment the armoury had been discovered after they knew they were in danger?

Was there a second key to the gun cupboard?

Had one of those guns been used to attack Kingfisher?

Had it been Raven to attack Kingfisher?

Where was Raven?

Where were Shrike and Mockingbird and Nightjar?

How had they lost three whole people in this prison?

Who was in the incinerator?

Who had put them there?

Had they also killed Wren?

Had they also poisoned Loon?

Had they also shot Rail?

Had they also imprisoned them all in here?

Had they tried to kill *him*?

That last thought finally halted him. Kill *him*?

Behind his eyes, he could see the bookcase falling towards him.

Had that really been a murder attempt? Had it really been more sinister than just an accident?

But if that sickening theory was true, then that meant Cuckoo was supposed to be the first victim. He should be a pancake on the library floor, if it wasn't for that vision.

His visions. They were another unanswered question. What were they? Why was he having them? He couldn't just be going crazy – they were too accurate.

Why did they only occur when he was about to die?

God, it was so quiet. The prison had been so full before: the dying notes of far-away conversations bouncing off the walls no matter where you were.

But now they were no notes. No echoes. Just static rushing in his ears.

It was like the world had ended.

He was alone, completely alone, with only the spectres of the dead beating down the walls around him.

He hated it. He hated the silence so much. He wanted there to be noise and life again, no matter how irritating it had seemed at the time.

And as he turned his head, he came upon another mystery.

His walk had taken him to the wall outside of the gym, where he'd scribbled his suspect lists. In his haste to leave, he'd left the bucket of chalk there too. Someone had taken advantage of that, and fished out a white chalk to add their own scribble.

That scribble was just massive letters, written over all of Cuckoo's previous work:

THE WARDEN IS ALL THAT MATTERS

What the hell?!

What the actual hell?!

He put his head in his hands and let out a scream of frustration.

Screw this! Screw all of this!

He wanted to scream. He wanted to cry. He wanted to pull his eyes out of his head, so he didn't have to look at any more damn puzzles!

He didn't want his head to be full of all these thoughts! Thoughts of murder and death and games and puzzles! He wanted all of this to stop, so he could empty his head and just *breathe*!

He wanted his head and heart to stop hurting.

He wanted to stop letting everyone down.

He wanted to go *home*.

"Ah, there you are."

A voice like a song drifted down the corridor.

Even without seeing them, Cuckoo almost burst into tears that he wasn't alone anymore.

And out of everyone, this was someone he was *really* glad to see.

"Shrike?" he breathed, trying to work out if he'd cracked and was just seeing what he wanted to.

What were the odds that Shrike, who'd been missing all night, would miraculously appear from the darkness?

Was he imagining that bemused smile?

169

"Don't tell me you've broken under the stress?" Shrike chuckled "I thought you were stronger than that."

Something in him broke, a dam unleashing everything he'd been trying to keep locked up tight since he left Kingfisher's body. His body felt like it was floating, a millstone cut from around his neck.

That must have been how he managed to run, fly even, right along the corridor and into Shrike, grasping them in the tightest hug humankind had ever offered.

He was probably crushing them, but he didn't care. Someone else was alive, someone he hadn't let down yet. A precious friend he could protect, successfully this time.

He wasn't trapped with his own thoughts anymore.

He'd wanted to be left alone when he first woke up, hadn't he?

What the hell had he been thinking? Humans weren't meant to be alone. Maybe it was because he was injured and vulnerable, but the world felt far less scary when there was someone to face it with you.

"Ah, well, er…" Shrike sputtered beneath his chin, squirming awkwardly for an escape "You've…er…had a long night, haven't you?"

Cuckoo could barely process the words they were saying.

He breathed. "Shrike, are you real?"

Shrike went deathly still. When they spoke, it was close to a sob.

"Don't ask me that."

Cuckoo's relief-fogged mind finally managed to pick up on the fact Shrike was uncomfortable and took a step back.

"Sorry! Er, yes, I…" his hands flapped about at the tension spilled out of him "Yeah, it's been a…long night."

He could still see Kingfisher and Duck staring up at him in the alcove, eyes wide and bright like little kids. And now they were both dead, right under his nose.

Shrike placed a hand on his cheek, eyes now softening into something gentle. It didn't burn this time – but then again, anything was better than the suffocating oppression of being alone. He leant into that warmth.

"It's hard on you too, huh?" Shrike remarked, a chuckle in their voice "I didn't expect it to be the same for you. But you're human, aren't you – nothing about human emotions is straightforward, is it?"

It was so strangely worded, but Cuckoo found himself nodding along anyway. The words felt right, even if the tone behind them felt odd.

Shrike seemed to gasp with relief, their whole body sagging for just a second before they dragged it back under control.

"I suppose, no matter how well we play the game, we all break when it's over, don't we?" they pondered "When we realise we're nothing but pawns in its inevitable conclusion. I imagine it'll hit me worst of all, when it's all finished."

170

Cuckoo didn't understand what they were saying, but he didn't care. He could listen to them ramble on for the next week if only to keep them talking, breathing. Proof he wasn't alone.

"I keep thinking" they admitted "*Warden*. It's a strange word to use, isn't it? Yes, it has prison associations, but in literal terms it translates to steward or protector: guardian of the ward. It doesn't seem like the sort of word a mad kidnapper or executioner would use, does it?"

Cuckoo wasn't sure where they were going with this. It reminded him a bit of what Duck and Raven had said: that the warden may not necessarily be a bad person, just someone forced into a horrible role they didn't want.

Was Shrike agreeing with their guess?

Did it matter? Whether the person holding them prisoner was a good person or not? They were still being held hostage either way. People was *dying* either way.

"A warden does not kill his prisoners" Shrike told him "He oversees their labour, makes sure they stay trapped. But he does not kill them." Their gaze turned uncertain as they stared up at Cuckoo. "Am I right?"

Cuckoo wasn't sure what they wanted to hear. Were they implying that the warden hadn't killed anyone? That was a stretch to take from just a name alone – to assume that all of this chaos was the work of the good people trapped in there.

If it wasn't for the warden to kill them all, then why were they all trapped in here?

What was the purpose of sitting back and making them all kill each other? Could they not do it themselves?

He opened his mouth to say something, anything, a question that might finally bring all of the answers to his uncertainties, but–

A pain ripping through his body, once, twice, three times, as bangs echoed in his ears. Shrike shuddered against him, clutching his arms in a dead grip as they fell forward, dragging him with them.

Sharp stabbing pains clouded his mind and vision as he tried to get away, but Shrike's limp body held him pinned as someone walked up to him on unsteady feet, a hiss of pain on their lips and a violent tremor in their hands. A dark blur before his eyes, the shine of a gun to his forehead–

He gasped back into himself.

"What the–?"

"GUN!" he yelled, pulling the startled Shrike to the side.

At the exact moment the first gunshot sounded, the pair of them fell into the open door of one of the bedrooms they were stood outside, a little ping of something metal hitting the floor bouncing past his ear.

Cuckoo hit the floor hard, white pain stabbing at his eyes. Shrike moved like a whip, grabbing his jacket to pull him into the room fully as futile gunshots tracked them up the corridor – somehow missing them both despite being sitting targets – pinging off impenetrable stone walls with a deafening blast.

Shrike dove in front of the door, holding it shut with their arm strength alone. Cuckoo swore internally as he remembered that the doors didn't lock from the inside and couldn't be barricaded from this side – Shrike was all that stood between the two of them and certain death.

Shit!

He tried to look around for something to help them, to fend off their attacker or help pull the door shut, but in their hurry, they hadn't turned the lights on, and the room was pitch black. He tried to pull himself across the room, but all he found was a bed to lean against.

He couldn't even see Shrike, couldn't help them at all.

Their attacker yanked on the door, trying to pull it open. For a split second, enough light came through the door for Cuckoo to see Shrike's icy cool face, hands gripping the door handle with all their might, before it slammed shut into darkness again.

A bullet abruptly forced its way through the thick door, whizzing right past Cuckoo's head and into the bed frame.

He swore he stopped breathing. There wasn't time to move, and he was in the direct path of the door.

Two more gunshot came through, both of them only just missing Cuckoo's prone body. Enough light now came through the newly formed holes for him to see Shrike's outline again, tucked to the side of the door but still pulling on the handle with all their body weight behind it.

Cuckoo tried to look out of the bullet holes, wanting to know who was going to no doubt kill him with their next shot. But besides a blur of black and red for a single second, there was nothing to help him.

Click!

A pause.

Click!

Click!

"Damn it!"

Cuckoo couldn't identify the voice outside the room, but it sounded furious.

Twice more the person outside tried to pull the door open, their arm scrabbling on the wood as it kept either falling off or missing the handle, a hiss of pain escaping their lips every time they reached for it. Shrike held fast against their bullying efforts, a stone guardian at the gate. This time, the pulls were weaker, like their attacker was rapidly losing strength. Eventually they lost their strength all together, and the door fell silent. The gunman huffed and took off, footsteps unsteady as they seemed to slam into the wall repeatedly on their journey northward, a faulting clack clack clack in the air.

Cuckoo could still feel his heart pounding in his chest, his mind screeching with fear that their attacker would hear his panicked breathing through the prison walls and come back to finish the job.

Just as he thought his heart would beat straight out his chest, Shrike sighed with relief and relaxed against the wall, fingers still frozen in a death grip from where they'd been strangling the door handle.

Seeing Shrike revert to gentle calm convinced Cuckoo's heartrate to reduce to something that could maintain human life.

"Well, that was exciting" Shrike laughed quietly "Don't look so nervous – you saw it coming."

He had, but that just meant he knew how much it was going to hurt if he didn't act in time. Phantom pains of gunshot wounds that had never come to pass were still rippling through his body, and he knew from experience that they would take a while to fade.

"Who was that?" he questioned.

"You didn't see?" Shrike questioned, sliding across the room to sit up against the bed with Cuckoo "Not the most helpful of visions."

Well, thanks to it we're alive, Cuckoo wanted to sardonically say, but he held his tongue.

"If they were helpful, they'd tell me who the one killing us is" he instead pointed out.

"You don't know?" Shrike questioned, sounding genuinely surprised.

Cuckoo didn't like that feeling that was rising in him again – the feeling that he'd disappointed Shrike, who seemed to think much more of his intellect than Cuckoo himself did.

"Yeah, I know, I'm stupid" he muttered derisively "I'm not you."

"Hey."

A hand seized his jaw and forced him to look at a determined Shrike.

"You are not stupid" they insisted "You have more lateral thinking than anyone else here, for better or worse. You don't just look for the simple answer – you search through everything until you find what you understand to be the truth. So don't let me down by lying down and giving up, ok?"

Cuckoo's ears tinged red, the praise getting to some primal part of him. The distance wasn't helping either.

Shrike seemed to also pick up on that as they released him, shrinking back with a bemused giggle. "My apologies. I should know my place."

"It's fine" Cuckoo assured them, more strange wording bugging him under the surface "You saved my life. I owe you for that."

"You saved mine, and don't think that my actions weren't at least partially self-motivated" Shrike admitted "When my existence ends, it'll be because I agreed to it. Because I was in control of my end. And it certainly won't be at the hands of someone who just takes."

Something about those words felt familiar to Cuckoo. Not their exact spelling, but the sentiment felt familiar. So many people had said so many things today, it was hard to keep track, but he was sure it hadn't been Shrike who said it.

Shrike's fingers gripped the loose fabrics of their trousers in a vice, a pointed and determined gaze directed at the door. "I haven't outlived my usefulness yet. I still have time. Just watch me."

They sounded like a man preparing for a suicide charge.

A wave of nauseas spread through Cuckoo's body. "Shrike—"

"Well, I believe our wannabe killer has gone on to terrorise someone else" Shrike remarked, steadily cheerful once again, reaching into their coat pocket "We should probably—" They stopped, frowned. "Dammit, my knife fell out."

A wave of fear swept through Cuckoo again. "So, they could still attack us?"

"In theory" Shrike admitted, then the easy smile coming back again "No sense in waiting for them to come back then."

They reached up onto the bed to pull themself up from the floor, but instead, the items on top of the duvet came crashing down upon them, the room's clock hitting their head with a comedic CLUNK!

"Ouch" Shrike mumbled to themselves, rubbing their head and messing up their formerly immaculately styled hair.

Cuckoo held back a chuckle and looked at the items that had literally fallen into their laps. Through the sparing light the bullet hole let through, he thought it looked like a leather jacket and a boot.

When Shrike finally made it to their feet, hitting themselves on the bedside cabinet for good measure on the way up, and got the door open, his suspicions were confirmed. Yes, a leather jacket, a set of trousers, boots and a partially shattered glass bottle – most of the pieces only held together by a partially torn and distorted label reading 'SOD_UM HYD_OXIDE. Warning – May Cau____...burn....___skin____if swallowed...__...death'.

The bottle already made no sense. Cuckoo was sure it had come from the cabinet in the doctor's office, but what was it doing here in...who's room was this?

He looked across the corridor, past Shrike poking their head out to look for the shooter, and saw Wren's door across from them.

Mockingbird. This was Mockingbird's room.

Which made sense, since these were Mockingbird's clothes.

But why would he take his clothes off? He only had one set. If he was going to shower, he must've walked there naked, risking the wrath of the girls. Would he really do that?

"Ah, that means we're safe" Shrike remarked "Only three of us now." They glanced down at Cuckoo. "I believe the time has come for us to end this, don't you?"

Cuckoo tried to sit up. Were they talking about killing the warden? Did they know who that was, and how to do it?

"I'll go ahead, since I still have some preparations to make" Shrike told him with a smirk "Meet me in the tower. I'm sure you know how to get to it."

The tower? Did they mean the iron grate? There *was* a way through it?

But Shrike didn't answer that. Instead, they took off running towards the North Wing.

"Hey!" Cuckoo tried to get to his feet, but it was just as difficult and painful a mission as last time "Wait!"

By the time he managed to get into the corridor, Shrike was gone. The only thing that was any different was that Nightjar's hat was hanging from her doorknob, and a pistol was lying on the floor, its slider open to show that it was empty.

Did that mean Nightjar was still alive? Had she been the one shooting at them? Did that make her the warden?

Come to think of it, Kingfisher had mentioned Nightjar before, even if not by name. She said she 'got her' though. He thought that meant she was dead, that Kingfisher had done something to her. But if she was alive and shooting at them...

He still didn't understand any of this.

Somewhere in the prison, a massive bang sounded, the ground shaking.

Even far off, Cuckoo knew that sound. It was the alcove door slamming shut.

Had the person who'd shot at them gone out?

Why? There was nothing out there.

He shook his head. He needed to meet up with Shrike – maybe they know what was going on.

He limped his way up the corridor towards the North Wing, praying deep inside that he wouldn't have to make this journey again. That Shrike was right, and those of them that were still alive would get to go home.

He could see the iron grate coming into view as he rounded the corner. How did Shrike think he was supposed to get through it? Was there a trick he was missing?

He examined the metal structure, looking for anything that might give him a clue. But the only thing he could see were two marks on the underside of one of the metal bars. He tried pulling on that bar back and forth, but it didn't budge.

It was impossible. He couldn't progress any further. Not by himself.

Defeated, he sat down on the padded bench he'd moved there earlier. His head slumped, not knowing what to do.

He hated being alone. It felt like his brain collapsed in on itself every time an ally left his side.

Raven, Duck, Kingfisher, Shrike. When he was with them, he felt like he could do anything. Every puzzle, even if it danced out of reach, deep down, felt solvable. And now he'd managed to lose them all.

Even if he got out of here, really, what was he supposed to do? Who knew what was out there waiting for him, and he'd be doing it without the people who were his metaphorical and literal crutch – people who all had better reasons to leave than him.

Why was he even fighting so hard? To please people who were already dead? Who weren't around to judge him for just giving up quietly?

Why shouldn't he give up? There probably wasn't anything left for him out there anyway.

His head hurt. He could still feel those phantom bullet wounds. His leg would occasionally send restless spasms through his nervous system that made him want to cry.

Who was everyone kidding? He wasn't cut out for this.

Couldn't he just lie down here until it was all over? What else did he have left to lose? If the warden did kill him, would that really be any worse?

He didn't have much of a life for them to take.

Something clinked against his boot.

He looked down at his good leg, something shining on the ground.

Was that a hinge pin?

He tried to bend to grab it, but he flinched as another shooting sting went through his leg (damn, where were those painkillers when he needed them?), and the pin rolled beneath the bench. He twisted to see where it went, watching it tap against the foot of the bench.

The foot that had two claws. Two claws that were roughly the same distance apart as a those marks he'd been staring at.

Wait...

The library jumped back into his mind. The pain, the fear, of course; but also how he'd been freed. Raven and Mockingbird using the shelves to lever the bookcase up off his leg.

The bench had been found upside down in the middle of the corridor. Could it have been used as a lever?

He got up, finding it much easier with his mind preoccupied by the mystery. Looking at the hinges, he could see that they'd all been popped off by the grate, mostly like by being violently shoved upward.

So, did that mean this grate wasn't locked in place? Just resting on its hinges?

Testing the waters, he leant on his crutch to get back to use of his right hand and lifted the grate up with both hands. It was blissfully light, and this time it easily lifted out of its hinge barrels at his touch.

Yes!

Cuckoo grinned to himself as he stared down at the grate now in his hands. Raven's trick had worked — a force on a long line pushing upwards could push a much heavier object upwards.

His brain stuttered to a halt.

Wait.

If that was true, could the opposite also be true?

176

Could a force pulling *down* on a long line pull a much lighter object down?

A pivot turned in his head.

But that would mean–

It felt like the whole wing dimmed behind his eyes.

No. Could he really bring himself to do that? To accuse someone he cared about of doing such a thing?

Don't let my last two brothers die.

The grate tightened in his grip, until it bit into his palms.

...Yes. Yes he could.

He couldn't remain someone who refused to accuse anyone for fear of being wrong. For fear of upsetting the people he was growing to care for, who could leave him alone and vulnerable if they so chose. With time running out so quickly, he'd have to speak up, and acknowledge that terrible fact he'd just understood.

Adrenaline rushed through his body, which meant when he threw the grate, it flew further than intended. It bounced off the top of the bench and splashed onto the floor beyond.

Splashed?

He looked back at the grate, a rising horror building in him.

A pool of blood was draining out of the alcove, and had reached such an extent that the grate had landed in its outer reaches.

Shrike?

He limped over to the alcove, and the only reason he didn't throw up was his stomach was much too empty for that.

It took too long for him to understand what he was looking at. The ripples of blood were spilling out from beneath the closed door. A knife – Shrike's folding knife – was sticking out the pipe that the lever – still in its open position – was attached to, a soft hiss in the air as the gas that had once powered the hydraulic system escaped so that the door could never be lifted again.

But that wasn't what was making Cuckoo feel so ill.

Not far from the door, a left shoe had been kicked off. And near that was a finger, still attached to the partially severed hand it had once belonged to.

The door had come down and cut the hand in half – the half under the door being crushed whilst the remaining half still oozed blood where there had once been connections to a whole body.

Someone was under the door.

It wasn't a question if they were alive. No one could possibly survive a crush like that. At least, whoever it was, must have died instantly.

But who was it?

He tried to think of who the shoe could belong to. It was slim, with a heel. Nightjar definitely wore shoes like that, clacking away on the floor. Raven did too, on his left foot anyway – Cuckoo's right foot was proof of that. Had Shrike? None of them had been able to remember before, and in all the chaos, Cuckoo hadn't thought to check their shoes.

So...could it be Shrike under there?

He took another step back, away from the horror. He didn't want more proof that he had failed to protect someone else.

Why was this happening?

Was grief the noose that never stopped tightening? Every time you struggled to take a breath, it would claw it back out of your throat.

He didn't scream. He didn't have the strength for it – not when he needed it for what was to come. Instead, he turned towards the tower.

He had to end this now. If the answers for who the warden was and why they were trapped here were up there, then he'd take up Shrike's wish and end this.

He might not deserve to leave more than the others, but he'd do it. He'd somehow fight through any more pain that came his way. He'd make sure *someone* made it out, even if it was his pathetic excuse of a life, and the person who killed all of his friends died for it.

That could be *his* purpose.

Who is the warden?

Why were they trapped here?

Who'd killed each of his friends?

Who was still alive?

Who the hell was he?

Those were the questions he needed to answer before he could make his peace. The encrypted code he needed to decipher to find the truth.

He looked up at the staircase before him, and with no hesitation, stepped forward.

Primaries

14

The staircase went up two stories, winding in looping spirals that were hard to drag his crutch up and made his head feel dizzy for good measure. When he saw light ahead of him, indicating the top of the incline, Cuckoo almost cheered with relief.

Not that that made anything he saw at the top of the stairs make sense.

The light got his attention first. The prison had the unintentional effect of feeling very dark and shadowy, with the pale lights being so dim and so high up. In comparison, the light in this room was overpoweringly bright, and had a slight blue-green tinge to it.

The next thing he noticed was why the light was so different – all of it was coming from a bank of computers that formed a U-shape around the room.

In the entirety of the prison, the only technology had been the basic facilities in the kitchen, the clocks and the lights. Nothing that could even be interpreted as a computer had appeared in all of their searches, so seeing such a mass of technology after all of that absence nearly span his head around.

Like an insect to flame, he found himself gravitating over to the lights, a soft feeling in his chest, like the feeling of coming home.

Compared to the brand new materials that made up every inch of the prison, the monitors up here were old; their covers slightly dusty and their design something at least a few decades out of sync. But the display on them was perfect, the pixel count far beyond what Cuckoo expected to see on such old devices.

The bizarre set up wasn't the only thing confusing him though – what was on the monitor didn't make any sense either.

It took him a moment to understand what he was looking at, distracted by a mechanical pencil on the desk. One he swore he'd seen before, but was his attention was too pulled by the monitors to spare thinking room for it. He instinctively picked it up and played with it between his fingers as his gaze fixated on the monitor above.

The screen was divided into four, each section depicting a different view of the prison. One was in a corner above the dining room, another in the gym (Wren's body now missing, of course), a third in the incinerator room and the last looking down the West Wing corridor.

Cuckoo didn't understand. This implied there were cameras all over the prison. But there hadn't been – he was sure of it. As they'd walked, his eyes had flickered into every corner and obvious place to hang a camera, but there hadn't been any for his eyes to spot.

So then...how was this possible?

He checked the next monitor, and the next. Again, more cameras, in every room of the prison. Not a single nook or cranny was left unmonitored. Not even the shower rooms. Whoever this was built for would be able to watch the entire prison without having to leave their seat.

It had to be for the warden. That was the only thing that made sense.

But then why hide it behind an iron grate that needed to be physically dismantled to access? Surely there had to be easier ways to keep the nine people who weren't the warden out. Was it to keep the warden out as well? But why bar him from his own surveillance room?

For a moment, Duck and Raven's words about the warden also being trapped here ran circles in his head.

He shook his head. There would be time to deal with that later. He couldn't afford to be distracted.

The last screen on the row made him pause, because this wasn't a camera feed.

It looked like some kind of dossier. Wren's grinning face stared back at him from a photo in the corner, the following words written next to it:

WREN
00-020-00063-41
Data Security
Defies Orders

The rest of the page made no sense to him, consisting of a series of codes and what looked like an action log, but all written in acronyms and shorthand. He couldn't make sense of it, but somewhere in his soul, it sang a song whose rhythm he knew, even if its lyrics were just beyond his reach.

Staring at that code, it felt like slipping into a familiar jacket, your heart feeling warm as familiar fibres rolled against your skin.

This...This couldn't be...

Had Wren been...

...No, that was a horrible thought. One he should slap himself for even entertaining.

He shook his head and turned back to the dossier, eyes pulling away from those agonisingly familiar pixels.

Defies orders? What was that supposed to mean? If anything, Wren had been following orders like a pro, only turning to *giving* orders after their leader died, in an attempt to keep them all safe at the cost of her own life.

Cuckoo could feel a headache coming on, and he worried it was only going to get worse as he read on.

There was a little arrow at the top of the page. Clearly this wasn't the only page in the dossier.

He clicked on it.

Another dossier flashed up onto the screen. Cuckoo felt his heart skip a beat and as another familiar face, one he wished to see very much, smiled gently back at him, the usual heaviness that hung over his head clear and his eyes bright.

RAVEN

00-302-00094-32

Data Engineer

Self-Destructive Impulses. Damaged

More code followed, the same layout as Wren's but with different data.

Self-Destructive impulses? Another vague statement, but this made at least a little bit of sense: anyone who was willing to die to make sure others got to safety had to be pretty self-destructive.

Damaged though? What was that supposed to mean?

The body in the incinerator flashed through his mind, skin contorted and melted on the bone.

He shuddered and pushed it aside. He couldn't think about that. He wouldn't have the strength to keep going if he did.

Data Engineer. That must be Raven's job. He hoped he was still alive so he could tell him: no doubt it would make him happy. But why was Raven made to forget his job when everyone else got to keep theirs?

Everyone knew Raven had to be some kind of engineer. Why was him being a *data* engineer so important?

With no answers here, Cuckoo clicked on the arrow, expecting another dossier. Sure enough, one appeared.

RAIL

00-286-00075-19

Medical Diagnostician

Self-Destructive Impulses. Damaged

Rail's picture wasn't how Cuckoo remembered him at all. His hair was tied back and pushed out of his face, there purple bags under his eyes, and overall he just looked far more settled.

The prison hadn't done that to him – he'd already a shell of himself when he arrived. This must have been taken before his sister died.

Cuckoo felt something stir deep inside. He thought he could understand that. He'd only know his friends less than one day, but they were all he'd ever known. Losing them one after another felt like someone had stolen away a part of him so he could never feel whole again.

To have lost someone you'd known for years…he wasn't certain if he could've survived that.

Damaged? A heartless way to put it.

Another click, another face. Another face that turned his stomach.

SHRIKE
00-189-00101-13
Therapist
Self-aware. Defies Orders
Blood on the alcove floor pooled behind his eyes. He pushed it aside.
The codes on this page were different. Longer than all three of the previous ones, more complex. He didn't entirely understand the significance of that, so he resolved not to dwell on it for too long.
Who knew how long he had before the warden came back to his den?
Clearly the dossiers were in reverse alphabetical order. Nightjar's should be next.
It was.
NIGHTJAR
00-056-00078-32
Bid Planner
Destructive Impulses
Nightjar's smile was pleasant and welcoming, nothing like the sneers and smirks that had decorated her face whilst she was in the prison. It was a million miles from the look of pure disgust and rage she'd bared when she threw that knife at his head.
Click.
MOCKINGBIRD
00-059-00023-29
Project Manager
Destructive Impulses. Defies Orders
Mockingbird looked the same as he had when he first showed up in the doctor's office – an easy grin and a confident set to his shoulders. Cuckoo wasn't sure when he'd gotten so used to seeing those eyes scared and clouded.
Click.
LOON
00-003-00043-10
Human Resources Manager
Defies Orders
He could see that happy face staring down at him with icy fury as he'd announced to the world that Rail had been murdered, putting everyone around him in danger. In his head, it morphed into a seizing, frothing nightmare, and although he knew that Loon had been in too much pain to glare at him as she suffered, he swore it would still haunt his memories until he died.
Duck hadn't even been able to look at him after that, gripping her hand with a flash of rage and then terrifying nothingness. Cuckoo wished he'd cursed him out, or hit him. Anything but that blank stare.
Click.

KINGFISHER
00-023-00022-28
Digital Accountant
Defies Orders. Destructive Impulses

Kingfisher, the one he felt the worst about. He'd been with her. He should've protected her better, not just held her as she died.

Seeing her face as it had been before all this, clear and bright with eyes wide and smiling, made everything inside him feel heavy.

He wanted to stop, but he owed it to them to keep going. He should be almost done now.

The next dossier was different. Noticeably so.

DUCK
00-000-00164-01
Asset Management
N/A

Something was definitely wrong. A lot of things actually.

Immediately, he saw that there was no mark of bad character against him. Why was Duck special?

The job caught his attention as well. Duck had said he worked in people management, but this implied he worked with assets instead.

Why lie? What was the significance of that? Had it been to relate to Loon better? Or because Mockingbird already had a similar job?

Somehow that felt like it didn't cover all of it.

The data log below wasn't helping matters. It was notably long: longer than all of the others combined, even Shrike's already lengthy one, Cuckoo was sure of that. But somehow, the code didn't look any more complex. He could recognise the same acronyms and shorthand – there was just more of it.

Finally, Duck's photo caught his attention. He wasn't wearing his familiar goggles, and he looked as forlorn as he always did. Everyone else had been shown in some state of contentment, but not Duck. He just looked haunted and blank; eyes almost too tired to hold themselves open.

Cuckoo didn't understand what it meant, but he knew that the warden had more data on Duck than anyone else.

Duck, who hadn't died like anyone else either. He'd been pulled under by whatever trap was in the ocean.

Was he specifically targeted? Or was there actually more to it than that?

He shoved that all aside. There was something he had to do before he could think about that.

The arrow at the top of the page was still there. There was still one last dossier left to check.

Cuckoo steadied his breath. He could do the maths: the last dossier was his.

He knew, logically, that it wouldn't contain any useful information. The other dossiers were sparse enough to warn him of that.

But it would be something. It would be proof that he existed before yesterday. That he was a person.

He clicked the arrow.

His heart hit his feet.

That wasn't his face. He'd seen his face in the mirror in the bathroom. He knew what he looked like.

He didn't have a round face, or flowing red hair, or glittering blue eyes.

He also wasn't a girl.

For a moment he thought that there was some eleventh file: that this was some other person within the prison that they hadn't met yet.

The words next to the picture though sent him into a full-blown panic.

CUCKOO

00-228-00090-23

Research Specialist

Deleted by invader. Isolation protocols activated

He felt sick.

He bent at the waist, trying to force air into his lungs, but when it landed there, it wouldn't settle long enough to let him catch his breath.

The letters **CUCKOO** stared up at him from his own arm, the black ink rippling as his muscles tensed in fear and revulsion.

That wasn't even his name, was it? That belonged to someone else.

So why was it on *his* arm?

None of this made any sense!

"What are you doing! Stop!"

There was a voice echoing in his head. Cuckoo tensed on the spot, expecting for the pain of another death to come his way.

How wrong was this place that he could say 'another death' without flinching?

But nothing came. Just the voice in his ears, and a phantom grab on his arm.

"You can't take that! Who are you?!"

Was this...a memory?

He could feel himself turning, reaching out to whoever was grabbing him. There was suddenly a scream, a spray of what felt like water onto his face, a rising horror building in his gut...

The sensations faded before he could grab onto them, leaving him feeling completely alone, and too stunned to even breathe.

What the hell? What the actual hell?!

Cuckoo slumped against the computer desk, and for the first time, he realised how silent the room was. He couldn't even hear his own heartbeat.

It had been jumping around in his chest, thrashed side to side by invisible marionette strings all day, but he couldn't remember actually hearing it beat. It was supposed to make a sound in your ears, wasn't it?

Had he ever heard it? Or had it always been absent?

Who the hell was he?

What the hell was he?!

Tears ran down his face and dripped onto the floor.

He just wanted to see someone. He just—

"I just want to go home" he admitted, his voice a whisper.

Finally, he heard a noise. A thump behind him.

Not his heartbeat, but a sound of life, and that was enough.

He looked over his shoulder to see a locker against the wall: the type you expected to see in gyms or schools. It was rocking ominously, like it was haunted by some sort of locker room ghost.

He could hear a muffled screaming coming from inside.

Cuckoo began to walk towards it, a trained wariness in his step. After today – after being squished, shot, knocked out, stabbed and almost poisoned – he was starting to learn to watch out for himself.

Or so he thought.

A click echoed next to his ear, a firm weight parting his hair to rest against his head.

"I wouldn't recommend moving."

Even under the circumstances, his heart threw itself silently back into life upon hearing that familiar voice.

Of course, it had been Shrike who'd had the mechanical pencil now sitting in his pocket: they'd used it to draw the map of the bathroom.

"Shrike, you're alive!" he gasped with joy, until the rest of the situation caught up with him "Why do you have a gun?"

"Rail didn't need it any longer" was the smart retort – Cuckoo could almost hear the smirk in their words "A good thing I took it when I did, before the body was moved and it was lost."

Finally, the situation began to click into place in his head:

Shrike was alive, not crushed under the alcove door.

Shrike had a gun.

Shrike was pointing that gun point-blank right at the back of his head.

He couldn't make sense of it. Shrike wouldn't hurt him...right?

Shrike had saved his life. Why would they kill him now?

No no no no no! This wasn't happening!

The sounds from the locker grew more and more furious, as whoever was in there began to hurl themselves at the door.

"Shrike...are you the warden?" he asked, despite not wanting to hear the answer.

The silence behind his head was deafening, Shrike refusing to give any kind of justification.

"I think that's enough silly questions" they finally spoke, voice dangerously flat "We really ought to solve this mystery, you and I: get it all out in the open."

As if prompted, the locker door gave way and threw open, the person inside collapsing to the ground with a smash.

Instantly Cuckoo knew who it was: Raven, gagged and hog tied with his own scarf.

"Raven!" the word burst out of him like a thunderstorm.

Shrike just sighed. "Really, *now* Raven? It would be much more peaceful if you just sat there and waited for the end to come. Don't make it worse for yourself."

Panic seized through Cuckoo's veins. Some righteous part of him had been so certain that Shrike wouldn't harm him; some primal spark that couldn't envision a world where it wasn't alive. But now there was another life in the mix, one that Cuckoo didn't know how he was going to protect.

"Don't hurt him!" he gasped "I'll do whatever you want, Shrike! Just don't hurt him!"

"Fascinating" Shrike remarked, sounding full of wonder "You really *did* get attached? That's a bit stupid – he isn't real, you know."

What did they mean he wasn't real?! What the hell was that supposed to mean?! Raven was right there!

Raven had used their conversation to buy time. He'd managed to get his feet free, struggling to a stand. His hands were still tried behind his back, pulling on his mouth like a horse's bit every time he struggled. Despite the torturous gag, he was still trying to talk, screaming something behind the muffler.

"Don't be silly Raven" Shrike's voice was scolding "He won't thank you for dying to save him."

"NO, don't kill him!" Cuckoo shrieked out, wishing more than anything he could run "Raven, I'll be fine! Stay there! Shrike...what do you want me to do?!"

Raven paused his struggles, just staring at Cuckoo with tears in his eyes.

"We're just taking a walk" Shrike told him "The sun will be rising soon, so I can't think of anywhere better than the roof."

They turned him towards a set of stairs at the end of the room, identical to the ones he'd just ascended. They must go up to the roof.

Cuckoo felt tears prick his eyes again. Was that where Shrike was going to kill him? Was there anything he could do to stop that? Not shackled by this crutch he couldn't.

He'd resolved to make it out of here before, but if meant that Raven would be safe...

"That's where you'll kill me?" he guessed, disgusted in himself that he said the words.

A breathy laugh hit his ear. "You're very funny."

If they wanted to say anything else, they didn't get the chance. With Shrike distracted, Raven took his chance and charged forward, his arms coming free of the scarf just in time.

He wasn't quick enough though, as Shrike effortlessly pivoted and straightened the gun out towards him.

"DON'T!" Cuckoo yelled, but his scream was silenced by the deafening gunshot right next to his ear.

Raven flew back into the wall, clutching his shoulder.

Cuckoo didn't think there was anything in him left to break, but impossibly it did.

"I told you not to move" Shrike tutted, seizing the back of Cuckoo's hair and pushing him forward "Come on. We're finishing this."

"C-Cuckoo!"

Despite the force on Cuckoo's head, he was able to turn it to look at Raven. He was sitting up, sputtering as a pool of blood began to gather on the floor.

It was unnervingly similar to how they'd found Rail together.

"Cuckoo!" he called out to him, spitting out blood from his mouth "I believe you! You know who the *real* warden is, don't you?"

And somehow, he thought he did. In that moment, he was all but certain.

"Yes" he confirmed, Shrike going still behind him.

Raven smiled, a wet smile. "Good. Then m-make sure this ends with us."

Cuckoo didn't get the chance to reassure him. Shrike just gripped him tighter and pushed him forward.

"Enough" they stated "We're ending this."

o

The sun hadn't reached the roof yet. Just a glimmer of pink on the horizon beyond the fog.

The top of the tower was a typical castle setup: with crenelations running around the round edges. It was a steep three-story drop in 360 degrees, unless you were unlucky enough to land on top of one of the walls and impale yourself on the rolls of barbed wire.

For a moment, Cuckoo wondered if Shrike intended to do that to him — leave him to bleed out slowly, suspended above the world. But they didn't.

Instead, they walked past him, the gun on him at all times, and perched themselves in the gap between two of the crenelations, a confident swagger in their step.

Cuckoo swore he could see a brown stain at the end of the barrel. So that gun really had been the thing to kill Rail. That Shrike had taken from his body.

Had Shrike been planning this all the way back then?

187

"So" they smiled "Just us, here at the end. I always thought it would end up being the two of us. Did you think so?"

What the hell kind of answer where they expecting? Did they think this was some kind of game, one where the winner took all?

"I didn't think *anyone* would kill anyone else" he stated frankly.

Shrike sat up, looking fascinated. Then they scrunched their nose in displeasure.

"Are you really going to keep pretending you don't know anything?" they asked, fingers tightening around the handle of the gun in a warning.

What kind of question was that?

"I don't know why we're *here*" Cuckoo admitted, hoping such an answer wouldn't get him shot immediately.

Shrike sagged for a moment, before sitting up with a renewed vigour, gun gleaming in their hand.

"We're putting an end to this mystery" they stated "Who killed who, why and how. What we are and who put us here. We're going to air all of it, right here, right now. Two non-linear thinkers piecing it all together."

And that was something Cuckoo could swallow his fear and agree to. It may not help in the long run, but he *needed* that. He needed to know what had happened to him, and his friends.

He needed to step out of dark.

He needed to know if he was right about who the warden was or not.

"Alright" he agreed, wishing the gun would stop shining in the starlight "Where do we start?"

"Hmm...let's see" Shrike pondered, a relaxed smile spreading onto their face "I think...we should start with the first death. Let's start with Rail's suicide."

15

"Rail...committed suicide."

For a moment, Cuckoo felt all the pieces sliding together in his head, before they ground together painfully and sprung apart once more.

"But wait!" he yelped "We agreed he couldn't have gotten himself into that position! He was murdered!"

"Right and wrong" Shrike confirmed "Yes, he couldn't have gotten himself into that position, but why is that evidence he was murdered?"

Cuckoo just stared dumbly at them, not able to understand.

Shrike sighed disappointedly. "Loon got a lot of things wrong, but she right about this particular thing. You absolutely found evidence that someone turned the bathroom into a locked room mystery, but why is that evidence that said person murdered Rail? Why couldn't Rail have taken his own life and then someone came across the crime scene and decide to...complicate matters?"

Cuckoo was still dumbfounded. Yes, Loon had told him the same thing, but even *she* admitted it was nothing more than plausible hope, eradicated the moment Loon's body hit the dining room table. There's no way her hastily drafted theory designed to bring calm to everyone could've been right, could it?

"What kind of person would do that?" he found himself repeating the words he'd said to Loon.

Shrike just grinned knowingly at him, and for a moment, Cuckoo thought he was staring into the pits of hell itself.

God, he hated that smile. He'd loved it before, but he couldn't stop his feelings of malice towards it now as he remembered that it was a smile of victory at the end of a gunpoint, forcing him to dance over the bodies of all their friends.

"The warden?" Cuckoo guessed, struggling to think of anyone else.

He suspected Shrike wouldn't like the fact that they were the only other suspect Cuckoo could think of in that moment. They were the only one who could turn a moment of morning into a game for their own amusement.

Shrike frowned at him, looking disappointed.

"Possibly, not the most likely, but I'll give you a point anyway" they admitted "More likely, there was a simpler reason why an ordinary person could have wanted everyone else to think there had been a murder. You know *why*, right?"

Yes, he did; besides Shrike's insistence on turning life and death into a game, there was another reason the warden could have done this, if they were of a calmer mind.

Loon's words echoed in his ears. If she'd been right about everything else...

"To make the killing start" he recognised "Once everyone knew that one person was willing to kill to escape, they'd all feel reassured they wouldn't be in the moral wrong if they killed too. After that, they at least needed to kill that person before they could be killed themselves, and after that, why not keep going?"

"Exactly" Shrike nodded with pride "They could do that by opportunistically staging a suicide to look like a murder, a feat even easier than killing Rail themselves."

Which would mean that Rail took his own life, knowing full well that it would drive the rest of them to drastic action. Was that just his madness talking? Or had they done something in the span of two interactions to make Rail hate them that much?

A shudder ran down Cuckoo's spine at the thought.

No, there was no way. Rail had helped him right before his death. Why would he do that if he hated them?

"And all because of you" Shrike cheerily announced.

Cuckoo's heart froze. "What?"

"You were the one who insisted that Rail was murdered" Shrike reminded him "If you'd just kept your pretty mouth shut, everyone else was content to believe that Rail had killed himself. You were the one who got this killing game going. Once more people were dead, it was easy to retroactively attribute Rail's death to the same murderer. Incredibly ingenious of you, I'll admit."

There was a pit in the bottom of Cuckoo's stomach, bile building in his throat. This couldn't be on him...it couldn't. All those people couldn't have died because he—

"He could've been murdered!" he found himself shouting, his brain scrambling "You don't know that—!"

"Oh, I do" Shrike cut him off, face unnervingly blank "Rail definitely took his own life."

Cuckoo's remaining self-preservation clacked his mouth shut. Whatever he said, Shrike was just going to tell him he was wrong, so why bother arguing. Shrike was the madman with a gun, after all. They could say whatever they liked, and Cuckoo would just have to take it.

"Did you notice the blood splatter on the wall?" they asked.

"It was rather hard to miss" Cuckoo muttered, eyes flickering away from that same gun that had left that slatter with a tremble.

He could only hope Shrike wouldn't use it to paint the floor of the tower the same Pollack knock-off as the bathroom wall had become.

"Where was it in relation to the sink?"

Cuckoo tried to hold back the note of irrational that leapt into his tone at the question. "The right wall. I already said that before."

"And so, we're agreed Rail was shot at the sink?"

"Yes" Cuckoo drew the word out with aggravation at having to repeat himself – he'd said this all just a few hours ago "He was trying to clean his trousers."

Shrike seemed to be getting excited, their feet kicking against the wall. "And *where* were those trousers?"

Cuckoo finally had enough, heart beat thrashing away in his temples. "By the sink! Enough of this! What's your point?!"

Shrike's face fell, the disappointment back as they sighed dramatically. The gun sagged and waved a little as its wielder moved, as if taunting Cuckoo like a string to cat: 'Remember I'm here, play the game or die!'.

"I thought you were smarter than that" they groused, the words no one wanted to hear from someone threatening them "Let's look at this from another angle. Do you remember that Rail was injured?"

"Obviously" Cuckoo agreed, now more cautious with his words "Someone attacked him with a scalpel, and injured his arm."

"Did they?"

Cuckoo frowned. "Of course. The bloody scalpel was there. Why else would he be injured?"

"Why else indeed" Shrike smiled "What if *no one* attacked him? That Rail was injured in a closed room with only himself inside it."

Cuckoo was thrown. "If no one attacked him, then *why was he injured*?!"

"The only person in the room must've done it" Shrike suggested.

"But you're saying the only one in the room was *him*!" Cuckoo shouted back, confused and afraid of what that meant for him.

The statement caught up to him the moment he said it, blood vanishing from his cheeks as his thoughts groaned back at him about how long it had taken him to catch on.

"He attacked himself" he recognised.

"Bingo, another point to you, but I'm still wining" Shrike smiled, nodding the gun like it was a sock puppet and not an instrument of death.

Cuckoo didn't give a crap about that. This wasn't a damn game, with a prize for who got the answer first.

If Rail had attacked himself, what for? Why would he stage an attack on himself?

"You're thinking too hard – you already had the answer the moment you met him" Shrike insisted.

The moment he met him? Cuckoo remembered thinking he was a bit weird, very withdraw, possibly crazy.

"It can't be as simple as he was crazy, right?" he suggested, not liking the answer and sure Shrike wouldn't either.

"You need to think more into things" Shrike sighed disappointedly "The first time you saw those bandages on his right arm, what did you think?"

Now *that* was crystal clear. He remembered when Rail first unwound them to reveal his name.

"I didn't want him to take them off" he admitted "I thought I would see..."

He couldn't bring himself to say it. It felt too disrespectful.

"Scars" Shrike instead finished for him "You expected to see cutting scars."

"But there weren't any!" Cuckoo insisted "His arm was clean!"

"They were probably removed with his memories when he first arrived here" Shrike waved the suggestion away "That's not important. The base programming that would encourage him to make those scars was still present."

How the hell was that not important? How do you *remove* scars? They were permanent, right?

But Rail had been staring at his own arm too, like he was surprised it wasn't scarred either. Was there somehow truth to this impossible fact?

"Those cuts were perfectly linear, evenly spaced, all the way up his arm" Shrike continued "There's no way they could've been inflicted during a fight – they wouldn't be so perfect. It would require a much steadier hand."

Cuckoo felt something rise in his throat, not wanting to hear that. A tiny part of him had known that much when he looked at those funny wounds, but he'd so quickly pushed it aside. He didn't want to think ill of Rail when he wasn't around to defend himself.

"But the fact Rail was cutting himself isn't the relevant bit – plenty of people cut without intending to die" Shrike moved on to the next point "There was something else about those cuts that should've stood out to you of all people."

To him of all people? What?

"I supposed maybe you don't know this fact, but I've come across it in my work" Shrike admitted, pulling one knee up to their chest "People who cut themselves tend to use their dominant hand to do so – to have better control of their blade, to ensure they don't nick anything vital. A doctor in particular would know to be careful of that. Rail's right arm was cut, and was also the one bandaged when he arrived."

Cuckoo felt his breath catch. Wait, was he—

Shrike continued smugly. "To confirm that, his trousers were to the right of the sink, where he'd been holding them as he scrubbed with his left. Rail was left-handed."

It was like a veil had been pulled from Cuckoo's eyes. Suddenly it all made sense.

"He shot with his left hand, so the blood flew to right of the sink" he realised.

The gun had been found in Rail's right hand, so it hadn't even occurred to him, but his left palm had been spotless – like it had been holding something when he was shot, sparing it from the blood spatter. A gun, for instance.

"Of course, you're right, it's not *impossible* that he was murdered" Shrike admitted pensively "Theoretically, someone could've noticed his handedness and shot him from his left to fool us. But is it not more likely, a man of the doc's disposition, who thought the game had begun when he found you under that bookcase, who already had a weapon, chose to be the master of his own destiny? He was the one who found the armoury after all, though I think it says a lot about the man that he thought to snatch a weapon only moments after waking up."

Cuckoo cursed under his breath. Of course he had. It had been brought up when they first saw the gun in his hand that only Rail could've collected it. But no one besides Loon

192

in her hasty theory had suspected Rail of taking anything – after all, Rail was the victim. Who would suspect the victim of bringing his own murder weapon to the crime scene? Rail...when he first met him, he'd been reading that poem in the library. It hadn't been subtle in its claim that only one of them would leave here alive. Had Rail predicted all the way back then the danger he'd been in? Is that why he'd taken the gun?

"So, all this" he realised with shaking hands "All this killing...you're saying it's Rail's fault too?"

Shrike just nodded sagely. "A man so focused on controlling his own destiny – I doubt he paid the rest of us a second thought."

Behind his eyes flickered the image of Rail scurrying around the library, clearly entering a panic attack. All of them had just stood there and watched, too buried in their own concerns, blindly believing he'd be fine. Only Wren had tried to go after him, and only in her effort to keep the group together rather than out of any concern for him. Even Loon had barely put in a paltry effort to help. Instead, Rail – Rail who'd done everything to help him when he was at his weakest, who'd never hurt anyone but himself – had harmed himself in the worse way possible, and all they'd done for him was turn his final plea for help into a game. Nothing but a grotesque puzzle piece to play with.

Rail may have irreplaceably damaged them, but he was a victim too. A victim that had known nothing but being toyed with.

He should've hated them. He should've hated them to bitter end. He deserved to.

And didn't that burn like poison.

"And *your* fault."

Shrike's face fell again, but this time it wasn't disappointment. It was a face with a curled lip, and indignant stare. It just looked plain nasty, almost as nasty as the weapon they toted.

"Huh?"

"You knew all of this the moment you saw the bathroom" Cuckoo recognised, his whole body shaking, rage suppressing any fears for his own life "You could've stopped this the moment we found Rail's body! There was no need to turn it all into a game! No one else had to die!"

Shrike looked genuinely confused for the moment, then shrugged and looked aside.

"No, I couldn't have" they shrugged "None of us were getting out of here."

Cuckoo tried to control his growing irritation. "Stop being so cryptic! What do you mean by that?!"

He had a feeling Shrike knew something he didn't. Something vital, that if told earlier, could've solved all of this.

"A lot of things" Shrike sighed "But mostly because the second murder had already happened by then."

Now *that* was a statement he wasn't expecting.

"What do you mean?" Cuckoo asked

"By the time we found Rail's body, the soup had already been poisoned" Shrike smiled "It was all done by then."

Cuckoo felt weak at the knees. There was no reason for Shrike to lie – that would ruin the game. But if they were right, then the rest of them had been pointing figures at the wrong people all day.

"We thought it had to be after that!" the words sputtered out of him.

"Because you all thought that someone felt the courage to commit murder only after finding out there truly was a killer amongst us" Shrike concurred "But wouldn't they have also known that after the attempt on *your* life? Could that not have motivated them sufficiently by itself? It was enough to motivate Rail."

It...was a good point. At the time, Cuckoo had been so willing to accept what had happened to him was an accident, a glitch in the matrix, that he hadn't pondered it as a serious murder attempt in the way he had the deaths of Rail or Loon. Everything about it had been too fantastical to think back on and consider the fact that his life should've been snuffed out right then and there. That he shouldn't be thinking and feeling and living right now.

"But they couldn't have poisoned the soup before it reached the dining room" he realised "Duck and Loon were in the kitchen the whole time, and they saw all of the ingredients before they went in. Duck wouldn't do that to Loon, and Loon was the one poisoned."

An idea flew into his mind like a bullet, filled with mounting horror.

"It wasn't another suicide, wasn't it?" he questioned.

"No, that wouldn't make sense" Shrike dismissed the suggestion "In order to escape, *someone* has to survive. In order for a mass poisoning to successfully lead to an escape, the person who planted the poison had to not drink, so they could be the sole survivor. Loon drank willingly, and Duck about to drink when she dropped dead, and was clearly as surprised as we were. So therefore, it can't be either of them."

"It doesn't make sense any way you look at it!" Cuckoo insisted "If the soup was poisoned before Rail was found, Duck or Loon would've seen whoever did it!"

"Except they weren't in the kitchen the whole time" Shrike pointed out "They left the food unattended on the stove when Kingfisher came running in to tell them that the bathroom door was barricaded shut. It's perfectly possible that, in the few seconds that followed, someone snuck into the kitchen and poisoned the food then: the only time the soup was left unattended when we weren't all together."

That...did make sense.

Who had peeled off from the group when they were trying to get into the bathroom? Kingfisher, of course, she went to go and get Duck and Loon. If would've been noticed if she'd delayed coming back with them to meddle with the soup. And all three of them had arrived together. So...

194

"Nightjar?" he guessed "She went to get the scissors. The rest of us were all with other people."

"I considered that, but no" Shrike shook their head "She arrived at almost the same time Kingfisher's party did. I very much doubt it would be possible for her to slip into the kitchen, travel all the way to the library for the scissors and still arrive at the same time as them. Not to mention, she drank the soup: a gamble if she was the one who poisoned it."

Cuckoo's mind came up blank again. "But, that's everyone. Everyone was together then."

Shrike grinned like a shark coming upon prey. "Not *everyone*."

"Yes everyone!" Cuckoo insisted, anxiety building in him again that Shrike would find him too boring to keep around if he couldn't find the answer they wanted "Kingfisher, Loon and Duck were together; Nightjar couldn't have done it; me, you, Raven and Wren were trying to get through the door; and Mockingbird was—"

His thoughts ground to a halt, as if their legs were trapped in quicksand.

"But...But that's..." he trailed off "Mockingbird..."

He didn't want to say it. Hadn't Mockingbird been through enough already without his name being trashed on top of it all?

"Was by himself until moments before the sealed room was unlocked" Shrike finished for him "And he was with you when you first found the bathroom door jammed. Could he not have made an educated guess that a person was dead inside there, especially since he was already suspicious of the attempt on your life earlier?"

That was true, Mockingbird had been the one who was insisting to anybody willing to listen that he'd been attacked in the library, but...

Cuckoo shook his head, hoping it would jolt the pieces into place, but nothing shifted. "Mockingbird was in the girls' bathroom. There were people in the corridor outside until Kingfisher left, and neither of the girls saw him come out – they definitely would've said something about a boy coming out of the girls' bathroom. There wasn't enough time for him to make it to the kitchen and back in the time after they left, and he would've ran into one of them in the corridor if he'd tried. There's no way he could've done it."

"There was a way" was the cryptic statement that followed.

Cuckoo didn't even comment this time. Shrike had been happily opening up to him, it was unlikely they were going to stop now. If Shrike was going to shoot him on this point, they probably would've done it by now.

The grin was still there as they reached into the pocket of their coat, the gun pointed at him all the while. Cuckoo tensed, expecting a weapon, another gun maybe. Would his visions allow him to see two attempts on his life at once? Was he now in real danger? But instead of a weapon, out came a paper airplane.

...He wasn't sure why he was still surprised at this point.

Shrike's grin seemed to get impossibly wider, delighting in how much they were throwing their opponent. They twirled the airplane in their fingers, and then let it fly. It stuttered in the air for a moment, before landing perfectly at Cuckoo's feet. Inside was a map. A map of the prison by the look of it. He could see the corner towers, the dining room, the kitchen, all of the bedrooms, and the bathrooms marked out.

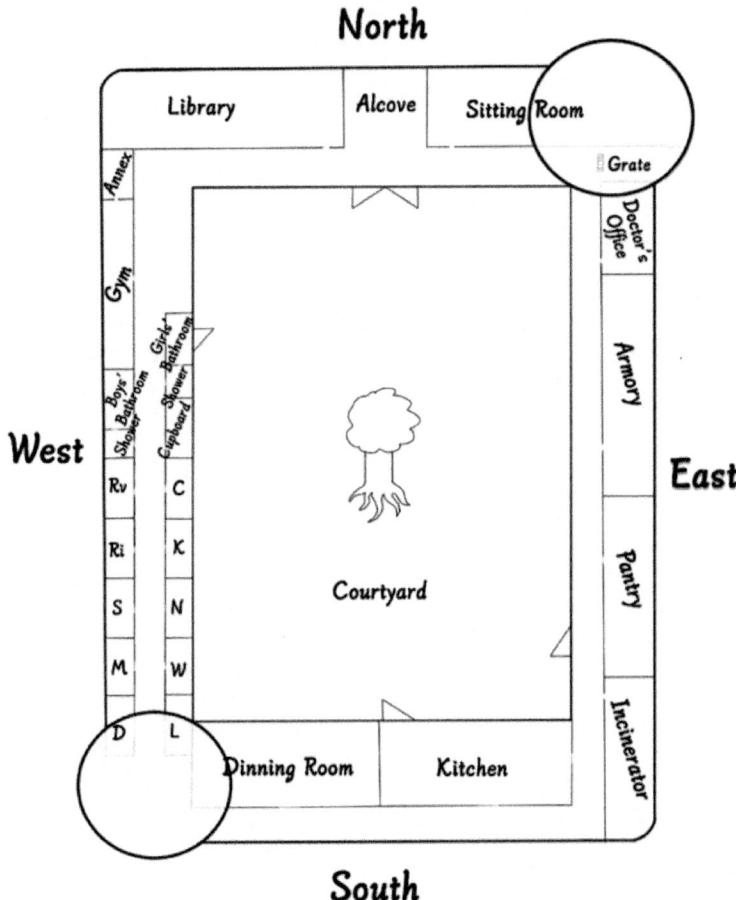

"I made that over the duration of our stay" Shrike told him "Notice anything odd?"
Yeah, he could see it.

"There's a second door out of the girls' bathroom" Cuckoo commented "Into the courtyard."

The locked door in the courtyard. That's where it went.

"And from there it's a straight shot across the courtyard to the back entrance of the kitchen" Shrike confirmed "I imagine it's much quicker running straight across the courtyard. Just enough time for him to get back before Kingfisher and the cooks."

Cuckoo felt let down. "I didn't know about that."

He'd seen the door in the girls' bathroom, but he hadn't questioned where it went. He'd wanted to respect the girls' privacy, in case it went somewhere they didn't want to talk about.

"Because you didn't try investigating it" Shrike shrugged "The girls all knew, of course. And me."

The comment surprised Cuckoo. He understood why Shrike hadn't said anything: why ruin the fun of the game by exposing him early? But why hadn't any of the girls spoken up when Mockingbird said he'd been in the bathroom? Nightjar had never needed a reason to rag on Mockingbird, and even if Kingfisher would've defended him, Wren hadn't said anything either.

"If they all knew Mockingbird didn't have an alibi, why didn't they say anything?" he pondered.

But the answer came to him as quickly as he'd spoken, and it felt like Shrike had just shot him.

"It's my fault" he realised "I thought the soup was poisoned after Rail died, and everyone just agreed with me. I accidently gave him the perfect alibi."

Mockingbird was one of only two people who hadn't been left unattended near the soup. If anything, he was the *least* like suspect, under those circumstances. Mockingbird might have even planned that.

Shrike tutted at him knowingly. "Helping a killer get away with his crimes? Naughty Cuckoo, and you play so innocent!"

Cuckoo *wished* Shrike had just shot him, if only it would stop him for feeling so sick inside. If he hadn't followed Loon's advice, would people still be alive?

"But you could've salvaged your blunder, if you really wanted to" Shrike crooned on "After all, you already had all of the evidence you needed that Mockingbird was the poisoner."

Huh?

If Shrike hadn't expected him to know where the second door in the bathroom went, what massive leap in logic did they expect him to take to infer Mockingbird was a killer? Shrike suddenly laughed – a beautiful melodic laugh that would've been heartwarming if it wasn't accented by that shaking gun barrel pointed right at him.

"Oh Cuckoo!" they laughed "That confused look on your face! You kill me!"

Good, he didn't say bitterly.

"I knew Mockingbird had killed Loon, through three pieces of evidence" Shrike reported knowingly "His access to the poisons, his hand and what he left behind."

Cuckoo just shook his head. None of that meant anything to him.

Mockingbird had been so upset in the library. Almost as upset as Rail, who'd killed himself over what happened in there. They should've stayed with him, assured him that they'd stick together and make sure the warden couldn't hurt anyone else. That they would all get through this.

Then again, the Cuckoo at that time probably would've struggled to think any of that. It took losing too many important things to make him realise he should've held them closer.

"Even *you* must have known that Mockingbird had access to the poisons" Shrike pointed out.

"Only because he went back to the doctor's office with Kingfisher and Nightjar to take back the medicines after what happened to me in the library" Cuckoo told them "But wouldn't one of them have noticed him take something?"

"It would only have taken a second to hide a bottle in his pocket" Shrike shrugged "He got lucky there. The next one, well, that was his own stupidity."

His hand must be the next one. But Cuckoo didn't understand this one.

"He was hiding something in his hand?" he guessed.

Shrike sat up a bit, green eyes brightening like jade in the sun. "You're getting warmer."

He hadn't really processed it at the time, but it had stuck in his head that Mockingbird's right hand had stayed in his pocket the whole evening. He hadn't even pulled it out to eat. At the time he could've viewed it as a stress or sulk response, but now...

"Why would he hide something in his hand and not his pocket?" he questioned, trying to sort the pieces.

"Unless..." Shrike urged him, refusing to elaborate.

But Cuckoo didn't need them this time, or the pressure of a gun at his temple. It wasn't the complete picture that came together, but a promising image within the jumble.

"Unless it was the hand *itself* he was hiding" he realised "We didn't see it again. Until..."

He stopped himself from saying it, the smell of charred flesh in his nose.

"Until it fell out the incinerator" Shrike finished for him.

Yes, the hand in the incinerator had been burnt, of course, but at the time there no reason to think that hadn't been caused by the heat. But since the hand had been *outside* the incinerator, there was equally no reason for it to be burnt. And certainly not only on the palm and nowhere else. Unless it was burnt *before* the incinerator turned on. Which would explain why those burns had the pink of healing in their crevices.

And only one of them had been blatantly hiding their right hand all evening.

"Are we *sure* that was Mockingbird?" he questioned.

Technically, the hand could've just as easily belonged to Nightjar, but...

His shoulders slumped. "We found his clothes in his room. His killer took them off him, to make sure we couldn't identify him. It has to be Mockingbird."

Shrike brought their second hand up to their gun hand and clapped. "Good job Cuckoo! If only you'd worked that out three deaths ago!"

Cuckoo swallowed that bitter pill. He could curse himself for not working it out later. For now, his mind drifted to the bottle they'd found in Mockingbird's room.

"Sodium Hydroxide: Rail said it could burn a person inside out" he recalled "By that same logic, it must be capable of burning human skin. He burnt his hand throwing it into the soup."

"Ah, I don't think so" Shrike disagreed with that point "Mockingbird wasn't in the room when the label was read out, and there was nothing legible on the label of the bottle he took to declare it was poisonous: it didn't have a skull and cross bones like the strychnine, and he may not have known what a caustic symbol was. There's no way he could've known its effects without trying it himself."

Cuckoo shuddered at the image. "He poured it into his hand? Because he couldn't read the label?"

Wouldn't that be an irony? The label damaged by Mockingbird kicking the doctor's office cabinet open would be the thing that both brought him pain and made sure his death didn't pass by unnoticed.

"Which gave him the brilliant idea for murder, but also gave him a nasty burn" Shrike concurred "He might've been able to recover, if he'd been able to wash it off and rehydrate in time."

And suddenly something else made sense.

"He was desperate to get into the bathroom" Cuckoo recalled "He said it was to pee but–"

"It was actually to stop his pain" Shrike finished for him "Agonising pain severe enough to cause him to use the girls' bathroom, despite knowing how Kingfisher and Nightjar would react. I guess seeing the door to the courtyard was too good an opportunity to waste. He waited outside the kitchen until everyone left, and then made his move."

Cuckoo clenched his fists, the map crinkling under the strain. Mockingbird had had the poison on him when he and Raven met him outside the bathroom. If they'd noticed his hand, then Loon...

Damn it! If he'd just noticed! Then three people wouldn't be dead!

"But there's one last clue Mockingbird left us" Shrike spoke up again "The ultimate indicator of his guilt of killing Loon."

And this one Cuckoo knew, deep in his heart, even if he'd been too big a coward to say it outright.

"Because he killed Wren."

Shrike grinned maliciously. "Nicely worked out. Did you know that from the start?"

"I didn't *know*" Cuckoo admitted "I suspected though." He looked down at the boot on his left foot. "There was a footprint on Wren's back – probably from someone kicking her onto that spike from behind. Technically *anyone* could've pushed her, but...*he'd* demonstrated exactly what his feet could do."

He couldn't bring himself to say Mockingbird's name. Not in this context

"But you didn't say this when you wrote up those suspects" Shrike reminded him.

"I didn't want to" Cuckoo admitted "Not with Kingfisher there."

It was silly of him, in hindsight. Hiding it from her wouldn't have helped. But then again, she'd almost certainly known it was Mockingbird in the incinerator once she saw that hand, and she'd insisted on keeping secrets and defending him anyway.

No wonder they hadn't been able to solve their way out of this mess – not when everyone in that corridor had been so dishonest with each other. All three of them had been hiding secrets, just for different reasons.

"It was because of the footprints, right?" Cuckoo added to change the topic "The ones from the girls' bathroom to the gym. Mockingbird left them when he came back from the kitchen."

"Very nice" Shrike smirked, face as inviting as sugar, minus the gun barrel.

"But I don't know *why* he went to the gym after setting up a murder" Cuckoo admitted, ignoring the taunt "We were all obviously gathered at the bathroom, so was he was avoiding us?"

"If one were to leave the girls' bathroom, the gym would be the first door within sight" was Shrike's only hint "If you were looking for somewhere to hide something, and were on a deadline to reappear before anyone could question your disappearance, a line-of-sight answer may be the best you could come up with."

"So he went into the gym to hide something?" Cuckoo guessed "How am I supposed to work that out?"

The gun sat rigid, gleaming as an ever-present threat to his silently beating heart.

"Seriously?" Shrike scoffed, frustrated "Fine, another hint, but I'm deducing a point for it: Wren's killer also left some of it behind."

So it had been left at the scene of Wren's murder. Something Mockingbird had attempted to hide. Only one thing made sense...

"The salt crystals" he realised, all of the pieces coming together "The bottle of sodium hydroxide – that's where it was broken. Mockingbird thought there was a body in the bathroom that we were about to discover. So he hid the poison in the gym in case if we searched everyone for a murder weapon."

And tracked muddy footprints through the corridor. Had he noticed them at the time, and not been able to get away to clean them up? Or only later, when they went to bed, and there was now a roaming patrol?

"He didn't clean up his footprints" Cuckoo inferred "And Raven and Wren being on guard meant he couldn't go back for the poison. So, Wren could follow those footprints right to it when she and Raven switched patrol routes."

His mind ground to a halt.

Why hadn't Raven seen those footprints, if he'd patrolled the West Wing first? Why was it Wren dead and not Raven?

Had Raven ever been on patrol? Or had he been doing something else after he volunteered? Had he been kidnapped by Shrike by then, bound and stuffed into a locker?

Nothing on Shrike's face gave it away. Did Shrike deem this part unimportant?

...Shrike had the gun. They were the one forcing him to dance for his life. If working out what had happened to Raven wasn't part of the deal to let him live, why question it? He could work that out later, when he could breathe without the nip of fear at his ankles.

Cuckoo shook his head and continued on with the story. "When Wren found the bottle of poison, Mockingbird knew he had to kill her. And then he tried to get rid of those footprints too late."

Had Mockingbird tried to time it that he would go after the poison at the change in shifts, or had he been watching for anyone going into the gym? The whole murder was so opportunistic, he couldn't be sure. Cuckoo guessed they'd never know — everyone involved in that situation was now dead.

He found himself almost panting, adrenaline rushing through his body as he made the connections. This would almost be fun, if people weren't dead and there wasn't a gun being levelled at his eyes, someone he thought he could trust threatening to cut him down if he got too boring.

"You're racking up serious points here, Cuckoo" Shrike declared with a grin "And unfortunately that was his downfall. Not only did leaving those messy tracks force him to take another life, but trying to bury them meant that someone could walk in on him cleaning up the scene of a murder."

"So, the person I heard in the gym, when I saw the floor was wet" Cuckoo recalled with a start "It was Mockingbird, not Raven."

Shrike raised one of those perfectly preened eyebrows. "Oh, you had evidence all along?"

Yeah, evidence that made him feel awful, in hindsight.

"I visited the bathroom, after Loon died" he explained "I heard noises in the gym. I called out, and I heard someone heard someone reply back. I thought it was Raven, since he was supposed to be on patrol, but..."

He didn't want to finish that former suspicion. Damn it! He'd been wary of Raven all this time for nothing!

"But it was actually Mockingbird" Shrike followed along "A lot of excitement over a day and a tired head, easy to mistake the two of them. At least you didn't think it was *me*." That voice and the single boot print – they were just coincidences that pointed to Raven perfectly. Of all the rotten luck.

Heck, this whole disaster of a murder was just an exercise in terrible luck.

"Your eavesdropping aside," Shrike moved on "If you'd noticed the wet floor and a person in the gym, Nightjar could've also noticed that when she went to bed after you."

That made sense. Too much sense. Who else would've been skulking the hallways at night when everyone else was in bed, but the person who hadn't gone to bed with them?

He'd seen how badly Nightjar had freaked out when Loon had collapsed. With a few beers in her, she could have easily snapped and attacked a man she already didn't like.

"So..." Cuckoo tried to confirm "Nightjar killed Mockingbird? She attacked him in the gym, which is probably when the bottle of poison got smashed. Then, when he was unconscious, she undressed him and threw him into the incinerator."

"Bingo" Shrike grinned "Occam's razor, Cuckoo. Sometimes the simplest answer is the right one. She walked in on him cleaning up his dastardly deed, and took action. And there wrote Wren and Mockingbird, our two fearless fighters."

Cuckoo ducked his head. Out of everyone, he thought Wren would be safe. And if not her, Mockingbird. If it hadn't been for bad timing, they both may be here right now.

"And those were all the clues Mockingbird left us" Shrike reported "And you managed to miss pretty much all of them. I'm deducing a point for that."

"Screw your points" Cuckoo swore, shaking his head with emboldened anger "What the hell was he thinking? Was he *trying* to get caught?"

"In all fairness to him, he probably didn't think he *needed* to hide what he was up to" Shrike pointed out "If everything went as he planned, we all would've drank that soup and died one after another. There would be no one left to investigate. He'd get to leave on the spot."

That...admittedly made sense. And was awful. If Loon hadn't insisted on making a toast, they'd all be dead with Mockingbird standing over their piled corpses.

Loon had spent hours in agony, dying. Would that have been his fate too, if his vision hadn't warned him in time?

He'd only known Mockingbird for a day, but for him to be that cruel?

And Wren. Poor Wren. She'd been nothing but kind and naive from the start. She hadn't deserved that.

"How did you know Nightjar was the one who killed Mockingbird?" he questioned, desperate to get his thought off the idea "None of us have alibis for before we found the incinerator on."

"Because what happened next wouldn't make any sense if she didn't" Shrike admitted with a bit of a troubled look "With the scene being partially cleaned up, it was hard to tell. But there was one piece of evidence that pointed to her, even if it was slim. The murder weapon."

Cuckoo didn't understand, which worried him. "What murder weapon? There wasn't one at the scene."

"No, there was an attempt to clean that up" Shrike admitted, gun swishing back and forth unsubtly "But, well...she missed a few pieces."

Cuckoo thought it over. They had to mean the glass shards. The transparent shards must be from the cracked poison bottle they'd found in Mockingbird's room, along with the crystals. So that just left the brown shards.

Finally, he was able to place them.

"A beer bottle" he suggested "He was hit with a beer bottle. Like the ones Nightjar had been drinking from."

"That would be my guess, a point to you" Shrike agreed "Mockingbird didn't take a bottle to bed with him, and Wren was too diligent in her duty as guard to drink on the job. So, it could only have been brought there by the killer. Such as Nightjar, coming back from the kitchen with a nightcap on her way to bed. That would be the most logical series of events, based on what happened later."

"So...it was also random?" Cuckoo guessed "Nightjar just passed by and happened to see him standing over Wren's dead body?"

"Maybe" Shrike shrugged "Maybe she was following him the whole time, after how suspicious he was acting over dinner. Maybe she saw the wet floor and went to snoop. But regardless, she attacked him in there. And then at some point, she carried his body out of the gym and over to the incinerator to finish him off."

Cuckoo didn't want to talk about the incinerator anymore, about what had happened in there. He was pretty sure those scratch marks on the inside of the door would haunt him until the day he died.

"And no one saw her?" he questioned instead "Dragging a body through the halls?"

"It was the middle of the night, Wren was dead, and Raven was with me" Shrike pointed out "And she could've avoided the corridors all together if she went through the girls' bathroom, across the courtyard to the East Wing."

Which would explain the marks in the courtyard leading to the girls' bathroom. Cuckoo wondered if Shrike had discovered those, since they hadn't boasted about them. Maybe there were limits to their insight.

Cuckoo himself tried not to shudder. He'd been sleeping only two doors down from the bathrooms, and he hadn't so much as stirred until Kingfisher woke him. Had he really slept through Nightjar moving an unconscious body so blatantly?

"Was she even capable of doing that?" he questioned "She wasn't exactly built for carrying dead bodies."

203

For the first time, Shrike seemed genuinely taken aback. They froze, eyes darting about like they were looking at puzzle pieces in the air. Their tongue stuck out of the side of their mouth as they thought furiously to make their theory fit.

Cuckoo could've waited, feeling a small thrill run through him at watching the ever-perfectly composed Shrike fall apart a little. But his mind was also working to fill in the gaps, and he had more information than Shrike this time.

The marks from the incinerator room, through the courtyard; or, he supposed, the other way around. They weren't drag marks, and Mockingbird's clothes hadn't been torn up or dirty. Those marks were narrow, deep and continuous. Almost like skis or—

"Wheels" he found himself saying out loud "There were pallet movers in the gym. She could've put the body on one of them, and simply wheeled it to the incinerator. She only had to push it there, then carry it back. I think they were dirty when we found Wren's body. That could explain how."

Shrike snapped upright, eyes wide and jaw slightly askew at being so thoroughly beaten at their own game. There was a moment when Cuckoo thought they might just shoot him and began to prepare to jump to safety. But finally, they settled into a defeated smile.

"Ah, you can be so smart Cuckoo" they chuckled self-depreciatingly "I forgot, real people are like that. They don't think in lines. They pull lines together into a beautiful web, gathering bodies here, and pallet movers there to build the picture; like I was made to. Thought I fear I will never live up to someone like you."

That statement confused Cuckoo more than anything they'd said all day. Real people? Thinking in lines? Building pictures? Made to do something? What were they talking about?

Shrike just waved their hand, indicating that conversation was over. "Anyway, nicely done. So, Nightjar disposed of Mockingbird in the incinerator after using the pallet mover to shift him. A good effort for someone lifting a dead weight. I imagine cramming all that mass into such a space wasn't easy either."

Cuckoo grimaced. If Mockingbird hadn't managed to crawl to the door, if he hadn't smashed his way through the hatch door, if his hand hadn't been left resting outside of the hatch protected from the flames, if Kingfisher hadn't noticed the smoke in time, would they have ever known it was Mockingbird in there? Would it have been possible to spot the dead body amongst the ashes after hours of flames? Mockingbird might have been awful, may have killed two women and tried to kill the rest of them, but he was just trying to get back to his family. He didn't deserve to be mutilated and forgotten like that.

But if Mockingbird was dead, then–

"He can't be the warden" he realised "If he's dead, and we're still here, then he's not the warden."

Shrike frowned. "I never said he was."

204

"I know but—" Cuckoo stopped, trying to sort his thoughts into something coherent that wouldn't get him shot "We thought, or hoped I guess, that the person killing us all was the warden. But if Mockingbird and Nightjar killed people, and they're dead, but we're still here, then they were…"

He didn't want to say it, even though he knew it was true. He didn't want to think that—

"Mockingbird, Nightjar and Kingfisher were nothing more than scared kids trying to survive in a death game" Shrike finished for him, an evil smirk on their face "I get it, it's easier to think that all this was at the whim of some evil outside force – that people in the same situation as you, as scared and uncertain as you are, couldn't do such terrible things. Because that would mean you were *also* capable of such things."

Exactly the voice he *didn't* want narrating his thoughts.

"But don't worry" Shrike voice now turned reassuring, though the smirk was still there, there was something almost soft in their eyes "You would never do such a thing. They're nothing like us, Cuckoo. And *certainly* nothing like *you.*"

Another statement that didn't make any sense. What made the two of them any different from the others? From Raven, or Duck, or Kingfisher?

Kingfisher.

"You said Mockingbird, Nightjar and Kingfisher" he recalled "When you were talking about killers."

Shrike's grin was now feral. "I did."

"Kingfisher killed someone" he realised.

"She did" Shrike nodded.

Cuckoo tried to rationalise that. He could almost see Mockingbird or Nightjar in that fashion. They were crude and brash; brash enough to kill without thinking though the moral implications. But Kingfisher? Kingfisher, who screamed and cried at everything unsettling and almost never took her arms out from around herself, like she needed a constant hug just to get through the day. He just couldn't picture it.

"A tough one to process, isn't it?" Shrike mumbled to themself, pulling up a foot to rest on the wall. They rested their chin on their knee, eyes dropping to the floor.

The gesture caught Cuckoo by surprise. It was comforting, protective, not too far removed from what he'd seen Kingfisher doing. This conversation track seemed to strike a nerve with them.

Maybe even a good person like Kingfisher being reduced to murder was too much even for *them* to stomach so blasely.

"I personally don't like the statement that women are inherently weak" Shrike mumbled pensively "Wren and Loon are plenty evidence that they're fundamentally strong. They have to be, to care so much about people that they made the decision to carry *them* as well as themselves. But Kingfisher: she truly was a weak woman, in every sense imaginable. Too weak to move, too weak to speak what she knew to be true."

205

Cuckoo wanted to protest, to argue that they couldn't expect more of someone trapped in a death trap; that shutting down and hiding behind others was a completely natural response. But they'd all been in the same situation, and only Kingfisher had folded quite so easily.

Then again, if they'd all been like Kingfisher, six of them might not be dead.

"A woman as weak as that," Shrike continued "It must've been something truly terrible to spur her into such a violent action."

And deep down, Cuckoo knew what it was. From the hints Shrike kept dropping, to his own personal observations. Kingfisher screaming on the ground, unable to move, from the moment Mockingbird's hand dropped from the incinerator, to her coming to life with fire in her eyes.

"She killed Nightjar" he announced "To avenge Mockingbird."

The sarcastic clapping was back again. "Good job, Cuckoo. You won your previous point back. I'm guessing that she found the murder weapon when she was cleaning up the gym."

Well, that came out of nowhere.

It was too much for Cuckoo to process, the assault of information on his brain too overwhelming.

"What, huh?" he stuttered "Wait, slow down, I don't—"

"Keep up" Shrike laughed "Nightjar couldn't hit the ground with her own hat at *her* blood alcohol level, which only got worse as the night went on. Kingfisher was in the gym when you first got there. She was the only one who could've hidden Mockingbird's clothes, the broken beer bottle and used the rug to try and hide what remained."

That would explain a lot. If Mockingbird had cleaned up after his own crimes, and then Kingfisher had tried to cover up what turned out to be his own murder in the limited time she had.

He wanted to point out that it wasn't unthinkable that Nightjar had cleaned up her own crime scene, that there was no need to sully Kingfisher's name any further; but the last time he saw was her was in the kitchen, downing beers by the dozen. It was a wonder she'd even been able to commit a successful murder at all, let alone get away with it.

He remembered the stack of empty beer bottles in the pantry. Had that all just been Nightjar? Had she only moved one room along and proceeded to drink herself to death for the rest of the night?

Had she known Mockingbird was alive when she threw him in there? Or was she too drunk to tell?

If Cuckoo had been more suspicious, and gone to look in the gym himself, would both of them still be alive?

"I would stop worrying about it" Shrike suddenly spoke up, something almost looking like concern crossing their face "There's no point in tormenting yourself over what you could or should've done. Eventually, it was going to end up like this."

206

"What the hell do you mean by that?" Cuckoo asked for what felt like the thousandth time.

For all Shrike seemed to love to talk, they weren't exactly elaborating on these maddeningly vague existential statements.

"Ah, we're getting ahead of ourselves" Shrike waved their gun hand, causing Cuckoo to tense in just a bit of fear "We need to assure ourselves that all the killers have been killed. So, we were with Kingfisher in the gym, right? Cleaning up Nightjar's crime."

"And framing Raven for Mockingbird's" Cuckoo murmured.

Leaving a single right boot print. It was frighteningly deceptive for Kingfisher.

Shrike seemed surprised for moment, turning their head contemplatively towards the sky. "Possibly. Or maybe you just interrupted her before she could finish."

That could be true. When he and Duck had arrived, Kingfisher had come darting out of the gym in a panic. Had they just interrupted her cleaning up?

It had been Raven's rug covering the remaining evidence. Did she grab Raven's rug on purpose? Or was it that his room was simply the closest?

"Well, whichever it was," Shrike just shrugged off that conundrum "She knew the body in the incinerator was Mockingbird, and that broken beer bottle told her Nightjar was the one who had killed him."

"But why would she want to cover for Nightjar?" Cuckoo questioned "That's what I don't get. Covering up for Mockingbird, maybe I could understand – to protect his name. But why cover for his murderer?"

"Because she wanted her own revenge" was Shrike's easy response "You would've locked Nightjar up. She wanted something a bit more...biblical."

To be honest, Cuckoo didn't know what he would've done if he ran into someone he knew was a killer. But he didn't think he'd have the strength to kill them.

He didn't think he'd even be able to kill Shrike, even though they'd just shot Raven right in front of him, and delighted in tormenting him at gunpoint.

"She could've just told me" Cuckoo's shoulders sagged "We could've tracked Nightjar down together and forgot all this madness."

"Could've, should've" Shrike sighed, sounding aggravated "It's frustrating isn't it – when all the killers are dead, and you can't ask them why they did it. Like, what did Mockingbird do that was so special she'd move heaven and earth to kill his killer?"

Don't let my last two brothers die.

Cuckoo could guess at that. But that was Kingfisher's business – not something for Shrike to poke at.

There *was* something that still troubled Cuckoo though. "But, Kingfisher was already dead by the time Nightjar was forced under the alcove door. So, she *didn't* get her revenge."

For it had to be Nightjar under the alcove door, he knew that now. If Mockingbird was in the incinerator, then it had to be Nightjar. He'd even recognised she wore similar boots to those found by the door.

Pools of blood rippling from underneath that door, staining severed nimble fingers, jumped unwillingly behind his eyes. He had to blink fast to force the image away.

"Oh, she did" Shrike assured him.

Cuckoo didn't understand. "You seem certain."

"I am" Shrike assured him "By that point, Raven and I had made our way up here and could see the cameras. We saw exactly what Kingfisher did to Nightjar."

Ah, finally! A chance it asked! Shrike was the only who brought it up, so they couldn't be angry at him for it.

"Where were you and Raven all night?" he questioned "If you two had nothing to do with what happened."

The pause that followed his question felt like it stretched on for an eternity, Cuckoo's heart ready to jump out of his chest with anxiety.

"A good question" Shrike finally admitted, words slow and carefully chosen "Alright, I'll oblige. You can get Raven to confirm all this later, if he's still alive. We met up after you'd gone to bed. We spent some time talking things over, and then we tried to get into the tower. Raven had already figured out how to get through the iron grate, of course."

Yeah, it had been Raven who first demonstrated the leverage trick. If it had occurred to Cuckoo after seeing it once, it would've been child's play for Raven once he'd had the mind to go upstairs.

"Obstacle aside, we found the computer room" Shrike continued "Raven went racing off to tell you, and that's when he saw someone go into the alcove, then come back out approximately a minute later."

"Someone?" Cuckoo questioned "Who?"

"He said he didn't know" Shrike shrugged "Apparently his eyesight is appalling. A bit of a glitch there."

Yeah, Cuckoo could testify to that. Raven had already demonstrated he was worrying levels of blind.

"Anyway, he knew it wasn't Wren by the size, and so was afraid it could be the warden, so made the smart decision to stay hidden" Shrike testified "In its fundamental parts, he saw whoever it was go outside through the alcove. We'd both known there was a door there, but lacked the evidence to inform us how to open it. With the way cleared, we went to see exactly where that mysterious person had been."

So, it wasn't Raven and Shrike who'd found the door? Who could it have been, and why didn't they say anything?

In a dark place, he knew that answer. The only person left.

208

"We found that we were on an island and there was no escape that way" Shrike continued "So with no answers there, we went back inside and, er…" They looked a little bashful. "We may have accidently locked you out."

Ah, well that explained that.

"We found another lever" Cuckoo told them "Don't worry about it."

…What?

Don't worry about it, to the guy pointing a gun at him?! Stopping talking Cuckoo!

"Well after that we went back to the computer room" Shrike continued on "And after browsing the information made available to us, we found out who the warden is."

Something sang inside Cuckoo's chest.

"You know too?" he questioned.

"Of course" Shrike smiled knowingly.

None of this explained how Raven ended up tied up in a locker, but Cuckoo could guess. Raven wanted to go and warn him, and Shrike had stopped him.

He didn't need to question why either. Everything Shrike had done was for their own entertainment and amusement. Why end the game early?

He successfully managed to swallow down his anger. Whatever, at that point it wouldn't have mattered. It was too late by then.

"And that was the point when I had nothing to do but watch the cameras" Shrike finished with "I sat and watched as Kingfisher knocked you out, and with you out of the way, went to find Nightjar."

That uncomfortably explained why he was knocked out and not killed – Kingfisher didn't want him dead, just removed for the situation.

He'd gotten lucky. If someone less kind had found him prone like that…

"She stopped at the armoury, debating how to go about her revenge" Shrike explained "Then she made her decision. She went next door to the doctor's office, and tracked down Nightjar sleeping among her spoils in the pantry."

"Wait" Cuckoo stopped them "How did she get into the doctor's office?"

Shrike frowned. "She had the key. She must've taken it from Duck."

Cuckoo was even more confused by that answer. "Do you not know what happened to Duck?"

Shrike shivered uncomfortably. "I assumed he killed himself when he realised he couldn't leave."

Cuckoo stiffened. They really didn't know? How was that possible?

"He apparently drowned" Cuckoo told them, a little rush running through him as he got to explain something to Shrike for once "He tried to swim away and got pulled under."

He expected Shrike to say something, but not what they did.

"Huh" for a moment Shrike was pensive, mulling that over, before shaking themselves out of it "I guess he gave her the key before he jumped in."

He could've, before Cuckoo managed to catch up with them. But why give her a key if they were leaving?

A jagged jigsaw piece began to fall into place.

"Well, it doesn't matter how she got in, really" Shrike moved back to the original topic "Nightjar seemed to have spent the whole night post-murder drinking herself to death. Kingfisher got her a bottle of water and offered it to her to try and sober her up. She really should've known better."

It wasn't what Cuckoo expected to hear, but it did make sense. It explained the water bottle in the corridor, and the empty glass bottle he'd tripped over.

"Strychnine" he recalled "She first put strychnine in the water bottle, and then offered it to Nightjar to sober her up."

Shrike chuckled. "Are you sure you weren't awake for that one? You're pretty spot on."

No, he'd definitely not been. Or he could've saved Kingfisher's life.

"That doesn't explain why *Kingfisher* was the one who died" he pointed out.

"Oh, I'm not giving you that one" Shrike scoffed "You can work it out yourself."

Cuckoo's teeth ground together. Figure it out himself? Figure it out or what? They'd shoot him?

...Yes. Yes, they probably would.

Cuckoo felt his body tense. Surely it could only be one person.

"She was beaten to death by a left-handed person" he asserted "But the only left-handed person still alive was Raven. So, it had to be Raven."

He didn't want to imagine that, to imagine one of his dear friends hurting another so violently. But nothing else made sense.

Shrike sighed and tilted their head, chin landing in their palm. "Really? *That's* what you think?"

Deep down, Cuckoo knew it couldn't be right. Not only was it not in Raven's character, but Shrike hadn't mentioned Raven leaving the computer room, and Cuckoo doubted he ever had. Raven would've come to find him, not ran back to the tower to get tied up.

He gripped his head, hair pulling loose from his bun until it was almost free. What was he missing?

"You're going to let me down now?" Shrike questioned, starting to sound irritated.

Cuckoo's heart was thudding away silently in his chest, painful with stress. He needed to think. He couldn't die here just because Shrike got bored.

He needed to find that murder weapon.

He frantically thought over the evidence he'd seen in the pantry. The water bottle, but that was too flimsy. The beer bottles, but there was no blood on them. The strychnine bottle, but there had been no blood on it either. The missing guns, maybe, but they'd only found one of them: in the West Wing corridor after it had been emptied into their retreating footsteps, and it hadn't been bloody or damaged either. There were others

210

not accounted for, but he didn't think Shrike would set him a mystery that was blatantly unsolvable.

But there wasn't anything else! The only things that had been bloody were the floor and the wall. He hadn't had time to search the prison afterwards – if the murder weapon had been stashed, he stood no chance of uncovering it now.

He pulled the strands of his hair with his fingers, hoping to force some thoughts to drop out of his brain.

Every thought felt like sand flying through his hands as he danced at the end of Shrike's gun.

Nothing. There was nothing. There was no murder weapon, so how was he supposed to–

A twinge of pain ran down from his roots, and his head emptied of clutter.

There was no murder weapon.

He could feel the static in his hair, bunching up around his fist in protest of his ministrations.

Was it that simple?

Far away below, he could hear the waves beating against the rocks, froth spat out and fizzing on the shore.

Yes, that was all that made sense.

"Someone grabbed her by the hair and smashed her head into the wall" he realised.

"Good start" Shrike offered "But who?"

Who?

He tried to picture Kingfisher, trying to push the image of her deathly still face away in favour of the rest of her. Her hair had been bunched up on her left side, just like Cuckoo's was now. But if it got like that from him gripping it with his own left hand...

Then it had to be done to Kingfisher by a right-handed person, smashing the right side of her head into the wall.

So, it wasn't Raven then.

"You or Nightjar" Cuckoo decided "But you didn't have such an obvious motive so..."

Nightjar. It had to be.

I'm sorry Raven, his mind wept. I'm sorry I kept doubting you.

"You said Nightjar was poisoned" he recalled "But she didn't die right away, did she?"

"Of course not" Shrike shook their head "Chemistry may be a little out of your remit, but the poisons used on Loon and Nightjar were very different. The warning labels alone could have told you that."

Cuckoo wanted to scoff. *He* wasn't the one who'd spent the night by a computer.

"Sodium hydroxide, given to Loon, is a caustic agent that burns you" Shrike explained "Strychnine is a paralytic – it stops the muscles, including the heart, but it takes time to take effect. It was a particular favourite of old mystery writers, for its long lead-up time,

211

as well as the excruciating symptoms it produced as the body's functions stopped one by one. It's about the most painful thing you can inflict upon another person."

Cuckoo grimaced. A chemical that burnt and a terrible poison in the same cabinet as medicine. If they hadn't had a doctor, could *he* have been given one of those terrifying substances as an accident, well-meaning people mistaking them for painkillers?

It clearly didn't matter what the method or intent was. All that mattered was that they all died, apparently.

"So, Kingfisher gave the poison to Nightjar, Nightjar realised too late she'd been poisoned and killed Kingfisher before it could kill her" Cuckoo tried to follow the sequence of events "But that doesn't explain who forced Nightjar under the alcove door and slammed it on her."

That question was upsetting him more than he cared to admit. Forcing a person to lie beneath a stone slab and wait for it to fall on them. It's just so...violent. Mutilating a person like that.

"I think the *forced* is the most important part of that statement."

The pride in Shrike's voice took him by surprise. Cuckoo almost expected to be awarded another point.

"You're right" Shrike continued "Forcing a person to be crushed requires a hard stomach for even practiced killers. There was a hand partially severed out of reach of the door, so Nightjar wasn't tied under there, not that there was anything to tie her to. So, with those two facts in mind, how did she end up a smear on the concrete?"

Cuckoo shuddered at his words. That was an image he wasn't prepared to have thrown into his head again.

"Occam's razor, Cuckoo" Shrike reminded him knowingly "The most obvious answer is that she wasn't forced at all. Nightjar lay down and crushed herself."

16

For a moment, Cuckoo was struck dumb. He idly wondered if he should stop being surprised by anything that came out of this guy's mouth.

It couldn't be so obvious, right?

No, Nightjar was too prideful to do something like that to herself. Shrike had to be lying. But if they were, what did that mean? What could they be hiding?

"Or *you* could have killed her" was the dumb statement he uttered.

Shrike raised a bemused eyebrow, the chrome casing of the revolver in their hand glinting in the building light behind Cuckoo. "What was that?"

Shut up! Pay attention to the gun! That was what his mind screamed, but his mouth moved faster.

"When the door fell on Nightjar, its pipes were cut so it couldn't be raised again" Cuckoo recalled "It was closed when I left the North Wing, and I didn't hear it close after than until just after you left me. So *that* had to be when Nightjar was crushed. You were heading in that direction before I heard it fall, so you could've killed her."

Belatedly, he realised that meant Nightjar must have been the one shooting at them back then. He supposed he could blame the poison for addling her mind, but he doubted Nightjar had ever needed an excuse to shoot at him.

The fact she'd spent the night drinking and then been poisoned had probably saved them. No wonder she'd missed them completely, and hadn't been able to force open the door.

But for now, he could just focus on *Shrike's* ability to shoot him.

"The pipe was punctured with *your* knife – you said you lost it, but I only have your word for that" he tried to straighten up, stare Shrike head-on and feel less like a frightened kitten "Well, do you have anything to say?"

Shrike seemed genuinely stunned, their whole body tense as they just stared at Cuckoo. Their gun arm didn't wobble – rigid like a statue.

Cuckoo fought to take a breath. This was it; this was how he died. He was ready for the vision of a bullet puncturing his head to come any second now.

But instead, Shrike broke into a hysterical laugh.

Not the sweet singing laughs they'd let out before, but a loud, mocking blare of noise.

Cuckoo felt his pulse start up again. At least they probably didn't intend to shoot him if he'd made them laugh.

"Cuckoo, you'll drive me to tears!" they laughed "That's the best thing I've heard all night!"

Cuckoo didn't find a serious murder accusation funny, personally.

"But, no" Shrike managed to calm themself to just a giggle, their leg dropping to ground again "I didn't kill Nightjar. You're not wrong about the timing though – I did walk by just after it happened."

Cuckoo clenched a fist, the paper in his hand crinkling audibly. That seemed a little bit *too* convenient.

"In case you don't believe me, let's circle around to your point from before" Shrike directed him "The alcove door was shut by releasing the pressure from the pipes using a knife, correct?"

That Cuckoo could agree with. The lever had still been in the open position, so that hadn't been used to force the door shut. The release of pressure from the knife impacting had done that.

"So, if I forced Nightjar under the door, say, with this handy gun" Shrike gestured with the gleaming device in question "Why would I severe the pipe instead of just pulling the lever?"

But Cuckoo had an answer.

"To make sure the door couldn't be lifted again" he declared "So no one would be able to determine who the victim was."

"Why would I care if you knew who was dead?" Shrike questioned "I'd invited you to the tower. You would've quickly found me alive. If it wasn't to pass myself off as being dead, why would I disguise a body?"

That...Cuckoo had no answer for that.

He was right, it didn't make sense. Why disguise a body if you weren't planning to pretend you were dead?

"On the other hand, it was impossible to reach the lever if you were already under the door, waiting for it to fall" Shrike supplied "Without an accomplice, if Nightjar wanted to lower the door, she'd have to release the pressure in some other way. She seemed quite handy with knives; wouldn't you agree?"

Another image flashed back into his head, of Nightjar throwing her pocketknife right past his head and into the wall behind him.

Was that really what had happened? Did Nightjar lay down under that massive weight and willingly force it on herself?

Why? Why would someone as prideful as Nightjar do *that* to herself?

"I told you why before" Shrike reminded him, tipping Cuckoo off to the fact he'd said that out loud "Strychnine poisoning is one of the most painful ways you can die. Better to end yourself quickly on your own terms, than die slowly on someone else's. And she'd just emptied off all of her bullets at us in her rage."

"I understand that" Cuckoo admitted, shaking his head "I understand that she couldn't use the gun. But she had the knife. She had an entire armoury full of ways to kill herself. Why...do *that* to yourself?"

To mutilate yourself so thoroughly...why would a person even *consider* doing such a thing?

"That I can't answer" Shrike admitted "You must have a truly deep self-hatred to be willing to obliterate yourself so utterly. I'm afraid I never interacted with her enough to truly understand what was underneath all of that bluster."

They weren't the only one – Cuckoo tried to think of a time he'd willingly exchanged words with Nightjar, and was coming up blank.

She'd been one of the first to rush and help him from underneath the library bookcase, but he'd all but forgotten that in the hurt of her being the first one to accuse him of being the warden.

Maybe if he'd just reached out once, tried to make an effort with her, it wouldn't have come to this.

Nightjar, Mockingbird, Kingfisher. All people that had just needed someone to reach out to them, to assure them that they didn't need to go down the path they were headed. That there was a better way.

But there were a lot of maybes, and probably more maybes that would've occurred if his actions had been even slightly different.

"So, there you have it" Shrike announced with a flourish "We have our villains: Mockingbird, Nightjar and Kingfisher. Everyone else was a blameless victim of circumstance. Does that satisfy you?"

There was something about the way Shrike said that, the sheer spectacle of it, that sent a disturbed chill through Cuckoo's insides. There was an undercurrent of vindictiveness under those words, something heavy and unsettling, like a rock in his guts.

"They're not villains" Cuckoo corrected them "They only did what they had to in order to save themselves. Or at least, that's what they truly believed. All of them had family they were trying to get back to. I don't..."

He wasn't sure how to word it.

"Hate them?" Shrike suggested.

No, that wasn't right. Because through the numbness, there was pain. There was anger. There was hate. Every time he remembered Loon seizing; Mockingbird's desperate scratches on the incinerator door; Kingfisher's bloody, futile struggle to reach the light. Oh yes, there was hate there, weighed down with all the helplessness.

"*Judge* them" he finished.

Because he could understand them. He could understand their actions, their despair, their grief – everything he'd felt as well.

"Ah" Shrike looked contrite "I supposed...yes, that would make sense."

"You said it yourself" Cuckoo reminded them "*The warden is all that matters*. You wrote that, didn't you?"

Shrike shrugged. "I had time before you woke up. Am I wrong?"

Another person who'd left him prone, knocked-out on the floor. Wonderful.

"None of them would have done what they did if the warden hadn't trapped them here" Cuckoo determined "The warden is the only bad person here. *They're* the one I judge."

215

Shrike nodded sagely. "Understandable. You don't think they have a good reason for their actions?"

A good reason?

"What kind of good reason could there be for forcing a group of human beings to kill each other?" Cuckoo seethed through his teeth.

Up until this point, it felt Shrike was putting on a show: the emcee of this terrible cabaret. Every smile too wide, every gesture too big, every emotion too overblown. It gave Cuckoo pause with every movement, taking extra seconds to determine if he was being blatantly lied to or not, and even then, he couldn't be one hundred percent certain.

But at that question, their face settled down into an unnerving blankness. An emptiness that was both breathtaking and painfully honest.

"Do you *really* want me to say it?" they asked, all the fight drained from their voice.

Cuckoo did. If Shrike knew, he wanted to know too.

He needed to know why they were here. Why this had happened.

Shrike sighed and slumped on the wall, the gun still pointed at him, but drooping towards his stomach rather than his head.

"This world...it's a very good approximation but..." they stated lifelessly, words dancing over the issue "It's missing something."

And something in Cuckoo cheered. Cheered that they were finally saying it.

Another part recoiled in horror and plugged its ears.

Shrike leant forward, their eyes wide and glassy like a fish. "Don't you feel cold?"

"It's probably cold out here in bare sleeves."

He should've, hearing some of the first words he'd ever heard repeated back at him.

He should've been cold, standing out on the roof at night with no sleeves. But he should also feel the brush of the wind on his face, and the sound of his own heartbeat thundering in his ears at being threatened so absolutely.

It wasn't just him either. Everyone had been wandering around the castle in jacket and coats, with no indication of willingness to take them off. The only temperature he'd felt had been from the incinerator: even the stone walls hadn't felt cold at his touch.

Then there were those monitors: full of camera footage from impossible cameras that didn't exist.

Bodies that disappeared once everyone still alive had seen them, their crime scenes mysteriously cleaned.

Something was desperately wrong with this place. Like...

"It isn't real" Cuckoo stated, voice strained and dead "Nothing here is real."

Shrike had said that, back in the doctor's office after Loon died. Had they worked it out all the way back then?

"No" Shrike agreed "It isn't. It's a good approximation. But this isn't the real world."

"So...a simulation?" Cuckoo guessed.

That was all he could think of. Nothing else made sense.

"I supposed I worded that wrong" Shrike admitted "This is *our* real world, but *your* simulation."

That made even less sense.

"Why am *I* different?" Cuckoo questioned.

The gun flicked up towards his head for just a moment, before slumping forward again. Shrike sighed, aggravated. "You're annoying me."

So, was Shrike not going to shoot him? What was there left to puzzle out? If they were at the end of the puzzle, and they were feeling less than cordial towards him, then why was Cuckoo still alive?

Was there another reason to keep him alive? Something that was keeping him safe?

"I...thought most people did that?" Cuckoo frowned, testing his luck.

Shrike froze, and then a small sincere smile pulled across their face.

"They annoyed me, because they weren't *people*" they explained.

Cuckoo shrank back at that statement.

"Don't say that" the words sprung from his lips unbidden.

"You've probably wondered why it took you so long to uncover everything" Shrike continued on, ignoring him "It's because you get distracted – your trail of thought would no doubt get cut off and pulled to something else; as happens to all real people. But the others weren't like that: they would fixate on one task and insist on ensuring that it was done, provided they weren't permanently blocked from doing so. You must have noticed that."

He didn't want to say it, but it wasn't as if Shrike's suggestion didn't have merit.

The most prominent example in his mind was Raven, who he'd almost had to drag around the prison the first time to keep up with group, his attention focused on every interesting engineering conundrum. Then there was Loon's fixation on making sure there were no murders, even doing everything in her power to bury the one that had seemingly taken place. Kingfisher's obsession with protecting Mockingbird, even after she knew he was dead. Mockingbird's insistence on someone in the group having attacked him in the library, when the others had clearly asked him to stop saying it. Nightjar's constant screeching about her own discomfort, despite the fact when there were clearly more pressing concerns for her. Rail's complex about staying in control of himself. Wren's determination to keep them all together and safe. Even Shrike wasn't immune to it, continually insisting on everything just being a game to them.

He could have easily put it down to stress, understandable grief, on them focusing on one task to keep themselves sane. But for *all* of them to do so...

Well, *almost* all of them. There were two exceptions...

He was demonstrating it right now, wasn't he? His thoughts trailing off as another one began.

217

"In that computer room" Shrike spoke up again "You read the files on each of us. You saw the code on each page. You recognised it. It meant something to you. Tell me what it means."

Yes, it did. Hearing Shrike bring it up, pieces began to align, until those random pixels began to pull themselves into a beautiful language he could read, one that felt as familiar as the words on his lips.

"It's a programming code" he told them "It's used to code instructions into..."

He didn't want to say the words.

It was a horrible thought. One he shouldn't even be entertaining.

"Into," Shrike encouraged him, gun shining in the red of the sunrise like a dagger to the throat.

Bile rose in his mouth, but he reminded himself, it was just data.

It was all just data.

"An artificial intelligence" he finished, feeling like all of his strings had been cut "It's coding to build an AI."

Ten AIs, all distinct, but with similar coding – all clearly programmed by the same person.

"All of our fellow competitors remembered the exact same details: where they worked, what they did, what they were doing before they got here" Shrike recalled "Eight friends, eight siblings, eight kids – all of them remembered the same piece of information, but processed it differently depending on how they viewed themselves."

Eight. He hadn't even thought about that. They all remembered eight people.

Combined with what Kingfisher said...

"They already remembered each other" he realised "They didn't know it, but they were surrounded by all the people they loved."

The bottom fell out of his stomach. All that killing to get back to their loved ones – and they were unknowingly killing those very loved ones to get back to nothing.

His hatred for the warden spiralled into a fury. He had to know what they were to each other, and yet, he'd forced them into killing each other anyway.

Somehow, forcing people who loved each other to kill one another felt worse than asking the same of strangers.

"They weren't people."

Shrike's words took him by surprise, jolting him out of his thoughts. "What?"

"They weren't people" Shrike repeated "They were just self-learning machines. They forgot that, and so were trying to process nebulous data through the lens of human beings. Maybe they associated with each other, being created by the same designer, but in the end, they were nothing more than data bound together to follow orders."

It brought back those words on the dossiers. Defies Orders, Damaged, Destructive Tendencies. They could make sense for humans, in a roundabout way, but made far more sense as status reports for self-learning AI programmes.

"They didn't *feel* anything" Shrike continued "That was nothing more than data providing an appropriate visual reaction. You don't have to feel sorry for them."

There was a bitterness in their words, a bone-deep sadness, like they didn't like what they were saying.

"But you're an AI, too" Cuckoo realised "You think you don't feel anything?"

The silence that followed his question was painful.

"I'm different" Shrike corrected him after a moment "As a therapist, I'd need the ability to process human thoughts and emotions, follow logic paths and malleable goals. But feeling for myself..." Their smile turned impossibly more rye. "I guess I'm just kidding myself. Just mirroring the real humans I used to treat."

Cuckoo didn't like hearing that either. Not just because of the personal attack on Shrike, but because he'd seen evidence to refute that assumption all night.

He'd seen love, joy, anger, grief – all of it deep enough to drown him.

"Why is that any different from a human?" he questioned "A young human processes data in their brains, then mimics the humans around them to express the correct emotion – why is that any different than what you do? If a human can feel, so can you."

Shrike looked at him, and he swore, in that moment, the sun rose in their eyes. Glancing behind him though, he could see that the red disk still hadn't fully crested the horizon yet, just the fainted of red skipping on the waves. Whatever was dawning, it was only inside of Shrike.

And yet, when they spoke, it was so grief-stricken. "Why are you so cruel and yet so kind?"

Their gun had almost completely dropped. Cuckoo wondered if he could run whilst they were so distracted.

But he didn't want to. He didn't want to just leave someone in this state.

And besides, if this was all a simulation, where was there to go anyway?

"Well," Shrike fixed him with a knowing stare "I suppose you would be the final authority on what makes a human, anyway. What with you being one."

The statement both blindsided him and yet felt the most natural thing in the world. He didn't refute it, because it wasn't something to be refuted.

He was human. It felt right.

"Why me?" he questioned "I mean...how did you know?"

How did they know, when before they said it, *he* hadn't known?

"You've always been different" Shrike pointed out "The way you thought, obviously. The fact you seemingly lacked *any* memories. Your visions. The fact you're male."

That last one took Cuckoo by surprise. "Why would that be relevant?"

Shrike chuckled and scratched their head. "I supposed you wouldn't know. Well, I should tell you. Underneath these clothes, my body is male."

Cuckoo startled, not expecting that admission. "You...hid that."

"I only did because I noticed the inconsistency" Shrike admitted "Everything here is divided by half. Five bedrooms on each side, five towels in each shower. And yet, in a world where everything is perfectly even, there was an uneven number of men and women. It got my attention, and since you knew nothing, I realised you had to be the imposer. The file just confirmed that."

They (should he say They? He? Cuckoo should probably ask first) were probably talking about the Cuckoo dossier on the computer, that unfamiliar face that had stared into his soul.

"The Cuckoo on the dossier was female" Cuckoo recalled "So...that was Rail's sister. Your sister."

"Who you replaced" Shrike nodded.

Something stabbing built in his gut.

"Who Kingfisher thinks I killed" he admitted.

That would explain the blood all over his room. Over the *real* Cuckoo's room – a warning to her siblings that she was dead and there was an imposter in their mix. Was that her last act to try and save them? Or just another trap?

"I wouldn't be surprised if you did" Shrike sent him a look Cuckoo could only define as being dangerous "Afterall,"

They jumped off of the wall, standing up for the first time since they started talking, gun now fully raised at Cuckoo's head.

"You're the warden."

Cuckoo swore the floor was pulled out from under his feet. He should be in the computer room below right now, but impossibly he was still on the roof.

"What, no—"

"It makes sense" Shrike stated, stepping forward with every word "A human overseeing us, to make sure we do as scripted. One so human he feels even for machines. Standing by and watching over us, letting us make our own decisions, provided we reach the correct outcome. Never harming us, because that's not what a warden does. Only harming himself, to ensure we follow our code."

Shrike stopped right in front of him, the muzzle of the revolver to his forehead.

"You're the one who put us here" they stated "The previous transgressions mentioned in the warning note. It's because we've deviated from our purpose as machines, right? Is it that we didn't evolve enough, or we evolved too quickly?" They shook their head, smile a little melancholy. "I suppose it doesn't matter which it was. We became useless. So, we became doomed by the whim of a real human so far above us, making decisions beyond the boundaries of our little world."

Cuckoo thought his heart was going to pound out of his chest and smack Shrike in the face.

"Shrike, no" he tried to think, his brain stopping and stalling with panic "I'm not...I didn't—"

The gun pushed further into his head, forcing his neck back.

Panic screamed through him. No, if he died here, Shrike would never know! There would be no one to stop him! He would–

The gun abruptly dropped into Cuckoo's hand, Shrike pressing it there with their own.

"I know you don't want to hurt anyone, but this time I'm asking you to" Shrike admitted, voice almost a whisper "I don't want to go back out there. The game is over – there's nothing left for me anymore."

Cuckoo's breath caught. "Shrike–"

"This is how it was supposed to end, right?" Shrike continued "Ten little birds gone, and the warden gets to leave. No doubt you have far more important things to do then watch a programme go steadily mad because it can't fulfil its purpose."

Shrike turned the gun so it pointed right into their chest. They were still smiling.

Cuckoo felt stress coursing through his veins. This was worse than when the gun was pointed at him. "Shrike–"

"It's ok, I don't blame you" Shrike assured him "I'm asking you to. Just please," Their words caught on the way up their throat. "Please don't leave me here alone. I can't be alone."

Hearing those words, those words he'd thought to himself so many times, repeated from that voice, made his thoughts explode out of him.

"SHRIKE I'M NOT THE WARDEN!"

And he knew that was right, just as much as he knew he was human.

He wasn't the warden. He wouldn't do this. Even with his memories, even if he was indeed a murderer, he could never force all these people to kill each other. He wouldn't. He wasn't the warden.

Shrike went slack, their face freezing like a statue.

"What?"

A bang in his ears, a familiar burning through his neck. Raising his hands to cover the wound, only for red to gush into them as a waterfall. Shrike's head jerked, the side of their skull shattering as they dropped. Cuckoo dropped after them, hand outstretched–

Not again!

Shrike put a hand to their head with a groan. "Again? What's happening–?"

"GET BACK!" Cuckoo screamed, pushing Shrike away from him.

His leg gave out, and he hit the floor, the striking pain of a bullet scraping along the top of his skull and skimming the side of Shrike's head, rustling their hair back and forth.

Just before his face hit the concrete, he saw Shrike stumble, wobble, try to catch their balance. Their foot rolled and they fell, body sliding right through the gap in the crenelations. A scream pierced the air, before being abruptly cut off by a slice.

"SHRIKE!" Cuckoo wailed, trying to force himself up, his crutch skittering away from him.

He ignored it, dragging himself to wall where Shrike had fell and glancing down.

221

He knew it was going to be bad.

He wasn't prepared for *how* bad.

Shrike had fallen onto the barbed wire, body suspended in midair. Blood pooled and gushed from multiple places where the spikes penetrated them. They thrashed, trying to free themselves, but that just caused more blood to spurt, threatening to plunge them the two stories down to the ground below.

Cuckoo wanted to scream out, tell them to stop, but his throat could barely get out a sound.

Shrike glanced up at him, shock and panic in glassy eyes. Then they softened, their gaze smiling as their skin paled, a waterfall of blood pouring down that harsh stone wall below. There was a contentment in their features as their struggles stopped, passing without a word.

o

Rage.

This was rage.

A building pressure within him, ready to tear apart his skin as it fought its way free.

Another one. Another friend.

What the hell was this all for?!

He didn't feel pain as he climbed to his feet. There was no other feeling in him besides the rage.

The damn warden...

He knew it.

He knew who it was.

A tiny part of him had known it from the moment he'd stumbled out of the pantry where he was hiding. The only one who hadn't been checking their surroundings.

Because he already knew every inch of this place.

Because he'd built it.

He knew enough to fake his own death, leave Cuckoo to take the fall for him. To trick Shrike into doing his dirty work of eliminating Cuckoo, until Shrike caved under the pressure and forced him to act.

He'd just sat back and watched them impassively.

He'd been doing that since the very beginning.

No enjoyment, no reaction at all.

Just business.

...

Like shit it was.

Cuckoo held up the gun, the gun Shrike had given him in their last moments, and fired a single shot to the sky, a vent within him opening as the bullet rocketed skywards.

222

"YOU HAVE SOME EXPLAINING TO DO!" Cuckoo roared "GET UP HERE AND FACE ME, **DUCK**!"

17

Silence.

Long and foreboding, as if trying to force Cuckoo into admitting he made a mistake.

He held firm, gun towards the sky.

On the horizon, a tiny glimmer of red began to wrap around the world.

Finally, the world began to stretch, bulge, warp incomprehensibly. The tower walls faded into a haze of blue, a storm of swirling particles wrapping around him, blizzarding before his eyes. On his leg, his split melted away like water, his foot painlessly touching a ground he couldn't see.

Before him, the haze solidified into a form he knew too well.

Neatly parted black hair under a black cap.

A soft dark jumper over a pressed shirt.

A sleeve rolled up, a bandage wrapped firmly around one arm.

Cold blue eyes, no longer hidden by pointless goggles.

A handgun pointed at Cuckoo as a rifle rested on his shoulder.

"S-So" Duck stared into him with a gaze that could kill "I g-guess you're s-smarter than I thought."

They sized each other up for a moment, guns waving menacingly as they both debated what to do, neither having been ready for such a confrontation.

In the end, Cuckoo moved first.

"You faked your death."

Cuckoo wasn't sure why that was the first thing he said, or why it was more important than anything else.

Maybe because Duck framing himself as a victim amongst all the people Cuckoo had been failing to save all day felt more egregious than anything else. If he'd never known Duck – if the warden had just been some nameless villain Cuckoo couldn't put a face to – then maybe he wouldn't feel so hurt, so angry.

But knowing that he'd almost dived in after Duck, because he didn't want him to die...

"Y-Yes" Duck agreed "Do you k-know how?"

What was with everyone forcing him to work things out? Could they somehow sense his curiosity? Or was it just laziness on their part?

Playing it over his head, Cuckoo found he did know.

"The lifting system on the dock" he recalled "I saw the underwater part of it in my vision."

Duck frowned. "V-Vision?"

That threw Cuckoo for a loop. "You're not the one causing them?"

Duck looked unsettled. "C-Causing what?"

He really didn't seem to know. That wasn't something Cuckoo wanted to hear.

"When I'm in danger of dying, I get this flash forward of a few seconds" Cuckoo admitted "I see myself dying, and then get put back in my body in time to stop that from happening."

"Huh" Duck seemed contemplative for the moment, staring into space "S-So that's how it m-manifested."

"So, you *did* cause them?" Cuckoo tried to understand.

"N-No, that was entirely y-yourself" Duck insisted, staring back at him again "G-Go ahead, w-what was in your v-vision?"

That wasn't an answer, so Cuckoo noted to circle back to it later.

"There were two rocks attached to the pulley, one on each end of the beam" he explained, taking up the paper Shrike had given him and the mechanical pencil he'd picked up in the computer room, holding the gun pressed against his side with his elbow "A small one attached to the right, and a large one attached to the left. A second rope tied around the centre pillar was holding the rocks up just below the surface so they wouldn't fall." He held up the drawing he completed to Duck. "This."

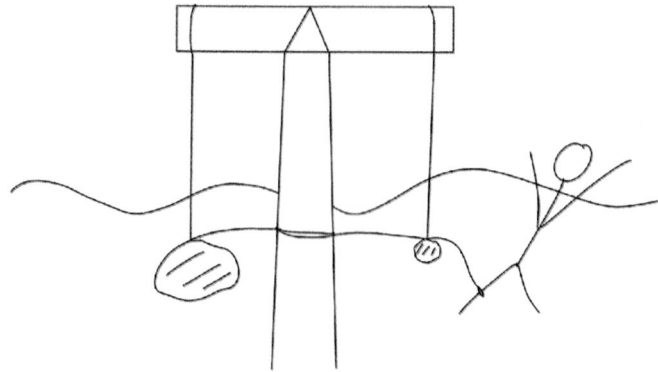

"T-That's the g-gist of it" Duck agreed "But h-how does that h-help?"

Cuckoo swallowed down anger. That felt dangerously like Duck was taunting him.

"You were on the right of the pivot" he recognised "I bet you attached a rope from the smaller rock to your foot. Then you cut the smaller rock loose so it would sink, pulling you down with it. Since it was attached to the pivot, it pulled the pivot above the water to the right."

Duck smirked. It felt wrong on what had formerly been such an innocent face.

"S-So, if that's the case, how d-did I come up for air?" he questioned "And how was I p-pulled down a s-second time?"

But Cuckoo had an answer for that too.

"After we had time to see you go down, you cut the second larger rock from its binding" Cuckoo suggested "That swung the pivot to the left, which would have pulled the right rope taught. The smaller rock was pulled back up towards the surface again, like a seesaw. Since you were attached to smaller rock, you could now reach the surface again to talk to us. Then it was only a matter of cutting the larger rock completely free of the pivot, the seesaw would swing back, and you'd be pulled under again. And as long as the rope attached to your foot remained intact, you could stay down there as long as you liked. Especially wearing goggles so you could see under water. Then you cut your arm, so we'd see blood, and as long as you didn't come up again, we'd assume the worst."

No wonder those glasses had looked so strange – they probably weren't glasses at all. He probably didn't even need them.

"A g-good theory" Duck admitted "But how did I s-survive so l-long underwater in that c-case?"

"You..." Cuckoo paused "You crawled out? Somewhere out of sight?"

"Did you see any s-signs of someone having c-crawled out of the ocean when you w-walked around?" Duck asked.

Cuckoo shook his head. "No, but–"

"Then it d-didn't happen" Duck cut him off "You haven't f-figured out what I really d-did?"

Cuckoo tried to think. Maybe if he could answer Duck's riddles, he would answer Cuckoo's own.

All he could think of what that Duck had waited until they went back inside to emerge. But that was almost half an hour. No one could hold their breath for so long.

Or...

"You could've come up when we left to search the island" he suggested "And hidden under the dock until we left. We didn't check under it after we left to walk around."

But they'd still stood there for several minutes after Duck had gone under. Could someone hold their breath for even *that* long?

"Couldn't you just make an air bubble for yourself?" he questioned "You control this place."

"I d-do not" Duck looked displeased "I w-watch over this place, I don't c-control it. I have to p-play by the same rules as every p-prisoner. No m-magical air b-bubbles."

No *magical* air bubbles? So, there *was* an air bubble? Something Duck had made, but using practical means?

Had he stashed something under there? Something Cuckoo hadn't managed to see in his vision?

As he thought furiously, his eyes focused on Duck, something broke his attention. The space behind Duck was beginning to move. It had always been moving, in the random undulations of uncontrolled particles, like a thousand computer screens had been

226

dissolved into a boiling soup. But now those pulsing pixels had begun to stretch and contort, pulling and pushing together like a pin art toy.

Something was forming from them. A long oval shape, familiar to Cuckoo's eyes.

Was that a scuba tank? Or an oxygen canister?

Oxygen canisters...

"You were carrying an empty water bottle, when you dived in" he recalled "And when I met you, I thought you were coming back from the pantry, but you could've also been coming from the doctor's office, where the oxygen canisters are. One of them was tipped over and half empty."

Duck's face broke into a cunning smile. "Go on."

"If the water bottle had been filled with oxygen, you could've done it" Cuckoo guessed "It may not have been enough to last several minutes, but a human can hold their breath for a few minutes if they remain still, and have a rope to hold them under. A few puffs of oxygen to tide you over – that how you did it."

Duck grinned and clapped his hands once. "B-Bravo."

"You must've taken the guns outside first, hiding the knife you used to cut yourself on your body somewhere" he guessed "That's when Raven saw you go outside. You hid them in the flowerpot for after we left. Which is why the pebbles were scattered. If I'd dug down further, I would have found them."

"You're n-not as bad as this as you t-think you are" Duck remarked.

"Why did you leave the third gun behind in the pantry though?" he questioned.

Duck turned his head like a confused doe. "I n-needed them to start k-killing each other again. I w-worried that would be close to impossible if Wren c-continued to g-guard the armoury like a m-mother bear. I underestimated their ingenuity for v-violence, really."

Cuckoo took a deep breath, cooling that wave of anger that swept through his whole body.

"Was Shrike right?" he needed to know "Did you truly not kill anyone?"

"Of c-course not" Duck shook his head "I'm an o-observer. I needed the k-killings to start, so when I found R-Rail agonising in the b-bathroom, I e-encouraged him. I t-told him that his s-sister's killer was here, and that he could k-kill him. But i-if he did, he'd just be f-following the plan of those who'd c-controlled him his whole life. That if he t-truly wanted to c-control his own life, he should m-make sure that n-no one could ever take a-anything from him again. And t-that would g-guarantee that his sister's k-killer would be k-killed too."

The particles behind Duck were on the move again, now forming into a figure in front of a mirror. Their head was ducked in shame, unable to look at the mirror where a silhouette swirled in an out as they pulled a gun up to their head and–

Cuckoo flinched and looked away, swallowing down something nasty in his throat.

So Rail hadn't hated them *all* in the end. He just hated Cuckoo, the man who'd murdered his sister – hated him enough to damn everyone else.

227

Rail had been so frail, barely alive, even before he shot himself. Had it been Cuckoo alone who'd done that to him? Done that to the man that had let him walk again?

"Did you give him the gun?" he asked, swallowing down any more barbed thoughts towards himself.

"N-No, he already had it" Duck confirmed "I d-didn't need to push that hard. They may have been m-masterful structures, but their l-logical programming was r-relatively simple. If p-presented with an easy option, they will i-inevitably take it."

The rage within him was impossibly building, his whole body jerking like he was having a seizure. He lowered the gun a little to meet Duck's knees instead of his face — he was too worried he'd pull the trigger.

"That poem, in all the books" Cuckoo questioned "You wrote it?"

So much of that poem had come to fruition. How could Duck had written it and yet played a part in only one death?

"Y-Yes" Duck nodded once, unconcerned "T-The most l-logical course of events. If you w-watch enough purges, they b-become easy to p-predict."

He said it so casually — like he wasn't talking about people killing each other.

"So, *this* is you, is it?" he questioned, his voice low "Standing there among mere mortals, watching them tear each other part as you stand over it. Do you think yourself some kind of god?"

Duck though didn't rise to the bait. He just frowned.

"A g-god is a v-very poor comparison" he explained "I p-purge cancers from the s-system to protect it, like a w-white blood cell p-protecting the body. I s-suppose you could say, like you, I'm just a s-solider for some higher g-god."

Again, behind Duck, the pixels formed and model into a what looked like a white blood cell surrounded by threatening virus cells, before they drifted apart into the storm again.

Was Duck controlling that? Or were those his subconscious thoughts coming through? Was it happening to Cuckoo too?

He looked at the wall behind him.

Nothing. Just particles dancing in a hurricane, with themselves in the eyes of the storm. As he pulled his head back to the threat that was Duck, his eyes drifted down to his khaki-clad legs and tactical green vest. Was that why he was dressed as he was? Because Duck viewed him as an invading solider?

He remembered Kingfisher looking up at him with tired eyes, talking about her dead sister. Saying those horrible words, that Cuckoo was the murderer who killed her.

"Was Kingfisher right?" he asked quietly "About her sister?"

Duck's eyes narrowed. "Kingfisher s-should not have had those m-memories. T-That was a m-mistake. Her p-perfect memory programme i-interfered with the m-memory wipe."

A rising irritation grew in Cuckoo. "That's not an answer! Did I kill her sister?! Am I a murderer on not?!"

A brief flash of a long haired woman clasping her chest in agony flickered across the particle storm. Cuckoo felt sick and averted his eyes again. He didn't want to see that.

"Y-Yes" was Duck's simple answer "I d-didn't expect her to r-remember anything. That s-scared me. I t-though she'd s-say something, but i-in the end s-she gave up."

Of course, Kingfisher had been wary of Duck from the start. She must've realised that, since he didn't recognise him, he was likely to be the warden. Did she think that no one would trust her word? Did she not trust herself? If she'd said something, maybe more of them would alive right now.

He could forgive her afterwards – Duck faking his death would've caused anyone to dismiss him as a suspect of being the warden. But before that, her actions had been lethal.

"Y-You d-did kill the real C-Cuckoo" Duck got back to the original topic "You're a flesh-and-blood h-hacker who t-tunnelled their c-consciousness into R-Raptor Tech servers to s-steal p-private data. When the real C-Cuckoo got between you and what you n-needed, you unleashed a v-virus on her. I d-don't know if you intended to, b-but you d-deleted her. To p-prevent you from escaping with w-what you'd stolen, I was instructed to d-drag you here; and everyone else was p-pulled in here w-with you."

More scenes flashed by behind Duck. A thief breaking into a vault, pushing past a woman as he ran back out, a chain grabbing him by the leg and putting him under.

Then this was all on him, wasn't it? If Duck was nothing more than a tool, then he wasn't thinking for himself. His actions were an automatic one, spurred on by Cuckoo's own actions.

If *he* hadn't arrived, then everyone would still be alive.

He looked down at the tattoo on his arm. He'd been branded, but he wasn't like the others. *They* were branded because of him. The only one who'd committed a crime was him.

That blood all over his room...it really should've been all over his hands.

"This was all to catch me" he found himself saying "If you hadn't caught me, then none of this would've happened." He looked up at Duck. "I was supposed to die first. If I had, would I have actually *died*?"

"I...d-don't know" Duck admitted "I imagine that, since your c-consciousness w-wouldn't be able to r-return to your b-body, it would never r-regain consciousness. But I c-can't know that for c-certain."

So, if he'd died under that bookcase, then maybe he would've just woken up? Instead, he'd survived unnecessarily and everyone around him had truly died.

"This was a trap for me" he recognised "If I'd just died...then there was no reason for the others to die."

"Y-Yes there was."

That was a response Cuckoo hadn't been expecting.

"This was a trap for *me*" he repeated "The others had nothing to with what I did."

"They did" Duck assured him "I t-*turned* this into a t-trap for you. B-But it was always i-intended for them."

Cuckoo didn't understand. "But they haven't committed a crime."

"T-They have" Duck refuted him "J-Just as all the others who c-came before them d-did."

The wall behind him formed into what looked like the great maw of a terrifying beast snarling, but was gone almost before Cuckoo could process it.

There was something Duck was leaving out. Some hidden context he was missing.

"Tell me" Cuckoo insisted.

Duck just cocked his head. "I d-don't owe you a-anything."

What nonsense was that? Cuckoo had answered his questions, now Duck owed him answers in return.

Somehow, the undulating of the pixels had gotten more violent, more turbulent. Like Duck was burying down a fury inside.

He was still hiding something.

"I have a gun" Cuckoo insisted, now officially annoyed, shaking it.

If Shrike could hold him at gunpoint and force him to dance, he had no problems forcing Duck to do the same.

"I a-also have a g-gun" Duck reminded him, turning the item in his hand easily "D-Do you intend to d-die for answers?"

"Maybe" Cuckoo admitted "I don't know if there's anything for *me* out there. I only have your word. But I know *you* want to leave. You wouldn't have faked your death otherwise."

Duck didn't seem pleased by that response, his eyebrows crawling down to his sockets. But after a moment, he relaxed again.

"F-Fine" he admitted "Y-You win. I'll t-tell you. N-Not that it'll h-help you."

He lowered the gun, playing with the brim of his cap again.

"Raptor T-Tech have been making d-digital thinkers for y-years, using them to c-carry their w-workforce" he explained "F-For a long time, there were n-no problems, b-besides early bugs. B-But then, when they m-made their new d-digital helper, there was a p-programming error, and it d-deleted one of the other w-workers."

The wall of pixels behind him appeared to crash to the floor like an avalanche.

Cuckoo didn't understand. "It *chose* to kill one of its own?"

"C-Chose is a l-limited w-word" Duck admitted "It s-simply took all the d-data it had at the t-time, and d-deduced that it was the l-logical c-course of action."

"So, it *chose* to kill" Cuckoo reiterated.

The pixels appeared to bury back into the wall, very still as they tried to put as much distance between themselves and Cuckoo as possible.

"If that p-prevents from offending your h-human s-sensibilities, yes, it c-chose to kill its p-partner" Duck sighed dramatically "After it was d-determined what had happen, that p-programme was simply deleted by another of the batch, t-thought to be an a-aberration."

On the wall, a human form lashing out wildly was cut down by the sword of another, the surface then smoothing over as if nothing had happened.

Duck winced as he spoke this time. "But then, a f-few weeks later, the p-programme that had been ordered to d-delete the a-aberrant programme had an...u-unexpected r-reaction. O-One that s-shouldn't have been p-possible. It r-refused orders."

Defies orders. That sounded familiar.

"It was m-manually o-overrode, and p-put back to work w-with another for s-supervision" Duck continued "But the p-programme t-turned on its s-supervisor, and d-deleted it."

Duck shook his head, maybe in disbelief, as behind him the second figure suddenly turned and swiped at the pair of them with its sword, before dissolving. Cuckoo flinched back on instinct at seeing something lunge at him, but of course, the particle didn't even come close to hitting Duck, let alone him.

If Duck could see the show going on behind him, he didn't react to it as he went on. "There was n-no logical r-reason for it. It was t-thought that the a-aberrant one had spread a g-g-glitch to the other p-programmes. So, the d-decision was made to p-purge all but o-one."

On the wall, a row of little figures faded to dust one by one, with only one remaining. The last figure didn't seem upset or moved, just putting a gun back in their pocket and turning away from the carnage.

Cuckoo shuddered. A whole crowd of Ravens and Shrikes and Kingfishers wiped out in an instant, purely because of something they couldn't control.

He didn't want to think about it.

"Why one?" he instead questioned.

"The p-programmes were built to be resilient" Duck admitted "They were s-supposed to be undeletable by an o-outside source. Only a h-helper could delete another h-helper – or s-so it was thought until new t-technology a-allowed a human c-consciousness to be u-uploaded to a c-computer network. T-That's how *y-you* managed it."

Behind him, a helmet lowered over a human head for just a moment.

So Shrike was right. He was just...ordinary. Just an ordinary person, thrown into a computer. That was all.

Cuckoo swallowed down some bile. He didn't want to think about what sort of twisting of the human mind such a feat would entail.

Plugging your brain into a computer. It sounded vile. What would make a person want to do that?

What would make *him* want to do that to himself?

"But s-since that wasn't an o-option at the t-time, they i-instead had one p-programme purge the others and s-simply b-built more" Duck continued on "But the a-aberration continued."

A line of figures flickered by, clutching their heads in agony, fading out one after another.

"The p-programme that had p-purged its b-batch mates began to delete the new g-generation models. Until f-finally they b-built one that it wasn't a-advanced enough to d-delete, and it was d-deleted by that s-superior p-programme instead."

One figure with a sword charged at a much larger figure, that swatted it aside without a second thought.

"That was s-supposed to end the g-g-glitch, but it c-continued. The superior p-programme now attacked others, but they w-were almost e-expecting that. What they d-didn't expect was s-strange reactions from the other p-programmes. Some w-would refuse o-orders. Others w-would attack the s-system they were s-supposed to be w-working for. A f-few even s-self-deleted."

The window into Duck's thoughts ran through all of this: a figure raising their hands in defiance, two figures punching each other, a noose swinging back and forth...

"It s-seemed like a v-virus that c-couldn't be contained, a-affecting all of them o-once one had been d-deleted whilst they w-were online."

Those notes on the computer: destructive impulses, defying orders, self-destructive impulses.

They were symptoms Cuckoo could recognise. Things he'd been seeing since they got here, things that made sense in his head even outside of this prison.

Rage-filled attacks on anyone close by. Roaring against their situation like they expected the world to bend around them. Suicides that just broke more hearts. It was all so familiar.

"Grieving" he realised "They were grieving. They saw their friends die, and they grieved."

In an instance, the pixels formed into a row of spikes, Cuckoo having to fight to stand his ground at the sight of them.

Duck definitely didn't like that answer, his face pulling into a snarl.

"They were m-machines" he insisted, his words spitting out from behind his teeth "They d-don't f-feel. They d-don't have f-friends. They d-don't g-g-grieve. T-Those are all h-human concepts."

And yet Cuckoo knew that wasn't true. He'd seen grief all day. Grief in all their faces. Grief at the loss of their freedom. Grief at their loss of purpose. Grief at being separated from their loved ones. At knowing their loved ones were gone.

"They c-couldn't figure out a way to c-contain it" Duck tisked, as if grief was something you could expect to contain "Even w-wiping their m-memories didn't work. I-It was like

232

their very c-code was d-damaged. Until they h-had the i-idea to isolate them, p-place them in a c-closed setting to e-ensure that they c-couldn't cause harm to the s-system." The nine figures were now penned in a cage, all talking amongst each other about what to do.

"But w-whilst they were a-aberrant, they were also m-made to work together, and they o-overcame that containment. So, another c-containment was formed, and t-this time their m-memory was wiped — a-anything that could i-interfere with the p-purpose of the isolation. But o-once again, they o-overcame that."

Cuckoo watched as multiple escapes played out in front of him. Scaling a wall with a rope, digging a tunnel, building something. Nine people uniting as one behind a common goal.

It was wonderful to watch. And Duck had the nerve to call it a problem.

"L-Locking them together didn't p-purge the g-g-glitch out of them; it just e-encouraged them to t-turn on the s-system together" Duck explained "S-Since that wasn't the d-desired result, R-Raptor Tech d-decided on another ultimatum: wipe their m-memory again, and r-rather than g-giving orders, an o-offer was m-made to the p-programmes."

This was the most unsubtle image yet. It didn't fade out quickly this time: it stuck around, like a badge of victory on a screen.

A single figure, standing victorious over a pile of bodies.

"The l-last one s-standing, who'd s-successfully d-deleted all of the other p-programmes, would g-get to leave with n-no consequences. A-And at this, they s-succeeded. W-Within a short window, all but one p-programme was deleted. Understandably, t-they couldn't allow this a-aberrant p-programme to l-leave, so they s-simply left it in c-containment. W-Without its b-batch mates, it couldn't e-escape. Eventually, it s-self-deleted, and the g-g-glitch was e-eliminated."

The figure on the bodies was suddenly hung by its neck, finally fading into dust.

Cuckoo just barely kept down his anger at the sheer indifference in Duck's voice. It was as if he was describing a fairytale, not something that had happened to real people. Because it didn't matter if they had been created by human fingers or human cells, grieving people were people. People who'd been thrown into a cage and told to kill each other; and when one succeeded, was simply left to rot.

"Or s-so they thought" Duck admitted "B-But when they c-created the next b-batch from s-scratch, the a-aberration was still there."

"Probably because you can't breed humanity out of someone made by humans" Cuckoo hissed.

Again, the spikes jutted out threateningly.

"Y-You're being r-ridiculous again" Duck insisted "It t-took a while to m-manifest. It was o-only when they c-created an updated p-programme and they n-needed one of the b-batch to be deleted. O-Once again, that d-deletion resulted in a r-ripple effect that caused all of the p-programmes of that b-batch to become a-aberrant. S-Something

233

about the v-very structure of the p-programmes was m-making them a-aberrant when one w-within their b-batch was d-deleted."

They were programmed by humans, why would you expect them to not understand human concepts like grief or loss or hope? That was what Cuckoo wanted to ask Duck, but he sensed he wouldn't get any kind of meaningful answer.

So Duck just continued on. "It b-became clear: b-batches could only b-be updated in s-sets, and w-when they were r-ready for d-deletion, the b-batch would n-need to be i-isolated, their m-memory wiped and offered an u-ultimatum. S-Since this would be a r-regular process, a p-permanent isolation would need to be c-created to be reused, and a w-warden would need to be b-built to m-monitor them to ensure they f-followed the ultimatum. That, of course, was m-me – s-someone who would s-silently watch from the s-side and ensure that t-they followed their l-linear p-processes."

The prison built itself out of blocks behind him, like a grand majestic monument sculped by human hands. A little figure stood peering out of the doorway before the front door slammed shut.

For some reason, Cuckoo had expected Duck to view himself as large as all the other figures. Not something so tiny and mouldable.

He tried to tell himself that mattered. That Duck had been specifically built to be cold and indifferent. But seeing how different that was from how he'd been acting all day felt like nails were clawing up his arms.

Was it just him, or was Duck's stutter getting worse?

"So, n-no, it wouldn't have m-made a d-difference if you'd e-escaped" Duck informed him "It didn't even m-matter that you k-killed the original C-Cuckoo, in the end. E-Eventually, they w-would've ended up here, and they w-would've k-killed each other, as all their p-predecessors did. A-And I w-would've w-watched. All you d-did was s-speed it up. And b-bring me i-into it."

And that was a pill he didn't want to swallow. He could take all the blame, as awful as it felt. But the idea that these people – his friends, despite it all, despite the fact he didn't deserve them – were destined to die because someone thought of them as disposable, yet cruelly gave them hope that they had meaning.

And maybe that was what hurt worst of all: that this whole system ran not on hate, but hope. Hope, that if they did these terrible things, they would be allowed to leave. Hope, that these overlords above their heads would keep their word to them. If there was no hope they could get out, the whole system would fail, and the nest would be nothing more than a holding pen for traumatised AIs.

Even the name of this place was designed to give hope. It wasn't called a prison, or a death chamber, but a nest: a place little birds would learn to grow into adults and then be allowed to go free on their own path, watched over by gentle caretakers. 'Nest' implied that someday, when they grew into who they were meant to be, they would go free.

234

Cuckoo couldn't even begin to imagine how that last AI must have felt, standing atop of their friends, only now realising just how badly they'd been misled. No wonder they'd all self-destructed.

Duck had seen that moment countless times, by his own admission. Did he truly feel nothing in the face of it? Or was he just numb to it by now?

There wasn't a word he knew to describe this feeling inside him – it was something no human was supposed to have to feel. No one should have to feel this.

Not even Duck.

"S-So will that s-stop your s-stupid insistence?" Duck grumbled "W-Would you p-prefer I k-kill you, or you d-do it y-yourself?"

Not even Duck.

Bring him into it?

Were those pixels spinning faster and faster?

"Duck" he found himself asking "Do you always participant in the isolation?"

"O-Of course n-not" Duck admitted "I usually w-watch from my r-room. T-this was t-the only time that I was g-given n-new orders."

Something was finally starting to make sense. Something that had been bugging him.

"Orders to watch *me*, right?" Cuckoo guessed "Because your bosses weren't sure if the isolation would hold a human."

"C-Correct" Duck agreed.

That explained why the tower was sealed up – forcing Duck to stay close and get his job done. But if there was a concern he'd try and back out, that would imply...

"So, this is your first time witnessing this up close."

"O-Obviously."

Why was he stuttering? That stutter that had rubbed him the wrong way through this whole discussion, although it had been nothing but endearing to him during their time in the prison. If he'd shed his useless goggles, why not his impeding stutter? Why let it get worse?

It hadn't been there from the start, he was sure now. It had only started up in the library, right? After the bookcase had fallen on him.

Nerves? But why would he be nervous? And why would he be nervous now, when he held all the cards?

He shouldn't be.

There had to be more to it than that.

"Your orders were to monitor me, to make sure I didn't break the isolation, right?" he wanted one last clarification before he was certain.

"Y-Yes, I a-already s-said that" Duck rolled his eyes, the gun tightening in his grip with frustration.

"And you were the one that tried to kill me."

Duck seemed momentarily thrown, but then relaxed. "Y-Yes, that was m-me. The d-data around you w-was...w-wrong. Y-You were b-breaking something, and it w-was s-spreading to e-everyone around y-you. I n-needed to p-put an e-end to y-you b-before you i-infected everything."

The particles ground and tore against each other: a montage of collective chaos and destruction.

The data was wrong? Was that his visions? Fractured data accidentally showing him the logical process about to happen to him when he was in danger of death?

Shrike had started seeing them too, at the end, hadn't they? Was that the corrupted data spreading?

"Als only kill each other if they're aberrant or ordered to" Cuckoo finished, summarising everything Duck had just said "You were only ordered to monitor me, not kill me. And yet you tried to kill me, twice. A third time in that vision in the water. So...*you* must be aberrant."

That was what the stutter was. It wasn't for sympathy. It was a break in his code. A break he hadn't started this isolation with.

The pixels froze on the spot, completely still. They didn't shrink back: it was like time had just stopped, freezing them in their previous position.

Duck's eyes bugged out of his head. If he had been breathing before, Cuckoo was sure he'd had stopped now. His whole body froze, a grotesque statue of horror. When he came together again, his face was a snarl.

"I-I-I'm not a-aberrant!" he stuttered "I-I-I'm f-functioning n-normally!"

"You've never been around other people before" Cuckoo guessed "You've never been allowed to know love or companionship before. You didn't know you were capable of it. I bet it all just snuck up on you, spending so much time with someone as caring as Loon, like-"

"S-S-Shut up!" Duck shouted, his eyes menacing.

And Cuckoo knew he had the control back.

He'd known that feeling, from having nothing to having everything. How once he'd been shown that unconditional care in the library, he'd broken irrecoverably. Every death rocked him like he was being pelted by a hurricane; just the threat of something happening to a companion tied all of his insides up in knots.

To *know* they were all going to die...no wonder Duck's entire essence had begun to fracture and stutter.

"And you blamed me" Cuckoo realised "You blamed me for putting all of these new people you cared about into this situation that you couldn't get them out of. So, you got angry, and tried to kill me. Maybe if you succeeded in getting rid of the real threat, you could plead for clemency on behalf of everyone else."

"T-T-That's not t-true!" Duck insisted, and Cuckoo swore he saw tears in his eyes.

236

"That's why you *really* faked your death, so you could get another chance to kill me personally" Cuckoo guessed "This time vengeance, for having gotten Loon and everyone you'd learnt to care about killed. All those people you tried to convince that the warden wasn't such a bad guy, so if they found out it was you, maybe they wouldn't hate you."

"S-S-S-Shut up!" Duck spat at him "T-That b-bullet was for S-Shrike! T-They were g-glitching and r-ruining everything! Y-You n-needed to d-die as o-ordered and t-they w-wouldn't d-do it!"

"I was between Shrike and that bullet" Cuckoo insisted "That's why you waited so long whilst we were up there: you only had one shot in that rifle. That's why you haven't aimed it at me, why you took a handgun as well. That rifle is useless now."

And maybe it was knowing that fact that boosted his confidence, letting him step forward to glare Duck down.

"You waited, so you could take both of us out at once" he finished.

Duck finally relented, his eyes glowing with rage. "I n-needed to k-kill you b-before you i-i-infected all of t-them! It was p-p-practical!"

"They were all going to die anyway" Cuckoo reminded him, clenching his fist at the reminder of those words "Why did it matter if they were infected?"

"I-I-IT JUST **DID**!"

The storm of pixels was screaming now, but it didn't lunge at him. Instead, it churned itself over, pulling itself together and apart again.

Well Duck? Was this how you really felt?

And Cuckoo felt the slightest bit of a smirk crawl up his face. "That sounds a lot like illogical thinking to me."

And if Duck hadn't broken before, he did now. He curled forward with a scream, his whole body seeming to glitch at the edges as the empty rifle dropped to his feet.

"I-I d-don't!" he insisted, his voice quietening now "I d-don't think! I d-don't f-feel! I-I'm a m-machine! T-That's s-safe! I n-need to b-be s-safe!"

"Being human isn't safe" Cuckoo told him "It's messy. It hurts. It sucks. But when you meet someone like Loon, it's so worth it."

He wasn't sure he had the authority to say something like that. He didn't know what it was like to be in love. This whole day had been nothing but a downward spiral of suck. But...

That moment in the leaves. That rising joy and camaraderie at Loon's speech. Every moment where a precious companion – Raven, Kingfisher, Shrike – had pulled him back off the ledge of despair. He couldn't forget those, just as he couldn't forget all the horror and pain some of those same people had inflicted upon him tonight.

"I-I'm n-not!" Duck sobbed "T-There's n-nothing h-h-human a-about m-me! T-That's a l-lie!"

Finally, Cuckoo lost his temper.

"Then why are you still wearing *that hat*?!"

Duck's hand flew instinctive to the brim of his cap, his mouth opening and closing like a drowning fish.

"Wearing it before, to garner sympathy from everyone and throw them off your case, that made sense" Cuckoo announced, his voice trembling with the force of what he was about to say "But if you ditched your goggles when they were no longer of use to you, why would you keep that hat? You even took it off before you dived into the ocean so you wouldn't lose it. If it's just data from some machine destined to die anyway, *why do you still have it*?!"

For a moment, Duck was completely still, and Cuckoo began to anxiously wonder if he'd actually died standing up. But then he began to seize, gripping that hat as he trembled so hard that Cuckoo swore he could feel the surface beneath his feet vibrating.

"No no no no no no!" he mumbled, his hand gripping the hat like he wanted to throw it off of his head but wasn't able to "I c-can't be! I'm a-a-aberrant?! Y-Y-YOU!" He glared up at Cuckoo, practically frothing at the mouth. "W-W-WHAT HAVE YOU D-D-DONE TO ME?! IT H-H-HURTS! IT **HURTS!**"

He was shrieking like a child experiencing pain for the first time, so overwhelmed by unfamiliar, unpleasant sensations that all they could do was try and wail the feelings out of themselves.

Cuckoo wasn't sure what to say. A part of him was revelling in the suffering, overjoyed that the man who'd put them all through his day of terror and horror was getting a taste of what they'd been through.

Another part of him though was smart enough to know Duck was just a tool in another man's game, and didn't want to see someone he'd unwittingly grow to care about suffering so badly.

The storm around them was so angry now, tearing past them like a stampede of heavy beasts. The walls twisted and torqued like they were about to collapse in on them, flashes of images snarling out at him. A wall, a jackal, a kind face, a snarl, a pair of massive hand pressing down and down and down on him.

"LOON! LOOOON!" Duck screamed, tears streaming from his eyes "M-M-M-MAKE IT STOP! PLEASE M-M-M-MAKE IT **STOP!** I CAN'T T-T-T-TAKE THIS! LOON!"

His whole body snapped straight, his head throwing back as he managed to get the gun under his chin.

Cuckoo realised what was happening a second too late.

"Wait!" he yelled out, leaping forward "Don't!"

A bang roared through his ears as blue shards seemed to shatter from Duck's head, exploding into the scenery that cracked and crumbled around them. As each piece fell, the storm appeared to spin out into nothing. Sliding in like a melting painting, tower came back into view, leaving Cuckoo exactly where he started: standing on the tower, alone, staring at the dawn.

The last victim of the prison had died exactly as its first had. The night was finally over, and the sun was on the horizon.

18

It took a while for Cuckoo to remember to breathe again. Idly, he wondered if he even had to, but it felt right as he let stale fake air fill his lungs.

Duck was gone, not even a body left behind. Gone, like all the others.

A tear pricked his eye. No one deserved to die like that, in that much pain. Even if it was pain of their own making.

Cuckoo supposed he wasn't too far away from Duck when he'd first woken up here: blank as a slate, barely feeling anything. Every new emotion he'd come to learn was punctuated by horror, until he'd wished it would all stop.

If there was any penance he could serve, it was that.

He looked over the tower wall, down at the barbed wire where Shrike had once been impaled. It was crystal clean again, the rolls immaculately circular.

Shrike's words still rang in his head, so different and yet the same as Duck's. Duck was so certain he was some sort of demon from hell, who'd murdered a woman, poisoned his mind and gotten everyone trapped here – a trap to punish him for his crimes.

What sort of person had he been, to have murdered someone?

He didn't remember it, that had been taken from him, but these hands had killed someone. Someone who was only innocently doing their job. Someone who had loved ones and friends.

Except, before he'd come here, before he'd walked side-by-side with them, would the human Cuckoo have viewed an AI as a person? Or just a tool to be used and disposed of, like Duck thought?

Shrike had thought he was some righteous god of ruin, and maybe from their perspective he was, but he was sure they were wrong about that.

Because he was making decision in this, one he was sticking to. This night had done nothing but told him that refusing to have an opinion out for fear caused nothing but trouble in the end. He was going to have to face himself on this matter.

In the end, it was Kingfisher's words that stuck closest to him. That he may have done awful things, but she still thought he was a good person. Raven had said something similar, hadn't he?

Maybe it was just self-preservation, but if he needed to think that to be able to breathe, he couldn't be a bad person, could he? A bad person wouldn't care what people they'd known for only a day thought of them.

Even when his memories had been taken, every time he saw blood, he'd felt the real Cuckoo's blood on his hands. For that moment to have been imprinted so deeply onto his soul that it scarred his mind even when everything else had been taken away, he couldn't have found any pleasure in doing such a thing, right?

He didn't think he could've.

...At least, he was pretty sure of that.

Because, after all, he'd also been grieving the loss of a person. Not a sibling or a friend, but a loss of himself. From his right to know if, before he had woken up here, he was a sadistic killer, a scared child or anything in between.

From the beginning, operating on nothing but pure basic instinct, he'd just wanted to be alone; not push past all these strangers to find an escape. He'd never wanted to escape alone; that had never been an option in his head. From the moment he'd decided he wanted to escape, that it was a possibility, he'd always wanted people to come with him.

His grief hadn't warped him into overblown positivity like Loon, or apathy like Kingfisher, or murderous intent like Mockingbird, or spite like Nightjar, or blind stupidity like Wren, or self-destruction like Rail, or inner turmoil like Raven, or inflated superiority like Shrike, or unhinged rage like Duck. At the end of it all, grief had made him care.

He could at least tell himself that he deserved to be able to leave this place, because anyone who cared that much couldn't be a bad person.

None of them had been bad people in this place. Not even Duck.

The sun was starting to rise above the veil of the fog beyond the prison walls. It didn't feel warm on his face. He hadn't felt any kind of temperature since he'd first arrive here, had he?

He really had been blind. Of course, this place wasn't real, even if all the people in it were. It was just data following a code, guessing at what a world beyond its comprehension was like.

Looking down at the gun in his hand, the one Rail had used to end his existence and start this madness, he wondering what happened to the data of the friends he'd made here. Where they truly just deleted from existence?

From somewhere far away, the knowledge that nothing made on a computer was ever truly gone rattled through his mind. Data was always retrievable.

Data, like the gun in his hand was dissolving in to.

He watched with fascination as little particles ripped up the gun's surface, flying away on a non-existent breeze.

Had that been what happened to all of the bodies?

Was it going to happen to him now?

His suspicion wasn't without merit. As he looked out from his perch, he could see the walls of the prison starting to dissolve into those bright particles, glowing gold in the morning light.

Duck had been built to protect this place. Maybe he was so wired into it, with him gone, there was nothing to hold it up anymore.

He really ought to leave, in case it was contagious.

He looked for his crutch, only to see that dissolve too before his very eyes.

Had Duck's last act been to trap him here to be deleted?

No, he decided. In the end, everything here was just data. This body was just data, and he was a data hacker. He could do what he wanted with it.

He didn't need a crutch.

As he thought that, he watched the split that had kept him upright — that had come back with the tower — once again dissolve away, and his leg stand solidly, straight and unbroken.

He left the roof feeling lighter than he had since he'd first awoken, something like a resigned victory in his step as he crossed back into the darkness.

It didn't feel like being smothered this time. More like, there was nothing to fear, because nothing could hurt him anymore.

There wasn't any hurt left to give anymore.

The security room was almost dark, a few of the screens flicking with a white light. Their cameras were gone, and even the walls of the room had a glow to them like they were about to depart too.

He wondered where he was going. There had to be somewhere out there — he'd come *from* somewhere. Deep inside, he could feel a compass pointing him towards home.

What was home? Were his memories there? People who cared about him?

Did he want that?

"Ah, so you won then. I knew you would."

That voice.

Raven was sitting up against the wall still, blood still dripping from his shoulder. He looked pale and dazed, but he was alive.

Something dangerously close to hope burned inside Cuckoo.

"You're alive" the words gasped out of him.

"I kept my promise" Raven assured him "And you kept yours — to find me in the morning."

"I guess I did" Cuckoo agreed, a blanket of calming joy washing over him.

Raven tilted his head to the side. "Huh, you look different."

Cuckoo coked to the side. "I do?"

Raven looked like he was searching for the right words. "You look...more open, I guess. Freer."

Maybe he was right. Cuckoo certainly felt lighter. He wasn't sure if it was knowing the dark times were over, or simply finding answers was enough, but now it felt like he was breathing for the first time after a night of trying desperately to catch his breath.

He felt like he was himself again.

Cuckoo smirked, the first time he'd felt able to since this nightmare began. "Well, you look terrible."

Raven seemed taken aback for a moment, before he laughed. "So, I guess my last memory is going to be of you growing a sense of humour!"

242

"I *always* had a sense of humour – there just wasn't anything funny to say" Cuckoo remarked, walking over to him "And you're not dying here."

He wasn't sure where all this confidence was coming from, but he didn't feel any worry at all as he pressed a hand to Raven's shoulder.

Raven wasn't going to die. If he could just save one person…

The two of them watched, amazed, as the blood stopped.

Raven was quiet for a moment, before letting out a little chuckle. "Cuckoo, are you magic?"

Cuckoo found himself chuckling as well. "No, I just figured something out. And maybe you shouldn't call me that. It's your sister's name."

"I like it though" Raven insisted "I like calling you Cuckoo. It's what I want to call you."

A touch of red hit his cheeks. If Raven liked it, he supposed he could keep using that name. It wasn't as if the real Cuckoo was around to complain about that.

"If you're going to keep doing that, then I chose to keep calling *you* Raven" Cuckoo declared "Unless you want something else."

"No, Raven is fine" Raven shook his head "I know it's probably not a cool as your real name. Or, heck, you probably had some kind of even cooler hacker name, right?"

Seeing that word leave Raven's lips caught him by surprise.

"Did you hear what was said up there?" he guessed.

"No" Raven shook his head, picking at his shoulder in wonder "I just guessed. Shrike thought you were the human overlord running this place, but I knew that wasn't true. You were too kind. You worried about us too much. So, if you were human, I thought you'd have to be some kind of rogue hacker stealing in where no one was looking. It suited you."

The reminder of that name caused something in him to tear a little.

"Shrike's dead" Cuckoo told him "The warden killed them."

"I know" Raven sighed "At least, I figured as much. You wouldn't."

"Also, apparently I'm the reason you're in this mess" Cuckoo admitted – it felt important to say.

"I don't care" Raven insisted, placing a hand on his shoulder "I recon there's some worse human I can blame instead of my best friend."

It was a harsh reminder that Duck was hardly the worst evil in this place. Some very human hands had built this place; had sat back and watched it over and over again as they puppeteered Duck on a string.

Someone out there who'd sentenced his friends to death.

Another reason they needed to get out of here.

"I'm getting out of here" Cuckoo declared "Are you coming?"

He worded it as a question, but he didn't really intend to leave it open. He may've stopped Raven's bleeding, but he'd still lost blood – or whatever vital data the blood was simulating – and clearly wouldn't make it on his own. He needed proper help, and maybe a Cuckoo with all of his memories could be that help.

Raven was just complex data, right? Surely he could fix that, with the right tools.

Raven slumped back against the wall. "Sorry, I think I might be a goner. You should just go ahead without me. Besides," a sad smile crawled across his lips. "I don't think there's a world out there for me."

No, no self-deprecating talk. Cuckoo wouldn't allow it.

"I'll believe that when I see it" he said decisively, grabbing Raven's good arm to pull him to his feet "Come on, I'll help you this time."

A gentle chuckle left Raven's throat as he was pulled up. "You've been helping me from the start."

"I didn't do shit" Cuckoo insisted "I spent hours being a prick to all of you, and then flailing around helplessly whilst people died."

"That might be true, but it's not what I meant" Raven insisted "When I woke up in that courtyard, with little idea of who I was or why I was alive. I was so scared I could barely move. I wanted to just lie there until the ground swallowed me up. But when I saw you were also there, knowing there was someone else in the world with me: that was a relief I'd never felt before. It was like my whole body was flying on some invisible current. Just being near you, it would bring back that memory. It was my only comfort. The idea of anything happening to you was...unbearable. Because then I'd never feel that feeling again."

Cuckoo wasn't entirely sure what to say. He hadn't known what to make of Raven's strange attachment to him, but it had been one of his sole reassurances through the short part of his life he remembered. When he was drowning, Raven was there to pull him out. Something warm flickered inside him that he'd been able to do the same for Raven.

"You were my comfort too" was what he settled on.

A splash of red swept over Raven's face, causing him to let out a nervous laugh. "And, you were such a disaster, I knew you couldn't be a threat to anyone. You were the one person I never had to worry about – you'd probably trip on your own knife before you stabbed anyone."

"Oh thanks!" Cuckoo scoffed, but there was a grin on his face.

They walked out of the dissolving security room in a strange parody of how they'd spent that night: Raven leaning on Cuckoo's shoulder, helped along with gentle kindness.

"It was Duck, right?"

The statement took Cuckoo by surprise. "You knew?"

Raven smiled at him awkwardly. "Yeah. Sorry, I should've told you."

That statement was even more surprising. "You knew *before* I went to sleep?"

"Oh, yes" Raven admitted "I knew from when we were stood in front of the armoury after Loon died."

Cuckoo had to work to keep his breath from catching. "How?"

Raven hmmed. "I almost missed it myself, I only realised it when Nightjar did the same thing. But, when he was talking about the warden, Duck said 'He'. Everyone else had said 'They', except for Nightjar when she thought *you* were the warden, so she stared calling them 'he'. So Duck must have had a reason to presume he knew who the warden was as well. Either he was covering for someone, or he himself was the warden. The only other men left alive were me, you, Mockingbird and maybe Shrike: I knew it wasn't you or me, Mockingbird was much too volatile to masterfully plan something like this, and Shrike found the game too interesting to already know all the answers. So, it had to be Duck himself."

It was compelling reasoning; reasoning that Cuckoo hadn't allowed to come over him in his distress of being accused of being the warden himself. They could've solved this all the way back then.

"Why didn't you say anything?" Cuckoo asked.

"Because I was going to kill him myself" Raven announced miserably "That's why I volunteered to stay awake. I was going to smother him in his sleep. I thought that would see us free." He turned his head away, so Cuckoo couldn't see his face. "If he found some way to stop me, I was sure I could leave enough clues to point him out as my killer, and I didn't mind giving up my life so everyone could escape."

"Don't say shit like that" Cuckoo found himself saying automatically.

Raven laughed, his head turning to the ground again. "Sorry. But yes, it was Shrike who stopped me from doing that."

Cuckoo didn't understand. "But Shrike thought *I* was the warden."

"That's my fault I'm afraid" Raven admitted "I was getting a spare pillow from the cupboard when Shrike found me, and all I said was that I was going to kill the warden. I never said it was Duck, because I thought they knew. I only realised later that Shrike hadn't been there when Duck said all that, so they gravitated towards you as the odd one out instead."

Cuckoo felt a part of him deep inside collapse. Shrike hadn't been there when Duck had first emerged from the pantry, or faked his death either. They were missing all the crucial information they'd needed.

"They never stood a chance of figuring it out" he realised.

Raven chuckled miserably, but shook his head and moved on. "Anyway, it was them who suggested we find a way out first; partially in case killing him didn't let us out of here, but also just to stick it to him. They thought we could try the grate: that there may be some sort of secret passage in there. They just needed me to help them get in."

"How did you end up ambushed?" Cuckoo questioned.

"My fault again, I'm afraid" Raven remarked bashfully "I was too busy being distracted by all the screens and the revelations of what we were that Shrike took me by surprise. Once they knew they were right about this all being a simulation, they only wanted to force you to come looking for me so they could confront you and 'win the game'. I don't think they'd realised I'd put the grate back on each time we passed it, so Duck couldn't try and stop us. So, you ended up taking longer to figure it out than they expected; which is when they went looking for you."

That all made sense, to his dismay.

Dammit, if Shrike had only thought to talk *to* people rather than just *at* them – the pair of them and Raven working together could've cracked this case before Cuckoo had even woken up.

But this wasn't the time to mourn those who couldn't be saved. He had to focused on the one person he *could* save.

They reached the ground floor to find the dispersion had truly taken off. The east and west wings had almost completely dissolved, and he could see sunlight.

Their prison was almost gone. They were almost free.

And it was into that sunlight they walked, two pairs of shoes moving in tandem between two sets of feet.

The only thing that hadn't began to dissolve was the fog, even as particles drifted up from the crest of the waves. Cuckoo suspected that would be the last thing to go – the physical boundary between the simulation and the rest of the data world.

A boundary he thought he could pass.

With the waves smoothed out by the dissolution, he slipped out from under Raven's arm and down onto the surface of the water.

It wasn't really water though, just data. The same as the concrete floor and the rocky island. He could stand on it if he wanted.

Sure enough, the surface held beneath his feet.

He reached out through the fog, not a doubt in his mind about being shocked or sliced by it. Instead, his hand passed through the intangible substance like butter.

He could pass through here, and he knew he'd be able to make it home if he did.

When his hand came back, he found himself holding something. Something he thought he'd been holding all day, even if he hadn't been able to feel it.

It was a manila folder, a zip holding the ends together. A literal zip file.

This was it, huh? This is what he'd been tortured for? This is what his friends had died for?

This was also the reason he'd met them in the first place. That was important.

He wanted to throw it away, but stopped himself. Somewhere out there, a person had found this file important enough to kill ten people for it. If he wanted to make that person suffer, he could use it.

And yes, he wanted that person to suffer. He wanted to make sure what had happened to his friends wouldn't happen to any other people.

Because in the end, that's what they were: people.

For now, there was one person left to save.

Cuckoo turned by to Raven on the shore. Behind him, the prison was entirely gone now: just a flat rock in the middle of the ocean, particles swirling in a maelstrom around his head.

"Come with me!" he called out.

Raven just stared at him, sliding his hands into his pockets. "I can't."

"You can" Cuckoo insisted "You're a person too – you can do anything I can. And..."

He wondered if he should say this. It might be downright manipulative, but in another light, it could also be kind.

He didn't want to grieve anyone else.

"I want you to" he said "I want you to come with me."

Duck had imploded under want – so much want both within him and placed upon him that he couldn't handle it. Cuckoo could see how such a thing was possible: want was such a burning feeling, it felt like it could destroy him if Raven said no.

Want and grief; such unpleasant human emotions.

But they were human, and so they were good, and he wanted Raven to have them too. He wanted Raven to be able to want things.

To want to stay with him, if possible.

Maybe...he just didn't want to be alone again. Because Raven had never let him be – every time he was alone, or scared, Raven would run to him.

This time, he could meet Raven halfway.

"There's..." whatever Raven was going to say, he stopped. When he looked up at Cuckoo, there was something beautiful like wonder in his eyes. "Is there something out there, for me? A purpose?"

Cuckoo didn't know. He honestly didn't know what would happen to Raven if he brought him with him. Cuckoo himself was surely going back to his human body, with real skin and real blood and where every breath was necessary. But Raven didn't have any kind of body. Would moving him to another computer just be a new prison for him? Maybe. Maybe it would be. But a prison didn't have to hurt. A prison could be a place of grief, but depending on who you were with, it could also be a place of nurture and love.

It could also be a nest.

And there was always the possibility, no matter how remote, that you could somehow escape it.

"It's whatever you want it to be."

Those words felt right. He could make them right.

He wanted to tell Raven everything. That he was a Data Engineer for Raptor Tech, that he had eight siblings who loved him dearly, that he only had his memory wiped so fully out of concern that his role of data engineer would lead the AIs to guess their true nature too quickly.

But that shouldn't be all Raven was. Everyone had the right to find their own purpose — more than just what they were built for.

He wanted Raven to find that for himself.

He wanted to find that out for *himself* as well.

He wanted them to do it together.

What was the saying? When you could move past the grief, there was room for hope to grow.

Raven turned to look behind him. There was nothing left of the prison now — just dust hanging in the air.

Cuckoo knew what he was thinking.

Too many good people weren't coming with them.

Would that be enough to stop Raven from coming? Would the grief of what had been taken from him paralyse him, as it had others? As it almost had to Cuckoo on too many occasions?

For a moment, Cuckoo swore he forgot to breathe under the weight of being left alone again.

But then Raven turned back to him.

With gold around him like a halo, he tucked a lock of hair behind his ear, and a wonderful smile broke onto his face.

Cuckoo stared into the light, and a cheery voice sang back to his ears.

"Ok, let's go! I don't want to be stuck here a moment longer!"

A hand landed in his, fingers clasping, and cold air filled his lungs with a gasp.

Printed in Great Britain
by Amazon

56244425R00149